# To Love a Spy

# To Love a Spy

Laura Beers

Cover art by Tugboat Design
http://www.tugboatdesign.net

## MORE ROMANCE BY LAURA BEERS

Saving Shadow
A Peculiar Courtship
A Tangled Ruse
A Deceptive Bargain
The Baron's Daughter
The Unfortunate Debutante

# I

## ENGLAND, 1813

Adrien Stanton, the new Earl of Camden, was infuriatingly bored in his small, crested coach. As he listened to the sound of rhythmic movement of the horses, his eyes scanned over the idyllic green countryside and he prayed for a cool breeze to help ease his suffering.

Heaving a sigh, he took a moment to contemplate how much his life had changed over the course of a month. He now had a title and three estates, and yet it meant nothing to him. He would gladly give it all up to be reunited with his family.

Leaning his head back against the plush carriage seats, he was resigned to his state of abject loneliness; a feeling with which he was all too familiar. With an immense desire to see the world, and serve his God and country, he freely made the decision to leave his family and go to France as an agent of the Crown.

Now, years later, he had no relations left to speak of, and he was forced to pick up the pieces of his family's tarnished reputation. The French spy, Michel, had killed his family, assuming the identity of his cousin, Lord Camden. He had even fired the entire household staff of Pratt Hall, his ancestral estate, to protect his ruse. His false predecessor had not even provided the staff with references, firing them through a solicitor, which made it nearly impossible for them to gain respectable employment again.

Within the past month, Adrien had done his best to right Michel's wrongs and hire back the household staff at Pratt Hall, located near Northumberland. After a thorough search, he was able to locate many of the former employees and rehire them at a substantial pay raise.

Touring Pratt Hall was bittersweet, because the estate had fallen into great disrepair. The stone was crumbling, the rotted wood windows were partially boarded up, and the façade details were falling off. Inside the estate, all the furniture was covered with faded white sheets, and a musty odor dominated the rooms. Even in its current state, each room still held fond memories of his family. He could almost hear his cousin's faint laugh as he walked around the dust-filled home.

The village near Pratt Hall had suffered tremendously with the loss of his familial connection. Many of the cottages that lay nestled at the bottom of the small valley had collapsed roofs. The storefronts of the shops were in desperate need of work, and the blacksmith's tools were inadequate to facilitate the repairs.

Not only did Adrien supply funds to rebuild the village, but he also pulled up his sleeves and helped with the work. Between chopping wood, fixing thatched roofs, and restocking the apothecary's shop, he felt useful, and truth be told, he loved the physical component of rebuilding.

But in the middle of his repairs, Lord Charles Beckett, England's chief spymaster, summoned him, so Adrien was currently traveling back to London. He could only dream of a new, dangerous assignment, since his days as a spy were gone. As an earl, he was not allowed to work for the Crown anymore. Although, Lord Beckett had been known to bend the rules. His niece, Lady Lansdowne, had been a notorious spy, known as *Shadow*, for many years.

Tugging at his cravat, Adrien silently cursed his decision to ride in a stifling coach, rather than ride his horse into London. Glancing at the empty bench opposite of him, he realized the thought of a wife did have some appeal. For starters, he wouldn't be so blasted lonely all the time.

On the rare occasion when his loneliness threatened to consume him, he pushed down his emotions, and hid behind a mask that he had perfected over the years. A spy never showed any weakness, for displaying even the tiniest weakness meant death.

Which was why he had not given much consideration to marriage while undercover in France. Even though he portrayed a jovial French officer, he refused to court a woman just to give credence to his cover. No, a relationship would have been too complicated and would have distracted him from his duties as a spy.

Although, at the age of twenty-nine, he was now an earl and was expected to marry. He needed an heir, or so he had been reminded, but the monotony of trying to find a good match seemed irksome.

Knowing that his friends, and fellow agents, Benedict and Jonathon, had marriages based on love, he intended to follow their example. However, he refused to be as sappy as they were around their wives. In their eyes, Eliza and Hannah could do no wrong, and his friends were constantly smiling like bloody fools. No, that would not be him. He would have a love match, but he would be in control of his emotions.

First, he had to find the perfect young lady, and that might take years. An image of Lady Camden, or Kate, as he was given leave to call her, flittered through his mind. She was exquisite with her light blonde hair, flawless skin, and an oval face that highlighted her wide, expressive blue eyes.

Kate had suffered much at the hand of her imposter husband, but they had struck up an unusual friendship while they both were confined within the walls of Beaumont Castle. It took some effort, but he managed to coax smiles out of her, and even had her laughing on occasion.

The last time he saw Kate, which was over a month ago, she had been frail and skittish, but when she laughed, her whole face briefly transformed, causing her blue eyes to sparkle. It always rendered him speechless to witness that transformation, even for a few moments.

Technically, Kate was now his responsibility as the Countess of Camden, but she chose to live at Eliza's townhouse in London. Now that he had a man of business, he would call on Kate and inform her of the generous monthly allowance he had allocated for her use. Even though Michel had spent much on gambling, mistresses, and other vile practices, the coffers were not quite empty.

The carriage slowed as it approached London, and the clean, fresh country air gave way to the pungent odor of horse dung. Fortunately, as they approached his townhouse, the cobblestone streets grew wider and cleaner. Ladies strolled down the streets with servants carrying their purchases. A few ladies glanced towards his crested carriage and fluttered their eyelashes at him.

I am not a fool, he thought, as he ignored the ladies' blatant flirtations. Although he knew he was a handsome man, most of the ladies of the ton were only interested in his title and fortune. He would need to be on alert as he started searching for a wife. Perhaps he should start with a dog to curb his gnawing loneliness. Yes, that would do for now.

The carriage jerked to a stop in front of his spacious, four-story townhouse located in Portman Square. Admiring the red brick frontage, wide windows, and iron railings that lined his property, Adrien knew this townhouse was highly sought after. Even though Michel was a despicable French spy, he'd had impeccable taste in properties.

Turning the handle of the carriage door, Adrien stepped out

onto the freshly-swept cobblestone street, not bothering to wait for the groomsman moving his way. As he walked up the few stairs, the main door stood open where his butler, Mr. Ward, waited for him.

"Good afternoon, my lord," Mr. Ward drawled as he extended his hand for Adrien's gloves.

"Ward," he nodded, "it is good to be back."

Mr. Ward, with his greased black hair and brown eyes, gave him a stoic stare. Adrien had the strangest urge to make a funny face at him. Instead, he said, "You are too serious, my good man."

"A butler's job is not to amuse you, my lord. My job is to ensure your household is running efficiently and is in proper order," Mr. Ward informed him.

"Right you are," Adrien agreed, stifling a smile. "I will be in my study until dinner."

"As you wish," Mr. Ward replied with a tilt of his head.

Walking across the marble floor of the entry hall, Adrien moved towards his study tucked back in the corner of the townhouse. A low-burning fire had already been set in the hearth, and the drapes were pulled back, showing off his spacious, well-manicured gardens in the rear. A large oak desk sat in front of dual windows, and one length of a wall was covered in shelving, with neatly arranged books.

A large pile of correspondence on his desk caught his eye. He inwardly groaned. Most of the letters were no doubt invitations to balls, soirées, and house parties, all with the intent of matchmaking. No, he refused to be hounded by overbearing mothers and simpering ladies. He was not that lonely. Hadn't he just decided to get a dog?

Before he finished tossing the correspondences out, his study door swung open and Benedict, the Marquess of Lansdowne, strode in. "Adrien, welcome back," he said, smiling.

Glancing at him suspiciously, Adrien replied, "I just arrived. How did you deduce I was in town?"

"I am a spy," Benedict reminded him.

"Are you not retired?"

"I am, but something has come up. Lord Beckett has sent me to fetch you."

Now Benedict had his full attention. "Is it a new assignment?" he asked, a little too eagerly.

"I don't know, but Lord Beckett wants to see us in his office posthaste."

"Let's go," Adrien stated, rounding his desk.

Benedict watched him with a knowing smile on his lips. "I take it that the life of an earl is a tad boring for the likes of you?"

"How do you handle the dreariness of being a marquess?" Adrien asked curiously.

"I married Eliza," he revealed slowly, as if imparting a huge secret.

"And?"

Benedict shrugged. "Being married to Eliza makes me happy and I do not want for more."

With a shake of his head, Adrien responded, "I was hoping you would provide me with real counsel."

"It is the truth."

Adrien was still curious about one thing. "In all honesty, how did you know I was home?"

"Oh, I saw your coach pull up. Did you not recall that we are neighbors?" Benedict asked, feigning disappointment. "We share a common wall…" His voice trailed off to emphasize his point.

"Why do you maintain two townhouses in London?" Adrien inquired. Everyone knew that Benedict's family maintained one of the largest townhouses in all of London.

"Berkley Hall is where my father would stay for the season, but Henry bought this townhouse just before he died. He bought it intending to watch Michel," Benedict revealed. "By residing in Henry's townhouse, I feel a connection to him."

"That sounds like a good enough reason for me," Adrien said. "It will be nice to have friendly neighbors."

"Who said we are friendly?" Benedict asked with a furrowed brow.

Adrien chuckled as he brushed past him. "Let's go see Lord Beckett."

ADRIEN DISMOUNTED HIS HORSE IN FRONT OF A WHITE, TWO-story, non-descript building on the outskirts of the fashionable part of London. A few ragged-looking men loitered out in front of the building. One ventured up to ask him for sixpence, but he knew these agents were tasked with keeping the building safe from intruders.

A young man approached them to care for their horses, and Benedict and Adrien walked into the building. A lanky man sat behind a lone desk, with his left hand hidden from view. Since no one came into this building solely by accident, no photos lined the walls, no vases sat on the tables, and no chairs were available for seating.

Taking command, Benedict announced, "Lord Lansdowne and Lord Camden request an audience with Lord Beckett."

The lanky man's countenance relaxed. "Lord Beckett has been expecting you, my lords. Please follow me," he said, ushering them up to his office.

Lord Beckett's office was a large square room, with a massive desk at one end. An ornate fireplace graced the opposite wall. Small windows allowed some natural light to filter in, but they were not large enough for anyone to climb through.

Bowed over his desk, Lord Beckett was in the process of writing. They took their seats in two upholstered arm chairs that sat directly in front of him. Once he placed the quill back in its ink pot, he acknowledged them and smiled. "It is a pleasure to see you so soon, Lord Camden."

"Thank you, Lord Beckett."

Tilting his head towards Benedict, Lord Beckett teased, "I am surprised that Eliza did not accompany you."

"You specifically requested that I not bring her," Benedict pointed out.

Lord Beckett laughed loudly. "As if that would have stopped my niece."

"Good point." Benedict offered a faint smile. "To be honest, Eliza has not been feeling well lately, but refuses to let me send for the doctor."

Turning towards Benedict, Adrien said, "I hope it is not serious."

"Thank you. I hope not, as well," Benedict replied, his voice betraying his concern for his wife.

"I am certain it is nothing, my boy," Lord Beckett assured Benedict. "Eliza will not let a sickness keep her down for long. I am sure she will be fencing by the time you return home."

Benedict just nodded with a pensive expression. Obviously, he did not feel as optimistic as Lord Beckett.

The spy master rested his elbows on the desk and threaded his fingers together. "I have an assignment for you two. As Benedict knows, we have searched every inch of Michel's properties." He hesitated, glancing at Adrien. "Rather, your properties now, and we cannot find the list of French spies that he referenced."

"How is that possible? Michel said it was on his property," Adrien stated. "When Michel stood on the deck of the *Brazen*

*Hine,* he announced that the list was on his property and bragged that no one would ever find it."

Shaking his head, Lord Beckett explained, "Agents have scoured your London townhouse, your estate up in Northumberland, and your country home, but we have found nothing that would give even the slightest hint of who the French spies are."

"Have you asked Kate to assist in the search?" Adrien inquired.

"Yes, Kate has been most helpful, considering what she has been through." Lord Beckett dropped his hands and leaned back in his chair. "If we did not have a full confession from Diana, the Duchess of Remington, and Michel himself, I doubt a barrister would have had enough evidence to even convict Michel of treason."

"Well, it is a good thing that *Shadow* killed Michel then," Benedict pointed out.

Giving Benedict a disapproving glare, Lord Beckett declared, "No, it was a horrible misstep! We never established who Michel's contact was, and we have not been able to pinpoint who the other French spies are. All we know is that there is a sinister scheme in the works, and members of Parliament and Prinny's staff have been infiltrated by French spies."

"Michel was going to kill Hannah. Eliza did not have much of a choice," Adrien argued, feeling a need to defend Eliza's actions.

Lord Beckett frowned. "I know, but I am not pleased by the outcome."

"I believe the best course of action, sir, is to turn in my resignation for the failure aboard the *Brazen Hine*," Benedict announced dramatically.

"Oh, do shut up," Lord Beckett said, good-naturedly. "You keep threatening me with your resignation, but I have yet to witness it, nor do I want it right now."

"As you wish." Benedict smiled, crossed his legs, and leaned back in his chair. "What would you like us to do?"

Lord Beckett's expression grew serious. "The House of Lords is considering a bill to end the war against France, by cutting off all funding, and initiating an immediate withdrawal of all British troops in Europe."

"Which would leave our allies to fight Napoleon alone," Benedict stated in a sharp tone. "And what of the Royal Navy? Are we to leave the channel undefended?"

"Luckily, the bill does not specify the Royal Navy," Lord Beckett informed them, frowning. "I need you both to vote down the bill."

"That is not a problem," Benedict asserted.

"That goes without saying," Adrien added.

Nodding his approval, Lord Beckett continued, "Next, I need agents on the inside to discover who the French spies are. Based on Diana and Michel's own confessions, we know at least one French spy has made his way into the House of Lords and one into the House of Commons." He leveled a stern gaze at them. "We need to find out who they are, what their ultimate purpose is, and stop them."

Adrien glanced at Benedict. "That sounds reasonable."

"I would suggest starting with Lord Devon, who orchestrated the bill. Recently, he has been an outspoken critic of the war against France," Lord Beckett revealed.

"I am not familiar with Lord Devon. Is he associated with the Whigs or Tory party?" Benedict inquired.

"He is a Tory," Lord Beckett stated. "However, both of his sons have died in the war. Many presume that is why he has turned bitter towards the war effort."

Lifting his brow, Adrien pointed out, "That sounds more like a grieving father, not a traitor."

"True, but he might have been approached by French spies and not even recognized the threat," Lord Beckett said. "The vote for the bill is in three weeks and Parliament is in session. I will expect you both to be in attendance." He stood up abruptly, pushing back his chair. "Now, if you will excuse me, I am late for another appointment."

As they departed the building, Benedict asked, "Would you care to join us for dinner? Eliza has been in low spirits since Kate moved out."

"Kate moved out?" Adrien repeated, momentarily shocked by the news. "Where did she go?"

Lifting his brow, Benedict replied, "To your country home. Did she not inform you of the move?"

"Blazes," Adrien muttered under his breath.

"Whatever is the matter with you?"

"I had planned to sell the country home. I do not need three estates, and my solicitor has already lined up a prospective buyer," Adrien confessed.

Benedict rubbed his hands together. "That is great news. Kate will be forced to move back in with Eliza, and my wife will be happy again."

Adrien chuckled. "Do you think Kate will be willing to move back in with you?"

"I hope so. She could also move in with Jonathon, or the duke."

"Did Eliza ever inform Kate that the duke is not her real father?" Adrien asked, after glancing over his shoulder to ensure no one could overhear them.

"No, we decided not to divulge that information," Benedict informed him. "The duke was especially insistent on not sharing the news."

Adrien disagreed with that, but kept silent. "I ensured Kate's allowance is generous, and I am returning her grandmother's inheritance to her possession. I will even buy her a smaller estate if she so desires."

"Good," Benedict acknowledged. "Will you allow her to keep her grandmother's jewelry?"

"Why would I not?" he asked, surprised by the odd question.

"I just had to ask. Poor Kate has suffered much at the hands of her mother and husband, and I will not allow anyone to mistreat her."

"Playing the part of over-protective brother, I see," Adrien said, amused.

"I don't play," Benedict answered back, his voice gruff.

Before Adrien could respond to Benedict's threat, the horses arrived, and they mounted. It appeared that he was going to take a trip out to his country home tomorrow and convince Kate to move out. That should not be too hard. After all, Kate would be reasonable once he explained why he wanted to sell the estate, wouldn't she?

# ❦ 2 ❦

KATE, THE LADY CAMDEN, RACED DOWN THE STAIRS OF HER country home at a most unladylike pace. She was dressed in an emerald green, high-waisted gown with puff sleeves, and wearing a pair of tan, kid ankle boots. Her blonde hair was piled high on top of her head, and ringlets ran down the side of her face.

Almost a month ago, she had decided that she wanted to be the mistress of her own home and announced she would move back to her country estate. Eliza and Benedict were not pleased with her decision, but they ultimately supported her. Benedict was even kind enough to remove all the staff at the country home who had been loyal to her imposter husband. With her permission, he replaced her household staff with kind, but efficient employees.

Since they were both killed while committing treason, Kate was free from the prison that Michel and her mother had so elegantly created for her. She finally had the freedom to discover what she was truly capable of, and it felt exhilarating, albeit a tad terrifying. What if her mother and Michel were right all along? What if she was worthless?

Banishing the burdensome thoughts from her mind, she adjusted her steps as she walked gracefully through the main hall. Her boots made clicking noises along the polished marble floor as she walked towards the dining room. "Mr. Oakes," she said cheerfully. "Is everything in order?"

Mr. Oakes, her butler, was a tall man with a small, protruding belly. He had learned early on to overlook her impropriety. Standing in the dining room with his usual relaxed countenance, he answered, "The cook has filled five baskets full of bread, cheese, and biscuits. Are you certain that you do not want me to send Sally along to assist you?"

"I am most positive. That is what Roger is for," she teased, glancing over her shoulder. "Isn't that right, Roger?"

Roger stepped into the room with an amused smile. "Yes, Lady Camden. When Mr. Larson assigned me to guard you, I was informed that my main task would be to carry baskets to and from the village."

With a quick smile at Roger, Kate turned back to Mr. Oakes. "You see, all is well."

"It really is kind of you to help those women, my lady," Mr. Oakes praised.

"I am pleased that my limited contribution will help ease their burdens. Please thank the kitchen staff for preparing the baskets," Kate responded, attempting to steer the conversation away from herself. Providing baskets to a few local families was simple and did not require any thanks.

Her deceased husband had tortured the household staff of the country home, and many of the women had fled in fear for their virtue. Sadly, a few of the women had become pregnant by Michel, and Kate had taken it upon herself to assist these poor women. Some of them had come back to work for her, but a couple of them were still heavy with child. Even though she had not caused these women pain, her husband had, and she wanted to right his wrongs.

Her father, the Duke of Remington, had provided her with an allowance since the new Lord Camden, or Adrien, as he had given her leave to call him, had not discussed funds with her. She was using part of her allowance to help these women and a few of the villagers.

Sally, a sweet, blonde-haired, freckle-faced young woman walked into the room with five baskets hanging off her two arms. "Here ya go, Lady Camden." She placed them on the large, wooden table.

"Thank you, Sally," Kate said, acknowledging her efforts. She lifted the white linen napkin off the top of the basket and breathed in the delicious aroma of freshly baked bread.

Reaching into the pocket of her apron, Sally pulled out a large chunk of bread. "Mrs. Palmer said you would best be wanting a piece of bread for the road."

Kate accepted Sally's offering, immediately taking a bite, and savoring the warm, fluffy bread. "Hiring Mrs. Palmer was the best thing I ever did."

Sally giggled, as she always did. "Mrs. Palmer has worked at this estate for almost twenty years. Ye did not hire her."

Giving her a conspiratorial smile, Kate stated, "Well, I best not fire her then."

Mrs. Palmer was one of the bright spots in her life. After a beating from Michel, she would escape to the kitchen and allow Mrs. Palmer to put ointment on her bruising. Not only did she help Kate with her physical pain, but she was a good shoulder to cry on, which was something she never had with her own mother.

Sally giggled again as she dropped into a curtsy. "I will tell Mrs. Palmer ye liked her bread… again."

As Kate reached to pick up the baskets, Roger was at her side, assisting her as he always did. "You take two, Lady Camden, and I will take three," he instructed her.

"All right," she said, giving him a mock salute.

Roger placed his baskets back down on the table and smiled at her. "You are happy here. I can tell."

Picking up her two baskets, Kate genuinely smiled at Roger. "I am. My husband cannot hurt me anymore. That alone provides me with immense joy."

"No one will hurt you again. I promise you that," Roger vowed, his voice reassuring.

Kate's eyes roamed her protector's aged face and crooked nose, a testament to his dangerous work. He was not as old as Mr. Larson, but his hair had started turning white around the temples. When Eliza had suggested sending a guard to protect her, she adamantly refused, but then Mr. Larson explained that her life could still be in danger. She agreed, once Mr. Larson informed her that Roger had been assigned to protect her.

"I know. I am truly blessed to have you here," she admitted.

Roger had started becoming her friend as he recovered at Beaumont Castle. He had been injured during the carriage wreck that resulted in Lady Hannah's abduction. They had struck up an unusual friendship as she read by his bedside.

A loud knock at the main door broke up their conversation. Roger lowered the baskets to the table again and walked towards the entry hall. Glancing back at her, he gave her a silent command to stay put. His hand went to the pistol he always carried in his waistband of his trousers.

Curiosity won out, and she dropped her baskets, edging her way to the entry hall. This was to be her first visitor!

As Mr. Oakes opened the door, a loud, but familiar voice boomed, "I am here to see Lady Camden."

Mr. Oakes' back was to her, but she could tell he accepted the visitor's card. "Yes, Lord Camden. Do come in," she heard him say as he opened the door wider.

Did he say Lord Camden? Kate felt the blood draining from her face as her knees grew weak. No, it cannot be. He is dead! A pitiful whimper escaped her mouth, and she leaned her back against the wall for support. She would never be free of him. Fear gripped her heart and she closed her eyes tightly.

"Kate," a rich baritone voice said next to her. "What is the matter? It is me, Adrien."

"Adrien?" she repeated as she opened her eyes.

A familiar, handsome face with a square jaw, straight nose, and warm green eyes greeted her. "Good morning, Kate."

"Oh, Adrien," she breathed, placing her hand to her chest. "I am relieved to see you."

He chuckled. "It is good to see you, too." His eyes roamed her face, his expression showing his concern. "What happened?"

"It was nothing," she said, suddenly feeling very silly.

Adrien's voice softened. "You were awfully pale when I entered. Why?"

"For a moment, I thought Lord Camden, my husband, was not dead. I thought," she paused, her voice hitching, "I thought he came back to punish me."

"Oh, Kate," Adrien murmured, gently. "You are safe. Your husband is dead. I saw his body floating down the River Thames," he spoke in a hushed tone for only her to hear.

"I apologize for my behavior," Kate said, straightening from the wall.

"You have no need to apologize."

Walking towards the drawing room, she asked, "May I offer you some refreshment?"

"No, thank you."

Kate sat down on a mahogany camelback sofa and smoothed out her dress. Once she was seated, Adrien sat down on an adjacent red wingback chair. "I came to discuss your allowance."

He stated a number that ensured she would be well taken care of, as would the women she supported. "Thank you, Adrien. That is most generous."

"I also intend to return your grandmother's lands to you," he continued. "Furthermore, your grandmother's jewelry will be yours to do with as you wish."

Her hand flew to her mouth in surprise. "Thank you," she proclaimed.

Kate allowed herself to relax in Adrien's presence. Whenever Michel had been generous, he always expected something in return, but Adrien did not ask anything of her. Maybe not all men were like her former husband.

Shifting in his seat, Adrien's face was expressionless. "There is another topic I would like to discuss with you."

"Whatever could it be?" Tightly clasping her hands in her lap, she dreaded his next few words. What could he possibly ask of her?

With a quick glance at her dress, he asked, "You are not in mourning?"

Kate shook her head adamantly. "No, I refuse to mourn him or my mother." She pointed at his right arm, which had a black armband over his coat sleeve. "You are choosing to mourn?"

"I'm mourning my cousin's family, nothing more."

"Oh, I am sorry for your loss," Kate murmured, genuinely heartbroken for him.

Her eyes drifted to his pin-striped waistcoat and cravat, then back to the olive tailcoat that fit his wide, muscular shoulders so well. Adrien and Michel shared an uncanny likeness, but the difference was in their eyes. Adrien's green eyes were warm and inviting, but Michel's eyes had seemed bleak, reflecting only sinister coldness.

"I have come to discuss your living arrangement," Adrien announced.

"My living arrangement?" she repeated, baffled. "I have been living here for a month now."

Adrien leaned forward, placing his arms on his knees. "Michel lived a life of extravagance as Lord Camden, and in so doing, he spent most of the coffers." He grimaced. "I have spent the last month with my new man of business, going over ledgers and expense reports, and I deem the best course of action would be to sell the country home."

"No," she spoke without thought.

Shifting so he was sitting on the front of the chair, he continued, "I have already spoken to Benedict and he indicated he would be pleased if you returned to live with them. Or, if you would prefer, you could reside with Jonathon and Hannah at Chatswich Manor while their estate is being built."

Again, Kate shook her head, causing her ringlets to swing back and forth. "I would prefer to stay here."

"I know you have suffered a great deal these past few years, and we feel it is best that you are surrounded by family." His tone was very diplomatic, almost as if he had rehearsed his words.

"We? And I assume everyone else knows what is best for me?" Kate asked, attempting to keep the sarcasm out of her voice. "I am happy here. The household staff of this country home have come to mean a great deal to me."

"I understand, but they are your servants, not your family," Adrien said, giving her a look filled with pity. "I will provide them with letters of recommendation and will assist them in finding new employment. If they are willing to move, I can offer them employment at my main residence, Pratt Hall."

Pressing her lips tightly together, Kate attempted to reign in the anger that was growing inside of her. Adrien was just like Michel. He was generous, but only if she did his bidding. What if she told him no? Would he lower her allowance or take back her grandmother's jewelry?

Her mother's voice came into her head. *A lady never raises her voice. A lady never reveals her irritation.*

Kate gave him a forced smile as she kept her hands clasped tightly in her lap. She did not want to leave the country home. It had become her refuge, a place for her to discover who she really was. Now Adrien wanted to take it away from her. No, she would not go!

"I fear you are wrong in your assessment, Lord Camden," she stated softly.

Adrien lifted an eyebrow. "Lord Camden?"

"Yes, it is improper for me to address you so informally given the circumstances," she explained.

"Kate, that is preposterous," he said, his voice rising. "What circumstances?"

*Oh no, she had angered him.* Adrien would never hit her, would he? She nervously glanced over her shoulder to look for Roger, but was unable to see him at this angle.

"You are now the Earl of Camden," she reminded him.

He frowned. "And?"

"And I am still the Countess of Camden, at least until you get married."

"I know all this. It doesn't explain why you are suddenly calling me Lord Camden again."

"All right, I will continue to call you Adrien, if you would like," she replied, trying to sound calmer than she felt.

"Yes, I would prefer it," he answered with a huff. "What has gotten into you?"

Kate rose and walked towards the window, creating more distance between her and Adrien. Now she could see Roger was standing in the hall, listening to the conversation, and it provided her with great comfort. She had never had cause for alarm around Adrien before, but she had made the mistake of not being afraid of Michel at first, either.

As she glanced out the window, she could see Adrien's reflection in the glass. He was gazing intently at her as if he was trying to sort out a puzzle.

Feeling brave, Kate turned to face him, and she could feel her legs start to quiver beneath her dress. "I would like to live here," she asserted, attempting to keep her voice steady. "If you would grant me some time, I would be willing to buy the country home."

"With what funds?" he asked, crossing his arms. "Did you forget that I control your allowance?"

"I could sell my grandmother's land or my grandmother's jewelry. I could also ask my father for funds," she said, her confidence faltering.

Kate placed her hand onto a side table for support, feeling as if her legs would collapse beneath her. She had never stood up to anyone before and it was quite unnerving.

Uncrossing his arms, Adrien rose from his chair and took a step towards her. She instinctively took a step backwards. Immediately, his steps faltered as his green eyes assessed her.

Could he see her trembling? Did he know how afraid she was to confront him?

Understanding crossed his features and his eyes softened. "I will call on you tomorrow to discuss the particulars. If you would like to remain living here, then I will not deny your request. However, I must beg of you to not consider selling your grandmother's land or jewelry, but it is yours to do with as you wish."

"Thank you, Adrien," Kate responded, gratefully.

He opened his mouth, but then closed it again. He bowed and said his goodbyes. As he walked down the front steps, Kate watched him stop and glance back at the window. He tipped his head at her and hopped into the black carriage.

Kate released a relieved sigh. Adrien had not gone into a fit of rage when she challenged him, nor did he strike her for being impertinent. While at Beaumont Castle, she had grown to consider Adrien a friend, but had been careful never to share too many details about her past.

*Do not boggle gentlemen's minds with your burdens*, her mother had told her. *They don't care one whit about women's frivolous concerns.*

She leaned her head against the cold window pane. She would never allow another man to control her as Michel had. No, she would rather die.

AS THE CARRIAGE LURCHED AWAY, ADRIEN SLAMMED HIS FIST against his thigh. Kate had been afraid of him! She had intentionally taken a step back when he moved to offer her comfort, and her eyes confirmed her distress.

He had watched Kate's body tremble as she told him no, and her voice had a slight tremor to it. She had thought he was callous enough to force his plans on her without listening to her thoughts on the matter. When she had placed her hand on the table for additional support, he would have given anything to see her smile, to make her smile.

It greatly unsettled him that Kate was afraid of him. The French were afraid of him, with good reason, but to his knowledge, he had never scared a woman before. If anything, women flocked to him and vied for his attention.

For some reason, the country home offered her solace, and he wanted to find out why. Tomorrow, he would call on her and extract a smile from her as he had at Beaumont Castle. He needed to be mindful that Kate should be treated as if she was a spooked horse. Not that she had any resemblance to a horse. Not at all!

Earlier he had reminisced on Kate's beauty, but his memory fell short of her actual comeliness. With her alluring emerald green dress, and her light blonde hair piled high on top of her head, she had reminded him of the Greek goddess, Aphrodite. When she spoke, he found he focused on her full, luscious lips, and he'd had to remind himself a few times to focus on her words.

It was apparent that Kate had a protector in Roger, an agent he recognized from Beaumont Castle, but she needed a friend. A true friend to help ease her back into polite society, after a proper mourning period, of course. With her beauty and connections, she would be popular amongst the ton and would have more friends than just her household staff.

Yes, and he was just the man to do it. He would be her friend.

# 3

DISMOUNTING HER CHESTNUT STALLION, KATE HANDED HER reins to the stable boy. "Thank you," she said, before swiftly walking the short distance to her country home.

Mr. Oakes held open the door for her as she removed her riding hat and gloves. Handing them to him, she asked, "Are the baskets ready?"

"Yes, Lady Camden. I have prepared the two that you requested."

"Thank you." She nodded her approval as she smoothed out her cerulean blue riding habit. She wouldn't have time to change. "Is Roger ready to depart?"

"He is in the kitchen talking to Mrs. Palmer," he answered with a knowing smile. "Those two seem to be on friendly terms."

She laughed. "You are quite the matchmaker."

Mr. Oakes glanced over her shoulder at the large window, overlooking the front entry. "It appears that Lord Camden is early today. Are you available for callers?"

Spinning around, she saw the familiar black crested carriage lurching to a stop and a feeling of dread formed in the pit of her stomach. "Oh no, my morning ride took longer than anticipated."

She started walking swiftly towards the kitchen. "Please send Lord Camden my regrets and inform him I am visiting families in the village."

"It has been four days since you first received him," Mr. Oakes reminded as he trailed after her. "Eventually, he will figure out that you are avoiding him."

"I am not avoiding him," she stated over her shoulder, ignoring Mr. Oakes' chuckling.

Was she avoiding him? At first, her morning ride took longer because her horse threw a shoe, so she missed Lord Camden's visit. In response, she had sent a messenger with a letter asking him to inform her in writing about the changes to her allowance, but the stubborn man had sent a return missive announcing he would call on her tomorrow. The last two days she had walked to the village at the precise time she knew Adrien would be calling.

Reluctantly, she admitted to herself that she was avoiding him. But why? They had been friends at Beaumont Castle and it had been easy to converse with him. However, now he was Lord Camden, and she was the countess, albeit the dowager, which allowed him to lord over her, enforcing his will upon her. She did not want him to have that control. So here she was, avoiding him at all costs.

In the warm kitchen, Roger was sitting on a stool, but rose when she strode into the room.

"Are you ready?" she asked him, reaching for the two baskets on the counter.

Roger smiled with a knowing look. "I assume Lord Camden's carriage has pulled up?"

Mrs. Palmer shook her spoon at Roger. "Oh, hush. If my Kate wants to run from a dashingly handsome man who resembles a pirate, who are we to judge?"

Kate's lips twitched in amusement, but she refused to take the bait. "He does not look like a pirate."

Mrs. Palmer started stirring the contents in the pot over the fire. "Are you finally admitting you find him dashingly handsome?"

"I will concede he is handsome, but that matters not. He is a man, and men cannot be trusted," she asserted.

"That is not a fair assessment," Roger stated in a bantering tone.

Kate moved towards the back door of the kitchen. "All right, I can trust *you*." She opened the door. "We need to hurry if we wish to sneak out before Lord…" Her mouth snapped closed when she saw Adrien leaning against the exterior kitchen wall.

He was looking entirely too pleased with himself as he watched her with a lopsided grin. "Good morning, Kate," he said, obviously amused.

"Adrien, it… it is good to see you," she stammered.

He straightened and glanced at the kitchen door. "I see you are resorting to escaping through the servant's quarters."

"I was doing no such thing," she lied. "I was searching for Roger, and he happened to be in the kitchen with our cook."

Adrien tilted his head towards the open window. "I overheard the entire conversation," he admitted with a twinkle in his eye.

"Oh," she mumbled, diverting her gaze.

"I especially liked the part where you admitted I was handsome," he declared with a smug smile.

She could feel her cheeks growing warm and ducked her head. What could she say to that?

Adrien took a few steps closer, but stopped to maintain proper distance. "Why have you been ignoring me?"

She bit her lower lip as she debated how to answer. She could not tell him the truth, or it might upset him, but lying to him did not seem feasible either. "I am sorry for my actions."

"Kate." He spoke her name so calmly that it momentarily disarmed her. "Nothing you say, or do, will ever upset me enough to lash out at you. It is obvious you are wary of me, but there is nothing to fear."

Kate met his gaze. His eyes seemed compassionate towards her, but that could be faked. Deciding to provide him with a submissive answer, she responded, "I understand."

Adrien shook his head. "No, I want truth between us. No more vague answers. I want you to speak your mind."

Turning her head slightly, she saw Roger nearby, but he was standing back in the kitchen, granting her and Adrien privacy. She turned her head to meet Adrien's gaze. "I will do as you ask."

Sighing, Adrien glanced over her shoulder towards Roger. "Did Michel ever strike you for being impertinent?"

Her eyes grew wide, fearful, and she took a step back, providing more distance between them. "Why? Do you think I'm being impertinent?" she asked, afraid of his answer.

"Impertinent? No. But exasperating? Yes," Adrien said, softening his words with a dashing smile.

"In what way am I being exasperating?"

Taking a step closer to her, he replied, "By answering my questions with responses that you think I want to hear."

"I do not," she replied softly.

"You do," he stated, giving her an amused smile. "But, I will ask my question again, and I want the truth. Did he ever strike you for being impertinent?"

Lowering her gaze to his blue riding coat, Kate whispered, "You already know that answer."

"He had no right to hurt you, husband or not." He stepped closer. "You should feel free to express your opinion without the fear of a rebuke."

Her eyes lowered to his buckskin breeches and black riding boots. She had no idea what to say to him. His words sounded sincere, but she was all too aware that men often used fancy, flowery words to achieve their purpose.

"I want us to be friends again."

"I would like that, too," she admitted honestly. She had

enjoyed his friendship at Beaumont Castle, but she felt safe there, surrounded by agents.

"Good, because I'm a spy," he stated matter-of-factly.

She glanced up at him with an arched brow, confused. "I am aware of that fact."

A smile played on his lips. "And yet you thought you could outmaneuver me?"

Kate's lips slowly turned into a smile when she realized he was teasing her. "I did avoid you for three days."

"No, I let you *believe* you had avoided me for three days." He glanced down at the baskets in her hand. "Where are you off to today?"

"I have two deliveries to make in the village."

"Excellent. I believe I shall join you," he said, extending his hand to hold the baskets.

The words 'that is very presumptuous of you' were on the tip of her tongue, but instead she simply smiled. "I would like that very much."

"Liar," he teased, as he offered her his arm.

"I beg your pardon?"

Giving her a charming smile, he revealed, "Whenever you are about to tell a lie, you press your lips together."

"I do not," she denied.

Roger piped up from behind them. "It is true. He does have a point."

She whipped her head towards Roger. "Traitor."

Roger shrugged. "It is a very tell-tale sign."

Removing her hand from Adrien's arm, she started walking towards the pathway to the village, ignoring the laughter behind her.

ADRIEN WATCHED KATE BRISKLY MARCH ON THE DIRT ROAD, HER riding habit swinging from hip to hip. He had not meant to cause her distress, but he wanted her to know that he knew when she was lying. He did not want a submissive friend, but one who voiced her opinions.

Increasing his steps, he reached Kate's side and offered her his arm. For a moment, he thought she would refuse, but her refined training won out and she placed her arm on top of his.

"What's in the baskets?" he inquired, breaking the silence between them.

"Mrs. Palmer packed them with bread, left-over ham, and biscuits," she informed him, as her eyes gazed at the green fields.

"And who are we visiting today?"

Kate pressed her lips together, and he was certain she was going to lie to him. "Just a couple of villagers down on their luck. Nothing to concern yourself with."

"I see," he replied, with a side-long glance. She was hiding something, but he would leave her be. "How are you enjoying the country air?"

Tilting her head towards him, she smiled shyly. "I do love the clean air and the wide-open fields. London was so congested and smelled awful."

Understanding her complaint about the London smell, Adrien could not help but return her smile. "Yes, London does take some time to become accustomed to. I find I enjoy my estate up near Northumberland," he revealed, then his smile faltered.

"What is it?" Kate asked, her hand tightened on his arm.

His eyes flickered towards her then straight ahead. "I should clarify and say I used to enjoy my time at Pratt Hall. Even though people surround me there, sometimes I feel so..."

"Lonely," she finished for him. "I know what you mean."

"Michel killed the remainder of my family," Adrien stated flatly.

With a look of contemplation, Kate murmured, "He destroyed many people's lives."

They walked in silence until he nudged her with his arm. "Technically, you are my last remaining relation as my cousin-in-law."

"I never was truly married to your cousin, Matthew," she said, frowning. "I married a French spy, masquerading as an earl. In truth, I am a fraud, too."

He patted her arm, attempting to reassure her. "The ton will only ever know you as Lady Camden, Countess of Camden."

"I would prefer not to be called Lady Camden," she sighed, her expression haunted.

"You did nothing wrong, Kate," he reassured her. "Your mother forced you into that marriage."

"I believe that is why I don't think of him as Matthew anymore. I do not want to tarnish your true cousin's legacy by associating him with the conspiracy," Kate admitted.

Her free hand rose to hold a large, round, gold locket that hung around her neck. She habitually reached for her locket when she was upset, something he had first noticed at Beaumont Castle.

Before he asked another question, Kate tugged on his arm and nodded towards a crude, shingle-board house, which at one point had been painted white. It sat next to a large oak tree, and one side of the house leaned onto the tree for support.

"If you will be so kind as to give me one of the baskets, I will go in and check on Mary," she said, glancing expectantly at him.

He handed her a basket and watched as Kate knocked on the door. A young woman, heavy with child, opened the door and peered out uncertainly. With a few words from Kate, the young woman smiled and opened the door wide enough to let her enter. As she started to close the door, her eyes met his. A look of fear flashed on her face, and she slammed the door shut.

His eyes roamed the tilted, shabby home, not sure what he should attempt to repair first. The roof was collapsing in on itself, the small windows were covered by tattered sheets, and the weeds were overflowing the yard.

As his eyes traveled towards a minuscule pile of wood, he saw an ax leaning against it. Chopping wood was something he could handle with his limited resources. He might as well make himself useful. He removed his coat, draped it on the fence, and started chopping the wood. Roger came to assist him by piling the wood as he chopped.

After they had created a large wood pile, Kate came out and walked towards him. All the exertion of chopping the wood was worth it when he saw the warm glow of approval in her eyes.

"That was most kind of you, Adrien."

"Roger helped, too," he informed her as he reached for his coat and shrugged it back on. "I do not enjoy being idle."

He offered her his arm, and they walked towards the next home in silence. As they approached the larger shingle-board home, he noted the similar disrepair as Kate walked towards the door. As before, he went to increase the wood pile.

A short time later, they started walking back towards the estate with Roger trailing behind. He was pleased to know that Kate was delivering baskets to the less fortunate, but his curiosity won out.

"Can you tell me who you delivered the baskets to?" he asked.

"Just two women that have been feeling ill lately," Kate murmured, her eyes focusing on the horizon.

Adrien wanted to shake her and demand to know the truth. Why was she being so stubborn? "What is the cause of their sickness?" he pressed.

Kate's focus now turned to the dirt road in front of her as her riding boots jetted in and out from under her habit. "They have been sick for some time now. A shame, really." She turned towards him with a smile on her lips. "Have you had a chance to see Benedict and Eliza lately?"

He studied her, knowing she was attempting to distract him. "Yes, I had dinner with them a few nights ago."

"You must send my regards," she said casually. "I look forward to…"

Adrien stopped in the road, and her voice trailed off. Turning to face her, he asked, "Do you recall that I mentioned I was a spy?"

Her puckered brow caused him to smile. "Yes."

"My power of deduction has allowed me to recognize that you are keeping something from me."

"Oh?"

"You are hiding something about those women that you visited," he tried to prompt.

She turned her head to glance towards Roger, then back towards him, but this time, she focused on the brass buttons of his coat. "You must promise not to be angry."

"Kate," he said softly. He placed his finger under her chin and gently tilted her head up. "I am not Michel. I will never hurt you."

Her face scrunched in sadness. "I know, but you two are very similar in appearance."

"In appearance, yes," he admitted, "but, in temperament, no."

She blew out a breath of air. "Whenever my husband would visit the country home, he took liberties with the female staff. I tried to help as many as I could, but he still managed to seduce some of the maids."

Adrien held in an expletive. "And the women we visited today?"

"They are carrying his babes," she responded weakly.

He dropped her chin and gently placed his arms around her,

pulling her into an embrace. At first, she stood rigid, but gradually she relaxed into his arms.

Of all the despicable things that man could have done! He seduced women in his employ, and right under his wife's nose. Poor Kate. Those poor women.

After a few moments, he stepped back and placed his hands on her shoulders. Slowly, she brought her gaze to meet his. "You have my blessing to continue bringing baskets to those women. Also, I noticed their homes are badly in need of repair. I will see that someone goes out and repairs their roofs and anything else they require."

Kate's eyes lit up and a smile broke across her beautiful face. "Thank you. That is most generous."

"Those women have endured a great hardship, and we will help them together, if you will allow me," he said.

"I would like that," she stated, her smile still intact.

She reached to loop her hand into his arm as they started walking once again down the dirt road. It was the first time she had initiated the touch, and it thrilled him. She was beginning to trust him.

This was a good start to their friendship.

# 4

"HAVE YOU CONVINCED KATE TO ABANDON THE COUNTRY ESTATE and move back in with us?" Benedict asked as they rode in his carriage for another session of Parliament.

Adrien stopped staring out the window and turned his gaze towards Benedict. "No, she is determined to stay."

Benedict crossed his arms, obviously displeased with his answer. "Eliza could use her sister right now."

"By all means, you try to convince her to leave," he stated, flipping his wrist.

"I doubt I could. Stubbornness is a trait that runs in their family."

"Kate is just beginning to trust me. I will not run the risk of alienating her because Eliza wants a roommate. She already has *you*," he said, pointing at Benedict.

"I cannot seem to figure Eliza out," Benedict admitted, frowning. "One minute she is laughing at my jokes, and the next she is crying about something she has no control over."

"Maybe she is crying because your jokes are terrible?"

Ignoring his witty retort, Benedict surmised, "Eliza was

happy when Kate was living with us, so naturally I have concluded she is devastated that Kate moved out."

Leaning back in the velvet bench seat, Adrien decided to change topics. "Kate informed me that Michel impregnated multiple maids at her country home and provided them with no means of support."

Benedict's brow elevated. "Did that man possess any shred of humanity?"

"No, I believe he did not."

Returning to the previous topic, Adrien revealed, "Kate has finally stopped cowering when I step closer to her."

"That is a good sign."

Adrien nodded his agreement. "I believe Kate should be reintroduced to proper society."

"I concur with that assessment," Benedict replied. "Eliza would be happy to help her."

"Technically, Kate should be in mourning for a year as a widow, but she has opted not to wear mourning attire. I believe the ton would not be supportive of her decision to forgo tradition."

Sighing, Benedict uncrossed his arms. "The ton would most likely give her the direct cut, even with Eliza's and my support."

"Exactly, which is why I propose we bring her to Lord Thornley's masquerade ball at the end of the week."

"That could work."

"Do you think Eliza would take Kate to order a new ballgown?" Adrien questioned, eagerly.

Benedict laughed loudly. "Even I know that a lady's ballgown has to be commissioned and will certainly not be available by the end of the week."

"What if I pay extra?"

"You could try," Benedict said with a shrug.

The carriage rolled to a stop in front of the Palace of Westminster, and they exited the carriage. As they walked through the large foyer, Benedict asked, "Have you located your seat yet?"

"Yes, I was here yesterday," Adrien grumbled, rubbing the back of his neck with his hand.

Benedict chuckled. "You will get used to the high-backed benches."

"They remind me of the benches at my parish."

Benedict's eyes darted around the foyer. "Today's schedule has Lord Williams, a Whig, speaking about the war against France. He's trying to garner support for the bill."

"The bill won't be voted on for another two and a half weeks," Adrien stated, his eyes assessing the foyer for all exits as a precaution. "Why is Lord Devon not addressing the House of Lords? After all, he was the creator of the bill."

"I do not know, but I intend to find out," his friend asserted, facing him, but continuing his scan.

"I was thinking if we discover who the French spy is in the House of Lords, it will be easy to discover who they endorsed for the House of Commons," Adrien explained as his eyes perused all the lords waiting for the meeting to start.

"Good point," Benedict agreed, slapping his back. "I will see you after the session."

Walking towards the rear door of the assembly hall, Adrien claimed his seat on the wood bench. Luckily, he was sitting next to the aisle, but to his left sat a heavy-set Lord Bryan, who spent more time sleeping than listening.

The lord speaker started the session with a booming welcome speech, and Adrien found himself looking over the men in the large room. He had not met many of the lords yet, but he knew he would eventually be introduced to the various members of Parliament.

While listening to Lord Bryan's light snoring, Adrien felt someone staring at him before his eyes found the person. An average-sized man, with brown hair, was glaring at him from across the room. He did not appear repentant when Adrien's gaze landed on him. Who was that lord? He wondered if Benedict knew his name.

After a three-hour speech on the debts being accrued from the war with France, the lord speaker called for a break. Adrien attempted to intercept the lord that had been watching him, but he was nowhere to be found in the main foyer.

Turning in a circle, Adrien kept his eyes open as he hoped to spot the mysterious lord. As he was about to give up and return to his seat, the man in question exited the main doors at a break-neck speed.

Adrien hastily followed him out the doors and through the streets of London. After ten blocks, the lord ducked into an alleyway without glancing behind him. Adrien stopped and retrieved his pistol from the back of his trousers.

He cautiously walked into the foul-smelling, narrow alley, keeping his pistol in front of him. The man stood under the light of a window, looking as if he was waiting for Adrien to appear.

"You can put that away, Lord Camden," the mysterious lord stated.

"Not until you properly identify yourself," Adrien commanded, as he kept his body on alert for a possible trap.

"My name is Lord Wessex, and I needed to talk to you," the man said, nervously looking at the pistol pointed at him.

Frowning, he kept his gun steady at the man's chest. "And you thought an ill-lit alleyway was a proper meeting place."

"I could not risk anyone overhearing our conversation," Lord Wessex explained.

Adrien lowered his pistol but kept it by his side. "You have five minutes."

Lord Wessex winced. "I received a threat against my sister's life."

"Why would you come to me with this information?" Adrien asked. "Why not the Bow Street Runners?"

Lord Wessex looked surprised. "I was told that you worked for the Crown. Was I misinformed?"

"Who gave you that information?" He was preparing to bring the pistol back up if Wessex had the wrong answer.

Lord Wessex lowered his voice. "I had first approached Lord Pembrooke, and he told me to seek you out. He gave me the impression that I could trust you. Was I mistaken?"

Adrien raked his hand through his nicely groomed hair. "No, but I will be verifying your story with Lord Pembrooke."

"I understand," Lord Wessex said.

"Please start from the beginning. Leave nothing out."

"I will just show you," Lord Wessex replied, slowly reaching into his coat pocket. He pulled out a paper and handed it to him.

Adrien read, *If you value your sister's life, you will vote Yes for the bill to end the war against France.* His gaze returned to Lord Wessex. "I consider this threat credible."

"As do I," Lord Wessex agreed, his concern evident on his brow. "My butler has mentioned questionable characters have been seen loitering outside our townhouse."

"Can you send your sister to a safe place?"

"I could send her to our country home in South Yorkshire, but I worry about highway robbers," Lord Wessex admitted.

"Your sister's life is in peril. You will need to keep her under lock and key till after the vote, whether at your townhouse or country home," Adrien stated.

"I understand."

"I will take the information and act on it. I will be in touch," Adrien said, ending the conversation as he turned and strode out of the alleyway.

KATE WAS TWIRLING HER LOCKET BETWEEN HER HANDS AS SHE stared out the window of her drawing room. On her morning ride, she had veered her horse near the village and heard the unmistakable sounds of workers repairing the shingle-board homes. It appeared that Adrien had made good on his word.

Adrien seemed to be nothing like her husband. When he had embraced her yesterday, she felt protected, and dare she say, cared for. He appeared to be interested in what she had to say and did not criticize her words.

For now, she would be his friend, until he grew tired of the façade and showed his true nature. No man could be as kind as Adrien claimed to be. Well, that was not entirely true, Benedict was a good man, and he adored Eliza.

"It is good to see you, my beautiful friend," Adrien said, his words disrupting her thoughts.

Kate smiled. "You are being kind this morning."

"There is nothing kind about it," he insisted, returning her smile.

Tucking her locket under her puce, floral gown, Kate walked towards Adrien. "I want to thank you for sending workers over to repair the women's homes."

"That is only the beginning," he stated. "I purchased the land and will gift it to the women. Also, the workers will repair their entire homes and add on another room."

Kate put her hand to her heart. "I cannot thank you enough."

Adrien's eyes roamed her face, his expression one of compassion. "Michel hurt a lot of people, and it is my duty to right his wrongs."

"I understand that sentiment all too well," she expressed, giving him a bittersweet smile.

With a slight lull in the conversation, Kate briefly admired

Adrien's attire of a black, cropped riding coat and dark breeches, with a white waistcoat. He must have ridden his horse and not taken the carriage, she mused.

"I was hoping to convince you to dine with me on the east lawn," Adrien said, a slow smile stretching across his face.

Not sure how to respond, Kate's hand went to her locket, and she absentmindedly twirled it in her fingers. Her eyes drifted towards the window to ensure the east lawn was visible from the country home. It would be nice to spend some time outside.

"If you would prefer, we could bring Roger along to chaperone," Adrien pressed, good-naturedly.

Turning her gaze away from the window, Kate saw his face held uncertainty. She smiled. "I do not think that is necessary."

"So, you will accompany me?"

"Yes, I believe I will," she answered, dropping her locket.

Adrien's face broke into a wide, relieved smile. Offering his arm, he escorted her outside to the east lawn where a blanket was already laid out with a large basket on top.

Adrien assisted her as she sat gracefully on the blanket, and he sat down next to her. "Let's see what Mrs. Palmer packed for us." He pulled out ham sandwiches and handed one to her.

After they spent a few moments eating, Kate turned her attention towards him. "How was your session of Parliament?"

Adrien shrugged. "I listened to a three-hour speech on the debts accrued from the war against France. It was an attempt by the Whig party to sway favor for the bill to end the war."

She gasped. "Oh no, that cannot happen."

Adrien wiped the crumbs off his hands. "I agree. Which is why I am voting against the bill."

"Do you think the bill will pass?"

He shook his head. "No, but the opponents of the war are working hard to achieve that end."

Thoughtfully, Kate took a bite of her sandwich.

Adrien leaned back onto his elbows, casually stretching on

the blanket. "I was hoping you would accompany me to Lord Thornley's masquerade ball at the end of the week."

Kate shook her head as she quickly swallowed. "No, thank you."

Turning towards her, he offered, "If funds are your concern, I will pay to commission a ball gown."

"That is not my concern."

"Chaperone, then?" he asked playfully. "We will be traveling with Eliza and Benedict."

"No," she said firmly.

"If you are worried that anyone will recognize you, don't be. You will be wearing a mask, and we would leave before the unveiling."

"I am sorry, but no."

"Did I ever tell you about how I pretended to be a French naval officer?" Adrien inquired with a lifted brow.

Surprised by the turn of the conversation, she shook her head in response.

"For three years, I lived on French frigates until I was called up to be an under-secretary for Admiral Garnier. During that time, I became friends with the other French officers as they spoke of centuries of hatred towards the British. I met their families and dined with them, all with the intention of betraying them, of protecting the Crown's interest in any way I could," Adrien revealed, glancing over the green field.

He sighed. "Sometimes we do things that take us out of what we are comfortable with, but that will allow us to grow. It shows us what we are capable of." He focused his gaze back to her, his eyes gleaming with concern. "Which is why I believe you need to be reintroduced into society."

Attempting to understand his logic, Kate scrunched her nose. "Are you comparing the ton to being undercover in France?"

Adrien chuckled. "They are very similar."

"I appreciate your efforts, but you do not understand my reservations."

"Then explain it to me," he said as he placed his hands under his head, laid down on the blanket, and closed his eyes. "And do not even think about lying to me."

Her hand went instinctively to finger her locket. She glanced over her shoulder to see if Roger was near, but she could not see him.

"I am waiting," Adrien stated, without opening his eyes.

Kate brought her gaze back to Adrien. She perused his handsome face, chiseled nose, and strong, square jaw, which made him far too attractive for his own good. A piece of his brown hair had fallen to his forehead, and she had a sudden desire to brush it aside.

Noticing one of Adrien's eyes was peeking open, she averted her gaze. "I was married at age seventeen, and except for being presented to the queen, and my engagement ball, I have not attended any social events held by the ton."

"None?"

"He preferred to attend such events alone," she admitted softly.

"We need to change that."

"No," Kate insisted, shaking her head. "I am happy here."

"You are twenty-three years old," Adrien contended, turning towards her. "You are too young to give up without a fight."

Kate drooped her shoulders. "Honestly, I do not have anything left to fight with."

"Yes, you do."

She turned her gaze towards the field, watching the long weeds blow in the wind. "Did you know that my sister was kicked out of the abbey by my mother when she was ten?" She watched as Adrien shook his head in response. "I envied her. She was no longer under the rule of Diana the Terrible."

"The Terrible?" he repeated, chuckling.

Kate glanced sheepishly at him. "That is what I called her in my head. I tend to think wicked thoughts in my head."

"Why do you not share those thoughts with those around you?"

She furrowed her brow. "A lady never vocalizes her criticism."

"Who told you that?"

"My mother. She was constantly tutoring me with words of wisdom."

Adrien huffed, "Those are not words of wisdom, but rather idiotic advice."

"I often thought so."

"Then I propose we do one thing a day that would have scandalized your mother," Adrien said, smirking.

"I already do," Kate confessed. "I take baskets to the women in the village. My mother thought that was beneath her station."

"What do you do for fun, Kate?" Adrien asked, leaning closer to her.

"I read, paint, and sometimes practice the pianoforte."

"What else?"

"I like to take walks," she added.

With a shake of his head, Adrien replied, "Just listening to you is making me bored. You need to have more adventure in your life."

"I beg your pardon?"

Ignoring her bristly tone, Adrien pointed west. "I noticed a stream running along those trees. I propose we remove our shoes and put our bare feet in the water."

Kate's eyes grew wide. "That is ridiculous and... and scandalous!"

"And fun!" Adrien jumped up and offered her his hand. With amusement on his features, he teased, "Don't worry, if anyone catches us then I will offer you my hand in marriage."

Kate's hands stayed firmly in her lap as she gazed at Adrien's face. His eyes were twinkling, but it was the way he was calmly offering her his hand that caused her to pause. He was allowing her to make the choice. He was not forcing her but encouraging her.

She slowly raised her gloved hand to place it in his, and he gently assisted her as she rose. He did not release her hand as he led her to the stream through a grove of trees.

As they came closer to the stream, her steps faltered. She could not take her shoes off in front of a man. As if Adrien sensed her hesitation, he glanced back and offered her an encouraging smile. With her courage bolstered, she followed him as he led her to a cluster of rocks.

By the time she had lowered herself down to sit on a large rock, Adrien had removed his riding boots and stockings.

Averting her eyes from his bare feet, Kate admonished, "If you want me to put my feet in the water, then you must allow me some privacy to remove my boots and stockings."

Adrien stood up and kept his back towards her, while humming a song she was unfamiliar with.

"Done," she announced as she stood. When she took a tentative step, she felt the wet leaves and pebbles on the bottom of her feet.

Turning back around, Adrien offered his hand, and they walked into the small stream. The icy water flowed around her feet, and the gritty sand squished between her toes.

Feeling rebellious and free, she could not help the burst of laughter that erupted from her. She dropped Adrien's hand, picked up her skirts, and started spinning in a circle. Kate felt the bottom of her dress become wet, but she did not care. It felt invigorating to do something so bold, yet so simple.

After a few moments, she stopped spinning and turned to face Adrien. He was watching her with an amused smile. "I had a feeling you might enjoy this."

"Thank you," she proclaimed, hoping to express her appreciation adequately. "I have never done anything so shocking."

Adrien threw his head back and laughed. "This is relatively tame on the scandalous scale."

Kate felt her smile grow. "To you, perhaps, but to me, it felt exhilarating."

His eyes latched onto her. "Do you trust me now?"

"No," she admitted, her smile vanishing. "I have been hurt too many times to give away my trust so easily."

"I understand," he replied, not seeming bothered by her admission. "Do you at least trust that I won't hurt you?"

"I can concede that point."

"Good." Adrien took a step closer. "Come to the masquerade ball with me."

Kate shook her head. "I cannot."

"It will be a new adventure," he asserted, his warm eyes looking earnestly at her. "It is a masquerade ball, and no one will know who you are. Besides, you will not be doing this alone. I will be by your side all evening, as well as your sister and Benedict."

"I don't think I can," she confessed, pained by her own admission.

"It is time to come out of hiding, Kate." His words were soft, but they pierced her soul. She realized she had been hiding out at the country home.

A night of dancing did sound more promising than dinner alone and reading in the library till her eyes drooped. "If I agree to come, then you must ensure I won't be left alone," Kate stated, her voice faltering.

"I give you my word," he said, his eyes confirming his emotions. He was telling her the truth.

Kate knew she had to make a choice. She could continue living as she had been, afraid to take risks. Or, she could trust Adrien and experience a masquerade ball. After all, her sister and Benedict would be there to help support her. She could do this. She would do this!

Feeling the sand swirling around her feet, she wanted to feel that sensation again. With her choice made, Kate smiled up at him. "I believe I have some shopping to do."

# 5

KATE WAS GREETED BY ADRIEN AS SHE STEPPED OUT OF THE carriage in front of Eliza's townhouse. He was looking especially dashing in a slate morning coat, white cravat, and buff pantaloons, which highlighted his muscular thighs. Even though he was impeccably dressed, it was his friendly face that she was anxious to see.

"I appreciate you arranging my transportation to London," Kate remarked to Adrien as he offered his arm.

"I trust my carriage was to your liking?"

"Oh my, yes," Kate gushed. "The velvet seating was incredibly plush, and it was a remarkably smooth ride."

Adrien nodded his approval. "That is good to hear."

He escorted her up the stairs and into Benedict's townhouse. Although she had stayed at the townhouse for a week, she was still in awe of the grandeur of the home. The main entry consisted entirely of marble, with white columns spaced throughout. Plus, the ceiling was painted with intricate designs.

"Kate!" Eliza proclaimed as she raced down the stairs towards her. Adrien dropped her arm as Eliza pulled her into a tight embrace. "I have missed you so much."

She was happy to see her sister looking so well and returned her embrace with much enthusiasm. "I have missed you, too."

Releasing her, Eliza turned her attention towards Adrien with tears in her eyes. "Thank you for convincing Kate to visit me."

Adrien just blinked, looking a bit bewildered at Eliza's tearful gratitude. After a moment, he cleared his throat. "You are welcome."

Glancing over her shoulder, Eliza acknowledged Roger. "I cannot adequately express my relief that you have been protecting my sister."

Roger shifted his stance by the door, glancing nervously at Adrien. "You are most kind, Lady Lansdowne."

For a moment, Kate thought Eliza would embrace Roger, but instead, she turned her attention back to her. "I have scheduled an appointment with Madame Lancaster to find you a new ballgown before the masquerade ball."

"Kate!" Benedict's voice echoed off the walls as he strode across the hall. As he embraced her, he whispered, "Your sister has gone mad. I cannot for the life of me figure out what I keep doing wrong."

Eliza huffed. "You insisted on eating the plum pudding even though the sight of..." Her face paled as her hand flew to her mouth, and she fled the room.

Staring at his wife's retreating figure, the concern on Benedict's face was evident. "Eliza refuses to send for the doctor, but she has been like this since you left us."

Kate glanced at Adrien and Roger who both also wore solemn expressions. It was apparent that the men in the room did not understand Eliza's condition. She decided to take pity on her brother-in-law. "I would summon the doctor for confirmation, but I believe Eliza may be with child."

Benedict turned to face her, his eyes wide. "Are you certain?"

Trying not to laugh at his shocked expression, she said,

"Based on what I just witnessed, I am quite certain."

Excitement filled his every feature, and he whooped loudly as he ran to follow his wife.

Adrien moved to stand next to her, his hands clasped behind his back. "It appears that Benedict is happy with the news."

"A baby is always welcome news," she murmured wistfully. If Michel had not beaten her, causing her to lose the babe she'd been carrying, she would have been a few months along herself.

Adrien's expression was filled with compassion as he leaned closer. "Their child will be blessed to have such a loving and caring aunt. I have no doubt you will spoil the little one."

She tilted her head towards him, feeling grateful for his words. "Thank you, Adrien. That brings me great comfort."

Nodding, Adrien's eyes roamed her face but lingered on her lips for a moment. Looking back in the direction Eliza had fled, she voiced her thoughts. "Maybe I should go see if Eliza needs assistance?"

Before either of them spoke, Eliza and Benedict walked back into the room, hand in hand, and both wearing bright smiles.

"Are you ready to go shopping?" Eliza asked her.

Kate eyed her warily. "Are you sure you are up to it?"

"Yes, I am. I could use a day out," she replied confidently.

Addressing Benedict, Adrien suggested, "Why don't you and I go to White's for a celebratory drink?"

Benedict shook his head. "No, I would prefer to accompany my wife to the modiste."

Eliza's smile grew wider as she gazed at her husband. "Go with Adrien. Kate and I will be content to go to the modiste alone."

"Not exactly alone. Roger and I will be accompanying you," Mr. Larson stated as he walked into the hall. "I heard congratulations are in order."

Benedict's mouth gaped. "How did you hear the news so fast?"

Mr. Larson tsked. "You disappoint me, Lord Lansdowne. I have suspected it for a couple of weeks now. I suppose that proves that my power of deduction is far superior to yours."

Kate giggled behind her gloved hand. She had grown to adore Mr. Larson and his teasing of Benedict. She knew both men had a deep love for Eliza, but it was apparent that they respected each other, as well.

Benedict glanced her way, making an odd face. "It is not funny, Kate. Larson has become delusional in his old age."

Eliza laughed. "You two behave." She leaned in and kissed her husband on the cheek, lingering for a moment. "Go have a drink with Adrien. We will be fine."

Kate's hand rose to grasp the locket around her neck. Eliza and Benedict were a love match and showered each other with affection and praise at every opportunity. How she wished she had been as lucky. To love, and be loved equally in return, was her greatest wish. However, her heart had been torn to pieces by Michel, ruining all hopes of loving another.

Feeling Adrien's hand on the small of her back, she tilted her head towards him.

"What is wrong?" he asked as his eyes seemed to look directly into her soul.

She attempted to give him a reassuring smile, but failed miserably. "I think it is wonderful how much Eliza and Benedict love each other."

Adrien frowned. "I find it quite revolting."

"You do?"

"They are constantly kissing each other, and Benedict will stare at doors attempting to conjure up Eliza," Adrien said, shaking his head. "It is madness, I tell you."

"That was Jonathon, you fool," Benedict stated, interrupting their interlude.

"We will be late for our appointment if we do not leave now," Eliza declared as she looped her arm around Kate's.

AFTER SORTING THROUGH PILES OF DRESSES AT MADAM Lancaster's exclusive shop, the famous modiste insisted on a rose dress, brocaded with white silken flowers, and worn over a white satin slip. As she tried on the gown, Madame Lancaster pinned and tucked the dress to ensure the correct measurements were taken so the dress could be altered. She was aware that the ballgown was urgent and guaranteed it would be delivered tomorrow.

When they were finished, Eliza and Kate strolled down the street intending to enjoy some lemon ice at Gunter's Tea Shop.

Walking down the street, Kate felt a bit self-conscious that she was not in mourning attire. Not because she mourned her husband or mother, but she knew the ton would judge her harshly for her actions. Technically, she wasn't even supposed to leave her country home for several months to demonstrate her grief.

Could she pretend to mourn her husband for a year, so the ton would accept her? No, she was glad he was dead. Besides, she could easily avoid London for the next year. Maybe she would avoid London altogether.

"Lady Lansdowne!" A sweet voice broke through Kate's musings.

"Lady Rachel!" Eliza proclaimed, quickly embracing her friend before turning towards Kate. "May I introduce you to my sister, Lady Camden. Kate… this is my good friend, Lady Rachel, daughter of the Earl of Exeter."

Lady Rachel dropped into a polite curtsy. "It is a pleasure to meet you." She glanced over Eliza's shoulder and waved. "I see Mr. Larson is as threatening as always."

Eliza swatted at her friend's puffy white sleeve. "He is protective of me."

Lady Rachel dramatically rolled her eyes. "Over-protective is the word I would use." She turned to Kate and informed her, "He threatened to kill me."

Kate's eyes grew wide. "Whatever for?"

Lady Rachel looked at Eliza for a moment, and Kate was certain something was being communicated between them that she was not privy to. "It was an unfortunate misunderstanding," she informed her with a wave of her hand.

"Oh," Kate mumbled, a bit disappointed.

"I've been doing some shopping," Rachel said energetically, "and I'm pleased to run into you two."

Eliza lifted a brow. "Not by yourself, I hope."

Rachel huffed, "Of course not." She glanced over her shoulder to acknowledge a woman, holding packages, and three men huddled back a few yards. "My father insisted I bring along three footmen, in addition to my lady's maid."

"Just three?" Eliza teased. "Oh, I recently purchased a book written by a lady and I thought about you. Have you read it?"

Kate stood idly by as Lady Rachel and Eliza engaged in a conversation about the books they had recently acquired. Lady Rachel was a beautiful woman with wheat-colored hair, pulled back into a low bun, and a straw hat with lace flowers sat slightly skewed on her head. Her wide, sparkling blue eyes lit up with excitement as she conversed with Eliza.

Glancing back at Roger, Kate felt melancholy as she listened to their happy chatter. She had always known that she paled in comparison to Eliza when it came to… well, to everything. When they were younger, Eliza used to sneak into her room at the abbey and tell her about the books she had read previously. Their mother would criticize everything that Eliza would do, but her criticism shifted to her when Eliza moved to live with Uncle Charles.

Kate was forbidden to go to the library without her governess. Her mother refused to let her daughter become a bluestocking, and limited the books she could have access to. Unfortunately, Michel shared a similar mindset as her mother. He would fly into a fit of rage if he caught her reading. He even slapped her when she dared to ask to read the newspaper.

"Kate?" Eliza asked, touching her arm. "Are you wool-gathering?"

"I'm afraid I was." She glanced up to see Eliza and Lady Rachel's expectant faces. "Did I miss something?"

Lady Rachel smiled warmly. "I was hoping to join you at Gunther's?"

"Yes, I would love that," she answered.

Leaning closer, Lady Rachel put her gloved hand up to her face. "I am glad to see that you are not mourning for your husband or your mother. They both were despicable."

Kate looked perplexed. "Did you know them?"

Lady Rachel dropped her hand but kept her voice low. "No, but I heard about their vile actions from another, and I daresay, I am glad that they are both dead." The corners of her mouth quirked. "I would mourn them no more than I would mourn the plague."

Eliza stepped closer and flashed Rachel a look of censure. "I apologize, Kate. My friend is a little blunt at times."

With a genuine smile, Kate replied, "I find that quality endearing in a friend, especially when she is accurate."

Rachel gave Eliza a haughty shrug. "I knew that Kate and I would become fast friends. It is evident who the *clever* twin is."

Feeling at ease around her new friend, Kate found herself relaxing. It warmed her heart to know someone as open as Rachel. Lady Rachel looped her arm around hers and started chatting away.

As they continued to stroll down the street, an enclosed carriage came barreling towards them with two men riding on top. Jerking the carriage to a stop next to them, a burly man jumped down from the top, grabbed Lady Rachel's arm, and yanked her towards the carriage's door.

In response, Lady Rachel began hitting the man with her reticule. Ignoring her feeble attack, he wrenched open the carriage door, keeping a firm hold on her wriggling forearm. A loud shot rang out next to Kate, and her head whipped around to see Eliza calmly placing a small, smoking pistol into the reticule around her wrist.

The man released Lady Rachel as his hand dropped to his thigh where a large blood stain was spreading on his trousers. As Mr. Larson and Roger stormed past them, the injured man jumped inside of the carriage as it raced away.

Frozen in fear, Kate watched the reckless carriage till it was out of sight. Did someone just attempt to abduct Lady Rachel off the streets of London? Did she imagine Eliza shooting a pistol into the man's leg as calmly as if she were eating lemon ice?

Finally turning her gaze, she witnessed Lady Rachel, Eliza, and Mr. Larson with their heads down, conversing privately.

"Are you all right, Lady Camden?" Roger asked with concern in his voice. At some point, he had moved to stand next to her.

Kate's hand rose to her locket. "Yes." She turned to him. "Did I just witness someone trying to abduct Lady Rachel?"

"You did."

"And did my sister shoot the attacker?"

"She did," he confirmed.

When did Eliza learn how to shoot a pistol? She knew Eliza excelled in archery and carried their father's dagger, but she had not drawn those weapons.

While Kate was mulling over these recent developments, Eliza's carriage pulled up next to them, and they quickly departed the scene.

# 6

As they drove towards Lady Rachel's townhouse at the edge of Mayfair, Eliza observed Kate was unusually quiet. It was not every day that someone witnessed an attempted abduction. As Rachel was being yanked towards the carriage, Eliza knew she needed to act without delay. She'd retrieved her overcoat pistol from her reticule, shot the attacker's leg, and replaced the gun before she thought anyone had witnessed her actions… but Kate had.

She would need to discuss this with her sister, but she did not have time to be distracted right now. Someone had boldly tried to abduct her friend in front of Gunther's. Fortunately for her, Rachel already knew that she was *Shadow*, because she had been one of the women abducted by Mr. Aaron Wade to be sold into slavery not so long ago. As Eliza had attempted to rescue the women from the brig, Rachel had witnessed the confrontation between Wade and herself, and even saved their lives by her quick thinking.

The carriage pulled up to the Earl of Exeter's townhouse. They exited the carriage and Rachel ascended the stairs ahead of them. She ushered them into her home, removed her hat, tossing it onto the entry table, and led them towards her father's study. She knocked once, before opening the door and waving them in.

"Father, I have an urgent matter that I must speak to you about," Rachel stated, forgoing the usual pleasantries. Except for her hair falling out of her chignon, which gave her a slightly disheveled look, her friend appeared calm.

Lord Exeter rose from his desk and eyed the group in his office suspiciously. "Will you introduce me to your friends?" he asked his daughter.

Rachel nodded and began to make the introductions. "Father, may I introduce Lady Lansdowne and her sister, Lady Camden."

At the name of Camden, she could see Lord Exeter stiffen, but he quickly recovered. "And the gentlemen with them?"

Rachel laughed. "Mr. Larson is the protector of Lady Lansdowne, but I am afraid I do not know the other gentleman's name."

Roger stepped forward. "My name is Roger Smith, my lord. I am under Lady Camden's employ."

Lord Exeter nodded his acknowledgement before turning back to his daughter. "What is the meaning of this interruption?" His words were formal, but there was an underlying concern in his tone.

"Someone tried to abduct me outside of Gunther's," Rachel informed her father.

Lord Exeter's eyes grew wide in shock as he muttered an expletive under his breath. He seemed to recover as he closed the distance between his daughter in two strides and pulled her into a protective embrace.

After a moment, he turned, but kept his arm around her shoulders. "Thank you for returning my daughter safely to me. I will take it from here."

Eliza could tell that Lord Exeter knew more than he was letting on. "Do you have any enemies that would profit from abducting Rachel?"

Frowning, Lord Exeter said, "Lady Lansdowne, I appreciate your forthright manner, but I do not believe you are equipped to handle such a serious matter." Rachel stifled a laugh, and her father tilted his head towards her. "I do not know what you could possibly find amusing, young lady."

"Lord Exeter, I know that you are considered a close friend to my uncle, Lord Charles Beckett," Eliza maintained.

He nodded. "I am friends with your father, as well."

"I also know that you are an influential man in Parliament, and if I'm not mistaken, you are the main opposition to the bill proposed to end the war against France," she stated.

Lord Exeter dropped his arm from his daughter, walked over to his drink tray, and poured himself a drink. "Lady Lansdowne, I do not mean to be rude, but I must go speak with your uncle immediately."

"And my uncle will then speak to me," Eliza countered firmly. "I am saving us time by coming to you directly."

Looking thoughtful, Lord Exeter took a sip of his drink before inquiring, "What do you want to know?"

Squaring her shoulders, she asked, "Have you been threatened recently?"

"No, I have not been." With his drink in hand, he pointed to Rachel. "But she has."

Rachel gasped, as Eliza pressed, "When?" Lord Exeter put down his drink and pulled a piece of paper out of his coat pocket, extending it to her. She took it and read, *If you value your daughter's life, you will vote Yes on the bill to end the war against France.*

Mr. Larson piped in, "When did you receive this threat?"

Lord Exeter sighed. "Three days ago."

Eliza saw Kate sit down on a chair towards the rear of the room, and Roger moved to stand next to her. It was clear that her sister relied on Roger's strength for her sense of security.

Focusing her attention back on Lord Exeter, Eliza informed

him, "You are being targeted because of your political voice. Most likely you will not be harmed, but it is apparent that your enemies will go to great lengths to get your vote. Can you send Rachel and Lady Exeter somewhere safe?"

With a shake of his head, Lord Exeter tried to dismiss her. "I apologize, but I would prefer to have this conversation with Lord Beckett."

"Father," Rachel said sharply. "Do not be ridiculous. Lady Lansdowne is a trusted friend."

Lord Exeter sat on the edge of his desk. "I understand that, but she cannot possibly understand the threat that is being placed on our family."

Rachel smirked. "You have no idea."

Lord Exeter frowned at his daughter, obviously confused by her words. "As I was saying…"

Cutting him off, Eliza spoke quickly, her voice taking on an authoritative tone, "Sir, do not dismiss me. I have the backing of the Crown. If you would like to waste time seeking out my uncle, risking your daughter's life in the process, then by all means, but I refuse to sit idly by." Not backing down, her intense gaze stayed on Lord Exeter as she continued, "If you do not heed my words, then I will abscond with Rachel right now, keeping her hidden until the threat has passed. Do I make myself clear?"

Her words had the intended effect, because Lord Exeter nodded, and his expression changed to one of respect. He straightened up and adjusted his waistcoat. "I believe I may have underestimated you, Lady Lansdowne. What would you recommend?"

Even if Lord Exeter didn't fully believe her, she did not care. "Do you have a place where you can send your wife and Rachel until the time has passed?"

"My wife is visiting our country home in Bath." He crossed his arms. "I could send Rachel there."

"No, not secure enough," she answered.

He furrowed his brow. "My brother has an estate in Scotland near a seaside village named Rockcliffe."

"That could work," Mr. Larson confirmed, as he walked further into the room. "Do you frequent his estate often?"

"Not as much as I would like," Lord Exeter admitted. "It has been over seven years since our last visit, but Rachel would be most welcome."

"We need to get Rachel out of the house undetected," Eliza asserted, turning to her friend. "I want you to pack your trunks quickly since you will be traveling tonight. If possible, your lady's maid should accompany you."

Rachel nodded, quickly striding towards the door.

"That is out of the question!" Lord Exeter shouted. "It will be dark soon."

Taking charge, Eliza turned back to him, ignoring his outburst. "I want your crested carriage brought out front, and have the servants make a big show of loading empty trunks." Turning to Roger, she requested, "Can you instruct our driver to move our carriage to the street closest to Lord Exeter's servant's entrance?"

"Yes, my lady." Roger bowed and walked swiftly out of the room.

"Stop! This is lunacy," Lord Exeter roared in disbelief. "My daughter will not be traveling anywhere tonight."

Deliberately keeping her voice calm and level, Eliza replied, "You have no idea what you are up against, Lord Exeter. French spies have infiltrated Parliament, and they will stop at nothing to achieve their goal. You are standing in their way. They will not hesitate to kill Rachel to force your hand."

"That is impossible," Lord Exeter sputtered.

"I need you to trust me," Eliza said, attempting to reason with him. "You can verify what I am telling you with my uncle, but you must follow my directives right now. I will ensure Rachel's safety."

With a resigned sigh, he conceded. "As you wish."

"Thank you," Eliza stated.

"What about highway robbers?" he asked, with a pained expression. "Lord Camden and your mother were just killed by a band of them."

"You have nothing to fear," Eliza reassured him. "Mr. Larson will accompany Rachel to your brother's estate in Scotland."

Mr. Larson stepped forward. "Sir, I am a former agent of the Crown, and I will assemble a group of men to travel with us. Lady Rachel will be well-guarded, and I will assign a guard to remain with her in Scotland."

Lowering himself onto a floral upholstered chair, Lord Exeter offered, "I will go with her."

Eliza dismissed his comment with a wave of her hand. "No, you need to stay and fight the bill. If you disappear, then the French spies will come one step closer to succeeding."

"My wife will not be pleased when she returns home to find Rachel gone," Lord Exeter admitted.

"When she returns, keep Lady Exeter indoors. She could be targeted next," Eliza stated, as she sat down on a chair near him. "I will ask my uncle to bring in *Shadow* to protect your daughter."

"You would do that?"

"Yes," she confirmed with a nod. "*Shadow* will keep her safe."

"Thank you," he answered, clearly relieved.

Eliza smiled at him. "I will send a missive over to my uncle, and he will contact you."

"You will need to bring footmen with you wherever you go, at least until after the vote," Mr. Larson added.

Arising, Eliza turned her attention towards Mr. Larson. "Go assemble a team of agents, and Rachel will be ready when you get back."

As she walked closer to her sister, Eliza saw that there was disbelief in Kate's wide eyes. "Kate, would you like to accompany me up to Rachel's bedchamber?"

With a slow nod, Kate rose with her hand clutching the round locket that she always wore. It appeared whenever she was deep in thought, her hands fingered the locket. Eliza decided she must ask about the necklace later, but for now, she had to get her friend to safety.

# 7

ADRIEN WAS GOING MAD! HE HAD TO BE. HE WAS STARING OUT the window, hoping to conjure up Kate and Eliza. After their celebratory drinks at White's, the men returned home anticipating they would see the ladies, but they were not home. Now, the sun was setting and still there was no sign of them.

"Mayhap I should go look for them?" Adrien asked Benedict for the hundredth time.

Benedict appeared calm as he sat on a wingback chair, but his clenched jaw betrayed his relaxed demeanor. "Pray tell, where would you look?"

"I would start at Madam Lancaster's."

Benedict shook his head. "Her shop will be closed."

His tone gave him pause. Where could they be? "Would they have called on a friend?"

"Perhaps, but Eliza gave no indication she was planning to do so."

"We have waited long enough. I will go alert Lord Charles that Eliza and Kate have been abducted," Adrien said, moving towards the door.

"Adrien, stop," Benedict yelled. "You are not thinking rationally."

He spun back around, raising his voice without intending to. "Are you not worried about your wife?"

Benedict huffed out a dry laugh. "I am petrified, but I trust my wife, and I trust Mr. Larson. We need to give them more time."

Adrien ran his hand through his hair and sighed. "What about Kate?"

"I trust Roger with Kate's protection. Do you not?"

Walking across the room, Adrien dropped onto a floral settee. "I should never have encouraged her to leave the country home. She is different there. She is more relaxed around her household staff. I thought by encouraging her to come to London she would open herself up to new experiences."

Benedict stood and walked towards the window. "Kate has been through hell and back, and you cannot force her to open up to you."

"I never said I wanted her to open up to me," Adrien grumbled.

"You did not have to." Benedict leaned his shoulder against the wall. "I can see the way you look at Kate. She is a beautiful woman, but you will need to be careful as you break down her walls. Take them slowly, one by one."

"And what would you know about breaking down women's walls?"

Benedict chuckled. "I married *Shadow.* I had to practically beg Eliza to take a chance on me."

"I do not think it matters. Whenever we are alone, I see Kate glancing over her shoulder to look for Roger. She doesn't trust me. She told me so."

"I disagree. When we were in the entry hall, I saw Kate only watching *you.*"

"That is good, but we are just friends."

Benedict laughed. "Yes, friends. Well, I think you are making more progress than you realize. What if..." His head turned to glance out the window. "Finally, they are home."

Jumping up from the settee, Adrien joined Benedict as they swiftly made their way towards the entry hall. The butler opened the door as Eliza and Kate glided in, with Roger trailing close behind.

Before Adrien thought rationally, he embraced Kate, protectively. He expected her to stiffen at his touch, but to his pleasant surprise, she placed her arms around his waist and rested her head against his chest. As she clung to him, Adrien marveled how perfectly she fit into his arms. He could stay like this forever. However, the reality of the situation caused him to drop his arms and step back.

"Are you all right?" Adrien asked Kate as he assessed her for any injuries.

Kate's eyes glanced over to Eliza and Benedict who were still in a tight embrace. "We had a... mishap."

"A mishap?"

Eliza's voice joined their conversation. "A *large* mishap." She tilted her head towards the butler and other household staff milling around, indicating she did not wish to share the news openly. "We should have this conversation in Benedict's study."

As they followed Benedict and Eliza through their townhouse, Adrien offered her his arm. Kate placed her delicate hand on top of his arm, and a surge of protectiveness washed over him. He had a duty to keep her safe, both as the current Lord Camden and as her friend.

When they entered the study, he expected Kate to drop her hand, but she continued to hold onto his arm firmly. He escorted her to the blue velvet settee and remained standing till she sat down. Claiming a seat next to her on the settee, he was overjoyed that Kate was watching him. Maybe he was making progress with her as Benedict had implied?

Eliza took control of the conversation as she explained about the attempted abduction of Lady Rachel and the follow up visit with her father, Lord Exeter. She informed them of the threat on Lady Rachel's life.

After Eliza stopped speaking, Adrien chuckled knowingly at Benedict. "I see that you informed Eliza about our meeting with Lord Beckett."

Benedict shrugged unrepentantly. "I don't keep secrets from my wife."

Nodding his approval, Adrien asked, "Have you informed Eliza about the threat sent to Lord Wessex?"

"Not yet," Benedict admitted.

Adrien took a moment to explain his strange meeting with Lord Wessex. He finished by saying, "Evidently, the French spies are resorting to threats to achieve their purpose."

Eliza's gaze grew thoughtful. "Most likely, they have threatened other lords, but we can't march into Parliament and ask who has been sent threatening letters."

"We are no closer to discovering the identities of the French spies, and the vote on the bill is in two and a half weeks," Benedict pointed out.

Kate's soft voice interrupted them. "What if you attempted to lure them out?"

"How so?" Adrien asked curiously.

Her eyes locked onto his for a moment, and he could see uncertainty on her face. He reached over and squeezed her hand in a show of support. She smiled at his reassuring touch, then continued. "Lord Exeter has been the main opponent of the bill, and his daughter was threatened, as was the sister of Lord Wessex, who is also a critic of the bill. What if Benedict suddenly became an outspoken critic of the bill, too?"

Eliza's eyes widened with surprise. "That is a marvelous idea. Why didn't I think of that? We could ask Lord Exeter to assist Benedict with this endeavor."

Benedict glanced at a large floor clock. "Speaking of which, we are late for Parliament." He rose and helped Eliza to rise. "I am relieved beyond words that you are home safe. I would prefer you to stay at home until Mr. Larson returns from Scotland."

Eliza did not disagree but smiled complacently at her husband. "You will receive no argument from me, at least for today. I am quite fatigued from our adventure."

"Good," Benedict murmured, leaning in to kiss her on her forehead.

Adrien rose and assisted Kate, resisting the urge to pull her close.

Kate's gaze slowly locked with his. "Thank you for being my friend."

"And I thank you for not slapping me when I embraced you earlier," he said. He watched Kate's lips grow into a smile as he hoped they would.

As his eyes lingered on her lips, a deep clearing of the throat caused the spell to be broken. "We should go," Benedict informed him.

KATE LOWERED HERSELF DOWN ONTO THE SETTEE AS SOON AS Adrien and Benedict left the room. Her sister came over and sat down next to her.

"How are you faring?" Eliza asked.

Kate smoothed out her dress, delaying her reply. She did not know how to answer. She had been asking herself that same question every day since she married Michel.

"Kate?"

Giving her an apologetic smile, Kate answered, "I am sorry. I am not trying to ignore you, but I do not know how to answer you honestly."

"What do you mean?"

Kate decided to start from the root of her problem. "Did you know I begged Mother to let me live with you at Uncle Charles's estate?"

Eliza shook her head. "No, I did not know that."

"When you left to live with Uncle Charles, you became free from Mother's scrutiny and wrath, whereas I had to endure seven more years." Kate cast her eyes down and slumped her shoulders. "I felt like a prisoner in my own home."

Putting her arm around Kate's shoulder, Eliza admitted, "I had no idea it was so bad for you."

"When Mother initially told me about the betrothal agreement with Lord Camden, I was thrilled to be out from under her rule, but I was wrong. It was worse."

"I am sorry."

"Do you remember the last time we went riding before my wedding?"

"Yes," Eliza answered, frowning. "I remember we talked about your upcoming nuptials and how dejected you appeared."

"The night before, I had approached Mother and pleaded for her to let me have one Season before I was married," Kate informed her, wiping a tear away.

"I take it the answer was no," Eliza said sarcastically.

Kate turned her body towards Eliza. "She slapped me. She told me not to ask any more idiotic questions, because Lord Camden would not be as sympathetic towards me as she was."

Eliza arched an eyebrow. "I dare say I would never classify Mother as sympathetic."

"I went from one prison to another, and I had no say," Kate stated dejectedly, her hand reaching for her locket.

Her sister embraced her tightly. "You are safe now."

Kate dropped her locket and wrapped her arms around her

sister. After a moment, she pulled back and asked the one question that plagued her thoughts. "How are you so confident?"

Eliza furrowed her forehead. "I beg your pardon?"

"Unless I was mistaken, you calmly shot that attacker, and you placed your pistol back into your reticule as if nothing had happened."

"Benedict has been teaching me how to shoot a pistol," Eliza explained.

Kate knew Eliza was lying to her, but continued anyways. "Then you marched into the study of Lord Exeter, who is one of the most powerful men in England, and you convinced him to send his daughter away to Scotland."

Eliza opened her mouth to speak, but Kate put up a hand to stall her. "I was at Beaumont Castle for more than a fortnight, and I saw you working with Adrien, Jonathon, and Lord Pembrooke. Furthermore, I caught you breaking into my country home, and later you informed me that you decrypted enemy codes. Please do not insult me by telling me that you are not an agent."

Eliza's lips tightened to a straight line. "It is not something that I can openly discuss."

"I know," Kate sighed, "and I am not asking you to. What I want to know is how are you able to be so confident? How can you stand up for yourself without the slightest tremor in your voice?"

One side of Eliza's lips curled. "Are you asking me how you can be more forthright?"

"I suppose I am."

Eliza's smile grew mischievous. "The most important piece of advice I can give you is to forget every word that Mother ever spoke to you. Her rules were ridiculous."

Kate smiled, sitting up straight in her seat. "I can do that."

"Good," her sister said. "Now, let me look at you." Eliza's eyes roamed her face, hair, and dress, before saying, "You are exquisite. With your beauty, you will outshine anyone in the room."

"You are too kind," Kate replied, taking a moment to admire her sister's auburn hair. "I have never met another set of twins that look and act as differently as we do."

"We may look different, but we are foremost friends." Eliza smiled, but it seemed forced. "My next rule is to speak your mind. I want you to vocalize your opinions and not just think them." To make her point, Eliza tapped her head with her finger.

"What if the gentleman does not want to hear my thoughts on a subject?"

Eliza arched an eyebrow. "Then they are not worth your time."

"But I should still avoid politics and religion, correct?"

With a shake of her head, she inquired, "Why can you not express your thoughts on those subjects?"

"It is improper."

"Improper to who?" Eliza questioned.

"To Mother," she answered, but paused before adding, "which means, I will disregard her advice."

Eliza laughed with a twinkle in her eye. "I am not encouraging you to go into White's and start a debate. I would strongly urge you to practice on Benedict and Adrien first."

"I think that is a fine idea," Kate admitted. She could not wait till she saw Adrien tomorrow and put Eliza's advice to use.

Later, in the privacy of her own bedchamber, Kate removed the gold locket from around her neck and shoved it into the top drawer of her dressing table. As she slid the drawer closed, she was flooded with old, painful memories from the past.

No, it was time to lock those memories away and start living in the present. Her past would not define who she was. No one could hurt her now, and starting tomorrow, she would start living the way she'd always wanted.

# 8

ADRIEN EXITED HIS CARRIAGE AND APPROACHED HIS COUNTRY home, his excitement growing in each step. He was anxious to see Kate. After last night, he felt as if something had shifted between them. He found himself dreaming of her and her sweet smile at the oddest times.

He strode into the drawing room and witnessed Kate reading a book. The sun was behind her, causing her hair to appear translucent. The scene was perfect. He walked over and sat down next to her on the settee.

Kate closed the book and laid it on her lap before she gave him a brilliant smile. So brilliant, in fact, that he was momentarily rendered speechless. "Good morning, Adrien."

The way his name rolled off her tongue made him want to kiss her. He cleared his throat. "Good morning."

"What scandalous activity do you have planned for today?" she asked, placing the book onto the table.

Again, he was tempted to lean over and kiss her. Would that be scandalous enough, he wondered? Instead, he replied, "I was hoping to take a stroll."

"A stroll?" Kate teased. "That does not sound scandalous."

Adrien found himself mesmerized by Kate. Something was different about her. Her eyes seemed brighter and her voice was more deliberate and confident. He leaned closer. "You do not know what I have planned."

Kate beamed at him. "Should I have Mrs. Palmer put together a basket for us?"

"It depends on how much time you want to spend with me," he answered, hoping she would opt for the basket.

She rose, giving him a lively smile. "I happen to find your company tolerable, so I will request a basket from Mrs. Palmer."

"I will go with you," he stated, jumping up, "assuming you do not mind."

"Not at all," she assured him, looping her hand through his arm.

As they left the drawing room, he remarked, "You seem different today."

Instantly, her face fell, her steps faltered, and she dropped her hand from his. "Oh," she murmured, back to her soft-spoken voice.

He placed his hands on her shoulders and hunched down to her eye-level. "What I meant to say, is that I approve of your behavior. You seem happier." He hoped that was the right thing to say.

A relieved smile graced her lips. "Eliza and I spoke last night, and she offered me some solicited advice."

Dropping his hands, he said, "I am eager to hear all about it."

"You are?"

"I am," he answered honestly.

Kate's eyes searched his as if gauging the sincerity of his words. After a moment, she offered him a faint smile. "Let us proceed to the kitchen."

Once they obtained a basket, they walked down the hill towards a cluster of trees growing on the far side of the property. Adrien had a blanket draped over his arm and the basket in the other as they neared the spot he had selected. He laid the blanket down and assisted Kate as she sat down, smoothing out her lavender dress.

She reached for the basket and removed the white linen napkin. "It appears that we have fruit and rolls." Then her lips curled with a pleased smile. "And lots of biscuits."

Adrien had no idea what had come over Kate, but he was captivated. He reached into the basket for a roll. "All right, lesson time."

Kate looked perplexed, which only made him want to tease her more. "Lesson time?"

He took a bite of the roll. "I want to prepare you for the masquerade ball."

"I am prepared. I have already secured a gown, gloves, and a mask," Kate listed, reaching for a roll.

Adrien grabbed the roll out of her hand and showed it to her. "Do you want *this* roll?"

"What are you doing?" she asked, arching an eyebrow.

He waved the roll in front of her. "Would you like *this* roll?" She tried to reach for another roll in the basket, but he repositioned the basket behind him. "This is the last roll. If you want it, then you have to tell me how much you want it."

"I would like the roll, please," she said, holding her hand out flat in front of her.

He shook his head. "Not good enough." She eyed him and made a quick grab for the roll, but he put it out of her reach. He leaned forward, drawing her attention towards him. He was close enough to see the fascinating green flecks in her blue eyes. "How badly do you want this roll?"

A smile touched her lips as he hoped it would. "I demand the roll," she paused, "please."

Adrien chuckled as he leaned back. "Try again."

"I demand the roll... *now*!" she exclaimed loudly, her words echoing in the wind.

He handed her the roll triumphantly. "And that is how you deal with the ton. If you are weak then they will dismiss you as unimportant and not worthy of their esteem. But, if you command authority, you will be deemed worthy and accepted."

"I am not sure I want to be accepted by the ton," Kate admitted, nervously glancing at her roll.

Adrien reached out and touched one of the ringlets that hung down the side of her face. As he rolled the piece of hair through his fingers, he expressed, "How could the ton not love you? You have the face of an angel and the heart of one, too. I have no doubt that the ton will fall at your feet and worship you, if you are so inclined."

Kate gave him a tight smile. "I fear you may be a little biased."

He shrugged as he reluctantly let go of her hair. "True, but I am being honest."

Before Kate could reply, Roger came sprinting down the hill with his pistol in his hand. Adrien shot to his feet, retrieved the pistol from his right boot, and placed Kate behind him. His eyes searched the field for signs of danger.

"I heard Lady Camden shouting," Roger yelled as he ran closer. His eyes kept darting to the surrounding areas.

Quickly arising, Kate dropped her roll into the basket and muttered under her breath, "This is all your fault."

Roger stopped before the blanket, breathing hard from running. "Are you all right, Lady Camden?"

She stepped out from behind Adrien. "I am sorry, Roger." She cast a sideways glance at him out of the corner of her eyes. "I got carried away because I really wanted a roll."

Roger's eyebrows knitted together. "You shouted because you wanted a dinner roll?"

Adrien could see the corners of her lips twitching in amusement, as Kate replied, "It was the last roll."

Roger glanced at the basket overflowing with food, including rolls. "Right," he mumbled under his breath as he placed the pistol into the waistband of his trousers. "Would you like me to stay to guard the rolls, or may I be dismissed?"

"It was my fault," Adrien stated. He did not want her to accept the blame for his lesson. "I was teaching her how to deal with the ton."

Roger roared with laughter. "With a roll?"

"I think it was quite productive." Adrien smirked.

Roger shook his head. "Mrs. Palmer will enjoy hearing about this. Carry on." He spun around and walked back up the slight incline towards the country home.

Adrien waited till Kate was situated and placed the pistol back in his boot. He lowered himself down on the blanket and was rewarded with the sound of Kate laughing. The sound of her carefree laughter was like music to his ears. It was the most beautiful sound he had ever heard.

Attempting to distract himself from his growing feelings for Kate, Adrien picked up his roll and started eating again. His eyes gravitated towards the trees, and he could hear soft chirps coming from the branches.

"I believe I earned this roll," Kate declared as she picked up the roll from the basket. She made a show of taking a bite and rolling her eyes as if she was eating the most delicious thing in the world. "I love Mrs. Palmer's rolls."

Adrien had never been so jealous of food as he was of that roll. He found himself staring at her mouth and willed himself to look away… again. The memory of Kate at Beaumont Castle came to his mind. Her cheeks were thin, and her eyes were sunken into their sockets.

Kate's face grew serious as she asked, "What made you so reflective just now?"

Adrien swiped his hands together to wipe the crumbs off. "I was thinking about the first time I saw you at Beaumont Castle. You were standing in the doorway as Hannah's ransom note was read to the group. Michel demanded your life and Jonathon's in exchange for Hannah. You were painfully thin, with remnants of bruises on your face, and yet you did not hesitate to volunteer to trade your life for Hannah's."

She swallowed the bite of food in her mouth, and her gaze lowered towards the blanket. "It was my husband who abducted her, so it was only fair that I took her place."

"No, that was not why," he said quickly.

"Then why do you believe I offered to trade my life for hers?"

He shrugged. "Because you are brave."

Kate shook her head, dismissing his comment. "I am not."

"Yes, you are," he insisted firmly. "You survived a brutal beating, but *you* were still willing to face Michel again."

"I do not feel strong." She gave him a sad smile. "My whole life I have been made to feel inadequate. I was the ignorant twin, the disrespectful daughter, and the disobedient wife."

Placing a finger under her chin, Adrien gently raised her head. "If you are comparing yourself to Eliza, then don't. Compared to her, I am a dumb fool who dabbles in espionage." He smirked. "Your mother and Michel were French spies, so I believe you should discount everything they said to you."

"Eliza said something similar," Kate confessed. "She told me to forget everything Mother ever told me."

His thumb slowly caressed her cheekbone as his hand cupped her cheek. "Eliza is exceptionally wise," he said, his eyes tracking hers.

Kate's blue eyes had a sheen to them. "I thank you for calling me brave. No one has ever said such kind words to me before."

He arched an eyebrow in disbelief. "I find that hard to believe."

A tear slipped out of her eye and he wiped it away with his thumb. "When Mother kicked Eliza out of the abbey at ten, I was left with no ally. I was at the mercy of my mother and the wicked governess she employed to ensure I was taught grace and poise."

More tears streamed down her face, as she continued, "Then I was given to Lord Camden, a man I had never met until my engagement ball, as if I meant nothing to my mother. My father refused to attend the wedding because he was against the marriage, but he did not stop it. After our wedding tour, Michel shipped me off to his country home and..." Her voice trailed off as a sob escaped her lips.

Adrien dropped his hand off her cheek and pulled her into an embrace. "You are safe now. No one will ever hurt you again." He kissed the top of her head. "I give you my word."

Kate cried into his white shirt, and he could feel the moisture from her tears. His hands started rubbing circles on her back, attempting to comfort her. After she stopped crying, she kept her head on his chest, and they sat in comfortable silence.

"Are you ready for our first scandalous outing of the day?" Adrien asked.

"Having a lady sob into a gentleman's chest was not the outing you had in mind? Because Mother would have been mortified had she still been alive," she murmured into his chest.

He slowly rose with Kate, ensuring she was on solid footing before he released her. "I propose we climb that tree," he stated, pointing to a tree that he had scouted out earlier. It had plenty of low-hanging branches to make climbing ideal.

Kate spun around, her mouth agape. "You want me to climb a tree?"

"Have you ever climbed a tree before?"

Her brow puckered. "I do not believe I ever have."

"Well, I think you should," he replied, extending his hand towards her. He wanted to ensure that Kate made the choice. He did not want to force her into doing anything she did not want to do.

A large smile played on her lips as she eagerly clasped his hand. "I am ready."

Adrien wondered if her comment referred to more than just climbing a tree.

MUCH LATER, KATE AND ADRIEN SAT IN HER DRAWING ROOM enjoying afternoon tea. She had thoroughly enjoyed climbing trees. At first, she had been nervous, but slowly she had learned to climb up the tree by using the large branches as foot holds. Adrien patiently followed behind and assisted her if she slipped.

Kate looked over the rim of her teacup to observe him. He was a handsome man. She loved the color of his dark brown hair and longed to run her hands through it. Would he mind? No, touching him without his leave would be too bold. Maybe she could suggest that as their scandalous activity tomorrow? She stifled a giggle at the thought.

"What are you smiling at?" Adrien asked, breaking through her thoughts.

"I am not smiling," she claimed, deliberately frowning.

He had the nerve to smirk at her. "Now you are frowning, but you were smiling just a moment ago."

She placed her teacup down on the table next to her. "It was nothing. I was just thinking about tomorrow."

He scoffed. "You are quite impertinent to believe I have so little to do that I would call on you every day."

Suddenly, the urge to coil into herself threatened to overtake her, but she resisted. She noticed the twinkle in his eye and realized that he was joking with her. "Pray tell, what occupies your time, my lord?" she questioned primly.

Adrien's face broke into a huge smile as he placed his teacup on the table in front of him. "I would have you know that I am attempting to root out French spies in Parliament."

"Sounds boring," she replied in a teasing tone.

"Spying can be boring at times. I have been filling my time calling on lords to determine their loyalties and meeting with Lord Beckett to compare our findings. These past few days, I have been going through pages of lords' financials to look for suspicious payments."

Kate covered her mouth and yawned intentionally. "I see why you prefer spending your time with me."

Adrien chuckled, but before he said anything, his eyes drifted to the floor clock. He rose and bowed. "I have thoroughly enjoyed our time together, but I am afraid I must leave."

"I was hoping you would stay for dinner," Kate said, attempting to hide her disappointment.

He adjusted his tailcoat and cravat. "Unfortunately, I must attend a rally protesting the war with France, then I have to go to Parliament for the evening."

"May I join you at the rally?" she asked as she rose. "I have never been to one."

"I am sorry, but it is no place for a lady," he stated, his voice firm.

"Where is the rally being held?"

"Timpleton Square, near the east docks," he informed her as he adjusted his gloves.

Kate wanted to go to that rally. She had never been to Timpleton Square, and she was downright curious about what transpired during a rally. How could she convince Adrien to take her? Her old self would have accepted what was expected of her and would have spent a quiet evening at home. However, the new Kate wanted to experience something new.

"What is going through your mind right now?" Adrien asked, stepping closer to her.

She pressed her lips together, then smiled, feigning ignorance. "Nothing, just thinking about what book I should read next."

"Liar," he said, his smile growing.

She had witnessed Eliza getting her way with Benedict when she initiated a touch. Would Adrien welcome her touch? Her touch did not work on her husband, but maybe it would on her friend. She stepped forward and placed her hand on his chest. "Would you please allow me to accompany you to the rally?" She kept her gaze steady, enjoying his green eyes.

Adrien's eyes widened a bit, alight with passion. She had not expected such a reaction. If she was not mistaken, he seemed to welcome her touch. In fact, never had a man looked at her as Adrien did in this moment. Her heart was beating so fast that she feared he could hear it or feel it through her hand.

Adrien cleared his throat, breaking the silence. "I cannot grant your request. Timpleton Square is no place for a lady," he insisted hoarsely, but she heard the regret in his voice.

Even though she was disappointed in his response, the fight was not over. "I understand that *you* cannot take me to Timpleton Square," Kate said, dropping her hand.

She walked over to the bell system and pulled on the brass handle mounted to the wall near the fireplace. Pulling the brass handle would ring a small chime outside the room alerting Roger that she needed him.

Adrien studied her face and furrowed his brow. "Timpleton Square is foul smelling and will have thieves roaming about. I am only going because Lord Charles has assigned me to do so."

Kate nodded. "I understand," she responded, as Roger walked into the room. She turned to acknowledge her protector. "We are going to a rally at Timpleton Square. Please arrange for my carriage to depart immediately."

Adrien turned towards Roger. "Do not arrange for her carriage. She is not going to the rally!"

Roger gave her a look of disbelief. “I must agree with Lord Camden. Timpleton Square is no place for a lady.”

This was it. This was when she would stand up for herself. Her legs started shaking slightly, but she kept her voice firm. “Lord Camden, are you my husband?”

“No, but…”

“What right do you have to lord over me?”

“I am the Earl of Camden. You are the Countess of Camden,” he stated, pointing at her.

Kate placed her hands on her hips as she had seen Eliza do before. “Earlier today you told me I was free to make my own choices, did you not?”

He raked his hand through his hair. “You are free, but Timpleton…”

“If I am free, then I will do as I wish,” she demanded, tilting her chin up.

For a moment, they stared at each other, neither willing to back down. With a deep sigh, Adrien conceded. “You do not fight fair. I will escort you to the rally.”

Kate felt like cheering, but she kept it inside. “Thank you for your invitation, but Roger and I already have plans to attend.” She felt like giggling as she saw Roger’s face blanch at her comment.

In two strides, Adrien closed the distance between them, leaning close to her. “Stop being a minx. You have outwitted me,” he said, his warm breath on her ear.

My, that is distracting, she thought!

She made the mistake of turning her head, and now their faces were only inches apart. Every thought was wiped from her mind as her eyes roamed every line of his handsome face.

“Lady Camden.” Roger’s voice caused her to jump.

Stepping back, Adrien clasped his hands behind his back. “Lady Camden has agreed to accompany me to the rally,” he announced proudly.

Roger glanced suspiciously between the two of them, but eventually nodded his head. "Yes, my lord. I will be accompanying you to ensure Lady Camden's safety."

Adrien's lips formed a crooked smile. "I am beginning to think she can protect herself." He slowly perused her dress, making her feel even more desirable. "You will need to change into something less alluring."

Roger started coughing loudly. He obviously did not approve of Adrien's comment, but she did. She nodded at him. "I believe I can find something suitable."

"That is wonderful news," Adrien replied, gazing at her.

"If you will excuse me, I will be down as soon as I have changed," Kate said, exiting the room.

As she walked towards her bedchamber, she realized that standing up for herself was exhilarating and more fun than she'd anticipated. Now she was going to go to a rally! What did one wear to a rally?

# 9

ADRIEN SAT ACROSS FROM KATE IN THE CARRIAGE AND WATCHED her gaze out the window. He was mad to allow her to accompany him to the rally. They were trying to root out a traitor, and now he would be responsible for her protection. Well, Roger would also be there, but he wanted to be the one who protected Kate.

When Kate had stood up to him, he could see the vulnerability in her eyes and could practically hear her legs shake. He wanted to run up and embrace her, but he knew she had to stand up alone. She had to prove to herself she could do it. And she did! He had never been so proud of her, or so frustrated. Of all the times for her to decide to be brave, why did it have to be now when it was so dangerous?

Starting at Kate's blue bonnet with a wide and rounded front brim, his eyes trailed down her slim, elegant neck and soft shoulders. His perusal paused when he reached her red spencer jacket, because something seemed different. Her primrose dress cost more than what the working class earned in a year, but that was not the issue. His eyes tracked the small pearls that ran along her neckline, briefly distracting him from his initial purpose.

Suddenly, it hit him. She was not wearing her gold locket. "What happened to your locket?" he asked.

"I took it off," she told him, turning her gaze from the window.

"Why?"

She took a moment to smooth out her skirt. "It reminds me of a chapter in my life I would rather forget."

Now he felt like a cad! "Michel gave it to you."

Her lips tightened into a thin line. "Yes. He gave it to me on our wedding tour."

"Why did you keep wearing it?"

She gave him a wan smile but turned her head to look out the window before answering. "He commanded me never to take it off." Her voice held a sad tremor.

"Never?"

"Never," she repeated. "I suppose I got used to wearing it."

He could tell that she was reluctant to talk about it, but he wanted to understand. "Why did you not take it off when you got to Beaumont Castle?"

Her eyes grew wide at his words. "I did not dare. When I first got the locket, I took it off for a bath, and when Michel found out…" Her voice trailed off.

"He hurt you?"

"Yes," she whispered. Her hands were balled into fists as they sat on her lap.

He sighed in frustration. Poor Kate! What must she have had to endure during those years of marriage? Although, his instinct felt like he was on to something important.

"Do you know why Michel placed such importance on you wearing the locket at all times?"

"He said I was his property, and this marked me as his." She spoke hesitantly, as if she could make those words disappear.

Could it be? Could the list of French spies be in Kate's locket? Michel's words from the ship came back to haunt him…

*The list is on my property.* He leaned forward in his seat, attempting to keep the eagerness out of his voice. "Have you ever opened the locket?"

She shook her head. "No, it was locked."

"Did Michel ever open the locket in front of you?"

"No," Kate stated. "Although, on a rare occasion, he would request the locket and sequester himself in his study."

"Is there anything else you could tell me about the locket?" Adrien pressed.

She lowered her gaze as anguish and pain filled her delicate features. "He told me that the locket was more important than my life, and if I lost it, I would forfeit my life."

Now he was certain the list was in the locket, but where was it? "Where did you place the locket?"

Her gaze lifted, and she eyed him suspiciously. "Why?"

"I have a hunch about something, but I need the locket to prove it," he answered honestly.

She shrugged one shoulder. "I placed it in the top drawer of my dressing table. You may have the locket, if you so desire."

"I will retrieve it when I drop you off this evening," he said, leaning back against the bench.

She relaxed back into her seat and leaned her head up against the wall of the carriage. Adrien watched as she drifted in and out of sleep. He quietly moved to sit next to her, placed his arm around her, and brought her head to rest on his shoulder.

Adrien relished the closeness of her and started to realize his feelings might be deeper than he was admitting. He had always enjoyed his time with Kate, but now he found when he wasn't with her, he longed to be. He enjoyed her smile, her wit, and her determined spirit.

He enjoyed how she would stand up to him, even though her legs would shake with trepidation. He loved her compassion towards those poor women that Michel had taken advantage of. Most women of the ton would dismiss them as harlots, but she recognized the plight of those women was not of their own making.

His feelings were growing for her. How could they not? Besides her beauty, she was compassionate, kind, and could charm a lamp post, if she wanted to. He glanced down at Kate as she breathed out a soft snore.

Adrien could not reveal his feelings because Kate was in a fragile place. She needed a friend more than a man to court her. Maybe over time, she would see him as a potential love match?

He needed a plan, because this could take some time.

KATE FELT THE CARRIAGE LURCH TO A STOP. SHE OPENED HER eyes to discover that Adrien's arm was draped over her shoulders, and she had been leaning against him. Rather than dwell on the impropriety of this situation, she couldn't shake the sense of safety and protection that engulfed her.

"Good. You are finally awake. I was afraid I would have to carry you to the rally," he teased.

"If you had not supplied such a comfortable shoulder for me to sleep on, I would have been up much sooner," she said, slowly lifting her head. Was it her imagination or did he seem as reluctant to release her as she was to sit up?

The carriage door opened, and Roger stuck his head in. He had a solemn frown on his lips. "Lady Camden, the rally has already started, and some unscrupulous characters are milling around the area. May I urge you to reconsider attending?"

"I have not changed my mind, Roger," she stated, preparing to exit the carriage. Roger reached his hand out to assist her.

Adrien reached under his bench, slid out a metal box, and

opened the lid. He pulled out a pistol larger than the one he carried in his boot and hopped out of the carriage. He shoved the pistol into the waistband of his trousers and yanked his tailcoat back down to cover it. She had seen him carry a pistol before, but now he truly looked the part of a pirate. Mrs. Palmer was right. He was a dashing pirate!

Adrien was alert, his eyes roaming the square before his gaze landed on her. "I must agree with Roger. This is no place for a lady."

Kate's eyes scanned Timpleton Square, taking note of all the surrounding run-down, darkened structures, and the filthy, worn cobblestone streets. A stale, musty odor tinged with horse manure hovered in the air as a large crowd of the working class, dressed in threadbare clothing, stood restlessly near a large platform.

Continuous shouting denouncing the war and the monarchy filled the square, as the protestors used foul expletives to enhance their words.

She glanced nervously at Adrien. "With you two gentlemen as my protectors, I have nothing to fear." She hoped her words sounded somewhat convincing.

Roger did not look convinced as his head kept sweeping over the crowded square. When he seemed satisfied, he turned back to her. "You will not leave Lord Camden's side for any reason. If Lord Camden needs to leave, you will not leave my side. If any rioting begins, and you hesitate to leave, I will pick you up and throw you over my shoulder. Understood?" He barked his orders in a tone that she dared not argue with.

Kate just stared at him and nodded her head in agreement. She had never heard Roger speak to her in such a forceful manner. Maybe she had made a mistake? Maybe it truly was too dangerous for her.

Adrien placed his hand on the small of her back, providing

her with much needed reassurance. "Is that what it takes to keep you from arguing back?"

She stifled a laugh. "Do not get any ideas, my lord."

He offered her his arm as they began making their way towards the large group assembled near the platform. She was very aware of all the hostile looks being cast their way. Gripping his arm tighter, Kate leaned in to Adrien. "Why is everyone staring at us?"

He looked down at her then back at the square, smiling. "They are staring at *you*. Women of your social class do not attend political rallies."

Kate's eyes were drawn to a girl near the edge of the crowd, who seemed no older than sixteen years of age. She held a tin cup up as she begged for coins, but the protesters shoved her aside as if she wasn't worthy of their notice. Kate's steps faltered as she watched this young woman, meekly asking for coins, meeting with the same rejection every time.

She had a thin, pale face, with dark shadows under her eyes and dirt patches along her cheeks. She wore a battered dress that was faded to the point of colorlessness, and a thin shawl draped around her shoulders that wouldn't keep out the slightest chill. Even though it was abundantly clear that this girl was impoverished, it was her sad, resigned expression that gave Kate pause. It was the same look of defeat that she would see staring back at her from the mirror on her dressing room table, after Michel beat her.

Kate met her gaze and offered an encouraging smile. In response, the young woman's hollowed eyes lowered to the ground as her shoulders slumped even lower.

Without saying a word, Adrien reached into his pocket and pulled out a few coins. He walked over and dropped the coins into her metal cup, and she looked up at him in amazement.

Kate was pleased with Adrien's generosity and only wished she could do more to help that poor girl. Unfortunately, she'd been ordered to leave her reticule in the carriage. Her heart broke at the sight of her kindred spirit, and she longed to help her.

As if he read her mind, Adrien gave her a sad smile. "It is hard to see so many people suffer."

"It is," Kate admitted. She had a sudden desire to help the plight of these poor women, but how?

A burly man roughly brushed up against her as he passed. "Sorry, me lady," he drawled sarcastically, while offering her a lecherous wink.

Kate shuddered and pressed closer to Adrien's side as they continued their walk towards the platform. In response, he put his arm over her shoulder, tucking her against his side, and she put her arm around his waist. Once again, she felt protected in his arms and enjoyed the masculine scent of leather and musk that lingered on his coat.

Earlier, Adrien had explained to her that Lord Devon was speaking out against the war. Even though Lord Devon was a Tory, he was siding with the Whigs, who were also considered reformers.

A large wooden platform had been erected for the event where three wooden chairs and a podium sat. Currently, a tall man with thinning black hair shouted about the injustices that many people faced because of the war with France. He shared experiences about women and children starving while their men were off fighting, and the plight of men unable to find work because of the injuries they sustained during the war.

Kate found herself sympathetic towards his words. Adrien leaned over. "It is horrible, but it would be worse if we allowed Napoleon to invade England."

His words snapped her back into the present. "I concur, but you have to admit that many men and women are suffering, and our government is not doing anything to help them."

"I agree. I hope to do some good in Parliament," Adrien stated reflectively. "Something has to be done for the men that have served our country and their families that are left behind."

Kate tilted her head up to see Adrien's jaw clenched as his eyes remained alert, looking for any signs of danger. "You are a good man," she asserted, earnestly. "I have every confidence in your ability to enact change."

Adrien relaxed his jaw and turned to look down at her. His green eyes held such tenderness and care, that she couldn't help but gaze into them. "Thank you, Kate," he said, his voice hitching.

"Kate!" a woman shouted, breaking the spell.

Kate shifted her gaze and saw her sister wiggling through the large crowd of spectators. "Eliza!" Kate dropped her arm from Adrien's waist, so she could embrace her sister, but his arm held firm over her shoulder.

Kate gave him a questioning glance. "I cannot risk losing you," Adrien explained unapologetically.

Eliza and Benedict came to stand next to them. "I am so glad you are here. Benedict told me that no other ladies were attending the rally, but I insisted on coming anyway," Eliza remarked, smiling smugly.

Benedict put his arm around his wife's waist. "I tried to dissuade her, but she thought it would be exciting." He smiled at Kate. "I am surprised that Adrien brought you, though."

Kate smiled triumphantly. "He was eager to bring me."

Adrien huffed. "Eager is not the word I would use. Coerced would be a more appropriate term."

"Either way, you are here," Eliza said, leaning closer to her. "Did you stand up to him?"

Kate bobbed her head, proudly. "I did. It worked splendidly."

"Which one is Lord Devon?" Adrien asked, directing his question to Benedict.

"The one in the middle," Benedict pointed out.

Kate stood on her tiptoes to get a better look at the man in question. He was average height, not too fat or thin, and he had a full head of brown hair. He seemed rather plain to be an earl, though. His clothing was even more ordinary. His tailcoat was brown, with a buff waistcoat and cravat, and paired with brown trousers.

A hush fell over the crowd as it was announced that Lord Devon would speak. Adrien and Benedict kept their eyes trained on the speaker.

Lord Devon slowly walked up to the podium. He pulled out a pair of rounded reading spectacles and placed them on the bridge of his nose. Slowly, he removed some papers from his coat pocket and unfolded them. He squinted as he looked at the audience before turning his attention back to his notes.

His unexpectedly loud voice echoed through the square. "I have lost two boys in this frivolous war. They both had a desire to serve the Crown. Unfortunately, their lives were in vain," he stated, his voice surprisingly monotoned. "I have presented a bill to Parliament that would greatly reduce the money allocated for the war against France, essentially ending England's involvement, and ensuring an immediate withdrawal of our troops from Europe."

He flipped over the paper and began reading the next one, continuing to use a bland tone. "Napoleon is not our foe. He wants to work with England and become our greatest ally. Instead of spending the money on war, we need to spend it here in England. We need better housing for the poor, and the docks need repair. If we stop this war against France, then we will be able to trade with them again, thus bringing in more jobs for our economy."

Adrien leaned over to Benedict. "Does it seem that Lord Devon does not believe the words that he is saying?"

Benedict nodded thoughtfully. "I was just thinking the same thing."

"Who are the men on stage with Lord Devon?" Eliza asked.

"The man who just spoke is Lord Lexington, the leader of the

Whig party, and the one sitting next to him is Mr. Henley from the House of Commons," Benedict informed the group.

"It would be in our best interest to call on Lord Devon later," Adrien said.

A loud commotion started near the front of the stage as spectators were shoved back. A large brawl had begun, forcing Lord Devon to flee the stage.

"I believe that is our cue to leave," Eliza shouted over the noise.

## 10

ADRIEN AND BENEDICT POUNDED ON THE DOOR OF LORD Devon's townhouse near eleven o'clock that night. A tired butler answered the door.

"May I help you?" he asked in a disgruntled voice.

Benedict handed him his calling card. "Please inform Lord Devon that Lord Lansdowne and Lord Camden need to see him immediately."

The butler glanced at the card in his hand and fully opened the door, ushering them into the entry hall. "Please remain here. I will inform Lord Devon of your arrival."

Adrien watched as the butler walked away before turning to Benedict. "I hope our instincts are correct on this, or we have just walked into a French spy's home without bringing reinforcements."

Benedict shrugged casually. "I have been in worse situations."

Adrien chuckled as the butler returned. "Lord Devon will see you now. If you would please follow me."

As they followed the butler, Adrien's hand reached for the small of his back where a pistol was tucked into the waistband of his black trousers, hidden by his tailcoat. If Lord Devon did turn out to be a French spy, then he would be prepared.

They were led into a small room with a desk pushed up against the corner near a window. Wingback chairs sat near the fireplace and a round table held a decanter and snifters.

Lord Devon rose as they entered. “Lord Lansdowne and Lord Camden, may I offer you a drink?” They both murmured their thanks but declined. He lowered himself back into his seat. “What brings you by so late this evening?”

They each took a wingback chair which allowed them to face Lord Devon. As they sat down, Benedict said, “We appreciate your willingness to receive us at this hour, since our business is most urgent.”

“Interesting, and what would two young lords wish to discuss with me?” Lord Devon asked casually, taking a sip of his drink.

Adrien rested his arms on the sides of the chair. “We attended the rally today in Timpleton Square,” he stated.

Lord Devon’s surprise caused him to choke on his drink, but Adrien ignored his reaction and continued. “Lord Lansdowne and I were both riveted by your speech.”

Their host placed his glass down on the table next to him. “Can I count on your vote?”

“No,” they replied in unison.

“May I ask why you are here, then?” Lord Devon asked suspiciously.

Adrien smirked. “Lord Lansdowne and I have a bet. I bet that you did not mean a single word from your speech, and he bet me that you did not even write your own speech.”

Lord Devon’s eyes slightly narrowed but he did not say anything.

“I beg the question, who won the bet?”

Lord Devon picked up his drink and took another careful sip. “I think it is time for you two to depart.”

Benedict crossed his legs, indicating he was not going anywhere. "No. We are not finished here."

"Yes, we are," Lord Devon responded coldly as he placed his glass on the table. He started to rise.

Jumping up, Adrien walked over to him and pushed down on his shoulder forcing him to remain seated. "We are not leaving until you answer a few questions."

Lord Devon appeared flustered as he adjusted his waistcoat. "Depends upon the questions."

"You lost two sons during the war with France. Why are you attempting to stop the funding to a war that your sons gave their lives for?" Benedict asked.

"After the death of my second son, I came to my senses and realized we should be striving for peace, not war," Lord Devon tried to explain.

Benedict's eyes assessed him. "Do you truly believe that Napoleon will order his troops to cease fighting if England backs down from the war?"

"Yes," he replied, frowning. "Why would he not?"

Adrien laughed dryly. "Napoleon is an egotistical blackguard who will stop at nothing until he has taken over all of Europe."

Lord Devon turned his head and gave him a critical stare. "And how would you know that?"

"I was working undercover as an under-secretary for Admiral Garnier until three months ago," Adrien informed him.

Lord Devon shifted uncomfortably in his seat. "You worked as an agent for the Crown before you became an earl?"

Adrien walked over to the fireplace mantel and picked up a small floral vase, examining it slowly. "I never stopped." He returned the vase to its location and focused back on their host. "Why did you write the bill to defund the war, knowing the ramifications would be monumental?"

When Lord Devon did not answer right away, Benedict added, "You are a Tory. Tories are in support of the war, and yet you would defy your party's wishes by writing a bill that will weaken England's defenses."

Adrien leaned his back against the mantle. "Whigs are the reformers. Whigs do not want this war, but they do not have the power, or the support, to write a bill of this magnitude. So, we must ask ourselves, why would a powerful earl, such as yourself," he paused to point at Lord Devon, "write a bill that would go against everything he believes, or supports?"

Lord Devon reached for his drink with a shaking hand. "You are wasting my time and it is time for…"

"Are you spying for the French?" Benedict demanded, cutting him off.

Lord Devon shot him a look of disbelief. "Are you mad?"

"No," Benedict said firmly, "but you do side with the French."

Lord Devon's face paled slightly, but it was his red, blotchy skin that gave him away. "No, I do not side with the French," he sputtered.

Adrien crossed his arms over his chest as he continued to lean back against the mantle. "We are now at an impasse. Lord Lansdowne and I know you are lying and are withholding information. We do not like being lied to." He glanced at Benedict. "Do we, Lord Lansdowne?"

Benedict shook his head. "No, we do not. I find that liars make me angry." He pulled out his pistol and placed it on the table next to him.

Lord Devon's eyes grew wide. "There is nothing illegal about writing a bill and putting it up for a vote in Parliament."

Adrien uncrossed his arms and reached behind him to withdraw his own pistol. "True, but it is illegal to spy for the French."

"Lord Camden," Lord Devon declared franticly, "I do not work for the French. You do not understand."

"Then make us understand, because I found tonight's session

of Parliament extremely boring, and I long to end this meeting so I can go home to sleep," Adrien said as he walked over and sat down on the wingback chair. He kept his pistol in his right hand, resting it on his leg.

Lord Devon leaned his head back on the chair for a moment. "What I am about to reveal to you must stay in the strictest confidence." He glanced between the two of them as sweat beaded on the sides of his forehead. "I am being blackmailed."

"By who?" Benedict asked, leaning forward.

"I wish I knew," Lord Devon admitted, forlornly. "A few months ago, I was approached by a man that I had never seen before, and he offered me a small fortune to write a bill that would greatly reduce spending for the war in France. I knew the bill's ramifications would end the war, so I laughed at him and proceeded as if nothing had happened."

"Can you describe the man?" Adrien inquired.

Lord Devon shook his head. "No. He was waiting outside my townhouse after my wife and I attended the opera. He wore a cap low across his face and a heavy coat."

"Why did you not report it?" Benedict asked him.

Lord Devon huffed. "I have been doing this for a long time. Do you know how many people have asked me to write a bill for Parliament?"

Benedict arched an eyebrow. "I find it convenient that you are claiming to be blackmailed but cannot help to identify a suspect."

"They have my wife," Lord Devon blurted out. "And if the bill does not pass…" His voice hitched with emotion and he stopped speaking for a moment. "They will kill her. They will kill my Betsie."

Adrien leaned forward, sitting on the edge of his chair. "Who has your wife?"

"Six weeks ago, my wife went out to the modiste and never came home," Lord Devon replied as he stood up and walked towards his desk. "A note was delivered claiming responsibility for her disappearance. In order for me to have my wife returned unharmed, I had to write the bill and push it through Parliament. If the bill does not pass, they will kill her." He slid open the top desk drawer, removed a stack of papers, and returned to his seat. "These are all the notes I have received since my wife's disappearance."

Adrien accepted the pile of papers. "Do you have any idea who might have sent these?"

Lord Devon shook his head fiercely. "None."

"Why not go to the magistrate or at least the Bow Street Runners?" Benedict pressed.

"In a few of the notes, I was warned that my wife would be killed if I notified the magistrate." Lord Devon sighed as he slowly sat down in his chair. He leaned forward and placed his head in his hands. "If my Betsie dies, I have no one left," he uttered, his words filled with anguish.

After Adrien read the threatening notes, he handed them to Benedict for his review. "You are not the only lord that has been threatened."

Lord Devon's head rose to gaze at him.

"Lord Wessex and Lord Exeter both have been threatened. Furthermore, someone attempted to abduct Lord Exeter's daughter in front of Gunther's," Adrien informed him.

"Was she injured?" Lord Devon asked, appearing genuinely concerned.

Benedict put down the notes. "No, a bystander interceded on her behalf."

"How fortunate," Lord Devon responded, reaching for his glass. "Lord Wessex and Lord Exeter are both friends of mine and are furious that I even put forth the bill for a vote. They have been extremely vocal in denouncing it."

Adrien returned his pistol to the waistband of his trousers. "We are here on Lord Beckett's behalf. French spies have found their way into Parliament and it appears that they are using any force necessary to pass your bill."

"What can you tell us about Mr. Henley or Lord Lexington?" Benedict asked.

"Nothing other than that Lord Lexington is the leader of the Whigs. He has long been an opponent of the war against France, but I do not believe he is siding with the French," Lord Devon said. "He is a member of Prinny's inner circle."

"But Prinny sides with the Tories. Why would he bring a Whig into his inner circle?" Adrien inquired curiously.

Lord Devon took another sip of his drink. "In his younger years, Prinny sided heavily with the Whigs, but now his views are more in line with the Tories."

"And Mr. Henley?" Benedict asked.

"All I know is that Mr. Henley is in the House of Commons and is bitterly against the war. I do not know which lord supported his appointment or bought him his seat," Lord Devon said.

Benedict tapped his fingers on the table next to him. "Lord Camden and I have strategized a way to get the French spies' attention. I am going to become a staunch opponent of your bill. Tomorrow night in Parliament, I will be giving a speech advocating the war."

"Oh, please add some humorous anecdotes to your speech," Adrien pleaded. "If I hear one more lord give a dry speech, I will collapse from boredom."

Benedict chuckled. "Pray tell, what humorous stories could I share concerning the war?"

A mischievous smile grew on Adrien's face. "It was widely rumored that Napoleon is afraid of cats."

"Cats?" Benedict repeated, amused.

Adrien nodded. "If that does not interest you, then you could mention that Napoleon wrote a romance novel. Supposedly, he allowed some of his officers to read the manuscript."

Benedict rubbed his hand over his chin. "I will take that into consideration. Now, if you do not mind," he paused with a knowing smile on his face, "I think we should focus on the task at hand."

Adrien cleared his throat and focused his attention back on Lord Devon. "If Benedict becomes a harsh critic of the bill, the French spies should be forced to single him out."

Lord Devon frowned. "Are you not recently married, Lord Lansdowne?"

"I am," Benedict confirmed.

"Are you not fearful that the enemy might target your wife?" Lord Devon asked.

Benedict sighed. "I have considered that possibility, but we have to act fast. We cannot allow this bill to pass."

"Lady Lansdowne is exceptionally clever. I have no doubt she will take extra precautions when leaving their home," Adrien said.

Lord Devon closed his eyes for a moment. "And what would you have me do?"

"Continue as before. Do not let on that the Crown knows of the French spies in Parliament," Benedict ordered.

Lord Devon winced at his words. "I hope for your sake that you both know what you are doing."

Benedict rose from his seat. "We do. You will need to trust us."

A deep frown puckered Lord Devon's brow. "In your opinion, do you believe that my wife is still alive?"

Adrien gave him a sympathetic look. "I do. Your wife is valuable to the French. She will be kept alive until they ensure your job is done."

"What you are saying is I have a little over two weeks before those abductors will kill my wife?" Lord Devon grimaced.

"No, you have a little over two weeks before we find your wife… alive," Adrien assured him. He glanced over to see Benedict give a slight shake of his head. They both knew the odds of finding Lord Devon's wife were slim, but to find her alive would be nearly impossible.

Benedict started to place the notes in his waistcoat but stopped. "Do you mind if we keep these notes for reference?"

"By all means, take them," Lord Devon said with a flick of his wrist. He grabbed the decanter and poured himself a large dose of amber-colored liquid. After gulping down his drink, he slammed his glass down on the table. "I know that I have not had the privilege of making your acquaintances before this evening, but I would be eternally grateful if you could stop these French bastards."

Adrien exchanged a look with Benedict, both showing extreme sorrow for Lord Devon's situation. "Do not give up hope," Benedict advised. "Sometimes that hope is the only thing that can get us through our grief."

Lord Devon smiled faintly. "Thank you, Lord Lansdowne. After meeting you and Lord Camden, I find I have more hope than I've had in weeks."

As they left the room, Adrien felt a burning desire to prove to Lord Devon that his faith was not misplaced.

# 11

Adrien waited in Benedict's elegant drawing room as he drummed his fingers against the arms of an exquisitely-carved settee. The rich wallpaper highlighted the Brussels weave carpets, thick drapes and a large, gold chandelier. He wondered if Eliza could play the pianoforte that was proudly displayed in the room. Kate had mentioned a passing fancy for the instrument, and he was hoping to hear her play soon.

Kate had stayed at Eliza's townhouse last night, and he had called upon her after she broke her fast this morning. He had easily convinced her to take a curricle ride through Hyde Park, then spent a few cozy hours in the library as she read aloud to him.

While attending the session in Parliament, he had started counting down the minutes until he saw Kate again. As much as he wanted to declare his intentions, she needed a friend more than a suitor at this moment. How could he woo Kate without her realizing his intent? Her eyes seemed to light up when he came into the room. Maybe she would welcome his advances?

Benedict, dressed in full-dress attire, walked into the room and sighed. "Eliza is not feeling up to the masquerade ball this evening. Would you mind escorting Kate?"

Adrien's heart felt like it would leap from his chest at this unexpected, pleasant news. He attempted to reign in his excitement since he did not want Benedict to realize how pleased he was that he would have Kate all to himself this evening. "I do not mind in the least."

Chuckling, Benedict gave him a knowing look. "I assumed as much." He went to the drink tray and poured himself some brandy. After he took a sip, he sat down on a floral armchair. He leveled an intense gaze at Adrien. "Kate may be under your protection as the new Lord Camden, but I am her brother. Do not make me regret this."

"Do not fear," Adrien tried to reassure his friend. "We will depart prior to the unveiling of the masks."

Benedict frowned, raising his glass to his lips. "That is the least of my concerns. Perhaps I should have Roger accompany you? He could remain in the carriage."

Adrien rose and went to pour himself a drink. "I have no doubt I can protect Kate at a masquerade ball," he answered sarcastically.

"It is plain to me that you care for Kate," Benedict stated bluntly.

Adrien swirled his drink in his glass for a moment, debating how to answer. "It is… complicated."

"I imagine it is. She is the current Countess of Camden," Benedict said with a lifted brow.

He took a sip of his drink. "There is no law against that."

"True, but Kate is still a widow. She should be in full mourning for a year, and then in half mourning for another," Benedict reminded him. "There will be speculation if you two are married within the year."

Adrien's glass froze near his lips. "Who said anything about marriage?"

Benedict chuckled. "No one did." He shook his head, appearing amused.

Before Adrien could respond, Kate walked into the room and all the words he had been forming in his head to refute Benedict's comments disappeared. Her blonde hair was piled high on top of her head, with large ringlets cascading down her back, and small ringlets framing her face. The rose gown, with matching long gloves, fit her body perfectly and highlighted every glorious curve. Even though her dress was exquisite, it was the twinkle in her eye that caused his breath to hitch. He had never seen a more beautiful woman than Kate, nor did he suspect he ever would.

Benedict rose and walked over to him. In a hushed voice, he advised, "You might want to close your mouth." Chuckling, he walked up to Kate and kissed her on the cheek. "You look beautiful."

Kate beamed in response to Benedict's compliment. "Thank you. I checked in on Eliza, and she is still quite pale. It would be best if you go to her."

"There is no place I would rather be," Benedict said, giving Adrien a pointed look before he exited the room.

Adrien stepped closer to Kate, offering his arm. As they walked toward the entry hall, he asked, "Are you ready for your first masquerade ball?"

Kate gave him a coy smile. "I am, my dashing pirate."

He arched an eyebrow at her. "Dashing pirate, am I?"

"After seeing you with the pistol at the rally, I realized that Mrs. Palmer was correct in her assessment. You do look the part of a pirate," she admitted.

"Ah." He grinned. "Let's hope that I do not ravage you this evening."

"That is not amusing in the least." Benedict's harsh voice could be heard echoing throughout the hall. They looked up to see him glaring down at them from the second landing.

"Your voice travels, Lord Camden," he drawled. "Please avoid giving me a reason to kill you later."

Adrien gave Benedict a nod of his head as they moved towards the door. Kate giggled as they exited, and her hand shot up to cover her mouth.

As he assisted her into the carriage, he whispered in her ear, "Oh, the fun we will have tonight."

Kate's smile grew. "I cannot wait."

KATE COULD NOT SEEM TO CONTAIN HER ENTHUSIASM AS SHE glided into Lord Thornley's ballroom. Her wide, rose mask had feathers sewn to the ends, extending high above her forehead, but that did not block her view of the magnificent room. The large, rectangular room was lit up by the sconces on the mauve-colored walls and by three low-hanging, gold chandeliers.

Her eyes roamed the crush as they attempted to edge further into the room. She gasped as she saw a lady dressed in a sheer gown, leaving little to the imagination.

Adrien chuckled. "I forgot this is your first time attending a masquerade ball."

"That gown is downright disgraceful," Kate whispered.

"The freedom of the mask is exhilarating," Adrien informed her. "Ladies wear whatever, or as little, as they want, and no one can judge them."

Kate's eyes roamed the gentlemen who seemed to be flocking towards the half-naked women. They were in full dress, and only a few appeared to be in costumes. "Why are the men not dressed in costumes?"

Adrien slipped his arm around her waist, leaning closer. "Is that what you desire? To see me half dressed?" he asked hoarsely.

Her eyes grew wide, and her mouth gaped open. How could she respond to that?

He took pity on her and gave her a charming smile. "I am teasing you, Kate. You can stop looking so petrified."

The music started up again, and she desperately wanted to dance with Adrien. The last time she danced was at her engagement ball. She glanced up to his masked face. "Would you mind terribly if we danced?"

Adrien furrowed his brow in confusion. "Why would you think there was dancing at a masquerade ball?"

Kate stood on her tiptoes and attempted to look over the heads of the patrons. Towards the center of the ballroom, four couples were dancing together in the quadrille. She turned her head back towards Adrien. "There are guests dancing."

He chuckled. "You are fun to tease."

She swatted playfully at his chest. "Dance with me."

He removed his hand from her waist and reached for her hand. "It would be my honor," he said, as he led her towards the dancers.

After dancing the cotillion, the scotch reel, and a waltz, she followed Adrien towards the refreshment table. He handed her a glass of champagne, which she graciously accepted. She had not had this much fun in years.

A short while later, Adrien removed the empty glass from her hand and placed it on a tray held by a passing servant. "Come with me," he invited, offering her his hand.

He led her out of the crowded, noisy ballroom and into a lush, garden paradise. Along the well-manicured garden were rows of trees, providing privacy for clandestine lovers. The sounds of giggling rose from behind the trees.

Kate did not know if she should be offended or thrilled that

Adrien had escorted her out to the gardens. Did he plan on showering attentions on her?

He led her to a lone stone bench that sat near a large fountain. After they were situated, he asked, "Are you happy?"

Kate looked at him in surprise. "No one has ever asked me that before."

"Well, are you?"

She did not need to think twice about her answer. "Yes, I am happy."

He leaned forward, placing his arms on his knees. "That pleases me."

"And you?" she asked, putting her hand on his forearm.

"Am I what?"

"Are you happy?"

He engulfed her hand with his. "With you, I am happy."

"That pleases me," she said cheekily.

He chuckled. "You are quite a handful, my lady."

As they sat in comfortable silence, Kate saw a man chasing a woman down the pathway and into the hidden alcoves of the garden. Her eyes trailed after them, envying them.

Standing up, Adrien offered his hand to her. "Break time is over. We should have time for a few more dances before the unveiling of the masks."

"What was your first kiss like?" she asked unexpectedly, looking up at him.

With a puzzled expression, he dropped his hand and sat down next to her. "I was sixteen, and I kissed one of the village girls when I was home for the holidays. Neither of us had ever kissed anyone, so it was a learning experience." With a smug smile, he added, "I have vastly improved since then."

"Oh," she said, ignoring his attempt at humor.

Nudging her shoulder with his, Adrien asked, "What was your first kiss like?"

Scrunching her nose, she turned her head to focus on the

fountain. "My first kiss was on my wedding night, and it was followed by… well, you know." Her voice trailed off.

When Adrien didn't respond, she shared, "Sometimes when Michel used to kiss me, I would try to imagine I was kissing someone else, but I had no other experiences to compare with it."

As she kept her gaze on the fountain, she felt Adrien place his hand over her clenched fists. "Would it help if I kissed you?"

With wide eyes, she turned to face him. "You would do that for me?"

Chuckling, Adrien placed his hand over his heart. "Kissing a beautiful woman in the moonlight is a cross I am willing to bear."

Focusing back on the fountain, her fingers rose to her lips. "If I kissed you, it might wipe away the memory of Michel's lips on my own."

"I have been told I kiss very well," Adrien said, his lips forming a crooked smile.

"I shall be the judge of that," she responded, feeling slightly nervous as she shifted to face him. Closing her eyes, she waited for Adrien to kiss her.

"What are you doing?"

Without opening her eyes, she replied, "I am waiting for you to kiss me."

"Kate," Adrien murmured gently, his warm breath on her face. "You look as if you are going to the executioner."

She opened her eyes in surprise. "How does one prepare to be kissed?"

A strange expression came into his keen eyes. "Do you truly wish to know?"

"I do."

"All right. But first, I must ask," he hesitated, his voice displaying a vulnerability that she had not heard from him before, "do you trust me?"

She placed her hand onto his forearm. "I do trust you," she said, wholeheartedly.

Without saying a word, he scooped her up and carried her behind a large tree that was hidden from prying eyes. He gently put her down with her back resting against the trunk of the tree. He rested his right hand on the tree behind her and the other hand lingered on her left hip. There was enough moonlight to see his green eyes roaming her face, but his face was still partially hidden behind his mask.

Tentatively, she removed his mask, so she could see his handsome face, a face that she had grown to care about deeply. Her fingers lingered on his skin, and a soft sigh escaped his lips.

He gently took off her mask, tossing it aside. "Kate," he said breathlessly before he slowly started lowering his head. He kept his eyes open as if seeking permission to kiss her.

She closed her eyes and tilted her head up, silently giving him that permission. His lips met hers, and they molded together in perfect unity. Slowly, her lips parted, and he tenderly deepened the kiss. Her arms slid up around his neck as she savored the nearness of him. In all the years she was married, never had a kiss been so all-consuming as the one she was sharing with Adrien at this moment.

He broke the kiss and slightly leaned back. His eyes searched hers, once again seeking permission. Her eyes filled with tears at his thoughtful consideration. Never had someone shown such regard for her feelings.

"Did I rush you?" he asked, his eyes full of concern.

She shook her head. "No. It was perfect."

His eyes watched her carefully. "Then why are you upset?"

"I am not upset," she answered, attempting to reassure him.

"You are crying." His words were matter-of-fact, but his expression showed his confusion.

"You have been nothing but kind to me," she replied, hoping

to properly convey her gratitude. "I can never thank you enough."

Adrien smiled flirtatiously. "I can think of a few ways," he murmured, lowering his head.

After a few moments, his kiss turned more passionate, which she eagerly responded to. Her arms tightened around his neck, as her fingers threaded through his hair.

With a low growl from the back of Adrien's throat, his hands started roaming around her back, pulling her tighter. His sudden intensity surprised her, but she was just as equally pleased. She wanted him close. She needed him close.

Without warning, his head jerked up, and his hands dropped from her. Taking a step back, his features were partially shadowed, but she could clearly see the regret on his face. "I am sorry, Kate. I behaved in a most ungentlemanly manner," he stated, pausing as if searching for the right words. "And for that, I would like to ask for your hand in marriage."

Kate could not have been more stunned than she was at that moment. No, she must have misheard him. Why would he just blurt out a proposal after kissing her? And a bad proposal at that?

Adrien looked just as shocked. "I only meant to give you a chaste kiss, and I got carried away."

If Adrien's expression hadn't been so crestfallen, she might have laughed. Instead, she replied, "You cannot be serious."

"I am." He winced as his hand came up to rub his neck. "You are under my protection, and I acted inappropriately."

"No," she said, softly. "My answer is no."

He pursed his lips, obviously displeased by her rejection. "You cannot kiss me like you just did and expect me to believe you do not hold me in some regard."

She rested her back against the tree, hoping she could communicate her feelings. "I do hold you in high esteem, but I have no desire to ever marry again."

"It would be different this time." He still maintained his distance from her, which hurt most of all.

"I will not marry you because you feel bound by duty," she said adamantly. "If you remember correctly, I gave you permission to kiss me."

Turning his head away from her, he sighed loudly. "If you won't marry me, then please accept my sincere apology," he spoke with a voice almost completely devoid of any emotion, a voice she did not recognize.

Fear gripped her heart as she realized her rash decision to be kissed might cause her to lose Adrien's friendship. What would she do? She had come to rely on his steady encouragement and humor. Tears welled up in her eyes as she pleaded, "I don't want to lose you over this."

Closing the small gap between them, Adrien pulled her into a tight embrace. "I am right here. You will never lose me."

Tugging on his lapels, she placed her head on his chest. "You do not understand how much you mean to me."

He kissed the top of her head. "Then why will you not marry me?"

"You have become my best friend, my confidant," she murmured against his black coat.

Adrien chuckled. "Except for not agreeing to marry me, you are saying things that are good for my ego. Please do not let me stop you."

How could she make him understand that marriage would ruin everything between them? Maybe she should share with him how fickle love is between a man and a woman.

"You should know I loved Michel," Kate announced, half expecting Adrien to shove her away.

"Impossible." His response was quick and dry.

She shifted so she could see his face, but not leave his arms. "On our wedding tour, I fell in love with Michel. He was so attentive and kind and, in my mind, he had rescued me from my prison at the abbey." She wiped away the tears from her face with her hand. "Then he sent me to the country home, but he would visit for the weekends. I used to wait in the library to see his carriage from a distance, so I could race and meet him at the door. I thought we were so in love …" Her voice trailed off as she closed her eyes at the painful memories.

"What changed?" he asked, his voice full of compassion.

Kate laughed, but there was no humor in the sound. "I came across him attempting to force his attentions onto a parlor maid. The poor girl was screaming hysterically, her skirts hiked up to her knees. I ran into the room and started beating Michel's back, demanding him to stop. He flew into a rage and beat me for interfering." She lowered her eyes. "At least the girl was able to escape in time." Kate could feel the tension in Adrien's body, but she knew it was not directed at her.

"If Michel was not already dead, I would do the honors," Adrien growled through gritted teeth.

"You see, I fell in love with a monster," Kate said dejectedly. "I will not make that mistake again."

Adrien reared back in shock. "Do you think I could ever be like Michel?"

Kate shook her head emphatically. "No, but what if Michel did not start out to be a monster? What if I displeased him in some way, and he became a monster because of me."

"Oh, Kate. You don't believe that, do you?" Adrien asked, his eyes full of pity.

"My mother hated me, and my husband hated me. The only correlation between the two is… me."

Adrien laughed loudly much to her horror. "No, the only correlation is that they were both French spies and by all accounts, horrible, despicable people."

"It does not change the fact that I fell in love with Michel," Kate insisted.

Adrien's hand came up and rested on her right cheek. "You

were a seventeen-year-old girl. Your mother forced you into an arranged marriage with an older, experienced man. I do not believe you were ever in love. Confused, perhaps, but not in love."

"How can you be sure?" Kate asked, daring to hope.

"When you are in love, you long to be with that person always. You find yourself reliving snippets of previous conversations or situations that you have shared with them at the oddest times. You realize that you would do everything in your power to ensure the person you love is truly happy." He smiled down at her. "Did you feel that with Michel?"

She shook her head. "No, but surely not every love is as strong as you describe?"

Adrien took his hand off her cheek and ran it through the curls along her back. "My offer of marriage stands and not just because I am duty-bound. I have every intention of breaking through your barriers and winning your heart."

Kate smiled sadly at him, knowing she would never be worthy of a man like him. "You deserve a woman that has a whole heart to give to you. I fear my heart is too shattered to ever truly love another."

Adrien lowered his head till his forehead touched hers, his warm breath on her cheek. "You are stronger than you care to admit."

"Please stop talking and help me forget my past," Kate's breathless voice pleaded as she brushed her lips against his. She would much rather communicate in this fashion than talk anymore.

## 12

KATE SAT AT HER PIANOFORTE AND PLAYED BEETHOVEN WHILE her thoughts turned to Adrien and the previous evening. After kissing behind the tree, they had donned their masks and made a quick retreat before the time of unveiling arrived.

She thought her heart would burst when he escorted her into Benedict's home and bid her farewell. Somehow, she floated to bed and woke up before breakfast to travel back to her country home. As much as she loved being with Eliza, the country life suited her far better than London.

As the music she played became more dramatic, she couldn't help but think about Adrien's marriage proposal. It was made in haste and only because he felt he'd been inappropriate. Maybe she should have thrown caution to the wind and accepted it? After all, she did care for him.

No, she was right to reject it. She needed time to heal her wounds. Besides, she needed time to learn to be independent and not rely on the strength of others.

A smile graced her lips as she remembered parts of the conversation from the night before. Adrien could always make her laugh, and he encouraged her to trust her feelings, her instincts. He was her best friend, and she could not lose his friendship. He was the dearest thing to her in the world, and a hasty marriage would ruin that.

"Lady Camden," a voice said from far away, drawing her back into the present. "Lady Camden?" Mr. Oakes repeated from the doorway.

She removed her hands from the pianoforte and opened her eyes. "Yes, Mr. Oakes?"

Her butler stepped further into the room. "A Mr. Henley is here to see you, my lady. Are you taking callers this morning?"

"I suppose I am. Please see him in." She rose and moved towards a settee on the opposite side of the room. She had no idea why Mr. Henley would be calling on her, but she would soon find out. She marveled at the progress she was making, because a week ago she would have had Mr. Oakes turn him away. She was stronger now!

Mr. Henley strode into the room but stopped and bowed, giving her time to peruse him. He was a few years older than she, with a chiseled jaw, sculpted nose, and black hair. She had no doubt that some women might find him desirable, but she was not one of them.

"Lady Camden, thank you for agreeing to see me on such short notice." The words were appropriate, but Mr. Henley did not sound sincere.

"Of course, please come in. Would you care for some refreshment?" Kate asked, walking over to the bell system.

"No, thank you," Mr. Henley said as he straightened his plum waistcoat. "You are an impossible woman to track down."

"Oh?" she responded, wondering what he meant.

"It was widely assumed that you were residing with your father, the Duke of Remington, and his new bride. However, when I tried to call on you there, I was informed you were not in residence. It was a wasted trip," Mr. Henley complained, not even attempting to keep the annoyance out of his voice. "Fortunately, I did some inquiring, and I discovered your whereabouts."

"I apologize for the confusion." Kate felt no need to explain.

She gracefully sat on the settee and clasped her hands in her lap. "How may I be of assistance?"

Mr. Henley's eyes narrowed slightly as his gaze travelled down the length of her pomona green afternoon dress. "I know I arrived unannounced, so I will not chide you for your manner of dress. Would you prefer a moment to change before I speak on a sensitive matter?"

Kate gave him a perplexed look. "Why would I be required to change?"

His lips thinned into a tight, white line. "Are you not mourning the death of your husband and mother?"

She knew that the ton would judge her for not being in full mourning, but she was not in London, she was at her home. She lifted her chin as she had seen Eliza do. "Mr. Henley, how I choose to mourn, or not mourn, is none of your concern. I do not need to justify my actions to you," she said, hoping her voice sounded confident.

Mr. Henley's nostrils flared slightly, and his eyes seemed to spark with rage. He waited a moment to speak, his tone calculating. "Lord Camden was a good friend of mine. I do not appreciate your blatant disrespect towards him now that he is deceased."

Kate glanced over his shoulder towards the door, hoping to see Roger. However, he was not visible. He must be further down the hall. She looked back at Mr. Henley and gave him a slow nod. "I apologize if my words offended you. I am grateful to make the acquaintance of a man who was friends with my husband." She pointed towards a chair, far away from her. "Please sit and join me."

Mr. Henley nodded but bypassed the proffered chair, choosing instead to sit on the opposite end of the settee she was sitting on. She pasted on what she hoped was a cordial smile, unsure of the nature of his visit. He watched her closely, his expression foul, reminding her of the look Michel would have when he found her lacking.

Mr. Henley's eyes appeared black at first glance, but looking closer, she could see they were dark brown. "You have something that I want," he stated, in an abrupt, almost brutal manner.

"What could I possibly have that you want, Mr. Henley?"

"A round, gold locket." He scowled as he looked at her neck. "Lord Camden informed me that it would be around your neck."

Kate's eyes grew wide at his request. Why would he want the locket that Michel gave to her after they were married? Besides, she had already promised it to Adrien. "I apologize that you came all this way only to be disappointed, but I lost the necklace a few weeks back," she lied, hoping he could not see through her as easily as Adrien could.

Mr. Henley crossed his arms over his wide chest, his glare intensifying. "That locket is extremely important. I must insist that you find it, and quickly." His tone was threatening.

She was attempting to be brave, but she had just reached her limit. As Kate began to rise, she said, "If you will excuse me…"

Mr. Henley grabbed her wrist and yanked her back down. "You stupid chit," he hissed. Kate glanced towards the door, looking for Roger again, and Mr. Henley followed her gaze. "A small brush fire broke out on the east lawn before I arrived, and most of the men are fighting the fire. I would not be expecting anyone to hear your screams." He smiled menacingly.

"Screams?" she repeated nervously.

"Assuming you cooperate, I am just here to speak to you, but if you don't…" He let the implied threat hang in the air between them. After a long moment, he dropped her arm.

Kate rubbed her sore wrist. "I do not have the locket any…"

"Find it," he ordered. "That locket is very important to me."

Kate nodded. "I will search for it." She just needed him to leave.

Mr. Henley leaned closer, and the smell of tangy orange reached her nose. "I would search as if your life depended on it, because it does," he threatened calmly, as if issuing a death threat was a normal, everyday occurrence.

She bobbed her head up and down in understanding. Why had she insisted on angering him with her rudeness earlier?

"I understand," she murmured in the same submissive tone she always used when dealing with Michel.

Mr. Henley just sat there, intimidating her with his stare. Kate needed him to leave, so she could breathe again. "If you will excuse me," she said, rising slowly to avoid angering her guest in any way. "I will begin searching now for the locket."

He rose and blocked her retreat. "Lord Camden always had a soft spot for you," he grunted in a disgusted huff.

Did she hear him correctly? Did Mr. Henley dare imply that Michel showered any affection on her? Before she could stop herself, she blurted out, "How dare you!"

His eyes narrowed, but he kept silent.

"My husband was cruel and vindictive. The only attention he ever showed me was when he beat me."

Mr. Henley's eyes lit up in contempt as he took a step closer. "You served your purpose when you married Matthew. The fact that you are still alive is a testament to his feelings. I don't know why he bothered trying to mold you into something you could never be."

Kate refused to step back even though she was tilting her head to look him in the eye. "Michel never cared…"

Her voice was cut off as she was thrown against the wall, and Mr. Henley's hands seized her neck tightly. She attempted to remove them, but in vain. "How long have you known?" he hissed.

"Known what?" Kate gasped, trying to understand what he was asking.

"You said Michel. How long have you known?" he demanded.

Kate closed her eyes. How could she have been so careless? "He came home drunk a few months ago, and he told me to call him his real name," she lied, hoping it sounded believable.

"Does Lord Camden know?"

"No," she whispered, barely able to breathe.

His hands squeezed tighter, causing her to fight for air. Just when she was certain he would succeed in killing her, Mr. Henley loosened his grip a little. He moved his face until they were just inches apart. "Does the new Lord Camden know?" he asked deliberately.

"No, he does not know. Do you think he would let me live here and grant me a monthly allowance if he knew I married an imposter?" Kate pleaded, praying that she sounded convincing.

Mr. Henley's eyes bored into hers. She tried to relax under his scrutiny, but his hold on her was still unrelenting and painful. She slowly swallowed, and his grip tightened around her neck.

She clawed at his hands, attempting again to remove them from her neck. She wasn't strong enough. Mr. Henley was going to strangle her, in her own home. She had been freed from the terrors of her husband, only to die at the hands of his friend.

The sound of a cocking pistol and the loosening of her attacker's hands brought her focus back up. "Let her go and step aside, slowly."

Roger was standing behind Mr. Henley with a pistol to the back of his head. As Mr. Henley stepped back, Kate could see Mr. Oakes and four of her footmen in the room. "Run to your room, now," Roger ordered her, without taking his eyes off Mr. Henley.

Kate made the mistake of glancing at her attacker and saw

him glaring at her with ferocious hate. Why did he hate her so much?

Regardless, she was not going to stand around and ask him. She picked up her skirts and fled.

KATE SAT ALONE ON A ROCK NEAR THE STREAM THAT HAD granted her such a thrill a short while ago. Her bare feet were in the icy, flowing water, and she didn't care that her toes had gone numb. At least she still felt something.

She was a fool. She had allowed herself to fall into a state of false security. She had believed Adrien and her family when they told her she would never be hurt again, and yet she had been choked in her drawing room by a stranger.

The constable had been summoned after the attack, and he determined the matter should be referred to the magistrate, Sir Walters, because Mr. Henley was a member of the House of Commons, and she was the daughter of a duke.

She had watched from her bedchamber as Mr. Henley freely walked out her front door and hopped into his carriage. It did not matter that he had just strangled her, almost killing her. The meaning was clear… she mattered not.

Roger had attempted to talk to her after Mr. Henley had gone, but she could not formulate any words in response. Instead, she chose to flee from her usual refuge of the country home and seek out a safer space, a place where she had been the happiest.

"Kate," a smooth, baritone voice called.

Turning towards the familiar voice, she saw Adrien standing a few feet away, his eyes filled with compassion. She jumped up and ran towards him, launching herself into his outstretched arms. "Adrien," she cried, sobbing into his chest.

His arms held her tightly, his familiar scent of leather and musk instantly comforting her.

"I am so sorry," he whispered, repeating it over and over.

At some point, he picked her up and moved her to sit under a tree by the stream. His back was resting against the trunk of the tree, and she sat next to him with his arm wrapped around her shoulder, pulling her close.

Adrien's voice broke the silence. "Can you tell me what happened?"

She shook her head. She did not want to talk about it.

Adrien placed a piece of errant hair behind her ear. "Roger sent over a messenger to explain that you had been attacked." His voice hitched as he spoke. "But he did not know what happened prior to Mr. Henley strangling you."

Kate shifted slightly so she could gaze up at him, her lower lip trembling. "I tried to be brave like you showed me. I tried," she confessed, her tone resigned, "but I failed."

"Please tell me what transpired between you two," he said, his thumb gently caressing her cheekbone. "Before I ride over to Henley's home, I need to know how excruciatingly painful I should make his death."

"You shouldn't trouble yourself. It would appear the constable is not concerned with my assault. Why should you be?" she asked, lowering her gaze.

He placed his finger under her chin and lifted it up. His eyes then surveyed the bruising around her neck. "This was no mere assault," Adrien spoke decisively. "It was attempted murder."

"It matters not." Kate shook her head dejectedly.

His eyebrows shot up. "Of course, it matters."

"I am used to the beatings," she admitted, wiping a stray tear. "Although, I truly thought Mr. Henley was going to kill me."

She realized that Adrien had not replied, so she raised her head to look at him. It surprised her to see tears in his eyes. He watched her with such tenderness that she found herself unable to look away.

Finally, Adrien spoke in a small, desperate voice, "I have failed you. Please forgive me."

"You did no such thing," she assured him softly.

"I vowed that you would never be hurt again. Yet someone walked into your home, your place of refuge, and tried to kill you. I'm sorry," he said, remorse clearly present in his voice.

Lowering her head against his chest, she listened to the soothing beating of his heart. "It is not your job to protect me."

"It is. You are under my protection." As he spoke, his voice rumbled from his chest.

Reaching into the pocket of her dress, she pulled out the locket. "Mr. Henley came for this." She straightened up to show him. "I told him that I lost it, and he threatened to kill me if I didn't locate it immediately."

She handed Adrien the locket, but his gaze never left her face as he dropped it into the pocket of his coat.

"You just told me that you were not brave, but you were," he stated. "You could have retrieved the locket and handed it over to him without incident. But instead, you stood up to him and refused to turn it over to him." His eyes shone with pride. "You were incredibly brave."

Her breath hitched. Dare she believe him? She didn't feel brave. Quite the opposite, in fact. "But he almost killed me. I was so afraid."

Attempting to lower her gaze, Adrien's firm finger under her chin stopped her, forcing her to look at him. "Even spies feel scared when their lives are at risk. You should have seen Jonathon when someone snuck up on him in an alley, and Eliza had to save him. He was shaking and thanking Eliza profusely." Adrien smiled.

Kate returned his smile, albeit faintly. "I fear that you are teasing, because Jonathon would never behave in that manner."

"I may have embellished the facts to amuse you," he said with a crooked grin. "However, it is nerve-racking when you are so close to death. Being brave isn't about not being afraid. Being brave is doing what you have to do despite your fears."

"Eliza is the brave twin. Not me," Kate said solemnly.

Adrien dropped his hands, but his gaze did not waver from her face. "Please tell me what happened between you and Mr. Henley." His eyes pled for her to confide in him.

"You will be displeased with me when I tell you what happened."

"How could I ever be displeased with you?" Adrien asked with kindness in his voice. "Nothing you tell me will change the way I feel about you. Please trust me."

Kate gazed into his eyes, realizing she was unable to deny his request. So, she started with Mr. Henley's criticism of her lack of mourning attire and ended with how she accidently slipped and said Michel's name, causing Mr. Henley to attack her.

When she was finished with her story, she nervously glanced at her hands in her lap.

"I was wrong," Adrien stated, his voice slightly hoarse. "What you revealed has drastically altered my feelings towards you."

"It has?" she asked, her voice trembling.

He leaned closer. "I did not think it was possible to be prouder of you, but you just proved me wrong."

Kate's eyes grew wide as she turned slightly, causing their faces to only be inches apart. "You are proud of me?"

A smile crept onto his lips. "How could I not be? You stood up to a French spy as if he was an entitled child demanding a new toy."

"I did no such thing."

"No? Well, you lied to Mr. Henley about losing the locket,

which was quick thinking, I might add," Adrien acknowledged, acting impressed. "More importantly, you single-handedly discovered a French spy in the House of Commons. Agents of the Crown have been working tirelessly for the past month to accomplish what you did in a single conversation."

Kate furrowed her brow. "You make it sound like I did something that deserves praise, but I did no such thing."

Adrien leaned in and kissed her on her lips, taking her by surprise. After a moment, he leaned back and smiled. "I could stay here and whisper praises about you all day long, but I need to plot Mr. Henley's demise."

He spoke lightly, but she heard the anger in his tone. "May I walk you back home? Eliza and Benedict arrived with me, and I know they are anxious to see you."

Kate's heart lightened at the thought of seeing Eliza and Benedict. "I would appreciate that, my lord."

"My lord?" he asked with a raised eyebrow. "What happened to a dashing pirate?"

Kate's lips melted into a genuine smile. "Today you are acting the part of a gallant lord."

His eyes danced with amusement as he watched her. "I wonder what I will look like tomorrow."

Kate giggled at his words, grateful for his friendship. Adrien could always make her laugh even when it felt like her world was crumbling around her. "I look forward to you calling on me tomorrow, so we can find out together."

"Do you?"

"Do I what?"

"Do you look forward to me calling on you?" he asked deliberately, his eyes looking vulnerable.

"I do," she said, placing the palm of her hand on his chest. "It is my favorite part of the day." And it was!

# 13

Adrien stormed into the study of his country home, slamming the door behind him. Eliza and Benedict were sitting on the sofa, holding tea cups. Both jumped as the door slammed.

"Good gracious, Adrien," Benedict grunted, as he placed the teacup onto the table. "You caused me to spill tea onto my trousers."

"How can you be so calm? Your sister was almost killed," Adrien barked at Benedict and Eliza. He walked over to the drink cart and grabbed the decanter. After pouring himself a generous helping of brandy, he emptied the glass in one gulp.

"We wanted to give you an opportunity to speak with Kate privately first," Eliza explained from the sofa. "Where is she?"

"She went to lie down," Adrien said, turning to face them. "I told her that you would be up shortly, but I needed to discuss a few things with you."

"How is her neck?" Benedict asked. "Roger mentioned there was bruising."

Not able to contain his anger any longer, Adrien threw the glass into the fireplace, causing the sound of breaking glass to echo throughout the small room. His chest heaved with fury as he shouted, "He almost killed her! If Roger had not intervened when he had, she would have been strangled!" Striding to the door, he yanked it open. "Roger! Get in here!"

"Pray tell, what are you going to do when Roger arrives?" Benedict asked in a half-amused voice.

"I am going to dismiss him! His only job was to protect Kate and he failed. He failed!" Adrien exclaimed, not caring who could hear his tirade.

Placing her teacup onto the table, Eliza rose calmly from the sofa and walked over to him. She placed a hand on his forearm and spoke in a soothing voice. "You need to calm yourself. Do you want to upset Kate more than she already is?"

"She almost died," he replied, his voice hitching. "We promised that no harm would come to her ever again and we failed."

Bringing his eyes up to meet Eliza's gaze, he saw a fierceness reflecting in hers. "Kate is alive. From now on, we will never leave her alone. We will keep her safe."

Eliza's words gave him great comfort, but still his shoulders slumped from the mantle of responsibility he had for Kate. From the moment the messenger arrived at his townhouse to alert him of the attack, he had been overwhelmed with fear. Now that he saw Kate was alive with his own two eyes, albeit with a bruised neck, all he could think of was exacting revenge on those responsible ... starting with Roger.

"You called for me, sir?" Roger asked, his pistol tucked into the waistband of his trousers.

Dropping her hand from Adrien's arm, Eliza smiled, *actually smiled*, at Roger. "Please come in. We have a few questions."

Adrien clenched his jaw as he watched Roger walk into the room. He wanted to rail at him and demand to know why he had not protected Kate. Instead he walked towards the window and stared out, hoping to calm his racing heart.

Eliza offered a chair to Roger as she claimed the seat next to

Benedict. "We want to fully understand what transpired today. Can you explain how Kate was left unattended?"

"A large brush fire started on the east lawn," Roger started, "and all the footmen and I formed a line to stop the fire before it spread towards the village. I did not stop to consider it may have been set deliberately."

"And was the fire set deliberately?" Benedict questioned.

Roger nodded. "Yes, Lord Lansdowne. We found evidence to indicate foul play."

Adrien humphed. "And you call yourself a spy."

"Adrien," Eliza said in a warning tone. "You are not being fair to Roger."

"No, Lady Lansdowne," Roger acknowledged humbly, "Lord Camden is correct. I failed to recognize a threat and act upon it."

Benedict cleared his throat, directing the attention towards himself. "If you were fighting the fire, how did you learn about Mr. Henley?"

"Mr. Oakes came running down to the east field to inform me that Lady Camden had an unannounced visitor in the drawing room," Roger explained. "I dropped my bucket and started running towards the estate. By the time I arrived, Mr. Henley had his hands around Lady Camden's throat, and her eyes were closed. I thought I was too late." His voice dropped to a whisper.

"She almost died! Your job was to protect her!" Adrien advanced towards him, but Benedict jumped up and put a hand on his shoulder, effectively stopping him.

"You are relieved of your command. Get off my land!" Adrien shouted.

Roger's gaze was unyielding. "With all due respect, sir, you have no authority to fire me. I am employed under the direction of the Duke of Remington and report to Lord Beckett directly. You will have to speak to either of them first."

"Believe me, I will," Adrien growled.

Benedict's hand was still firmly placed on Adrien's shoulder, and his voice was even. "Roger is not the enemy. Mr. Henley did this, not Roger."

Adrien knew that Benedict was right. He needed to go see Mr. Henley and kill him. "You are correct. I will go visit Mr. Henley right now."

Without moving his hand from his shoulder, Benedict ordered, "First, you need to tell us what transpired between Kate and Mr. Henley."

Adrien's eyes narrowed at Benedict as he realized how much he hated his friend at this moment. How could Benedict ask him to stay and talk, when all he wanted to do was deal with the man who'd tried to kill Kate? Opening his mouth to share his displeasure, he noticed Kate walk into the room. Her eyes were red, and her hair had fallen from her chignon, causing her to look younger and even more vulnerable.

"I heard shouting." Kate's voice was unsure, glancing between Adrien and Benedict.

Adrien's rage fell flat at the sight of her. As his tension diminished, Benedict dropped his hand from his shoulder.

"That would be my fault. I am sorry to disturb you," Adrien said apologetically.

"Please do not be mad at Roger," Kate requested, her wide eyes pleading with him. "He saved me today."

Adrien's eyes flickered to Roger, who had stood when Kate walked into the room. "You heard that?"

"I did," Kate replied.

"The whole staff heard that," Benedict mumbled under his breath.

Walking closer to Kate, Adrien clasped his hands behind his back, attempting to avoid the temptation of pulling her into his arms. "Will you allow Eliza to escort you back to your bedchamber, and I will try my best to keep my voice down?"

"That sounds wonderful," Eliza stated as cheerfully as if she was planning a house party. "Besides, you will need to decide what to bring with you. We want you to stay at our townhouse for the next couple of weeks."

Kate placed her hair behind her ears. "I have no desire to go to London."

"You must go," Adrien urged, drawing Kate's attention back to him. "Henley won't be able to get to you at Benedict's townhouse."

A brief flicker of fear came to her eyes when he mentioned Henley. How he wished he could wipe away all her fears.

"I will go on one condition," she said, looking him in the eye. "I want you to buy me a pistol and teach me how to shoot."

"Agreed," Adrien replied without a second thought. "I think it is a grand idea for you to know how to use a pistol. We will buy you an overcoat pistol, and you can keep it in your reticule."

Kate's shoulders relaxed, and she smiled at him. "I am getting better at giving orders, aren't I?"

"That you are, my dear," he agreed, smiling back at her.

She turned towards Eliza. "Let us go decide what I should bring."

Unclasping his hands from behind his back, Adrien stepped aside as Eliza and Kate exited the room. He strode to the drink cart and helped himself to another glass of brandy. This time he took a sip, then sat down on the settee.

Benedict sat on a chair across from him with Roger next to him. "Start at the beginning," he commanded.

Adrien placed his glass on the table and repeated everything that Kate had told him. After he finished, he removed the large, golden locket from his coat and handed it to Benedict. "This is Kate's locket that I told you about yesterday. I was hoping Eliza could use her lock-picking skills to open it."

Benedict examined the locket before asking, "Do you truly

believe the list of French spies are inside?" He handed it to Roger for his review.

"I do. Michel viewed Kate as his property, and he went to great lengths to ensure she never took the locket off," Adrien said. "I don't know how Mr. Henley knew about the locket, but I intend to find out." He started to rise.

"Wait," Benedict ordered, frowning. "We are partners now and we need to rationally discuss our next course of action."

Adrien sat back down and reached for his glass. "I am not used to having a partner," he grumbled as his finger traced the top of the glass. "I learned a long time ago that to be an effective spy, you have to sever all ties with loved ones for their safety." Attempting to keep the bitterness out of his voice, he stated, "And what did it get me?"

"Adrien…" Benedict started.

"It cost me everything," Adrien exclaimed, slamming the glass down onto the table next to him. "The only family I had left, who I hadn't seen in almost seven years, were murdered by the French, while I was off serving my country… in *France*."

Silence descended upon the room as Adrien wallowed in his self-pity. Michel was already dead, so he couldn't exact revenge against him, but Henley was still alive. Standing up forcefully, he reached behind his back and pulled out the pistol tucked into his trousers.

"If you will excuse me, I believe I will call on Mr. Henley now," Adrien said dryly, returning his pistol to its proper place after ensuring it was in perfect working order.

"Sit," Benedict barked. "You are not thinking like a spy, but a fool who is only thinking about revenge."

"Henley dared to attack Kate in her own home," Adrien challenged, pointing at the ground. "Kate is under my protection."

Huffing, Benedict shook his head in response. "I am sure Kate's father might contend his daughter is under *his* protection."

He placed his hands out in front of him. "Or, as Kate's brother-in-law, I could assume she is under *my* protection."

Adrien narrowed his eyes at his friend. "Kate is the Countess of Camden, and thus I have a right to protect her."

"You are not thinking clearly," Benedict claimed, frowning. "Your feelings are clouding your judgement."

Adrien lifted an eyebrow in confusion. "What feelings?"

"Your feelings about Kate," Benedict pressed.

"That is ridiculous," Adrien said, dismissing the notion with a flick of his wrist. "My feelings for Kate have nothing to do with this."

His friend's eyes grew big as saucers as he stared at him. After a moment, Benedict pressed his lips together. "We have been afforded a unique opportunity here. If you rush in, threatening to kill Henley, then we learn nothing."

Roger added, "At least we now know that Mr. Henley is the French spy in the House of Commons."

"Yes, luckily," Adrien replied harshly, turning his annoyed glare towards Roger.

Arising, Benedict walked over to the drink cart and poured himself a drink. No one spoke as he tossed back his brandy and gazed at the empty glass. Turning to face Adrien, his friend's expression was unreadable. "You seem to think you are the only one who has suffered from working undercover. My brother was murdered by my step-brother, Aaron Wade, while I was on a mission."

Placing his empty glass onto the drink cart, Benedict crossed his arms. "I was bitter and wanted to extract the most heinous revenge I could think of, but if I had, we could not have saved all those women he abducted. Sometimes, as an agent, we have to look at the whole puzzle and not just the piece directly in front of us."

Feeling properly chastised, Adrien sat back down on the settee. "What do you propose?"

"You are *Hawk*," Benedict stated. "You spent years undercover as a French Naval officer, constantly surrounded by the enemy. I have great confidence you can outwit a French spy on English soil."

Adrien leaned forward, placing his forearms on his knees. "I could attempt to befriend Mr. Henley, and perhaps become privy to who the other French operatives are."

"If you don't, then I will," Benedict declared firmly.

"I will need to create a bloody good backstory," Adrien sighed, resigned to the fact he was going to befriend the enemy, again. "Are you sure I cannot just kill him?"

"Positive," Benedict asserted. "I will inform Lord Beckett of our plans. We will return to London separately, so you can call on Mr. Henley."

"Delightful," Adrien said sarcastically.

Benedict ignored his comment. "We will bring Kate back to our townhouse, and she will be watched at all times. I will even post a guard outside of her bedchamber."

Roger shifted in his seat. "I cannot even begin to apologize…"

Adrien interrupted him, "It is I who needs to apologize to you. You saved Kate's life, and I was out of line."

"You had every right," Roger admitted.

Adrien shook his head. "No, I did not. Please just keep her from being harmed."

"With my dying breath," Roger promised.

Adrien acknowledged his words with a nod of his head. "Well, it appears that I have a date with the devil," he announced with a humorless laugh.

As he went to find Mr. Oakes to request his carriage, he took a moment to dwell on his new assignment. He had spent most of his time as a spy completing undercover assignments. He found it was easy to make believe he was someone he was not. It had always filled a void in his life.

Now, Kate had filled that void, and he found he was content to be himself. Even though Kate had refused his impromptu marriage offer, he could see her softening towards him.

The way her eyes lit up when she saw him today, gave him hope. And today… hope was good enough.

A few hours later, Adrien was ushered into Mr. Henley's townhouse located on Gracechurch Street, not far from Cheapside. His townhouse appeared paltry on the exterior, but the interior had a look of order and cleanliness. The dark, papered walls gave the interior a regal appearance. The expensive furniture was well-made, but sparse. In fact, the townhouse seemed not only to have limited furnishings, but art work, as well. If he did not know any better, he would assume that Mr. Henley was in the process of moving in or moving out.

"Mr. Henley will see you now, my lord," the butler announced.

Adrien followed him through the narrow halls towards a back room. Before he walked into the room, he took a deep breath as he got into character. He had a job to do even though every fiber of his body wanted to simply kill the man. He adopted the spy persona that had served him well over the years and conjured up a smile.

"Thank you for agreeing to see me," Adrien said as he stepped into the room.

Mr. Henley rose from his desk chair and shuffled papers in his hand. "I admit I was taken aback by you calling upon me at such a late hour. I was preparing to leave for Parliament to hear the speeches."

Adrien wanted to mock Henley's plum waistcoat but instead smiled at him. "I do apologize for calling unannounced, but I wanted to thank you personally for taking Lady Camden in hand today. I do not approve of the visible bruising, mind you," he stated, with a raised brow, "but I do appreciate your directness."

Mr. Henley reached for another pile of papers on his desk. "Did Lady Camden mention what we discussed?"

He shook his head. "No, but she did request additional funds to buy proper mourning attire. After the previous Lord Camden died, I provided her with adequate funds to buy mourning gowns, but she spent it on frivolous nonsense."

Mr. Henley huffed, "Women."

"Without a firm hand, women are hopeless."

"I concur," Mr. Henley agreed as he grabbed a file and shoved all the papers in. "Lady Camden appears to be quite a handful."

Adrien laughed loudly. "You could say that. I inherited her as my responsibility since she is currently the countess, and she routinely takes advantage of my generosity. Even though her father, the Duke of Remington, owns many estates, Lady Camden insists on residing at the country home which requires a large household staff."

Mr. Henley put the file down on the desk, suddenly interested in what he was saying. "Is that a problem?"

Adrien scoffed. "I had secured a buyer for the country home in hopes of using the money to turn a profit at my estate near Northumberland. My cousin kept many women comfortable in London, and I'm afraid he spent more than what his estate brought in."

Mr. Henley slowly lowered himself in his chair as he indicated Adrien should sit. "Are you looking for a source of income?"

Taking his lead, Adrien sat down on an armed chair, facing the desk. "My man of business indicated I would not be in the red much longer if I can reduce my expenditures. However, I cannot seem to curtail Lady Camden's spending."

Mr. Henley placed his arms on the desk and leaned forward. "What exactly is she spending your money on?"

"I believe the term 'spending' should be 'wasting,' because she hands the villagers money. She believes she needs to provide restitution for the deeds of her deceased husband." He laughed cruelly. "As if my cousin was not able to do as he pleased."

"Why have you not forced your hand on Lady Camden?" Mr. Henley asked, eyeing him suspiciously.

Adrien pretended to pick off a piece of lint from his trousers, ignoring Mr. Henley's mistrust. "I was concerned she would go crying to her sister, Lady Lansdowne. But now," he said with a smile, "since your visit has subdued her, I intend to make up for lost time."

"You do not believe she will go to her sister or father now?" Mr. Henley pressed curiously.

Adrien leaned forward in his chair. "When I arrived at my country home today, Lady Camden refused to speak to me, would not look at me, and acted like a skittish mare. It was a refreshing change."

Mr. Henley smiled, looking quite self-satisfied. "I am glad to help."

Rising abruptly, Adrien bowed slightly. "Now if you will excuse me, I will see you at Parliament." He started to walk out of the room, hoping Mr. Henley had taken the bait. With each step he took closer to the door, the more confident he was that his plan had worked.

As his hand turned the door's handle, Mr. Henley called him back. "Before you go, please join me for a drink."

It had worked! He slowly turned around, smiling. "I would be honored."

Mr. Henley pointed to the settee near a small fireplace. He

sat down and accepted the glass of port. "Matthew and I were close, but he failed to disclose he had a cousin."

Adrien took a sip of his drink. "I am not surprised. After Cambridge, I took a tour of the continent. I even invited Matthew to go along, but he refused to go when England was at war." He frowned. "England is always at war with some country, sometimes multiple countries at once. Prinny is a blood-thirsty regent, who will stop at nothing till he dictates what the world can and cannot do."

Mr. Henley tapped his fingers against his glass. "You could be branded a traitor for saying that about our beloved prince regent."

Adrien took a long sip from his port, pretending to savor the drink. "I do not openly share my views." He narrowed his eyes at Mr. Henley, his tone becoming accusatory. "I would have thought you were a progressive thinker, since you are associated with the Whigs."

"Do not fear. Our beliefs are aligned," Mr. Henley assured him.

"I wish my uncle would have sided with me, but his hatred of the French clouded his judgement. When I wrote home describing the French countryside to be full of friendly, hospitable people, my uncle's letters became irate."

Mr. Henley took a sip of his port. "How so?"

Adrien snorted. "He cut me off when I informed him I wanted to stay and live in France. He thought it was distasteful that his nephew would side with the French when he was such a staunch Tory."

"And what did Matthew think?"

Adrien shrugged sadly. "I don't rightly know, but I fear he thought I was dead. The last letter I received from him was over six years ago, but I was too angry to write him back." He paused to sip his drink, reflectively. "I regret that decision now."

"Don't judge yourself too harshly, you were still young," Mr. Henley replied, his voice holding no compassion.

Pretending he found Mr. Henley's words comforting, he nodded thankfully. "A couple of months ago, I arrived back at my uncle's estate, only to discover a skeleton staff. They informed me of the death of my uncle, and I went in search of Matthew. By the time I made it to London, I learned he had died in a carriage accident while trying to outrun highway robbers."

"If you loved France so much, why did you return home to England?" Mr. Henley inquired.

Adrien did his best to look ashamed. "I ran out of money. I owed too many of the wrong people," he admitted as he took a sip of his drink. "Which is why I was pleased to learn I was the new Lord Camden." His face fell, then he shrugged. "What I lack in funds, I make up in property, supposedly."

"Where did you live in France?" Mr. Henley asked in French.

Adrien responded in French, "Strassburg mostly, but I loved Sexanne."

Mr. Henley continued speaking in French. "How did you occupy your time?"

"I lived with a few mademoiselles at their chalets until I grew tired of their company and moved on," he remarked callously. "I do not believe that every man has a soul mate, but it is amusing to look, no?" He smirked, doing his best to impersonate a French cad.

Mr. Henley smiled at his heartless response. "It appears that we have much in common," he declared, switching back to English.

Adrien placed his drink on the side table next to the settee. "I have enjoyed our time immensely, but I'm afraid I must go."

Mr. Henley lowered his empty glass onto the table. "I have a business proposition for you."

He stilled. "I am listening."

"Lady Camden has something that I want, and I am willing to pay for its return," Mr. Henley stated.

"Why not just ask her to return the item in question?"

"I did," Mr. Henley said, frowning. "That is what led to our… disagreement."

"Ah." Adrien nodded his understanding. "What exactly does she have of yours?"

"A round, gold locket," Mr. Henley answered.

Adrien arched an eyebrow. "A locket? That hardly seems worth your time."

"I am willing to make it worth *your* time."

Adrien looked incredulous. "You want to pay me to retrieve a locket from Lady Camden's possession?"

"Yes."

"How much?"

"Five hundred pounds."

Adrien gave a low, long whistle of amazement. "To retrieve a worthless locket?"

"It is not worthless to me."

"No, of course not," Adrien replied, pretending to mull over the request. "I will do it."

"Excellent." Mr. Henley smiled as he rose. "If you prove successful, I think we can become mutually beneficial to one another."

Adrien stood up, taking a moment to pull down his waistcoat. "I find I am very motivated by money."

Mr. Henley eyed him in approval. "I hope to see you soon."

"Where should I deliver the locket?"

"Bring it to me in two days, and I hope to have another task for you to complete," Mr. Henley said, walking him towards the door.

"As you wish." Adrien nodded his farewell as he exited the room.

When Adrien closed the door of his carriage, he had the

sudden urge to go home and soak in a bath. He wanted to rub his skin until he could become clean from the filth of Mr. Henley.

Now, he had to see if Eliza could pick the locket. What if the list wasn't in the locket? It had better be. Then they could arrest Mr. Henley and his accomplices and end this farce. He would seek out Eliza as soon as he arrived home. For the first time, it was nice having Eliza and Benedict as neighbors.

## ⁂ 14 ⁂

FROWNING, ADRIEN WATCHED A SHADOWY FIGURE SLUMP against the building across the street from his townhouse. He assumed Mr. Henley would send someone to tail him, but he was insulted at the caliber of the ruffian sent. An idiot would be able to discern that he was being spied upon.

At some point, the man fell asleep. When Adrien peered out of the window before heading to bed, the man was laying on the floor, curled up into a ball. To make matters worse, another shadowy figure was watching his servant's entrance, but Adrien could hear him snoring when he opened his chamber window this morning.

He chuckled to himself. Maybe he should approach the men and offer them some unsolicited advice about staying concealed while spying on someone? No, it was best to let the men report back to Mr. Henley and inform him of his whereabouts, without casting doubt on his identity.

He was playing the part of an English rogue, who seduced women in the French countryside, and who had only come home to secure more funds from his rich uncle. At no point would his character have become adept at espionage and learned the skill of sneaking up on people.

Rubbing the back of his neck with his hand, Adrien had hoped to see Eliza and Benedict upon his arrival last night, but he did not want Mr. Henley to know of his close association with them. It would cause suspicion if he was seen being ushered in to Benedict's townhouse at such a late hour. When would the men leave to report their findings to Mr. Henley?

He exited his bedchamber and walked towards his study. Coming to a stop at the end of the hall, he placed his palm on the mauve-papered wall. Benedict's townhouse mirrored his in the layout of the rooms and halls.

His hand roamed the wall. One wall separated him from speaking to Eliza and Benedict. One wall separated him from speaking to Kate, and slowly courting her without her knowledge. A spark of genius came to him.

"Ward," he shouted, "bring me a sledgehammer."

Mr. Ward, his butler, hurried up the stairs and stopped a few feet from him. "A sledgehammer, my lord?"

Adrien shrugged off his morning coat, dropping it onto a nearby chair. "Yes. Do we have one?"

Ward's lips tightened slightly, but he was wise enough not to frown. "What do you plan to do with the sledgehammer, sir?"

Adrien turned back around and surveyed the wall. "I am going to take down this wall, so I can speak to Lord and Lady Lansdowne."

Clearing his throat, Ward looked utterly confused. "Have you spoken to Lord Lansdowne about sledgehammering through the wall?"

Adrien removed a large portrait of a previous earl from the wall and placed it on the ground. "No, I have not."

"Do you think this is wise?" Ward asked, disapproval lacing his words.

"Bring me a sledgehammer," he ordered with a tone that

brooked no argument. He heard Ward running down the stairs to do his bidding.

Standing back, he looked at the narrow wall. It would only take a few well-aimed blows with the sledgehammer to open it. After it was open, he would widen the area, so he could eventually hang a door between the two townhouses.

Ward marched up the stairs with a young, lanky footman who was holding the sledgehammer. "Please step aside, Lord Camden. I have assigned Carson to complete the manual labor."

Adrien held out his hand to Carson. "I will do it."

His butler's eyes widened. "You are an earl. It is simply not done," he sputtered.

Adrien hid his smile at Ward's blatant disapproval. "Carson, go out the servant's entrance and ask Lord Lansdowne's housekeeper to remove any personal effects from the other side of this wall," he directed, pointing at the wall. "Do not state your business until you are inside Lord Lansdowne's townhouse. Understood?"

"Yes, my lord," Carson said, before he disappeared down the stairs.

Adrien removed his cravat, then rolled up the sleeves on his white muslin shirt. After waiting a few moments, he reared the sledgehammer back to gain momentum before slamming it through the papered wall. He was met with the crashing sound of splintering wood and a white cloud of plaster dust filling the air.

As he swung the sledgehammer over and over, he quickly created a large opening on his side. Next, he started hammering through the plastered walls on Benedict's side. The wood and walls were old, and he broke through without much effort.

As the light streamed through from the large hole on Benedict's side, he placed the sledgehammer down and started ripping off the remaining plaster with his hands. When he was satisfied there was enough room for him to squeeze through, he ducked his head and emerged on the other side. As he had predicted, he was standing in a hallway mirroring his own.

Benedict was leaning up against the wall, shaking his head. "What possessed you to sledgehammer a hole in my wall?" he grumbled.

Adrien dusted off his trousers. "I needed to speak to you and Eliza, but both entrances were being watched."

Looking down, Benedict placed his fingers upon the bridge of his nose. "You thought the rational course of action would be to create a passageway between your townhouse and mine?" he asked slowly, deliberately.

Adrien ran a hand through his hair, causing white plaster remnants to fall to the floor. "It worked splendidly, if I do say so myself."

Benedict's mouth gaped open. "You are a bloody fool, and you are paying for that wall."

"I already planned to," Adrien confirmed.

"My lord, your coat," Ward said, his perfectly groomed head peeking through the wall. He extended the coat through the opening, then attempted to brush off the fine white plaster dust covering the garment.

Adrien unrolled the sleeves of his shirt. "I do not require the use of my tailcoat."

"Yes, my lord." Ward nodded, then disappeared back through the wall.

Benedict chuckled. "He is attempting to make you more civilized."

"It is not working well, is it?" Adrien replied with a smirk.

Benedict glanced over his shoulder at the wall and shook his head. "Bloody idiot," he muttered under his breath, followed by a few choice expletives. After a moment, he leveled his gaze at Adrien. "Have you broken your fast yet?"

"Yes. I tend to eat earlier than most," Adrien informed him. "A habit I picked up in the French Navy."

"Fair enough," Benedict said turning away from him. "Follow me, we can talk privately in my study."

Adrien followed him as they headed down to the first level and into his study. He dropped onto a brown leather sofa and wiped his hands along his trousers, which were still coated in fine white powder. He attempted to brush them off as he chuckled. "My valet will not be pleased with me."

Benedict sat on the edge of his desk with a frown on his face. "What was so important that you felt you needed to create a large passageway through my wall?"

"I spoke to Mr. Henley yesterday, and we have an arrangement," he replied, then filled him in on their conversation.

Benedict placed his hands on the edge of the desk. "Mr. Henley is willing to pay *you*, a down-on-your-luck lord, five hundred pounds to retrieve the locket that Kate gave to you."

"Yes," Adrien confirmed. "Although, my instincts are telling me that this task is more of a test."

"As much as I hate the hole in the wall, I believe it will come in handy. It is vital that we are not seen together in public, especially since I am giving another speech tomorrow night in Parliament in favor of the bill," Benedict informed him.

"I concur. It must appear I am siding with the Whigs until the vote," Adrien admitted reluctantly. "I was thinking…"

"A dangerous pastime for you, no doubt," Benedict interjected, smiling at his own wit.

Adrien rolled his eyes at his friend's attempt at humor. "As I was saying, I was thinking about the vote to end the war. Even if the bill passes, it will take months, if not a year, before it takes effect. We have too many troops and ships deployed to assume there could be an immediate withdrawal from Europe."

Benedict tilted his head, his expression thoughtful. "That is a good point. Even though the coalition forces may have suffered two major defeats in battle, Lord Beckett is confident that the war will be over within the year."

Adrien leaned forward in his seat. "What are the French trying to accomplish by infiltrating Parliament and bringing a bill forward to end the war? It seems as if it is too late in the game for this scheme to work."

"Not necessarily," Benedict said. "Besides supplying troops, England provides our allies with financial support. Without our backing, Russia, Austria, and the rest of our allies would be unable to continue fighting Napoleon."

"And the bill specifically calls for an immediate ending of all financial support to our allies," Adrien stated, frowning.

Benedict rose and began pacing. "If the bill does pass, Napoleon would be unstoppable."

Adrien raked his hand through his hair, hesitant to ask his next question. "Have you considered that the bill might also be a diversion?"

Benedict stopped pacing and faced Adrien. "Meaning?" he asked.

"Every day, multiple riots break out all over England in opposition of the war and the high food prices. Women and children are starving while their husbands, and sons, are serving in an unpopular war." Adrien grimaced. "What if the French spies are using this bill to encourage an uprising?"

Benedict rubbed his chin reflectively. "France did attempt an uprising in Ireland in 1796, but they failed horribly," he pointed out. "Do you truly believe the French spies would be able to complete such a lofty goal on English soil?"

Adrien shook his head and snickered, amusement dancing in his eyes. "You are a spy, too. Do I really have to bring all the brilliant ideas to the table?"

Benedict laughed, as he hoped he would. "I agree with you that the bill seems ill-timed. Hopefully your interaction with Mr. Henley will provide us with more insight into their plans."

Adrien glanced over his shoulder at the closed door. "Is Eliza awake? I am curious to know if she was successful in opening the locket."

Benedict huffed sarcastically. "If you had not been preoccupied with destroying *my* property, you would have seen her leave in the carriage with Kate. Unfortunately, she was unable to open the locket, and is taking it to her jeweler."

"And you did not go with them?" Adrien asked, shocked by his friend's carelessness.

Benedict looked at Adrien with an expression of disbelief. "Is your brain always this addled in the morning?" After a moment, he shook his head. "Mr. Larson returned home from Scotland last night, and he accompanied the ladies to the jeweler, as did Roger and six footmen."

Adrien put his hands in front of him in a show of surrender. "My apologies. I am just worried about…"

"About Kate, yes, I know." Benedict nodded knowingly. "Need I remind you that my wife is the greatest spy in all of England?"

Adrien chuckled smugly. "Maybe in England, but my code name, *Hawk,* sparks fear in the hearts of the French. My intel saved thousands of Englishman's lives and secured many crucial victories for the Royal Navy."

Benedict gave him a crooked smile. "I will concede that you are a decent spy, at least according to Lord Beckett."

Adrien laughed good-naturedly. "Why do you not have a code name?"

Benedict shrugged. "I never was in a position that required one."

"*Sunshine*," Adrien exclaimed.

"I beg your pardon?"

"If Eliza is *Shadow*, then the opposite would be *Sunshine*," Adrien explained, laughing.

"My code name would not now, nor ever be, *Sunshine*," Benedict growled.

"What about *Shadow's Keeper*?" he jested, pointing at him with a bright smile.

"It is time for you to leave," Benedict declared, walking towards the door, and opening it.

As Adrien exited the room, he said over his shoulder, "I will see myself out, *Sunshine*."

He could hear Benedict slam the door shut. He could not help but laugh all the way down the hall.

KATE PEERED AT THE LARGE, GAPING HOLE AT THE END OF Eliza's second level hallway. "Eliza?" she asked loudly. "Where did this hole come from?"

Receiving no answer, and assuming it was an opening that led into Adrien's townhouse, she glanced over her shoulder to confirm no one was privy to what she was about to do. Quickly, she stepped through the wall.

"Kate?" Adrien walked across the hall to greet her. "How long have you been here?"

"I just arrived." Turning to examine the wall, she noticed that the opening had been originally created on Adrien's side. "Why did you create this massive hole?"

Stopping a few feet away, Adrien leaned up against the wall. "It was a way for me to converse with Benedict and Eliza privately."

Kate traced the outline of the hole with her fingers. "This seems rather excessive, does it not?"

Adrien smiled smugly. "I thought it was rather brilliant."

"I suppose exiting your door and walking ten feet to your

neighbor's entrance could be considered tiresome by some," she said cheekily.

"Kate," Eliza's pleasant voice called from the other side of the wall, "are you over there?"

Adrien placed a finger on his lips, encouraging her to stay silent.

After a moment, Eliza informed them, "Adrien and Kate, I can see you through the hole."

Adrien reached for her hand, and they raced along the hall and down a flight of stairs. He tugged her into a room, which she could only assume was a small library. Shelves, filled with books, ran nearly the length of the square room, except where two small windows were situated, providing adequate light. A stone fireplace sat along the wall opposite the door.

Kate flew to the shelves and ran her hand along the books. "Where did you acquire all these books?" she asked in awe.

Adrien smiled. "They came with the townhouse."

"Have you read any of them?"

Adrien walked over to the shelves and grabbed a book, glanced down at the title, and read, "*Rameau's Nephew*, by Denis Diderot, the French edition." He placed the book back on the shelf. "Sadly, I have read very few of these books."

"We must read a book together," she suggested, her excitement shining through. "Eliza bought me a new book titled *Pride and Prejudice*. It is by the same author as *Sense and Sensibility*." She placed her hand up near her mouth as if telling him a secret. "They are both written by a lady," she whispered.

"A lady, you say," Adrien said, smiling down at her.

Kate bobbed her head. "Would you allow me to read the book to you aloud?"

"I believe that is a grand idea," he replied with such enthusiasm that Kate knew he wasn't just placating her.

Eliza glided into the room, and her attention was immediately captured by the numerous books. "Oh, Adrien. Look at all these books!" She practically ran towards a shelf as her eyes perused the titles. "There are so many that I have not read before."

"You are welcome to any books in my library," Adrien offered, as he gave Kate a private smile. "As you are, too, Kate."

Benedict stormed into the room and stopped when he noticed Eliza perusing the books. A small sigh escaped his lips. "Oh good, more books for Eliza to read."

Kate started to giggle but threw her hand up to stifle it.

Benedict smiled at Kate before he asked Adrien, "Did Eliza tell you why we stepped through the hole in the wall, or did she get distracted by all the books?" He walked over to his wife, placed his hand on the small of her back, and whispered in her ear. Whatever he said caused her to blush and divert her eyes to the floor.

Kate glanced over at Adrien to see if he noticed the interaction between her sister and brother-in-law. But instead of looking at them, he was watching her, and his eyes were filled with tenderness. Benedict escorted Eliza to a settee near the wall as Kate sat on an upholstered armchair. Adrien grabbed a chair and placed it next to hers before sitting down.

"Kate and I just came back from my trusted jeweler. He was able to open the locket, and he found a small folded piece of paper," Eliza informed them, reaching into a pocket of her dress.

"Did the jeweler close the locket?" Adrien asked.

"He did," Eliza confirmed, giving him a curious look. "He also gave me a little tool that will open it again, if required."

Adrien looked pleased. "Excellent. I have an appointment with Mr. Henley tomorrow evening to deliver the locket, and I need it in its original condition."

Eliza nodded. "I could copy the details of the paper, then we could return the original to the locket. That way it would appear undisturbed to Mr. Henley."

"That should work," Adrien agreed.

Eliza unfolded the small piece of yellowed paper. "It reads, *E.H., Marthe, G.M., Rogue, 6/15.*"

Adrien wiped a hand over his mouth, attempting to interpret the cryptic words. "Do you think the initials indicate the first letter of their given name and surname? *E.H.* might be Mr. Henley."

"Perhaps," Eliza said, briefly biting her lower lip. "I have no reason to believe it is a coded message."

"Why would Michel keep this list of initials and a date in a locket around Kate's neck?" Benedict asked. "It must be important."

Adrien sighed. "I cannot turn this locket over to Henley if this paper provides him with information that could turn the tide of the war."

Eliza turned the small paper over and examined it. "I could reproduce the page, and we could alter the original initials and date?" she suggested.

Adrien shook his head. "I don't think that would work. We must reasonably assume that Henley already knows who the other French operatives are."

"What if Eliza just changed the date?" Benedict proposed.

"And if Mr. Henley already knows the date on the paper?" Eliza speculated. "We would likely get Adrien killed."

Adrien leaned forward in his seat. "We cannot risk changing the information. We might lose my only opportunity to partner with Henley. I will have to be extra diligent to ensure Henley will trust me."

Kate's hand flew to her bruised neck. "You are intentionally seeking to work with Mr. Henley?"

Adrien's eyes darted to Eliza and Benedict before they rested back on her. "I am an agent of the Crown. This is who I am," he replied softly.

Kate shook her head. "But you know he is a French spy. Why not have my uncle arrest him and force him to tell you who his co-conspirators are?"

Adrien shifted in his seat, facing Kate. "The Crown does torture enemy spies, but most of the spies do not turn."

Kate's temper began to rise. "Your plan is to go work for Mr. Henley, the man who nearly killed me, until he gives up his secrets?"

Uncertainty flashed in Adrien's eyes. "Yes, but it is much more complicated than that."

"And if he kills you?" Kate asked desperately, her eyes filling with tears.

Adrien placed his hand over hers. "He will not kill me."

Kate removed her hands from his and wiped angrily at her tears. "Do not coddle me. We both know there are risks associated with this plan."

"Eliza and I are working with Adrien, and we have the full support of your uncle," Benedict informed her.

Kate knew Benedict's words were meant to reassure her, but she was no fool. This was a dangerous plan and Adrien could be killed.

"I understand," Kate murmured, giving Benedict a faint smile. "If you will excuse me, I need to go lie down."

She quickly rose and fled the room without a backward glance. As she reached the base of the stairs, Adrien called out to her, "Kate, please wait." She stilled at the desperate plea in his voice.

Hearing his footsteps coming closer, she mustered up a smile and spun around to face him. "I do not…"

Without a word, Adrien pulled her into his arms and kissed her firmly on the lips. Before she had time to respond, he released her and stepped back. Her eyes grew wide as she waited for him to explain his spontaneous behavior. Although, she did not intend to complain.

The intensity in his eyes held her transfixed. "No one has ever cared enough for me to cry over me."

Kate stepped closer, longing to be back in the safety of his arms. "I find that hard to believe. You are the kindest, most compassionate man I know. I wager there are many people that worry about you."

His warm eyes crinkled, just a tiny bit in the corners, although it seemed forced. "You are wrong, but it is kind of you to say so."

Kate's heart lurched, sadness filling her chest at his words. How could he not see that he meant so much to her? "Promise me that you will be safe," she pleaded softly. It was on the tip of her tongue to ask him to come back to her, but she could not be so bold.

Adrien's cocky smile wiped away his vulnerability. "I am *Hawk*. I always survive."

"Adrien, stop wooing Kate and get back in here," Benedict's teasing voice echoed through Adrien's hall.

"Coming, *Sunshine*," Adrien called over his shoulder.

*Sunshine?* Kate mouthed to Adrien, her expression both amused and puzzled.

He chuckled. "It is Benedict's code name."

"It is not my code name," Benedict grumbled.

Adrien leaned over and kissed her cheek. "I will call on you later tonight," he promised, before turning and walking back into the library.

Kate stood and placed her hand to her cheek. Why would Adrien believe that no one cared for him? He apparently had no clue that he was constantly on her mind. His warm smile. His laugh. Those were the things that she dreamed about as she laid her head on her pillow every night. She cared for Adrien immensely, but maybe it was more? No, that was not possible.

Whatever she was, she was happy.

# 15

ADRIEN CHUCKLED TO HIMSELF AS HE WALKED PAST GARDEN Ladies, a high-class brothel near St. James's church, located in the central district city of Westminster. The two men trailing him should be ashamed of themselves for their lack of discretion.

After arriving at the brothel, he hired a scantily clad young woman and followed her up to her room on the second level. After paying her a generous sum to remain in her room for three hours, he opened the window and scaled down the building. He removed his dark blue coat and turned it inside out. The interior color was a bland brown, specifically designed to be inconspicuous, thus changing his appearance. He removed a cloth cap from his pocket and settled it on his head.

He pulled his starched collar as high as it could go and stuffed his hands in his pockets. He rented a hackney, two blocks over from the brothel, and within a few minutes he pulled up in front of Lord Beckett's building. After paying the hackney driver, he hopped out and walked into the building. He could not help but notice that three burley men, dressed in working class clothing, followed him in.

The men did not intimidate him, since they were ensuring he

meant no harm. As he walked closer to the lone desk in the foyer, he recognized the young man who had assisted him before. He put his hand up in a greeting gesture and said loudly, so the men following could hear, "Lord Camden to see Lord Beckett. He is expecting me."

Within moments, the men following him had disappeared, and he was left with the young man leading him to Lord Beckett's office. The office door was ajar, and he could hear Benedict's voice drifting through the hallway.

When he walked into the room, he noticed that Benedict was sitting with his legs crossed in an arm chair across from Lord Beckett, who was sitting behind his large desk. Their conversation stopped, and they both looked expectantly at him.

His steps faltered. "Did I interrupt something?"

Benedict shook his head. "No, we were just taking bets on when you would arrive. Neither of us expected to see you this soon."

Adrien claimed the chair next to Benedict. "The men followed me to Garden Ladies, where I hired a young lady's services for three hours."

"Define hired?" Lord Beckett asked gruffly.

Adrien's face fell flat. "Did you think I was referring to… no, that is not what I meant," he sputtered defensively. "I hired a young lady to stay in her locked room, with her window ajar, for three hours. Nothing more!"

Lord Beckett nodded approvingly. "I am glad to hear that since Benedict has informed me that you are paying court to my niece."

Adrien glared at his friend with displeasure. "Technically, Kate has not agreed to the courtship."

Benedict chuckled. "I am sure she is amendable, considering you two were spotted kissing at the base of the stairs yesterday."

To Adrien's surprise, Lord Beckett genuinely smiled at him. "It warms my heart to know that you are pursuing Kate. She has suffered so much in her young life at the hands of others. She deserves to be happy."

"I could not agree with you more, sir, but Kate has been harder to convince," Adrien admitted frankly.

Lord Beckett's smile grew wider. "In my experience, the ones that protest too much are the ones that are fighting a battle within themselves. From what Roger has reported, she is likely already in love with you and does not realize it."

"That gives me hope." Adrien smiled.

"Did Roger report these findings before or after Adrien tried to fire him?" Benedict teased, smirking.

Lord Beckett's expression changed to a deep frown. "You had no right to fire Roger."

"I am sorry for that misstep," Adrien apologized, putting his hands up in surrender.

Benedict chuckled. "Roger paid him no heed anyway."

Lord Beckett pointed his finger at Adrien. "Larson and I handpicked Roger to protect Kate, and they have formed an alliance. She relies on Roger, although I heard she is relying increasingly on you."

Adrien nodded his agreement. "Of late, she has not glanced over her shoulder to look for Roger."

"Of course not. You two only seem to have eyes for each other. It is revolting," Benedict ribbed good-naturedly.

Lord Beckett laughed under his breath. "It is the exact same way with you and Eliza," he informed Benedict.

Adrien extended his legs in front of him and placed his intertwined fingers in his lap. "Gentlemen, as much as I am thoroughly enjoying this conversation, I only have two hours before I have to seek out the men that are currently following me. It is exhausting to keep pace with those two. Sometimes, I have to stop and peer into a store's window just to give them a chance to catch up," he sighed.

"What a hard burden you are expected to bear," Benedict sympathized dramatically.

Adrien smirked. "Finally, some recognition."

Lord Beckett appeared less amused by their banter. "Per your request, my agents have done a thorough check on Mr. Henley and Lord Lexington."

Now, Adrien was paying attention. He straightened in his chair. "What did you discover?"

Lord Beckett opened a file on his desk and pulled out a piece of paper. "Mr. Henley supposedly made his fortune in trade, but the agents cannot verify any specifics," he reported, glancing up from the paper for a moment.

"That is not at all suspicious," Benedict muttered sarcastically.

Lord Beckett continued reading from the document. "For the past three years, he has been active in the House of Commons. His seat was purchased for him by Lord Lexington, which is no surprise to us. He sides with the Whigs and is vocal about his disapproval of the war against France." He put the paper down. "He is unmarried, and the agents could not find any information about him prior to 1809."

Adrien gave him a look of disbelief. "Mr. Henley shows up four years ago and gained a seat in the House of Commons a year later. Did no one find that suspicious?"

Lord Beckett shook his head. "Historically, the House of Commons has been made up of men supported by lords to push their agendas. It was only four years ago that the practice of purchasing seats was made illegal. Many men chose to look the other way since Mr. Henley was endorsed by the Marquess of Lexington, who is a close associate of Prinny's."

"What can you tell us about Lord Lexington?" Benedict asked.

Lord Beckett reached for another paper in the file. "Lord Lexington was Prinny's playmate when they were younger, and they stayed close for most of their lives. When Prinny started siding with the Tories, their relationship became strained, but not severed. He is also a heavy opponent of the war with France and frequently goes to rallies in Timpleton Square."

"Has Lord Lexington suffered any financial setbacks?" Adrien inquired.

"None. He has a London townhouse, a country home near Kent, and thirty thousand pounds in the bank," Lord Beckett read.

"Why would Lord Lexington betray his country, if not for money?" Adrien pondered aloud.

Benedict replied, "Men have betrayed their country for much less."

Lord Beckett reached for another paper in the file. "Lord Lexington has been married for twelve years to the eldest daughter of Viscount Wixton. They have two children together, a boy and a girl." He placed the papers back in the file, before saying, "He does keep a mistress in town, but that is not uncommon for the gentry."

"What is Mr. Henley's first name?" Adrien asked, reaching into his pocket for the locket.

Lord Beckett glanced down at the paper. "Edgar. Why?"

Adrien held the locket out to Lord Beckett. "This is the locket that Mr. Henley is paying me to retrieve from Kate." He took a moment to recount his meeting with Mr. Henley. "Inside, it holds the list that Michel referenced before he died."

A smile graced Lord Beckett's face. "What did the list reveal?"

Benedict handed him a piece of paper. "Eliza recreated what was on the paper."

Lord Beckett's smile dimmed as he read it, then flipped it over. "This is what Michel kept with Kate for all these years?"

Adrien shifted in his seat. "It appears the first set of initials belong to Edgar Henley, but after that we are at a loss."

"What is Lord Lexington's name?" Benedict inquired.

Lord Beckett shuffled through the pages. "Mr. Henry James Preston."

"Although his name is not on the list, he is still connected with this," Adrien insisted. "I propose agents watch his comings and goings and see who he is meeting with."

Lord Beckett bobbed his head. "I concur. What about Edgar Henley?"

"I am meeting with him tonight to deliver the locket and hope for my services to be retained," Adrien informed him. "But, I would recommend assigning agents to watch his every move. I have no doubt that he is a French spy, but we need to find his co-conspirators."

"I am giving a speech tonight in opposition of the war in a special joint session of Parliament," Benedict stated. "By calling a joint session, it will divert Mr. Henley's attention towards me."

Lord Beckett furrowed his brow. "And Eliza. Mr. Henley has no qualms about abducting women to push his agenda."

Adrien grinned. "I pity the fool who attempts to abduct Eliza."

"Mr. Larson has increased security at our townhouse and is taking the potential threat seriously," Benedict affirmed.

"Good, good," Lord Beckett repeated as he rested his hands on the desk and leaned forward. "I will assign agents to trail Mr. Henley and Lord Lexington. I would like to notify the Bow Street Runners and bring them into our confidence. They might prove useful to us."

Benedict tapped his trousers with his finger. "Since Adrien is being followed, I will send a messenger to your office with any information we uncover."

"How do you propose to communicate with both your townhouses under surveillance?" Lord Beckett inquired.

Benedict scoffed. "Adrien created a passageway between our neighboring townhouses."

"A passageway? How did he accomplish that?" Lord Beckett pressed.

"With a sledgehammer," Benedict said.

Lord Beckett turned to Adrien with a teasing smile on his lips. "Well, well, Lord Camden. It appears you were quite eager to call on my niece."

Adrien shook his head. "That was not my original intention."

Lord Beckett chuckled. "Do not take me for a fool, son. I have been in love before, and a passageway between two homes is of little consequence."

Wanting this conversation to end, Adrien rose quickly. "If you will excuse me, I need to climb back into the brothel before anyone notices my absence."

As he exited the building, he reflected on Lord Beckett's words, *I have been in love before*. Was he in love with Kate? He could not possibly be. He admired her strength and perseverance. He especially enjoyed kissing her and, if he was not mistaken, she enjoyed kissing him, too.

Now he just had to convince her to grant him permission to court her. Whenever he thought about the future, he pictured her as his wife. He staggered to a halt with that realization. The reason he was so obsessed with convincing her to allow him to court her was because he loved her! He loved spending time with her. He loved being the person who made her smile. He loved being the man he was when he was with her! Furthermore, he thoroughly enjoyed suggesting scandalous outings because he loved to hear Kate freely laugh, as if she did not carry any burdens from her past.

He needed a new plan. He needed to convince Kate that he was the man for her.

KATE WAS SITTING ON THE CHAISE LOUNGE IN HER CHAMBER, reading a poetry book that she found in Adrien's library. A soft knock at her door broke her concentration. She put the book down and walked to the door. Opening it, she saw a young maid who handed her a small note, curtsied, and made a quick retreat.

Opening the letter, she read, *Meet me in my ballroom.* No name was signed, but there was no doubt who it was from. She dashed to her dressing table to ensure her hair was still pulled back into the stylish coiffure that Martha had insisted upon that morning. She smoothed out the skirts of her high-waisted, jonquil-colored gown and pinched her cheeks to add color.

She quietly closed her door and moved silently down the stairs towards the hole that Adrien had created. To her surprise, the hole in the wall had been extended, and a door had been added. She opened it and rushed down to meet Adrien.

Adrien's ballroom was square-shaped, with gold-papered walls and decorative wall sconces spaced evenly throughout. The drapes were opened, allowing the large windows to let in an exorbitant amount of light. Adrien stood in the center of the room, dressed in his finery, watching her. Even though the ballroom was magnificent, it paled in comparison to Adrien.

She approached him until she was close enough to see the brown flecks in his green eyes. "This ballroom is exquisite," she marveled. If she'd had more courage, she would have said, '*you are exquisite*'.

"I thought you would appreciate this room." He smiled and took a step forward. Suddenly, there was no space between them.

Kate reached out and rubbed her fingers along the lapels of his black dress coat. "And you look very handsome," she said, nervously breaking eye contact with him.

"Do I now?" he asked, his eyes roaming her face.

Kate decided to bring humor into this suddenly serious

conversation. "I must admit you very much fit the part of an elegant lord today."

"And does that displease you?"

Kate bit her lower lip, pretending to mull over his question for a few moments. "No, I suppose not."

He chuckled as she hoped he would before he placed his hands on her shoulders. Slowly, he slid them down her arms until he grasped her hands. "Dance with me?"

Kate wrinkled her nose in confusion. "But there is no music."

Adrien gave her a mischievous smile. "Trust me," he said, as he slipped one hand around her waist and raised his other arm. Kate placed her ungloved hand into his. As soon as Adrien started leading her in the waltz, music filled the room.

Kate gasped as she looked around trying to find the source of the music. "Where is the music coming from?"

Adrien pulled her tighter to him, leaning down to whisper in her ear, "Look up."

Tilting her head, she saw a small balcony above the entry door where a few musicians sat playing their instruments. She turned her attention back to Adrien. "Did you do this for me?"

Adrien smiled at her. "I did. I specifically remembered you loved to dance." As hard as she tried to quell her tears, she was unsuccessful, and her vision was soon clouded by moisture. Adrien loosened his hold on her, his face etched with worry. "Did I do something wrong?"

She shook her head. How could she properly convey that he did everything right… completely perfect. "No, you could never do anything wrong. I was momentarily rendered speechless by your thoughtfulness."

Adrien puffed out his chest and smiled. "What has occupied your time today?" he asked, as he guided her along the dance floor.

"I played the pianoforte this morning for Eliza," she informed him. "My poor sister was not feeling well."

"I hope she feels better soon."

"Oh, she will," Kate teased, "in about seven months."

He laughed. "How silly of me."

"I noticed you stepping into your carriage this morning," she said. "What occupied your time today?"

Adrien's steps faltered, and he gave her a disapproving look. "Were you spying on me?"

"No," she replied, suddenly feeling silly. "I just happened to look out the window."

Tsking, Adrien started leading her to the music again. "That is a dangerous habit, my lady. Soon, you will be lurking in alleyways and meeting unscrupulous men in the pubs on the east side."

Feeling her heart lighten by his teasing, Kate feigned disappointment. "I fear you may be right. My spying days must come to an end."

As Kate danced to the music, relishing Adrien's arms around her, she realized she wanted to encourage him. She did not want to push away the one good thing in her life, the one constant she could always rely on. But she did want to open her heart and trust him. She wanted to marry him; maybe not right now, but in the future.

After dancing for what seemed like hours, Adrien slowed to a stop, before he kissed her cheek. "I have an appointment that I need to keep before Parliament. I will seek you out tonight before you retire."

"Most likely, I will be in your library."

"No matter where you are, I will find you," he whispered in her ear.

# 16

ADRIEN TOOK A MOMENT TO GET INTO CHARACTER OUTSIDE OF Mr. Henley's home. Never in his life had he wanted to just kill someone and walk away. Although, if he killed Henley, they risked losing the other French operatives.

In the past, this work excited him. He excelled at pretending to be someone else, hiding behind a mask of his own making. When he was undercover, he could pretend that he was not an orphan, who had been sent away to boarding schools from almost the moment he arrived. Even though he had an ally in his cousin, Matthew, he had only seen him for the holidays.

He sighed. He'd had no issues with being an agent of the Crown, because if he died, no one would truly mourn him. He had managed to send a letter out once a year to Matthew and his aunt, informing them that he was alive and touring the continent. They had no idea he was masquerading as a French Naval Officer.

Now, for the first time since his parents died, he did not feel alone. Whenever he was around Kate, he felt desired, loved. He smiled at the memory of dancing with her in his ballroom. She was warming up to him. Slowly, he was breaking down those barriers and it felt like his most important mission ever.

Adrien placed his top hat on his head and exited the carriage. After presenting his card to the butler, he was ushered into the study where Mr. Henley was sitting in a grey wingback chair, with a drink in hand.

Mr. Henley rose when he came in. "Lord Camden, it is good to see you." He walked over to the drink cart. "May I offer you something to drink? Brandy, perhaps?"

Adrien raised his hand in silent refusal. "I have acquired what you asked of me."

Mr. Henley placed his drink on the cart and stepped closer. "Give it to me," he ordered.

"I want my money first," Adrien demanded. "I had to rifle through Lady Camden's personal effects, and I believe I've earned it."

Mr. Henley walked over to his desk and pulled out a small pile of money, extending it towards him. "Five hundred pounds, as agreed upon."

Adrien collected his fee and placed it in his waistcoat pocket before removing the large, gold locket. Mr. Henley's greedy eyes widened with pleasure at the sight of it. He reached for the locket, and Adrien dropped it into his hands. After a few moments of examining it, he looked up at Adrien. "Did you open this locket?"

Adrien laughed wryly. "For what purpose? Do I look like a man that would be interested in a lock of women's hair?"

Mr. Henley smiled back at him. "No, you do not. Forgive me."

Adrien bowed, then nodded his farewell. "If you will excuse me, I have a few bets I would like to make at White's."

"Before you go, I have a business proposal for you," Mr. Henley said as he walked over to a chair and sat down.

"Does it pay as well as this job did?" Adrien asked eagerly.

"Infinitely better," Mr. Henley confirmed.

Adrien sat down near him. "I admit I am intrigued."

Mr. Henley eyed him for a moment. "You have an interesting past."

"What are you referencing exactly?"

"I had men tailing you while I made a few inquiries about you," Mr. Henley explained. "It appears your parents died when you were young, and you were sent to live with your aunt and uncle. After Cambridge, you disappeared for almost seven years, then suddenly you reappeared here."

Appearing unconcerned, Adrien shrugged. "As I told you, I was residing in France."

Mr. Henley nodded. "I know. Your French is superb, which proved that to me. I also discovered you have quite a bit of debt tied to your name, but that's not news to you, is it?"

Adrien sighed and tossed his top hat onto another chair. He was secretly pleased that Lord Beckett had succeeded in altering his financial records, giving credence to his cover. "I told you I inherited a failing estate, but I intend to borrow some money from the bank to make the estate more profitable."

"What if I gave you ten thousand pounds to turn your estate around?"

Adrien's eyebrows shot up. "Ten thousand pounds?"

Mr. Henley wiped a hand over his mouth. "Yes, ten thousand pounds *if* you complete an unusual job."

"Can you define 'an unusual job'?" Adrien asked cautiously.

Mr. Henley relaxed back into his seat. "This war against the French has gone on long enough. That is why passing the bill to end the war is so paramount. We are fighting a losing battle against Napoleon, and for what? Too many lives have been taken to save a king that is mentally inept. We need to ensure this bill passes at all costs."

Adrien nodded, carefully choosing his words. "I agree. This

war is futile, but we are in the minority as Whig supporters. The Tories are in favor of the war, as is the prince regent."

"We do have some Tories that are against the war. For instance, Lord Devon wrote the bill, and Lord Wessex and Lord Exeter will come around soon enough," Mr. Henley gloated.

Adrien shook his head. "Lord Exeter is a staunch supporter of the war. He would never agree to the bill, even if his life depended on it."

"Exactly," Mr. Henley agreed, "but if a loved one's life depended on it, then he would vote yes."

Adrien sat back in his seat, pretending to truly ponder Mr. Henley's words. "What are you suggesting?"

Mr. Henley watched him with a slow, calculating gaze. "We abduct a few of the lord's wives or children, ensuring their cooperation till the vote of the bill."

"And if the bill does not pass?" Adrien asked with a raised eyebrow.

Mr. Henley forced a chuckle. "Either way, we return them home."

"Are they returned unharmed?"

"Of course, unharmed," Mr. Henley stated. His words flowed so smoothly that Adrien might have believed him if he did not already know that he was a ruthless French spy.

"And what are you asking of me?"

Mr. Henley gave him an approving nod, obviously pleased that Adrien did not criticize his tactics. "Lord Lansdowne has started becoming a nuisance in Parliament, and his speech is starting to sway other lords to vote against the bill. I believe if his lovely new bride was abducted, then he would change his tune."

Adrien jumped up from his seat, feigning outrage. "I cannot abduct the wife of the Marquess of Lansdowne and the daughter of the Duke of Remington. If I was caught, I would be exiled, or worse, hung. No, that is ludicrous."

"We are not asking you to abduct her, but rather provide us with details that would allow us to apprehend her in a safe manner," Mr. Henley explained in a calming tone.

"Who is the 'we' that you are referring to?"

"No one you need to concern yourself about," Mr. Henley assured him.

Adrien loomed over Mr. Henley and glared. "You are asking me to risk death to abduct Lady Lansdowne, but I do not need to concern myself with who your partner is?" His tone was sarcastic, but firm. "Do not get me wrong, I find Lady Lansdowne to be quite irksome, but I do not wish any harm to fall upon her."

Mr. Henley took a sip from his glass, completely unaffected by Adrien's outburst. "And no harm will fall upon her," he paused, a slight smirk on his lips, "assuming Lord Lansdowne votes in favor of the bill."

Adrien raked his hand through his hair, feeling frustration pour throughout his body. Mr. Henley planned to abduct Eliza. They had thought that Eliza might become a target if Benedict actively protested the bill, but that had been just a theory. Now, Eliza was in real danger. No matter the costs, he would not allow her to be abducted. More than ever, he needed to go along with Mr. Henley's plan, so he could be one step ahead of them.

The only way to truly protect Eliza was to find out who Mr. Henley's partner was. It was most likely Lord Lexington. Maybe he should just call on Lord Lexington? No, if there was the slightest chance he was wrong, it could jeopardize everything. He needed Mr. Henley to trust him.

Adrien dropped onto the settee. He rubbed his hands over his face then sighed deeply. "I will help you abduct Lady Lansdowne," he paused, as he toyed with the idea of punching Mr. Henley's smug face, "*if* you arrange a meeting for me with your partner."

Mr. Henley lowered his glass to rest it on the chair's arm, eyeing him suspiciously. "And why would I do that?"

Adrien smirked. "If you don't, I will inform Lord Lansdowne of the threat on his wife."

Mr. Henley's eyes narrowed to slits. "You are trying to blackmail *me*?"

"Yes," Adrien confirmed. "I want ten thousand pounds and a meeting with your partner."

Mr. Henley leaned his head back and laughed. "You come into my home and you threaten me. I could just as easily have you killed. Pray tell, why should I let you live?"

Adrien casually placed his hand on the settee's armrest as if a death threat was nothing. "I am practically family to Lady Lansdowne. I routinely meet with Lady Camden to discuss her monthly allowance, and I frequently interact with Lady Lansdowne because of those meetings. I could establish her routine and help you find the ideal spot to abduct her, without any harm to her or bystanders."

Mr. Henley placed his drink on the table as he stared at him. There was a deadly twinkle in his cold, black eyes. "I will ask my partner about bringing you in, but I cannot give you any promises."

Adrien had seen that look in others' eyes. He knew Mr. Henley would kill him as soon as he served his purpose. At least, he would try. "I understand."

He started to rise as Mr. Henley said, "If my partner agrees to your terms, then I want something in return."

Adrien shrugged. "What?"

Mr. Henley slowly cracked his knuckles, one after another. "I want Lady Camden."

Adrien's heart pounded fiercely in his chest, hoping he misheard him. "Why would you want Lady Camden?"

Mr. Henley's lips curled into a cruel smile. "It is personal."

Adrien shook his head, trying to comprehend Mr. Henley's requirement. "What do you intend to do with her?"

"That is not your concern," Mr. Henley spewed.

Adrien's immediate reaction was to pull out his pistol and shoot the vile vermin. However, he had a role to play and a jealous lover was not the role. He was supposed to be a down-on-his-luck lord that did not care at all about Lady Camden or her worthless family. He pushed down the bile coming up his throat as he choked out, "Deal."

Looking pleased with himself, Mr. Henley nodded his head in reply. "Excellent. I will see if I can arrange a meeting. We will be in touch, Lord Camden."

As Adrien left Mr. Henley's townhouse, he wanted to race home and abduct Kate from her bedchamber. He wanted to carry her away to somewhere safe and never look back. Why did he have to fall in love with her? His feelings for Kate could jeopardize this entire operation. If he sent her packing, then Mr. Henley would know that he had tipped her off.

No, she had to stay in London, but she did not have to know the risks. He would protect her without her knowing that he had made a deal with the devil.

KATE SIGHED IN FRUSTRATION. SHE HAD REREAD THE SAME sentence five times, and she could not seem to focus on the book in front of her. All she could think about was Adrien. His kind eyes and warm smile. His rugged face and strong hands. Good heavens, she thought to herself, I am acting like a love-sick debutante.

Although, for the first time in her life, she felt as though she would burst from happiness. Finally, after enduring so much cruelty, she was in a position that allowed her to be free from the burdens of her past. After all, why would she ever need to look back when her future was so bright?

Adrien's voice broke through her musings. "I was worried you would have already retired for the evening."

Kate turned to face him and saw him leaning up against the door frame, watching her. "I almost did, but I wanted to speak to you before I retired."

A boyish grin came to his lips as he pushed off the door. "You certainly know how to inflate a man's ego," he said, walking towards her.

Watching him as he sat down next to her, she admired his fine, dark tailcoat and his loosely tied cravat. She reached up and slowly retied it. As she finished, she boldly allowed her fingers to trail above his starched collar and marveled at the softness of his skin.

Her eyes flickered up to meet his and the love she saw reflected back at her was her undoing. Adrien's eyes were so expressive, and they seemed to mirror his soul. How she loved this man! She wanted to learn everything about him.

She dropped her hands into her lap. "Tell me about your family."

Adrien furrowed his brow slightly. "I already told you that my parents died from influenza."

Kate wanted to laugh aloud at his response, but it appeared that he truly believed that was the end of his story. "What was your mother like?"

A smile formed on his lips. "My mother was my entire world while I was younger. She used to make up stories and would exaggerate every detail."

Kate smiled. "That sounds like someone I know."

"My mother used to steal me away from my nursemaid and we spent hours at the creek by our house. She taught me how to fish. It was our special time."

"That sounds divine."

"My father was firm but kind. He would allow me to sit in his office while he met with tenants, and he even taught me how to balance a simple ledger," Adrien said, wearing a silly expression on his face as he remembered his youth. Kate intentionally remained silent to allow him to continue. "After my parents died within hours of each other, I knew that my life would forever be darkened."

"How old were you?"

"Eight," came his pained answer.

"You were just a young boy."

He frowned as sorrow lined his features. "I thought that my aunt and uncle did not want a sad little boy, so I always worked hard to keep a smile on my face. I learned to use humor to mask my true feelings." He focused his gaze on the other side of the room. "It has also served me well as a spy."

She placed her hand on his cheek to direct his face to meet her gaze. "Do you enjoy working as a spy?"

Adrien huffed, but he smiled at her. "When I was approached at Cambridge by Lord Beckett, I leapt at the chance to see the world. Since my mother was half French, I grew up speaking the language and spent some summers of my childhood in Paris. Lord Beckett decided to use that to our advantage and tasked me with various assignments in France, discovering that I had a knack for undercover work."

"Do you still have family in France?"

"No. I was told they were all killed during the French Revolution," he admitted, sadly. "I am alone to face the world."

Kate kept her hand on his cheek, enjoying the intimacy between them. "You are not alone. You have friends that love you."

His hand reached up and covered hers. "When I go undercover, I reinvent myself. I am not a sad little boy, alone in the world, but a spy with an agenda." He stifled a pained smile. "I always create a backstory that enables me to have a mother and father that are still alive. For a moment in time, I can pretend that all is well in my life."

Kate's heart ached for Adrien and the pain he held onto. "Were your aunt and uncle cruel to you?"

Adrien gave her a startled look. "Of course not. They were kind and nurturing, but they mostly focused on Matthew. After his heart was weakened by influenza, he was the most important thing on the estate. Per my parent's instructions in their will, I was sent off to Eton at the first opportunity and wouldn't receive my parent's vast fortune till my eighteenth birthday."

"Were you envious of the attention Matthew received?"

"Heavens, no. I loved Matthew. Even though he was a year older than I, we got along with each other famously. I came to view him as a brother," Adrien revealed. "Matthew was a talented writer, and he would create stories of the adventures he wanted to have. Sometimes we tried to recreate his stories with the servants." He chuckled.

"That sounds wonderful," Kate said.

She saw Adrien relax at the memory of Matthew, but she was curious about one thing. She had to ask a question and was worried about his reaction. "Am I seeing the real you, or do you mask your true feelings from me?"

He slowly lowered their hands off his cheek as he gazed deeply into her eyes. His eyes reflected his vulnerability and, dare she hope, love for her. "You have always seen the real me, Kate. I have never had to hide who I was around you. I have been drawn to you because you always made me feel as if I was coming home."

She let out a relieved sigh. "I am glad. I feel the same way about you."

His eyes widened slightly at her words. "Do you?"

Kate boldly lifted her face and mustered all the courage she could. "Yes."

"Could you expand on that, my dear?"

Kate dropped her gaze to her lap. For all the freedom that she had acquired, she still found it agonizing to speak about her feelings. Her mother was not one to discuss feelings, and Michel only used them to entrap others.

Adrien put his finger under her chin and brought her gaze up to meet his. His eyes searched hers. "You are not ready, I see. I promised that I would not push you."

As he began to lower his hand from her chin, she reached out to stop him. Taking a deep breath, she knew it was time to express what she felt towards him, at least partially.

He was looking at her expectantly. She summoned courage she did not know she had and stated, "The first time I saw you at Beaumont Castle I found you irritating."

He quirked his brow but did not respond.

"You were constantly trying to get me to smile. After that, you became a pest until you made me laugh. However," she hesitated, "when you departed Beaumont Castle, I found myself missing you and your anecdotes."

"You missed me?" he asked, obviously pleased with her words.

"Hush, I am trying to bestow praises on you, if you would just let me finish," she said, pretending to chastise him. "You make me happy. The way you speak to my soul makes my heart forget the heartache of my past. More importantly, you remind me how strong I am, that I have a purpose, and my life truly has value."

"If I didn't know better, I would say that you are fond of me." Adrien smiled, leaning closer.

"I am more than fond of you," she confessed, "but that is all I can admit now."

"Ah. Good enough for me," Adrien murmured, his face inches away from hers. "If it helps ease your mind, I am more than fond of you, too."

"You are?"

"How could I not be?" he teased, his eyes twinkling in merriment. "I even proposed to you."

"That was not a true proposal," Kate pointed out, her hands moving up to play with the buttons on his coat. "You proposed to me after your most ungentlemanly conduct."

As his lips hovered over hers, he smiled most mischievously. "That was a fun night."

"Yes, it was," she agreed, just as his lips brushed against hers.

A loud clearing of a throat caused them to jump apart. Both turned their heads to witness Mr. Larson observing them from the entryway.

Adrien chuckled. "Did Benedict send you to chaperone?"

Mr. Larson stifled a smile. "Yes, my lord." He came further into the room and leaned up against the wall. "Please do not let me interrupt you."

Kate smiled amusedly at Mr. Larson. "Where is Roger?"

Mr. Larson gave her a sympathetic glance. "Lord Lansdowne expressed concern that Roger was shirking his chaperoning duties."

Adrien shrugged. "I found his chaperoning to be exemplary."

Mr. Larson huffed, "You have proven his point."

Kate let out a bark of laughter which caused both men to turn towards her in surprise. It was the most unladylike laughter she had ever expressed.

Adrien smiled proudly at her. "May I escort you to your bedchamber?"

Mr. Larson grunted loudly and shook his head.

"May I escort you to the door between the townhouses?" Adrien asked, altering his previous statement.

"I would like that very much," Kate said, smiling. As they walked out the door, she noticed that Mr. Larson was following closely behind.

# 17

TAKING A SIP OF BRANDY, ADRIEN WILLED HIMSELF TO STAY seated in his plush study. He wanted to jump up and start pacing, but that would be a waste of his energy.

Three days he had waited to hear from Mr. Henley. Three days, and he had heard nothing. He had expected a missive by now, whether granting his request to meet his partner or a denial. But, he had received neither.

He was tired of waiting. He wanted to storm Lord Lexington's townhouse and haul him off to Newgate for interrogation. Unfortunately, Lord Beckett forbade him because they only had circumstantial evidence against Lord Lexington. Furthermore, he was a member of Prinny's inner circle and if they were wrong, then they risked angering the prince regent. That was not something Lord Beckett was willing to do.

It was easier when he was undercover in France. Everyone was the enemy! In England, it was not as easy to distinguish between friend and foe. Lord Lexington had to be Henley's partner. Who else could it be? Lord Beckett confirmed that Mr. Henley was trailed to Lord Lexington's townhouse on multiple occasions and remained inside for hours. That information alone should be enough for an arrest.

Adrien rose from his chair, placed his glass on the table, and tried to think of something more pleasant. Almost immediately, he thought of Kate and smiled. In a few hours, he would escort her through Hyde Park on a ride. He had been impressed with her riding abilities and especially enjoyed watching her face light up while they rode. Kate had revealed that riding her horse was the one pastime that her mother approved of, and she took advantage of the freedom that came with racing in the fields around the abbey.

Stepping over to his desk, he flipped through the correspondence that his butler had organized into a pile. This was his life now. He reviewed the pages and placed his signature where his man of business indicated. He ensured his tenants were taken care of and sent monthly allowances to the women that Lord Camden had violated. When he had told Kate about the monthly allowances, she kissed him soundly on the mouth, which was a most pleasing way to be thanked.

Benedict walked in. "Lord Beckett is asking for an update. Has Mr. Henley or his partner made contact?"

"No," Adrien replied, his tone frustrated.

Benedict dropped onto a chair. "Do you think Mr. Henley discovered you are an agent?"

Adrien moved to sit on an adjacent chair. "How could he? He offered to hire me to abduct Eliza. If he even suspected I was an agent, then he would never have revealed the next step in his plan."

"True, but it has been three days," Benedict pointed out.

"If Henley didn't trust me, then why did he stop his two incompetent ruffians from trailing me?"

"Good point," Benedict agreed. "Poor Eliza has been quite restless since we have restricted her to our townhouse…"

"For her own protection," Adrien cut in.

"I concur, but Eliza hates being confined, even for her own safety."

Shaking his head, Adrien adamantly exclaimed, "No, she is a target. Do not let her leave the townhouse."

"That is not a feasible option," Eliza argued from the doorway. Her hand was planted on her hip, and she did not seem pleased.

"Darling." Benedict jumped up and kissed her on her cheek.

Any residual anger dropped from Eliza's expression as she leaned into her husband. "I heard that you just returned from visiting Uncle Charles. Is there anything new to report?"

Benedict shook his head. "No. Adrien and I were just discussing the possibility that his cover has been blown."

Eliza bit her lower lip, which she always did when she was concentrating on something. "Then why would Henley reveal that he planned to abduct me?"

Adrien had stood when Eliza walked into the room, and now he leaned against the chair. "I am still hoping that Lord Lexington will contact me."

"We have not confirmed that Lord Lexington is a traitor," Benedict said.

"Who else could it be?" Adrien's voice rose. "Henley has been seen entering Lord Lexington's estate, and they routinely appear together in public."

Eliza sighed in frustration. "We are missing something. You and Benedict have gone out of your way to avoid each other in public, yet Henley and Lexington are seen together frequently. If they were both French spies, why would they bind themselves publicly?"

Benedict nodded. "True. However, they might not realize that we have caught on to their scheme."

A knock interrupted their conversation, and Mr. Ward walked in bearing a letter on a silver tray. "My lord, a miscreant dropped off this missive at the servant's entrance. Per your instructions, I brought it up post haste."

Adrien scooped up the letter and opened the unsealed envelope. He read the cryptic message aloud, "*Rotten Row in Hyde Park, 3 pm.*" He looked up to meet their gaze. "This is what we have been waiting for."

"I will inform Lord Beckett, and we will have agents posted along Rotten Row," Benedict stated, putting his hand up as Adrien opened his mouth to protest. "They will not engage the traitor unless directly ordered to intervene."

Satisfied by Benedict's plan, Adrien handed him the note and started walking towards the door. "I will need to change for the outing." He suddenly stopped and spun around. "I was supposed to take Kate riding later."

Eliza practically jumped up and down in response. "I will take her!"

"Eliza..." Benedict's voice held a warning. "You cannot leave the townhouse."

"Do I need to remind you that you don't dictate what I can and cannot do?" Eliza declared as she put her hand back on her hip.

Benedict frowned at his wife. "I am trying to keep you safe."

"Please?" Eliza pleaded, dropped her hand, and looked forlorn. "I feel like I am suffocating here. I need some fresh air."

"You have fresh air in our lovely garden," Benedict pointed out.

Tears sprang to Eliza's eyes. "I would like to go riding. My poor horse has not been exercised in days."

Benedict softened his stance when he saw Eliza's tears. He stood in front of her and wiped away a tear that rolled down her cheek. "I will take you, but Mr. Larson, Roger, and ten, no, twenty footmen will accompany us."

Eliza swiped at another tear trailing down her face. "It might look suspicious if we take that many footmen. The French might realize that Adrien warned us."

"If you accompany Eliza, along with Mr. Larson and Roger, then the agents scouting Hyde Park can keep a watch out for any signs of danger," Adrien suggested.

Benedict trailed his hands up and down Eliza's arms. "That will have to suffice. However, I insist that you don't run your horse for the sake of our baby."

In response, Eliza gave her husband a smile of gratitude, proving again that they only had eyes for each other. Adrien knew it was time to bow out and get ready to meet Mr. Henley's accomplice.

KATE REACHED FOR ANOTHER BOOK IN ADRIEN'S LIBRARY AND sat down near the window. Before she opened her new treasure, Eliza glided into the room.

"Adrien was called out on an assignment, so Benedict and I will be taking you riding," Eliza announced in an enthusiastic voice.

Kate attempted to hide her disappointment as she replied, "Oh, good."

Eliza laughed. "Liar. I can tell you are disappointed, but Adrien should be back for dinner, since Parliament is not convening this evening."

Kate placed the book onto the table. "Do you think I'm mad to consider courting Adrien so soon after Michel's death?"

"No," Eliza stated plainly. "Are you having doubts?"

Kate's lips curled downward as she attempted to answer her sister's question. "I care for Adrien, but his reputation will suffer if he marries me. The scandal alone might cause the ton to give us the direct cut."

Eliza's face softened. "Is that what is truly bothering you?"

She shook her head. "No."

"What is the real reason?"

"I am afraid."

"Afraid of what?"

Kate's lips tightened into a line as she attempted to control her emotions. "My marriage to Michel was a farce, a horrible mistake."

"I will not disagree with that."

"What if Adrien tires of me like Michel did?"

Kate was surprised to see a wide smile grace Eliza's lips. "I asked a similar question about Benedict."

"You did?"

"I did. But do you know what I realized?"

Kate watched Eliza expectantly. "What?"

Eliza's eyes grew reflective. "I realized I had a choice, and I chose love."

"Can you expand on that?" Kate asked with a furrowed brow as she tried to grasp what Eliza was telling her.

Eliza came and sat down next to her on the settee. "Uncle Charles began grooming me very young to decipher codes and eventually write codes for the home office. Later, I became a field agent with Jonathon as my partner. Over time, I became jaded with society, and it caused me to trust only a select group of people."

Kate leaned forward, intently listening to Eliza's story. "What changed?"

Eliza's lips twitched for a moment, as if reliving a pleasant memory. "Uncle Charles and Jonathon decided to partner me with Benedict. At first, it was a disaster." Eliza laughed. "Benedict was under the impression that he was to train me."

Kate started giggling at her sister's infectious laugh. "What happened next?"

Eliza gave her a knowing smile. "From the moment I laid eyes on Benedict, I knew I could trust him. He helped me to overcome my past and made me remember how to smile, truly smile again." Eliza raised an eyebrow at her knowingly. "Do you trust Adrien?"

Kate's shoulders drooped in despair. "Yes… no… perhaps." She sighed. "Adrien makes me unbelievably happy, and he has helped me to find a purpose in my life again."

"Let me guess, you trust Adrien with your life but not your heart?" Eliza asked insightfully.

Kate's eyes grew wide in surprise. "How did you know?"

Eliza huffed. "I have been in your exact same position. In the end, I chose to open my heart to Benedict and allowed myself to love him. Without Benedict, I would have slowly withdrawn from my loved ones and would have grown bitter. However, with Benedict, my life has begun anew."

"And if Benedict ever betrayed you?"

Eliza bit her lip for a moment. "He would never betray me intentionally. I know that because I have made it my mission to learn as much as I can about my husband. He is loyal and kind, but most importantly, my best friend."

"I feel the same way about Adrien," Kate admitted. "But, is it all right if I am still frightened?"

"It is perfectly normal to have some anxiety about the future. If it helps, I believe that Adrien is a good man and would never betray you." With a playful smile, Eliza added, "And if he did, I would kill him for you."

Kate laughed. "I appreciate that."

"Besides, I guarantee your marriage with Adrien will be very different than with Michel," Eliza said with a bright smile. "For starters, you will be happy."

Another bubble of laughter escaped Kate's lips. "This time I will be married to an English spy and not a French spy."

"True!" Eliza laughed as she rose from her seat. "We should change if we want to go riding."

Kate jumped up and embraced her sister. "You are most definitely the wiser twin."

As they walked up to their rooms, Kate was grateful for her sister's wisdom. It was natural for her to be frightened, but she knew that Adrien would never betray her. He would never hurt her like Michel had.

# 18

ADRIEN SAT ON TOP OF HIS STALLION, TIPPING HIS HEAD POLITELY to the gentlemen and ladies passing by. Rotten Row was filled with glamorous carriages that held ladies wearing their finery, waving to their friends as they passed by. Gentlemen rode on top of horses as they flirted with the ladies, and occasionally couples would sneak off towards the cover of the trees.

His eyes traveled up and down the length of the road, noting agents protecting the perimeter. The missive that he received was vague, but he knew Mr. Henley's accomplice would make contact. He kept his eyes open for Lord Lexington, but so far, he had not seen his crested carriage. The French spy was late. Maybe he was not going to come? What if it was a trap?

If it was, then his pistol was tucked behind him in the waistband of his trousers. Furthermore, his boots held a small pistol and a dagger. He was ready to defend himself if necessary, but with the number of agents milling around, he doubted he would need to take any action.

A barouche pulled to a stop in front of him, and a scantily dressed lady addressed him, "Lord Camden, I presume?"

Before he replied, he noted that the driver appeared to be

assessing the situation in a way that he found suspicious. This was not the usual driver of a lady's barouche, but rather he appeared to be more of a personal guard to his companion. A pistol sat in his waistband, and he was sitting erect in his seat, surveying the surrounding area.

The woman's rich burgundy dress had a low, square neckline that exposed much of her bosoms and showed off a comely figure. Some of her brown hair was piled high on her head, but the majority flowed down her back. As he observed the lady's oval face, he noticed her crescent-shaped eyebrows accentuated her brown eyes perfectly. Her bottom lip was larger than the top, creating a pouty look. She was indeed a very striking woman, but paled in comparison to his Kate.

Realizing that he had not yet responded, he tipped his hat to her. "You have presumed correctly. May I be so bold as to ask your name?"

Her smile was coy. "You may call me Marthe."

Adrien sucked in a breath. Her name had been on the list that was in Kate's locket. This was Mr. Henley's accomplice. He took a moment to compose himself as his eyes continued to be drawn to her neckline. Obviously, she wore that dress for a reason. He noticed that she was watching him very closely and seemed pleased by his perusal.

"What a beautiful name," he said with practiced smoothness.

Marthe patted the bench of the barouche in a flirtatious manner. "Would you care to join me for a ride while we discuss a few things?"

He knew this was a ploy, but he would go along with it. He had seen female spies before, and they tended to use their bodies to their advantage. Most men's defenses were weakened by a willing woman that allowed certain liberties in exchange for information. He would need to be on alert, especially since they were in Hyde Park.

Adrien attached his horse to the back of the barouche and

hopped in next to Marthe. As soon as he was seated, she scooted over and placed her hand on his inner thigh. She leaned in and purred, "When Edgar asked me to meet you, I had no idea how ruggedly handsome you were." Her hand slowly caressed his thigh. "I cannot wait for our association to become more… personal."

The driver veered the barouche towards a cluster of trees just off Rotten Road. As they came to a stop, the driver jumped down and secured the horses before he disappeared. Apparently, Marthe wanted to spend some time alone with him.

Marthe removed her hand from his thigh and shifted to face him. Her eyes roamed his face as her hands started playing with the buttons on his tailcoat. Looking up through her long black lashes, she said, "Edgar told me that you refused to help unless you met me. I hope your curiosity has been satisfied now." Her fingers started trailing along his jaw, and she leaned forward, brushing her exposed bosom against his chest.

Adrien was no fool. This woman was attempting to seduce him and convince him to do her bidding. Her touch revolted him, but he could not push her away. He was a spy, and he needed to play along. He needed to extract information from her by using a similar tactic. He needed to play the rogue that she thought he was.

His hand trailed up and down her arm as his eyes watched her carefully. "I am more than satisfied. Henley failed to mention that his associate was such a beautiful woman. I am beginning to see why he has kept you hidden all this time."

Her hand stalled, and he swore he saw her blush. "Edgar is protective of me, but we work as a team." Her voice held a slight French accent, despite her attempt to mask it.

He switched into French as he asked, "How could a man work with such a beautiful woman and not work passionately together? It would be impossible, no?"

Her lips parted as her defenses seemed to weaken, but then her eyes sharpened. "You speak French well, Lord Camden."

His fingers weaved through her long brown hair. "I lived in France for a few years and had a few French lovers."

Marthe pressed her bosom against his chest and smiled seductively up at him. "Do you have a lover here?"

The image of Kate flittered through his mind before he shook his head no. "Sadly, I have not found one that can fully satisfy me, but it has been fun searching." He laughed as he brought his hand up to brush against her cheek. "Would you be willing to apply for the position?" he asked hoarsely.

A low sigh escaped her lips as she brought her face close to his. "I would be willing," she replied, keeping her lips hovering over his, "if you help us abduct Lady Lansdowne."

Adrien crushed his lips into hers, and her arms came tightly around his body. He needed Marthe to believe that he was gullible and would fall for her charms. His kisses were demanding, rough. He was playing the role of a rogue willing to betray his country for a chance to bed a beautiful woman. If his kisses were gentle rather than passionate, she might not believe his act. He had to appear as if he could not live another moment without this woman in his arms, and he would go to the ends of the earth for her.

Marthe broke the kiss and sat back. "Will you help us?"

His voice was breathless as his fingers traced the graceful length of her neck from ear to shoulder. "Yes, assuming you are a part of the deal."

She smiled broadly. "I am. As soon as Lady Lansdowne has been abducted, I will be yours." She leaned in and trailed kisses down his neck. When she arrived at his cravat, she untied it and kissed his throat. "I must admit that I will be looking forward to our liaison. You are quite the handsome man, no?"

"What would you like me to do?"

"All we need is Lady Lansdowne's schedule." She gazed at

him, her eyes twinkling. "We need to find the ideal time to abduct her."

Adrien tilted his head and trailed kisses down her neck. "You will not hurt her, will you?"

He felt a muscle in her neck twitch, and he knew the next words out of her mouth would be a lie. "Of course not. You have my word," she stated, lying just as smoothly as Mr. Henley had previously.

Adrien wanted to shove her away, but he needed more information from her first. "Is there another member of your group I need to meet before we proceed?"

Her hands slid up and looped around his neck. "There is no one else."

"And would I report to you or Edgar?" he whispered in her ear. He heard her breath hitch. It appeared that Marthe was more affected by his charms than she was letting on. He leaned back and looked deeply into her eyes. "I would much rather report to you."

"I am indisposed during the day, but I would be happy to stop by your townhouse for a visit."

"Why is this bill to end the war so important to you?"

Marthe stiffened slightly, then relaxed in his arms. "Too many English lives have been lost in this senseless war. It is time to put an end to all the death."

"But you are French. Why does it matter to you if English lives are lost?"

She sat back, a cold, bleak look filling her eyes. "Why do you assume I am French?"

Giving her a seductive smile, he answered in French, "Mademoiselle, I lived in France for seven years, and I recognize your distinct accent. French women are the most alluring, no?"

Her eyes lit up, and she leaned against him again. "You are quite the charmer, Lord Camden."

"Call me Adrien." He crushed his lips against hers once again. "Where shall I find you?" he asked when he broke free.

"That is not how it works," Marthe replied, in a slightly breathless tone. "Edgar or I will contact you."

"I agree to your terms, Marthe," he stated slowly. "More importantly, I will be dreaming of our next meeting."

Her hands started weaving through his hair. "You will also be paid handsomely for your assistance."

He wiggled his brow at her. "I would prefer you as payment. May I take you home now?"

In response, Marthe kissed him passionately. Her hands roamed over his body with an urgency he had not expected, and a shudder of disgust coursed through him. He broke the kiss and shoved her to an arm's length, unable to continue the charade.

Being mindful of the importance of his mission, he forced his lips into a seductive smile. "As much as I want to continue this, I am afraid we would become a spectacle to the pedestrians. Should we adjourn to my townhouse for a continuation of this… discussion?" Adrien knew that she would decline, but he still needed to act the part of a rogue.

Leaning back, she ran her fingers over her swollen red lips, before she smoothed out her dress. After composing herself, she snapped her fingers, and her driver appeared almost instantly. "We are ready to depart, Norman."

Marthe gave him a coy look. "Our meeting has run its course, Adrien. We need to know Lady Lansdowne's schedule for the next few days. It will be easy to acquire, no?"

"No problem at all. I will wait for you to make contact." He jumped off the barouche, detached his horse, and stood back while Marthe departed.

Then, he mounted his horse and turned back towards Rotten Row. As he rode, he adjusted his waistcoat, retied his cravat, and smoothed out his hair. He made the mistake of glancing at a few of the posted agents, and they were all smirking at him.

It's a good thing that Kate did not witness this meeting with Marthe, he thought.

KATE'S MOUTH WAS AGAPE AS SHE WATCHED THE SCENE BEFORE her unfold. Adrien was sitting in a barouche with a beautiful woman, and they were kissing passionately. No! This could not be happening.

Eliza reined in her horse next to her. "Kate, what is wrong? You look as if you have seen a ghost."

Kate raised her hand and pointed at Adrien because she could find no words to describe what she was witnessing.

"Oh!" Eliza exclaimed, shock filling her voice. "Is that Adrien?"

She nodded. "Yes, and with another woman."

"This might not be what it looks like," Eliza admonished.

Kate turned her fury onto her sister. "What it looks like is Adrien is kissing a woman in Hyde Park. How could it look any different?"

Eliza glanced over at Benedict as if asking for help. Benedict's eyes filled with compassion. "Why don't we go back to the townhouse and we can discuss this calmly?"

Kate tightened her grip on her reins. "No. I want to go back to my country home. I don't want to be anywhere near Lord Camden ever again."

"Kate," Benedict ventured, "it is not safe to travel to…"

"I do not care," Kate yelled, cutting him off. She turned her horse towards the townhouse and kicked the mare into a run. She could hear hoofbeats behind her, confirming that Eliza and Benedict were following her. If she had to guess, Roger and Mr. Larson were also not far behind.

It did not matter. She did not want to speak to anyone about this. Adrien had betrayed her! She was such a fool. She had believed him when he used his flowery words of love, and yet he was already keeping a mistress. Kate could feel the barriers returning to her heart. Never again would she fall for the charming words of a man. No, she was finished with men and their lies.

Blinded by her tears, she approached the front of the townhouse and reined her horse in. A groomsman came out to retrieve the mare, and she ran inside. She could hear Benedict and Eliza shout her name as she ran up the stairs and into her bedchamber. She did not want to discuss this with them. How could they understand her anguish? Once again, a man had tricked her. She was the same foolish girl, destined to make the same mistake repeatedly. Angrily, she brushed the tears away. Not anymore! She had learned her lesson.

Eliza opened her door and peered in. "May I enter?"

Nodding, Kate sat on the bed, and Eliza came to sit next to her. "Adrien went to meet Mr. Henley's accomplice, and it would appear the woman in the park is actually a French spy."

Kate huffed, "Am I to overlook the fact that he was practically mauling her because she is a spy?"

"A French spy," Eliza clarified.

Kate jumped up from the bed. "Why are you trying to justify Adrien's behavior? He was passionately kissing a woman in Hyde Park for anyone to see."

"I just feel that you should talk to Adrien before…"

"No! No! I do not want to wait around to hear Adrien's explanation. He will just lie to me." Kate paced, her outrage growing with each step. "How could he claim to care for me and then kiss another woman?"

Frowning, Eliza tried again. "I know it looks bad…"

Kate shouted over her sister, "Because it *is* bad! I caught Adrien kissing another woman. I will not be fooled by him again." She went to her trunks and opened them. "Please send Martha in to help me pack," she ordered over her shoulder.

"It is not safe to travel," Eliza admonished.

Kate's eyes filled with tears again as she turned to face her sister. "I finally convinced myself that I was worthy of Adrien's love, and I naively trusted him." Kate furiously swiped at the tears streaming down her face. "I am stronger now, and I will not be deceived. I want a husband who will love me unconditionally and won't stray, because I will be enough. It is obvious I am not enough for Adrien."

Eliza closed the distance and embraced her sister tightly. "You are perfect the way you are."

She sobbed loudly. "Adrien does not think so."

"Adrien is a fool."

"I just want to go back to my country home," Kate pleaded. She needed her place of refuge now more than anything.

Eliza conceded as she leaned back, "All right. I will send in Martha."

Kate tightened her hold on Eliza. "I am grateful you are my sister. I don't know what I would do without you."

"It will all work out." Her smile was tight. "It seems bad now, but it will work out."

Kate stifled her sob. "That is not true. Nothing seems to work out for me."

"Oh, Kate," Eliza murmured sadly as she embraced her tightly again.

Kate sobbed into her sister's arms. She was destined not to have a love match like Eliza and Benedict. She would rather be alone than be married to a liar again.

# 19

ADRIEN PLOPPED ONTO THE SETTEE IN HIS STUDY AND TOOK A SIP of his brandy. He had ordered a bath to be prepared as soon as he had walked through the door because Marthe's perfume was so strong he was sure it had permeated his clothing. He could not visit Kate until he bathed and changed his clothes. He hoped that she would be willing to continue reading *Pride and Prejudice*. He had to admit that he was interested in the outcome.

Before he took another sip, a large dagger plunged into the cushion between his legs. He recognized the dagger as Eliza's, but he had no idea how it had appeared there. He glanced up to see Eliza, her eyes blazing with fury. She held another dagger in her hand, and she appeared to be debating about throwing that one at him, as well.

He jumped up from his seat, nearly spilling his drink. "What is the meaning of this?"

Her glare deepened, and she raised the dagger into throwing position. Before she could fling it into his person, however, Benedict reached up and grabbed the dagger out of her hand. "Eliza, we discussed this. You cannot kill him." His tone sounded almost regretful.

Adrien placed his glass down on the table. "Why would you need to kill me?"

Eliza marched into the room and stood right in front of him. "What were you thinking? You are a bloody fool!"

Eliza's choice of words would have amused him if he understood where her anger came from. He needed to regain control of this conversation. He smiled kindly at her. "Will you please explain what I did wrong?"

Her fiery glare was palpable. "Did you forget that I took Kate riding through Hyde Park today?"

"Is that all?" Adrien asked, his shoulders relaxing. "I forgot to thank you for taking Kate on a ride."

Benedict shook his head in disbelief. "You are a bigger idiot than I thought."

With a furrowed brow, Adrien looked down at Eliza. "Just explain to me what I did wrong."

Eliza's eyes narrowed. "Kate and I were riding down Rotten Row until she veered off because she saw your horse attached to a barouche."

Adrien's eyes grew wide. "No, no, no," he muttered loudly. "Please tell me that Kate did not witness me talking to Marthe."

"We did not see much talking, but we saw plenty of kissing," Benedict accused.

Adrien threw his hands over his face. He had been so focused on Marthe that he failed to recognize someone might have witnessed his interaction. He had to go see her. He had to make this right. Dropping his hands, he started towards the door.

Before he reached it, Benedict grabbed his arm. "Wait. We need to hear about your meeting."

He shrugged off Benedict's arm. "No, I need to go speak to Kate and make this right."

Eliza's hand rose to her hip in a defiant stance. "Was it worth it?"

"Was what worth it?" Adrien asked.

"We saw you in the barouche," Eliza pressed. "Kate's heart is broken, and I fear that she might never recover from this. You have lost her trust."

Adrien's heart lurched inside of his chest. "No, Kate does not understand. Marthe was trying to recruit me to help abduct you, and she was attempting to seduce me."

Benedict crossed his arms over his wide chest. "It appeared that she had succeeded."

"No, by playing along, I was able to extract information from her. She informed me that I was to report to Henley but let it slip that there is no one else I would report to. Also, she knows the fate of the abducted women. She is busy during the day which means she must be doing something with her time. I'm guessing she's with them."

"Marthe was on the list in the locket," Eliza said. "We have now identified two of the French spies on the list."

"I will forward that information to Lord Beckett." Benedict walked over to the desk for a paper and quill. "However, where does Lord Lexington fit in all of this?"

"I have not figured that out yet," Adrien admitted.

"We will ask Lord Beckett to check into this," Benedict said. He wrote some information down on the sheet of paper.

Eliza's gazed softened a tad, but it still reflected residual anger. "I understand what you were doing with Marthe, but Kate does not. As an agent, you put a mask on when you are tasked to complete certain assignments, but Kate is not one of us and never will be. She feels betrayed, and I could hear the mistrust back in her voice."

A lump in his throat threatened to unleash his emotions. "What can I do?"

Eliza pressed her lips together. "I do not know."

Adrien turned his head towards Benedict, hoping his friend could offer some advice. However, Benedict just gazed at him with compassion in his eyes. "I cannot help you, either."

He placed his hands on the sides of his forehead as he tried to formulate a plan. Nothing came to his mind. "I have to try."

As he turned to leave, Eliza spoke up, "You should know that Kate is packing to go back to her country home."

Adrien spun around to face her. "She cannot leave. It is not safe."

"I told her that, but she is in an emotional state right now."

"Do not order a carriage for her," Adrien barked at Benedict. "If she leaves, she could fall prey to Mr. Henley."

Benedict came around the side of the desk. "I cannot keep Kate hostage. We have enough footmen to see her home safely."

"She is home!" Adrien roared.

He could not take the looks of pity from Benedict and Eliza anymore, and he started running towards Kate's bedchamber. Once he explained what he was doing in Hyde Park, she would see reason. She would forgive him! She had to!

"Would you like me to pack all of your dresses in the trunk?" Martha asked.

Kate placed her ivory gown on top of the pile of dresses on the bed. "Yes, all of them." Even though Martha was Eliza's lady's maid, she had begun to consider her a friend, as well. "Thank you for helping me pack."

Martha frowned at her. "May I ask why you are running away?"

"I am not running away. For the first time, I see clearly." Kate picked up another dress from the pile.

Martha placed a dress into the trunk. "And what is that?"

"Men cannot be trusted," Kate stated in a resigned tone. "I thought Adrien was different, but I was wrong."

Martha's face softened at Kate's words, and she walked over to give her an embrace. "I used to adamantly believe that all men were vile, deceitful human beings, with only one thing on their minds." She leaned back to look Kate in the eyes. "But, I became acquainted with Lord Jonathon, Mr. Larson, Roger, and Lord Lansdowne. These are men that can be trusted."

"I agree, but they are the exception to the rule."

Martha started to open her mouth as Adrien walked into her bedchamber. Martha leaned forward and whispered, "Give him a chance to explain before you run away." She turned to Adrien and gave him a slight curtsy before she departed.

Adrien's riding coat hung open, his cravat hung around his neck untied and his normally groomed hair was tousled about. She'd never seen him in such a state of undress before. He looked steadily at her with a strange, deep look that held vulnerability. Kate ignored his gaze and picked up a dress off her bed. She rolled it and placed it in the trunk, completely ignoring Adrien.

"Kate." Adrien spoke her name softly, as if it was infinitely precious. "I am sorry."

Without saying a word, she picked up another dress and flung it in the trunk. She should ask him to leave, but she realized she didn't really want him to go. Her treacherous heart was still choosing Adrien, even after she'd convinced herself that she was better off without him.

Adrien stepped further into the room, his hands in front of him as though he was afraid she would run past him. "Eliza tells me that you witnessed my meeting with a French spy this afternoon." He stepped closer to her but was still an arm's length away. "It must have been difficult to watch me kiss her, but it meant nothing."

Kate huffed loudly, as the fury inside of her raged. "How

dare you presume that it was merely 'difficult' to watch you seduce another woman in the middle of Hyde Park!" Her chest heaved with fury as she turned to face him. "You led me to believe you cared for me."

Adrien furrowed his brow as he watched her. "I love you, Kate. I want to marry you. Rest assured that has never faltered. However, I had to interrogate the spy, and she was bent on seducing me."

Kate threw her hands up in the air in frustration and ignored his ill-timed declaration. "By interrogate, you mean you had to trail kisses down her neck?"

Adrien had the decency to look ashamed. "I am a spy, Kate. My personal life is separate from my life as an agent of the Crown. My assignment was to discover who Henley's partner was, and I succeeded. That woman in the park is Henley's partner and a French spy." He frowned. "Do you think I enjoyed myself?"

Narrowing her eyes, Kate could not seem to contain her anger. Adrien saw nothing wrong with his actions, and he was asking her to just accept his infidelity. "No!" Kate tightened her hands into fists. "I am tired of the lies."

"What lies?" Adrien asked in confusion.

Kate marched up to him and poked him in the chest. "It is inconceivable to me that you claim to love me and yet allow yourself to be in situations where you are seducing other women. I will not tolerate it."

Adrien's eyes softened. "I do love you. However, I am a spy."

"Would you have bedded her if you thought it would have helped with your interrogation?" Kate asked intently.

"No!" he stated emphatically.

She fisted her hands on her hips. "Can you tell me honestly that you have never considered bedding a woman to loosen her tongue?"

Adrien swallowed slowly and diverted his eyes. That was all Kate needed to know.

She spun around and went to her bed to continue packing. Adrien came up behind her, putting his hands on her arms. "I have never bedded a woman for information," he declared, his fingers slowly trailing down the length of her arm. "Please talk to me."

Kate shrugged off his touch and picked up another dress. As she was rolling it, Adrien walked over to the trunk and started pulling out her dresses, placing them back on the bed.

"What are you doing?" Kate shouted. "I am packing."

Adrien leveled his gaze at her. "You cannot leave. It is not safe for you to travel."

Kate grabbed the pile of dresses he had placed on the bed and dropped them into the trunk. "You do not need to concern yourself with my safety anymore."

"You are under my protection…"

"Not anymore," Kate proclaimed, cutting him off.

Adrien's mouth gaped open before he managed to say, "Would you mind repeating that?"

Kate squared her shoulders and turned to face him. "I have no desire to be under your rule anymore."

Adrien sighed. "Kate, please be reasonable. Kissing Marthe meant nothing, it was just a means to an end."

Shaking her head, Kate stood her ground. "I do not care. Never again will I wonder where my husband is, or who he is with. I deserve better!"

Adrien placed his hand on her arm. "I am a spy…"

"I know you are a spy," Kate acknowledged, hesitating, "but I will not be a spy's wife again. I do not want a man that is faithful to me only when it is convenient."

With a calming voice, Adrien replied, "I will always be faithful to you. However, what I do in the name of the Crown is to keep England safe and protected. Sometimes I am tasked with assignments that are contrary to my beliefs and desires, but they must be done. Seducing Marthe was strategic, and it worked."

Kate closed her eyes and her lips formed a tight line. "If we were married, I would want the real you. The one who sneaks flowers into my room or the one who tells me I am brave." Tears came to her eyes as she continued, "Unfortunately, you hide behind a mask as you are unfaithful. You are just as bad as Michel was."

"I beg your pardon?"

Kate got a whiff of perfume that was not hers from Adrien's clothing, infuriating her even more. "Michel was a French spy who seduced women, and I am sure he would say that it was part of his cover."

Adrien reared back, his face reflecting shock. "I am nothing like Michel."

Kate leaned closer to Adrien and sniffed his coat. "You reek of that woman's perfume… Marthe was it? How dare you come speak to me when you still have remnants of your tryst on your clothing."

Adrien ran his hand through his hair and sighed. "It meant nothing. I was just…"

"'Doing my job'," Kate finished for him. "Well, England is grateful to have such an upstanding agent in a barouche, working hard to keep everyone safe." Her tone was filled with sarcasm. She scooped up the rest of the dresses on the bed and dropped them into the trunk. She did not care if they were wrinkled. Her lady's maid would press them for her.

Adrien put his hands over his face and leaned his head back. After a moment, he dropped his hands and moaned, sounding defeated. "I am sorry I hurt you, Kate."

Kate flicked her hand, easily dismissing his apology. "It matters not. I am just glad I learned the truth about your character before we were married."

Adrien's eyes were sad and weary. "I still want to marry you."

Kate walked closer to Adrien until she stood in front of him. "I care for you, deeply. I will always care for you, but to love a spy…" her voice hitched, "is not something I am capable of."

His eyes pleaded with her. "I am more than just a spy. I am a man who loves you immensely."

"You helped me to open my heart, but seeing you with that woman…" Her voice trailed off. "It shattered my heart even more. I fear I will never trust you again, and that would not bode well for a marriage. I am sorry."

Adrien placed his hand on her cheek. "You must understand that I had no choice in the matter. We are trying to stop French spies from pushing their agenda inside of Parliament."

"You did have a choice, and you made the decision that suited Adrien, the spy."

The sadness reflected in his eyes was undeniable. "Are you asking me to stop working as an agent?"

Kate shook her head. "No, I would never ask you to stop working as an agent, because that is your true love, your passion. But I do not want to be an afterthought."

Adrien brought his other hand up to encompass her face. "No, you are wrong. You are my true love."

Kate placed her hands over his hands and slowly lowered them. "It is too late. I have made my decision." She lowered her gaze to the floor, hoping Adrien would leave on his own accord.

Instead, he said, "I do not accept that. I love you and I want to marry you."

Kate brought her ardent gaze back up to him. "If you had truly loved me, then you would not have seduced a woman in Hyde Park."

Adrien groaned. "How many times do I have to tell you that it was part of an assignment? It meant nothing! She meant nothing!"

Kate narrowed her eyes in fury. "How can passionately kissing a woman mean nothing?"

Adrien shook his hands in front of him in obvious frustration. "I was interrogating her."

Kate tilted her head back and looked at the ceiling. "I do not care!" she exclaimed as she brought her gaze back to him. "I will not go into a marriage where my betrothed already has indiscretions."

"It was one time," he roared. "I do not have a mistress, nor do I have indiscretions. I was just acting the part of a spy."

Kate stood her ground and stared back at him for a moment. She could tell he was agitated, but she did not fear him or his anger. "Once was enough for me. I have been through too much to just give in. I will not marry you, not now, not ever."

Adrien pursed his lips before saying, "We are meant to be together. I will find a way for you to trust me again, and we will be wed."

Shaking her head in disbelief, she replied, "You protect England, and I will protect my heart." As Adrien opened his mouth to say something, Kate cut him off and shouted, "Roger."

Roger peeked into the room. "Yes, Lady Camden."

Kate tilted her head defiantly at Adrien. "Will you please escort Lord Camden out of my room?"

Adrien dropped his wide, muscular shoulders in defeat. "Please, do not do this, Kate."

She locked eyes with him. "You made your choice, and I made mine. Now we must live with those choices." She turned to the trunk and closed the lid. "Roger, could you also ask a footman to bring my trunks down to the carriage? We will depart for my country home within the hour."

"Absolutely not," Adrien declared. "It is not safe for you to travel. Why are you being the most obstinate female in all of England?"

Her jaw tensed, and she clenched her fists at her sides as her frustration grew. "You do not control what I do, Lord Camden."

Adrien stepped closer to her, his tone firm. "The roads are not safe for you to travel on."

As Kate glared up at him, she noticed that her legs weren't shaking. She was fully in control of this conversation, and she recognized how far she had truly come. "I do not answer to you." She turned towards Roger. "Please escort Lord Camden out, *now*."

Roger's face held a sympathetic gaze as he looked at Adrien. "Lord Camden, it is time for you to go."

Adrien's eyes roamed her face as if memorizing every line and nuance. "I will go, but this is not goodbye. I refuse to let you go."

"Goodbye, Lord Camden," she said before she spun around and kept her back towards him. She did not dare watch him walk out, for that might have weakened her resolve. She had made the right choice. She had caught Adrien in a tryst, regardless of the circumstances.

Still, even though in her mind she was doing the right thing, her heart was telling her something completely different.

# 20

ROGER STUCK HIS HEAD BACK INTO THE CARRIAGE. "I WOULD ask you to reconsider this hasty departure." He grimaced. "Dusk is approaching soon, and it is not safe on the roads at night."

Kate clenched her hands in her lap. Why did the men in her life try to control her? First, Adrien demanded that she stay. Followed by Benedict's long tirade about highway robbers. Now, Roger had asked her four times to reconsider. She was tired of being treated like a coddled female.

"I would like to go home now," she answered, attempting to keep her voice calm. "It is only an hour carriage ride."

Roger gave her a swift nod. "As you wish." He closed the carriage door firmly.

Kate blew out a breath that she had not realized she had been holding. She had almost fallen for Adrien's charms. Who was she kidding? She had completely fallen for his charms.

A tear ran down her cheek, but she did not move to wipe it away. It was a good thing she was alone in the carriage, because she could cry and no one would hear her. She had made the right choice.

The carriage lurched forward, and she leaned her head back

onto the cushion. Tears trailed down her face as she kept her eyes closed. Adrien's betrayal had ripped her heart into pieces. Never had she felt so deceived. He spoke of love and promises, but his actions proved otherwise.

His face appeared in her mind, and she remembered his jovial smile, his kind eyes, and his tender touch. But then she remembered the way Adrien had trailed kisses along that woman's throat. Her eyes jerked open. That scene was permanently etched into her memory.

Abruptly, the carriage lurched to a stop, and she fell slightly forward. The carriage door swung open, and Eliza, wearing a high-waisted blossom dress, jumped in. After she sat down on the bench opposite her, Eliza crossed her arms over her chest as the carriage started moving down the road again.

Kate furrowed her brow. "Why are you here?" Not that she was complaining, because she loved her sister.

Eliza's lips were curled into a frown. "I am here to protect you."

"That is what Roger is for."

"It was not safe for you to leave our townhouse. There are dangerous men afoot, and you made an impromptu departure at nightfall." Eliza gave her an exasperated look.

Kate crossed her own arms over her chest. "You know why I did."

Eliza huffed. "I know why. You are running away."

Outraged, Kate just stared at her sister like she was mad. "I am doing no such thing. I caught Adrien kissing another woman in Hyde Park."

"No, you saw *Hawk*, kissing a French spy in the park," Eliza countered.

She threw up her hands. "Adrien and *Hawk* are the same person!"

Eliza's eyes studied her for a moment as if attempting to peer into her soul. "Are you saying you cannot condone Adrien's actions even when he is acting as a spy?"

"Of course not. How could I?"

Eliza blinked, her look of disbelief settling into a tight press of her lips. "You would give up a lifetime of happiness with Adrien, because he was trying to extract information from a French spy, by any means necessary?"

Kate frowned. "I believe we have already established that fact."

Eliza uncrossed her arms and placed the palms of her hands on the bench. "Perhaps you find torture a more acceptable way of extracting information than kissing?"

Kate's eyes grew wide at the question. She did not know how to respond.

"Or, Adrien could have slit Marthe's throat and thrown her body into the River Thames." Eliza lifted an eyebrow, challenging her. "Would that have been a more permissible approach?"

She shook her head no but remained silent. Kate recognized her sister's point, but it was not going to change her mind. Adrien had been unfaithful to her! She could not condone that behavior.

"What has Adrien told you about his role within the agency?" Eliza asked.

Kate's eyes lifted to meet her sister's gaze. "I know he went undercover in France for a few years."

"Did he ever mention that *Hawk* is just as hated in France as *Shadow* is?" Eliza asked with a raised brow.

"No, he did not."

Her sister's eyes softened as she gazed upon her. "Adrien spent years undercover in France. Then he was forced to break cover and flee in the middle of the night. He arrived only to discover his family had been murdered by a French spy." Eliza's eyes pleaded for her to understand. "To him, you are his only family. He loves you, and I suspect you love him, too."

"How can I condone…"

"You are condoning nothing," Eliza said, cutting her off. "In your heart, do you truly believe Adrien wanted to kiss Marthe, a known spy?"

Kate bit her lip as she shook her head. "I see your point, but," she hesitated, "what if he does it again?"

Eliza let out a most unladylike snort of laughter. "I have no doubt that he will never kiss another woman again, interrogation or not."

Kate gazed out the window for a moment, trying to think of words to express her internal turmoil. She turned back. "I still think it is better if I go back to my country home."

"Better for who?"

She frowned deeply and drew her brows together. "I cannot get that image out of my head. I see Adrien kissing that other woman, and it reminds me so much of Michel. How can I ever trust him again?"

Eliza moved to sit next to her. "You have been taken advantage of horribly in the past, but I believe Adrien is your future. He loves you and is utterly devastated." Concern crept into her eyes. "I saw the panic on his face when he discovered you witnessed his meeting with Marthe."

Kate wrung her hands together. "I do not believe I am cut out to be a spy's wife," she admitted.

Eliza placed her hand over Kate's, causing her to still. "You can be anything you choose to be." She paused, her eyes filled with compassion. "And, if you are adamant in your decision to not marry Adrien, then I will support it. After all, you are my favorite sister."

A small laugh left Kate's mouth. "I am your only sister."

"I want you to remember that," Eliza said, with a tight smile.

"But, I truly believe you made a mistake by running away from Adrien."

"Is that so?" Kate asked warily.

Eliza nodded. "I understand how you could perceive Adrien's actions as an indiscretion," she held up her hand to stop Kate's retort, "but he was working as an agent of the Crown to sniff out the traitors within England. By seducing Marthe, he discovered more about the French's scheme."

Kate pursed her lips. "How could you possibly understand his actions?"

Eliza's face grew solemn, yet her eyes sparked with an intensity she had never witnessed before. "Because, I am *Shadow*."

Surprisingly, Kate was not shocked. All the missing pieces started fitting into place, and Beaumont Castle, Mr. Larson, and her black clothing made perfect, logical sense. Her lips twitched in amusement. "Now I see why you hired Mr. Larson as your butler, even though he is horrible at domestic skills."

"So, I have been told, repeatedly," Eliza stated good-naturedly. "He was initially hired to protect me on missions, but he now is responsible for my full-time protection."

"I am glad he is around. I do not want anything to happen to you."

Eliza withdrew her hand and leaned away. "And I do not want anything to happen to you." Her eyes grew sad, distant. "I have done horrible things as a spy. I am sad to admit that most of my actions would shock you, maybe even cause you to despise me."

It was Kate's turn to reassure Eliza, even though she knew she could not comprehend the mantle of responsibility that came with being a notorious spy. "Nothing you say or do would change the way I feel about you," she assured her.

"I have killed men, technically hundreds of men," Eliza said, her eyes devoid of emotion.

Kate's eyes welled with tears for her sister. "You have killed bad men who would not have hesitated to kill you." Suddenly, a thought dawned on her. "You were the one who saved Hannah, weren't you?"

Eliza shook her head. "We saved Hannah as a team. Jonathon, Adrien, Benedict, and other agents boarded the ship, and I remained in a building nearby with Mr. Larson." Her eyes flickered towards the small window. "My job was to take out the men guarding the gangway and any other mercenary that needed to be put down."

Kate briefly smiled at the memory of Adrien sitting at the dining table the morning after Hannah was rescued, and how he shared his skewed version of the events. A few days later, they were in the library, and he admitted to the true story of how Hannah was rescued. Ironically, in both accounts, she found herself dreaming about how handsome Adrien must have looked on the ship's deck, with his brown hair blowing in the wind, reminding her that he looked very much like a dashing pirate.

Her mind jolted back to the present. "Adrien told me that *Shadow* gave a few sailors warning shots in their shoulders rather than kill them outright." Kate watched her sister bite her lower lip, a sure sign that Eliza was upset. "That sounds like a compassionate spy who does not thirst for bloodshed."

Eliza gave her a tight smile. As she opened her mouth to respond, the carriage started swaying back and forth as it lurched forward at an alarming pace. Muffled shouting was coming from around the carriage, but no words were recognizable over the sound of pounding hoofbeats. Multiple explosions came from behind them, hitting the carriage with the distinctive sound of splintering wood.

Eliza turned and grabbed Kate's shoulders, forcing her to look at her. "These men want to abduct us, not kill us. Be calm and do not panic."

Kate's eyes grew wide as she attempted to take in what Eliza just told her. "How can I stay calm?" she asked in earnest. How did someone stay calm, knowing their life was in danger?

Eliza smiled reassuringly, although it seemed forced. "You have been in worse situations than this. Trust me. Adrien and Benedict will find us, unless I get us out of this scrape first."

More explosions came from outside the carriage until it started slowing down. Once the carriage was stopped, Eliza and Kate watched the door cautiously. They did not know which side had won, and time seemed to cease as they waited. Were Roger and all the footmen dead, or did they prevail?

The carriage door was wrenched open, and a husky man with sandy blond hair glared at them. He laughed cruelly. "I see that Lady Camden is not alone. I presume you are her sister, Lady Lansdowne."

"Please do not hurt us," Eliza pleaded. Her voice was shaky, and her eyes were full of tears.

Kate turned her head around to ensure that it was indeed Eliza that spoke with such uncertainty. How unlike her! The man laughed again and turned his head out of the carriage. "We scored tonight. We got two ladies from the list." A roar of applause came from outside of the carriage.

Flinching, Kate glanced back at Eliza and saw her wink. How silly of her. Eliza was playing the role of a simpering female.

"Get out of the carriage," the husky man demanded when he turned his attention back on them. He stepped back and allowed them to exit the carriage on their own.

Kate was not prepared for what she saw. Dead bodies were sprawled around the ground, their bleak, lifeless eyes staring at her. She scanned the bodies looking for Roger, hoping that he was still alive. As she glanced at the road, she saw Roger stretched out in the dirt, blood dripping down the side of his mouth.

"Roger," she shrieked as she ran the few yards and dropped

to her knees next to him. "No, no, no," she said as she tried to figure out what she could do to save him. "Please do not die." Her voice turned pleading as she ripped the bottom of her dress and tried to apply pressure to the wound on his chest. His shirt was saturated with blood, and it appeared her efforts weren't helping.

His hand rose, gently grabbing her hand to stop her. "This is…" He tried to say, before he coughed up blood. "This is… not… your fault."

Tears streamed down her face as she shook her head repeatedly. "It is all my fault. I should never have left the townhouse." She buried her head into his side, being mindful not to cause him anymore pain. "I am so sorry," she cried.

"I want you… to do… something for me," Roger gasped.

"Anything!" She brought her eyes up to look at her protector, who had become a dear friend.

"Be… happy," he said, his voice getting weaker with each word.

Gripping his hand, she could not keep from bursting into loud sobs. "I am so sorry, Roger."

Her sister's arm came around her shoulder, pulling her in tightly. "He is gone." Eliza whispered into her ear, "We need to act the role of weak women."

"It won't be an act for me," Kate replied with resignation in her voice.

As Eliza helped her rise, she glanced once more at Roger's lifeless body. She had killed him, almost as if she had pulled the trigger. She insisted they return home, even after he urged her to reconsider. She had made a poor decision again, and this time, it resulted not only in the death of her friend, but all the footmen who came along to protect her.

Without a word, she leaned up against her sister, knowing she did not have the strength to walk alone. How does someone move on, knowing they have blood on their hands? The men roughly tied their hands together and slipped a bag over their heads. As they were tossed carelessly into the carriage, Kate knew she deserved this treatment. In fact, she deserved far worse.

ADRIEN STARED OUT THE WINDOW, THE SNIFTER IN HIS HAND forgotten long ago. Currently, he was in a state of numbness, and no matter the drink, it would not ease his broken heart. He had lost Kate, the only good thing in his life, for doing his job as a spy.

It had never even occurred to him to attempt a different strategy with Marthe. His instinct told him to seduce her, and he always acted on those impressions. He had learned long ago to never doubt his instinct, and it had served him well in the past. Now, he did not give a damn about his instinct, or being a spy. All that mattered was Kate.

He flinched, knowing his instinct was telling him that Kate would never trust him again. How could she? He could understand her fury, or her need to rage, but he never expected her to dismiss him entirely. A weak smile came to his lips as he remembered Kate shouting at him, never once wavering in her anger. She had grown so much in these past few weeks. He was so proud of Kate… his Kate!

He loved her! Without her, his life was bleak and held no meaning. He needed to go and plead for her forgiveness. Society would mock his lack of pride, but he did not care about his pride when it came to Kate. She had given him purpose and restored his hope in a world that sometimes lacked humanity.

With a surge of resolve, he jumped up from his seat. The sun had already set, but he was determined to set things right with Kate. He placed his snifter on the tray and straightened his waistcoat. As he started across the room, Benedict strode in, stopping with a cocky smile on his face. "I recognize that resolute stance. You are going to fight for Kate."

"I am."

"It is about time," Benedict stated. "I was prepared to knock some sense into you hours ago, but it appears that is not necessary anymore."

"Why are you in my study?" Adrien growled. He really did not have time to chit-chat with his friend.

Benedict laughed. "Because some idiot put a door through my hall."

Adrien started walking towards the hall. "If you will excuse me, I will use that very door to beg Kate to give me another chance."

Benedict looked perplexed. "I thought you knew."

A cold shiver ran down his spine at his friend's words. "Knew what?"

"The carriage left over an hour ago with Kate."

"What?" Adrien roared. "And you are just telling me now?"

Benedict gave him a stern, knowing look. "It was not my call to stop her. Roger and five footmen went along for her protection."

"You only sent five footmen?" He was beginning to question if Benedict was a bloody simpleton.

"Eliza was so upset that she went to her room to lie down."

Adrien started pacing back and forth in a frenzy. "I need to go after her." He strode past Benedict and into the hall. "Ward! Bring me my horse! There is not a moment to lose."

"Don't be a fool." Benedict was suddenly in front of him, his hands out front, attempting to be the voice of reason. "You cannot race after her at night and risk having your horse go lame. Besides, the roads are crawling with highwaymen."

Adrien stopped, staring at his friend with a steely, hardened gaze. He was ready to face whatever came his way to see Kate again. "I do not fear highway robbers."

Benedict dropped his hand in defeat. "I wish you luck."

Near the entry hall, Adrien spun back around. His instinct was telling him something was amiss. He frowned. "Has Eliza ever retired to her room when she was upset?"

"Not that I can recall, but she is with child now."

"Did she wish Kate a farewell at the carriage?" he pressed. Something was gnawing at him.

"No, she went to lay down before the carriage departed." Realization dawned on Benedict's features as he sighed gruffly. "Giving her enough time to scale down the wall and join her sister in the carriage."

"Eliza would want to ensure Kate's protection, even if it meant enduring your wrath."

"If what we believe is true, I plan to lock her away in our estate," Benedict growled. "After I ensure she is unharmed."

Adrien knew his friend would never lock Eliza away. How could he? Benedict was just scared. He understood that emotion very well right now. "First, let's go see if my theory holds true."

They both sprinted towards Benedict's townhouse with a sense of dread. If Henley had targeted Kate's carriage, then he would have acquired both Eliza and Kate. That would be disastrous! Running down the hall, Adrien stepped aside as Benedict threw open his bedchamber door. The window was opened, and the drapes were fluttering in the wind.

"Larson," Benedict shouted with such venom that Adrien almost took a step back. He was glad he was not on the receiving end of that anger.

Scanning the hall, Adrien stated, "I do not see him. Where is he?"

"Larson is always with Eliza." Benedict's face was a grim

mask as he sorted through this puzzle. "It appears I will be traveling with you to your country estate to retrieve my wife."

They both raced towards the main entry where a group of servants waited to do their bidding. "I want my horse readied, now!" Benedict ordered as he ran out the main door.

Adrien followed closely behind, anxiously waiting for his horse to be brought up front. The sound of pounding hooves on the cobblestone street caught his attention. Focusing on the direction of the noise, he saw a horse barreling down the street with a rider who sat low, urging his mount to run faster. The horse pulled up in front of them, and he saw Mr. Larson dismount quickly.

"They took Eliza and Kate! They took them!" Mr. Larson yelled, his voice frantic. In all his days, Adrien had never witnessed Larson rattled.

Benedict grabbed his shoulders, looking directly into his eyes. "We will get them back. First, we need to know what happened."

Nodding, Mr. Larson took a deep breath, regained his control, then his eyes took on a deadly gleam. "Eliza asked me to order her some tea and biscuits. While I was away, she snuck out of the window, and I assumed she met the carriage at the corner."

"Why would you think that?" Adrien asked curiously.

Mr. Larson scowled at him. "Because that is what I would have done." He turned his attention back to Benedict. "I thought I had time to catch up to the carriage and bring Eliza home. Unfortunately, I arrived too late." He fisted his hands, and Adrien thought he might punch something.

"We need to know all the facts," Benedict pressed calmly, but Adrien was not falling for his brave facade.

"The carriage was on fire," Mr. Larson hesitated, "but I confirmed no one was in it." Noticing the black ash on his clothing, Adrien wondered how close Mr. Larson got to confirm no one was in the carriage. "Everyone was dead, including Roger..." His voice trailed off.

Adrien felt like someone just punched him in the gut. Roger was dead? Poor Kate. Roger was more than just her protector, he was her friend. Anger ripped through his body. Henley would pay for this! "I believe I will pay a visit to Henley's townhouse," he snarled. First, he would retrieve Kate and Eliza, and then he would make Henley suffer a gruesome death.

"Do you want me to go with you?" Benedict asked, snapping him back into reality.

"No, Henley is mine," Adrien declared as he mounted his horse that a groomsman had brought around front.

"I will inform Lord Beckett." Benedict gave him a pointed look. "Try not to get yourself killed, *Hawk.*"

With a firm nod in response, he tightened the reins in his hand and kicked the horse into a dry run on the empty cobblestone street.

"And don't kill him, yet!" Benedict shouted behind him.

Shaking off Benedict's words, Adrien knew he could not promise that. Right now, he would kill as many people as it took to get his Kate back.

# 21

On his ride through the foggy streets of London, Adrien mentally prepared for what needed to be accomplished. By confronting Henley, he was going to break cover without confirming who the French spy was in the House of Lords, or where Marthe resided. However, Henley would know where Kate and Eliza were being held, and he had every intention of rescuing them before they were injured or killed.

Knowing Lord Beckett had assigned agents to trail Henley's movements, he dismounted his horse near the alley where he had last seen them. Being vigilant as he approached the dark alleyway, he could see two hazy figures. His steps were deliberate to ensure he did not spook these agents.

He stopped a few feet away from the men, knowing he needed to announce himself. "Be on alert. Street urchins will likely pick your pockets."

Once he uttered the code, the hazy figures left the obscurity of the alleyway and came closer. The two relatively young agents wore dark coats and appeared to be unsettled by his presence.

"What is it that you want?" the agent with brown hair asked, keeping his hand on the pistol tucked into his trousers.

Stepping forward, he handed his reins to the agent. "Henley just abducted Lady Camden and Lady Lansdowne, killing six men who were guarding them, including a former agent."

Obviously offended at being relegated to the job of a groomsman, the brown-haired agent handed off his reins to the other agent with the bony nose. "Are we tasked with bringing him in, then?"

"No," he answered firmly. "I will go confront Henley, but I want you to track all of his movements."

"We are already doing that…"

Cutting him off, Adrien proceeded to give orders. "I want to know everything that happens with Henley for the next twenty-four hours." He raised his eyebrows to stress his point. "If he leaves that house, you both will follow him. Do not split up."

The brown-haired agent frowned, appearing frustrated. "With all due respect, we do not work for you. We work for Lord Beckett, and he ordered us not to leave this location. We are just to report who comes and goes from Henley's townhouse."

Taking a step forward, Adrien's voice turned deadly. He did not have the luxury of time to argue. "What is your name, agent?"

"Stearns," the brown-haired agent answered.

"Well, Stearns," he drawled, not bothering to hide his annoyance, "Lord Beckett has put me in charge of this investigation, and I will dictate what you will do." His eyes narrowed as his jaw clamped shut, resisting the urge to beat this agent into submission.

The bony-nosed agent nodded his consent, but Stearns was not as easily convinced. His eyes roamed Adrien's fancy clothes and shiny boots. With a look that clearly indicated his disbelief that an entitled lord was in charge of this investigation, he asked, "Can I get your name, my lord?" He huffed disapprovingly. "You know, in case Lord Beckett wants to know the name of the man who changed his direct orders."

A slow, satisfied smile came to Adrien's lips. "You can tell him that *Hawk* changed his orders."

"*Hawk*," Stearns repeated with newfound respect. "Last we heard, you were in France."

With a determined glance towards Henley's townhouse, Adrien replied, "Gentlemen, I do not have time for questions right now. Will you do as I ask?"

"Yes, sir," they both said in unison.

He started down the alley towards Henley's house. "Hold my horse," he ordered over his shoulder. "This shouldn't take long."

As he was ushered into Henley's study, Adrien ensured his coat was covering the pistol tucked in the back. He liked having the pistol hidden from view, giving him an advantage. As usual, his spare overcoat pistol and small dagger were in his boot. He never liked to be unprepared for a fight.

As much as he wanted to kill Mr. Henley, he needed him alive at this point. Lord Beckett would most likely send agents to arrest Henley tomorrow, but he hoped to have Kate back in his arms by sunrise.

"Lord Camden, it is a pleasure to see you this fine evening," Mr. Henley said with a hint of sarcasm as he laid the papers he had been perusing onto his desk. His tailcoat had been removed and was draped over the back of his chair.

Adrien strode into the room, ignoring Mr. Henley's gestured invitation to sit. He placed his hands on the desk and leaned forward. "Where are Kate and Eliza?"

Mr. Henley chuckled as he leaned away from his desk. "Kate, is it? Eliza? You must be quite close to be using their given names."

"Kate is my responsibility," he asserted firmly. "Not only did you abduct her, but you took her sister, Eliza, and torched the Marquess of Lansdowne's carriage." He leaned further over the desk. "Furthermore, you killed six innocent people, leaving their bodies in the road as if they were discarded waste."

"Is that all?" Mr. Henley asked, unconcerned.

Pushing off from the desk, Adrien's eyes narrowed. "You abducted the daughters of the Duke of Remington. Did you not think there would be an investigation?"

Mr. Henley seemed unaffected by his words. "Highwaymen frequent that road at night. It will be written off as a robbery gone bad." He reached for the papers on his desk and started rifling through them. "Now if you don't mind, I have work to do, and I trust you can see your way out."

Straightening his shoulders, he tilted his head as he watched Mr. Henley's attempt to dismiss him. After a moment, he crossed his arms, then spoke, his voice firm, leaving no room for argument. "I want Kate and Eliza back. I will not leave until you tell me where they are."

Without sparing him a glance, Mr. Henley put up two fingers, signaling someone to come into the room. He turned slightly and watched two large men, with pistols tucked into their trousers, walk up to the desk to stand behind Henley. It was obvious that these men were meant to intimidate him, which only infuriated him more. Did Henley really believed that these two men would stop his questions?

Focusing on Mr. Henley, his eyes were blazing with fury. "Where are they?"

Mr. Henley rose from his chair with the air of a man who believed he was still in charge. "You were hired to help abduct them, but my men took care of it. I owe you nothing."

Taking a deliberate step forward, Adrien was gratified to see a glimmer of fear in Mr. Henley's eyes. "And you thought you could cheat me?"

Mr. Henley sighed in relief. "If this is about money, I am sure we can come to an agreement."

Chuckling dryly, Adrien shook his head. "No, this is most

certainly not about money." Gone was the down-on-his-luck, selfish lord, replaced with the steely, determined agent he truly was. "I want Kate and Eliza returned, unharmed," he ordered.

Henley placed his hand on the desk, his finger tapping the pile of papers thoughtfully. After a moment, he met Adrien's gaze. "I am willing to give you back Lady Lansdowne, unharmed."

Adrien clenched his jaw tightly. "I want Lady Camden, too."

With a wave of a hand, Henley dismissed his words. "I am keeping Lady Camden," he said, his voice dripping with contempt. "She is mine."

*No, she is mine,* Adrien wanted to shout, but instead he pressed for more information. "Why do you want Lady Camden?"

A frown tugged at Henley's lips. "It is personal."

Adrien's hands were now balled into fists at his sides, and his knuckles were white. "I'm afraid I cannot let that happen. Lady Camden has agreed to marry me, and I want my fiancée back."

Henley's upper lip curled in disdain. "You are not really in a position to negotiate, are you?" He glanced at the two men behind him. "I believe Lord Camden has outlived his usefulness," he sneered. "Escort him out and deal with him."

Before either of the two men moved, Adrien whipped his pistol out from behind him, shooting the man to Henley's left, square in the chest. Almost simultaneously, he reached down to retrieve his spare pistol from his boot, shooting the man on Henley's right before the thug even uncrossed his arms. Pulling out his small dagger, he came around the desk and confirmed the two men were dead. Henley's stunned face would have been comical at another time, but he needed to keep him from retaliating.

Grabbing Henley's hand, he placed it palm down on the desk, and thrust his dagger through the center of his hand, embedding it into the desk.

Now that Henley couldn't move, he grabbed a chair and ran towards the open door. He closed it, locked it, and jammed the chair under the handle, effectively barricading himself in with Henley. Within a few steps, he was back to the desk and could see Henley's eyes were wide, bright with fear.

*Good, this is where I want him.* He leaned closer to him. "Where are the women you abducted?"

Henley's other hand held the wrist of his pinned hand. "I cannot tell you that. I can give you Lady Lansdowne back, plus the money." His voice was strained and coming out in gasps. "I can give you whatever amount you desire."

*He still thinks I am trying to negotiate for money? Unbelievable.*

Adrien reached for Henley's other hand and placed it palm down on the desk. Without saying a word, he removed the dagger from the one hand and jammed it through the middle of the other hand. But this time, he twisted it and was satisfied to hear Henley roar with pain.

"I can do this all night," Adrien stated flatly. "I want all of the women, not just Eliza."

Henley looked at him, his face devoid of all color. "I cannot give you Kate. She is not mine to give."

Adrien's eyes flickered towards the door as the sound of pounding came from the other side. He only had a few minutes before they broke through that door. "What do you mean by that?"

Henley didn't respond as his eyes took in the blood covering the desk and soaking into the papers beneath his hand. Adrien reached down and tugged the pistol out of one of the dead men's trousers. He placed it to Henley's temple. "Answer me, or die," he threatened.

"I was ordered to bring Kate back alive."

"Why?" he asked, digging the pistol into his head.

With a sudden outburst, Henley revealed, "Her father wants her back."

Adrien's gun faltered, and his eyes narrowed. Kate's father was alive? Before he could ask any further questions, he could hear the splintering of wood. They were almost through that door. He tucked the pistol into his trousers and yanked his knife out of Henley's hand. He collected the pistols from the ground and walked swiftly towards the window. Adrien gave Henley a smug smile before he jumped out of the window.

As soon as his feet hit the ground, he sprinted towards his horse and the two other agents. He had no doubt that Henley would attempt retribution. Not only did he anticipate it, but he looked forward to it. Next time he encountered Henley, he would kill that French spy.

ADRIEN RAN TOWARDS THE OTHER AGENTS. A THIRD FIGURE stood with them, causing him to slow his approach, and he instinctively reached for his pistol. As he came closer, he saw that it was Benedict and dropped his hand.

As he approached the group, Benedict asked, "Did you learn where the women are being held?"

"No, and I am tired of playing nice." His response was gruff.

Benedict chuckled softly. "You have never really played nice with others."

"Good point." Adrien moved towards his horse, reaching for the reins from the junior agent. Addressing the two agents, he ordered, "If anyone leaves that house, you will follow them and report their locations. Lives are at stake, and I do not have time for any incompetence."

"Yes, sir," the men said in unison. They had not stopped gaping at him since he'd left Henley's house. He was aware that his reputation preceded him, but he was not used to the approving stares.

"*Hawk*," Benedict said to his back as he mounted his horse.

"Yes, *Sunshine*."

Benedict shot him an exasperated look as he stepped closer and lowered his voice. "If you are going to pay a visit to Lord Lexington, then I am coming with you. We suspect that he is the third French operative, and he could very well kill you before you set foot inside his home."

"By all means, please join me," Adrien offered, with a flick of his wrist.

Benedict was staring at his hands. "You are injured."

Adrien took a moment to inspect his bloodied hands. "This is not my blood."

"Did you kill Henley?" Benedict asked, more curious than accusatory.

He shook his head. "No. I did not kill him, but I did take out two of his mercenaries."

"It sounds like you had all the fun," Benedict stated over his shoulder as he mounted his horse. "It is my turn to persuade the French spy to talk."

Adrien gave Benedict a baffled glance. How was his friend so relaxed? His wife had been abducted, too, yet he seemed amused by his antics. "Why are you not panicking? Aren't you worried about Eliza?"

Without giving him a glance, Benedict pushed his horse into a run down the dark, foggy street. After letting their horses run, he slowed to a brisk pace and turned his attention back to his riding partner. "Henley abducted Lady Lansdowne, the pampered wife of a marquess. They have no clue who she is and what she is capable of."

Benedict paused as his eyes roamed the street. "We will find them if I have to tear this city apart. I will not rest till they are safe. No one hurts my wife and lives to tell about it." His last few words were clipped and sharp-edged, leaving no doubt that he meant them.

Adrien gave Benedict a sideways glance, feeling exactly the same way. He would not rest until he had Kate back in his arms. As their gazes locked for a moment, unspoken words passing between them confirmed the lengths they were willing to go to get their women back.

A determined silence descended around them as they once again raced their horses towards Lord Lexington's. His massive, white stone townhouse was located on Grosvenor street with a wrought-iron fence surrounding his property. Dismounting in front, they took a moment to secure their horses before they charged up the steps.

Benedict started pounding his fist against the main door and did not relent until the butler opened it. He pushed his way in, and Adrien followed close behind.

The butler sputtered like a fish. "Get back here, or I will alert the constable."

Turning back to deal with the butler, Adrien glared at the man and was gratified to see him shrink back. "We are here to speak to Lexington on behalf of the Crown." He took a step closer to the man. "Where is he?"

"The study." The butler's eyes seemed fixated on his blood-spattered hands. "In the back."

Without further questions, they headed towards the study and briefly took in the scene. Lord Lexington was sitting on an armchair with a snifter resting on the table next to him, his attention on the book resting in his lap. In a few strides, Benedict picked up Lexington by the throat, knocking over the chair. He shoved him against the shelves with such force that books cascaded to the floor. "Where is my wife?" he demanded, his tone venomous.

With his eyes bulging, Lexington choked out, "Your wife? Why in the blazes would I know where your wife is?"

"No?" Benedict asked as he yanked the marquess forward using the hand around his throat, then he slammed him back against the shelving again. "Does that help jog your memory?"

Lexington tried to pry Benedict's hand off his throat. "Lord Lansdowne, let's be civilized about this," he gasped.

"You made the mistake of abducting my wife and my sister-in-law. There is only one scenario that will allow you to keep your life." With a smirk, Benedict leaned forward until he was nose-to-nose with the red-faced lord. "Tell me where they are now, and I will let you keep eight of your fingers."

Fear filled Lexington's wide eyes. "I did not abduct your wife or sister-in-law. Why would I? You have to believe me."

Walking over to Lord Lexington, Adrien leaned against the wall next to him, pulled out his pistol and started the tedious process of reloading. "Here is why we are not inclined to believe you," Adrien said, sparing him a glance. "You are good mates with a French spy."

Lord Lexington attempted to turn his head to look at Adrien but was hampered by Benedict's hand around his throat. "Impossible. I am not friends with any of the French, much less a French spy."

Benedict scoffed. "We saw you two together at the rally looking quite chummy, and you are both after the same thing." His eyes narrowed. "For us to withdraw our troops from Europe, enabling Napoleon to conquer England."

"It's true that I am against the war, but I am no traitor," Lord Lexington declared. "We have not exhausted our diplomatic channels with Napoleon."

Adrien saw Benedict loosen the pressure against Lexington's throat, but he did not release the marquess. "Do you deny being friends with Mr. Edgar Henley?" Benedict asked.

"Henley and I are not mates. I can barely tolerate the man."

The disgust in Lexington's voice was evident, but that did not mean he was innocent of aiding the French agenda.

"If you disliked Henley so much, then why did you purchase a seat for him in the House of Commons?" Adrien pressed as he tucked his pistol back into his trousers.

"Why are you questioning me about Henley?" Lexington's tone was full of arrogance. Suddenly, his face paled, and his voice was full of dread as he asked, "Henley is a spy?"

Benedict lifted an eyebrow. "You tell us."

All the fight drained out of Lexington, and he went limp. "I purchased a seat in the House of Commons for a French spy." He sounded mortified. "What have I done?" He closed his eyes and leaned his head back against the shelving with Benedict's hand still around his throat.

Frowning, Adrien's eyes flickered towards Benedict. His instinct told him that Lexington was telling the truth. *How did they get this so wrong?* "I think we should start over and discuss this over a drink."

Benedict dropped his hands from Lexington and stepped back. "I concur. I believe we have a lot to discuss."

For a moment, Lexington did not move, but then he opened his eyes and straightened his head. "I am ruined. Prinny will never forgive me for this."

Adrien walked over to the drink tray, poured two glasses of brandy, then handed them to Benedict and Lexington. After he poured himself a drink, he downed it in one swallow. Placing his glass back on the tray, he asked, "If you cannot tolerate Henley, why did you purchase him a seat in the House of Commons?"

Taking a sip of his drink, Lexington grimaced before answering, "Miss Henley requested it, and I complied. I saw no reason to deny her, since we both side with the Whigs." He moved slowly to the settee and dropped down, his drink splashing a bit onto his hand. "She will be devastated to learn of her brother's deceit."

Benedict grabbed an upholstered armchair and repositioned it directly in front of the marquess. "Who exactly is Miss Henley?"

Retrieving a handkerchief from his pocket, Lexington dried his hand. "She is my mistress."

Sitting on the opposite side of the settee, Adrien turned his body towards the marquess. "We will need to speak to her."

"Of course, I will call for her," Lexington said, standing. Walking over towards the door, he shouted into the hall, "Harvey, wake Miss Henley and ask her to join me in the study."

"Miss Henley is here?" Adrien questioned, attempting to keep the shock out of his voice.

Resuming his position on the settee, Lexington's lips tightened into a straight line. "Miss Henley insisted on spending the night with me tonight. Normally, she resides in the townhouse I maintain for her across town."

"How kind of you." Benedict's tone was curt, making it clear how he felt about Lexington's relationship. "Where did you meet Miss Henley and her brother?"

Lexington rubbed his chin as he recalled the facts. "About four years ago, I was at a house gathering for…" His voice faded off for a moment, then he announced, "Lord Camden! I was at Camden's townhouse, and he introduced me to Miss Henley. She was beautiful, and I must admit I was immediately smitten."

Adrien exchanged a pointed glance with Benedict. "And her brother?"

"Edgar is a bloody menace," Lexington stated, shaking his head. "Miss Henley introduced me to him shortly after she agreed to become my mistress. I bought him a seat in the House of Commons after she became quite insistent about it."

"Did you investigate Henley at all before buying him a seat?" Benedict challenged with narrowed eyes.

Lexington gave Benedict a perplexed look. "And why would I? Henley had the support of Lord Camden."

"I would like to remind you that it is illegal to purchase a seat in the House of Commons," Adrien stated dryly.

Lexington opened his mouth to respond, but quickly turned it into a wide, bright smile. As he rose, he said, "Dearest, thank you for coming down so quickly."

Turning towards the door, Adrien's eyes saw the last person he thought he would see… Marthe.

# 22

WEARING A TIGHT WRAPPER, MARTHE'S HAIR WAS TUCKED AWAY into a long braid, and she was swishing her hips back and forth in a seductive manner. Her eyes were trained on Lexington, but then realizing he was not alone, her eyes skimmed the room until they landed on Adrien. Immediately, her smile dimmed, and her eyes grew wide, showing a flash of panic before she blinked it away.

With a forced smile, she locked her gaze on Lexington, but her steps faltered. "I did not realize you had guests," she said, without a hint of her French accent. "I am afraid I am not dressed appropriately. Please allow me a few moments to change."

"Of course," Lord Lexington agreed with a bob of his head, completely oblivious to the tension in the room. Marthe's lips twitched in response.

"If you move, I will shoot you," Adrien warned, his voice clear and precise.

He had no doubt that if Marthe left this room, she would flee and be out of their reach forever. In a few strides, he stood in front of her and watched as she shrank back from him. Before she could object, he gripped her forearm and led her towards the settee he had just vacated. "Benedict, meet Marthe." He made the introduction through gritted teeth.

Benedict's face turned hard, impassive. "Ah," was all he said.

Lexington glanced suspiciously between the two of them. "How exactly are you acquainted with Miss Henley?"

Once Marthe was situated on the settee, Adrien turned his attention back towards Lexington, but kept her in his peripheral vision. She may be in a wrapper, but she still might be carrying a weapon. "We met in Hyde Park today to discuss a little business matter." His lips twisted in wry amusement as he glanced down at the French spy.

Throwing his hands up, Lexington shouted, "My mistress is a spy?"

Benedict crossed his arms over his chest, frustration pouring out of him. "You seem to be well acquainted with two known French spies, Lord Lexington. I am beginning to think you are either the world's biggest fool or a spy yourself."

"I am no spy," Lexington stated.

With a huff, Benedict quipped dryly, "Then you are a fool."

Adrien focused his attention on Marthe and studied her face for clues. "Where are Lady Lansdowne and Lady Camden?"

In response, Marthe sat rigid, but her expression became one of perfectly practiced innocence. "I have no idea what you are referring to."

"No?" Adrien asked with a disbelieving smirk. "I seem to recall that you offered me a generous sum of money, and yourself," he paused, "if I helped abduct Lady Lansdowne and Lady Camden."

Glancing between Benedict and Adrien, Marthe looked shocked by his suggestion. "I do not know what you are referring to. I do not know a Lady Lansdowne or a Lady Camden." She gave him a polite, but haughty smile. "We do not exactly run in the same circles."

Adrien grabbed a chair and placed it in front of her, with the intention of interrogating her properly. "Are you denying you met me at Hyde Park today for a liaison?"

Marthe's hand flew to cover her opened mouth. "Heavens, no. I was at the modiste all day. My driver can attest to that fact."

Adrien ran his hand over his chin while he debated how to proceed. Time was of the essence, and he did not want to waste any by slowly easing into his questions. He glanced sideways at Benedict, who nodded. It was time to press Marthe. "Prior to turning over the locket to Henley, we reviewed the list that Michel created."

With a stilled hand, her face became an expressionless mask. "I know nothing of a list."

"No?" Adrien asked. "It had your name on it."

"I am confident it is a case of mistaken identity," she said flippantly. "Marthe is a very common name."

Benedict pulled out his pistol and rested it on his thigh. "No," he replied firmly. "We do not have a case of mistaken identity. Besides, most of the ton saw your pathetic attempt to seduce Lord Camden in Hyde Park."

Marthe turned towards Lexington and shot him a look of mock indignation. "Are you going to sit here and let them make these lewd allegations against me?"

Lexington's face withered as he looked at his mistress. "Yes, I am."

Jumping up, she shouted, "Well, I am not going to stand for it." Her hand discreetly slid down towards a pocket in her wrapper. "If you come back tomorrow, we can rationally discuss this with my solicitor present."

Without hesitation, Adrien grabbed her hand tightly and twisted it behind her back. "Let's see what you are hiding, shall we?" Placing his other hand into the pocket of her wrapper, he pulled out a dainty overcoat pistol and handed it to Benedict.

Keeping her arm behind her back, Adrien asked, "Do you have any more weapons on your person?"

"No, I do not," Marthe replied with a shake of her head. "I only keep the gun for protection."

Benedict chuckled. "Who do you fear in a marquess' home? The butler, the chef, or the maids?"

With an exasperated sigh, Adrien started a more thorough search of Marthe.

Lord Lexington shouted in outrage, "Lord Camden, it is not proper for you to touch Miss Henley in such a fashion."

"Do shut up, Lexington," Adrien ordered as he ran his hand down her right thigh, finding a knife strapped to her leg. He pulled out the sheathed knife and handed it over to Benedict.

Once Marthe was searched, Adrien shoved her back down onto the settee. "The game is over for you, Marthe," he informed her as he retook his seat in front of her. "We know you are a French spy, as is Edgar Henley, your alleged brother. We have proof that there is a conspiracy to force lords to vote for the bill to end the French war by abducting their loved ones, and you are orchestrating the crimes."

"What?" Lord Lexington exclaimed. Turning his gaze towards Marthe, his eyes held misplaced compassion. "My dear, why would you do that?"

Marthe reached for Lord Lexington's hand, encompassing it with her own. Smiling softly, she gazed into his eyes, seeming to bewitch him. "I am not guilty of these crimes…"

"I am tired of this charade," Benedict declared, cutting her off. "I want my wife and my sister-in-law back. Also, I want all the women you have abducted over the past few weeks."

Marthe's eyes grew wide at his accusation. "I have abducted no women," she stated. "For what purpose?"

"Gentlemen, I fear that you may be misguided in your pursuit of justice," Lexington lectured as he squeezed Marthe's hand. "Miss Henley is merely a woman."

Making a clucking noise, Adrien ignored Lexington's words as he continued to stare down Marthe. "If you do not tell us the truth, we will escort you down to Newgate where agents will force you to share what you know."

Lexington huffed, obviously exasperated. "Surely, you are not implying that agents will torture Miss Henley."

"If need be," Benedict asserted with a raised brow, "but only if she refuses to divulge the truth."

"Britain does not torture women," Lexington said haughtily, as his gaze fixated on his mistress. "I will ensure you are treated fairly, my dear."

"Bloody fool," Benedict muttered under his breath as he gave Lexington an icy glare. "French spies are denied trials, since they are the enemy."

Leaning back in the chair, Adrien perused Miss Henley from head to toe. "I believe Marthe is truly Mr. Henley's sister. They have the same eyes and pointed ears."

Marthe gasped. "I do not have pointed ears."

"Drop the innocent act. It is not fooling anyone but your lover," Adrien stated as he pointed at Lexington. "Give me the location of the abducted women." He lowered his voice for emphasis. "I will not ask politely again."

Tilting her head coyly, Marthe appeared unruffled by his threat. "And I contend that I know nothing about the abducted girls."

With a decisive bob of his head, Adrien reached down into his boot and pulled out his knife. Yanking her free hand towards him, he promptly sliced off the tip of her pinky, causing her to cry out in pain. "If you lie again, I will cut off your whole finger." He lowered the knife to the bottom of her pinky as blood trailed down her hand.

"No!" Marthe shrieked out as she tried yanking her hand free, but he held tight.

As blood drops splattered onto the floor, Lexington's face

paled. "This is uncalled for, Lord Camden."

In that instant, Marthe's mask was stripped off, and her mouth thinned to a harsh, bitter line. "Go ahead and torture me," she spat in French, "but I will never reveal the location of the women to you English swine."

Adrien moved to slice off her pinky, but Benedict's hand on his shoulder stilled him. "I think it would be best if we turned her over to the other agents." Glancing over his shoulder, his friend added, "Besides, her screaming might alert Lexington's household, and I really do not want to explain to the magistrate why we were torturing Miss Henley."

Adrien placed his knife back into his boot. Pulling out his handkerchief, he wrapped Marthe's bloody finger and released her hand. "I had hoped it would not come down to this, but you refuse to cooperate, leaving us with no choice."

Grabbing Marthe's forearm, Adrien forced her to stand, keeping her tight against him. Turning to address Lexington, he said, "You will vote against the bill to defund the war."

Puffing out his chest, Lexington acted as if he had a choice in the matter. "I will not. Whigs are against the war, and I am the leader of the party."

Before Adrien could respond, Benedict jabbed his balled fist into Lexington's face, causing him to stumble backwards and collapse to the floor. "You are a blasted idiot," he growled in a low, threatening voice as he loomed over Lexington. "French spies have infiltrated Parliament to ensure the bill passes, and you still want to vote for it?"

Lexington's eyes scrunched in pain. "We have not exhausted peace talks yet…" His words faded as Benedict crouched down low next to him.

With undisguised hostility in his voice, Benedict gave him a venomous look. "You are wrong. If Napoleon continues to succeed in overthrowing European countries, then he will eventually conquer Britain."

"We do not know that for certain," Lexington argued, his voice still skeptical.

Adrien scoffed at the arrogant lord, annoyed at his ignorance. "I can attest that Napoleon has designs to conquer England."

Lexington shot him a look of disbelief. "Pray tell, how exactly would an earl be privy to Napoleon's plans?"

"I was not always an earl," Adrien informed him. "Before assuming the title of Lord Camden, I was an agent for the Crown and worked as Admiral Garnier's under-secretary."

Marthe turned her head, shock on her face. "You are *Hawk*."

"I am," Adrien confirmed, not relenting his firm grip on her forearm.

Closing her eyes, she muttered in a resigned voice, "I am a dead woman."

Not pausing to acknowledge Marthe's statement, Benedict continued his assault on Lexington. "If you do not vote against the bill and encourage the other members of the Whig party to follow your lead, then I will make it my mission to destroy you, including everything you hold dear."

With a reddened face, Lexington jumped to his feet. "You would not dare."

"I would." Benedict rose from his crouched position. "I would go to my father-in-law, the Duke of Remington, and together we would inform Prinny you've been harboring a French spy, and that you bought a seat in the House of Commons for the enemy. You would be ousted from Parliament, but I would not stop there," he said, with a deliberate shake of his head. "I would leak to the newspapers that you were conspiring with two French spies, and I would see that your name, and your family's name, would be tarnished forever."

Benedict tugged on his waistcoat, appearing deadly calm. "I would ensure that you would never be invited to another party, soirée, or ball within polite society, and you will live the remainder of your days in exile."

Lexington's eyes spewed with anger. "A true gentleman would never resort to blackmail."

"I never called myself a gentleman," Benedict retorted, with a crooked grin.

Lexington stumbled over to his drink cart and poured himself a drink. His hand was shaky as he brought the glass up to his lips. "I will do as you ask," he conceded, intentionally avoiding eye contact, "but only because of the extenuating circumstances surrounding this bill."

Leading a submissive Marthe towards the door, Adrien halted and spun back towards Lexington. "It is safe to assume that you would not be foolish enough to reveal our connection to the Crown, is it not?"

The glass hovered near Lexington's mouth, his lips frowning. "And if I do, then you will ruin me." His tone was mocking.

"No," Adrien said with a shake of his head. "I will kill you."

With eyes radiating fear, Lexington nodded his assent as Adrien, Marthe, and Benedict exited the room and passed by wide-eyed servants. No one dared to stop them as they left the townhouse.

As they descended the steps, Adrien tilted his head towards Benedict. "I am beginning to think that Larson is rubbing off on you."

"In what way?"

"Your threats are getting more devious."

Benedict let out an exasperated sigh. "You are a bloody idiot."

"Yes, *Sunshine*." Adrien smirked.

"I swear I am going to kill you," Benedict muttered under his breath.

Wiping the smile off his face, Adrien grew serious as he turned, forcing Marthe to face him. "Tell us where the women are, and we will not turn you over to the agents at Newgate."

Speaking in French, Marthe replied, "I will not betray my country."

"Your country has abandoned you," Adrien stated, switching to French. "You will die alone, a traitor's death."

"Either way, I will be killed," she replied. He could sense the turmoil, panic, and fear that she was feeling. Maybe she could be reasoned with?

"No, it does not have to be that way," Adrien assured her, in a soft voice. "If you tell us what we need to know, I will let you go back to France." He ignored Benedict's shocked expression as he pressed forward. "I just want my Kate back."

Marthe grew pensive as she surveyed Lexington's townhouse. "She is lost to you," she murmured as her gaze returned to his face. "You must accept that."

Adrien cleared his throat, swallowing back the deep emotion that had settled there. "No, I will never accept that."

Suddenly, a steel wall replaced the sorrowful look that was in Marthe's eyes just moments ago. "You Englishmen are fools, no?" she mocked in English. "You have the misconception that love is tangible, but that is a weakness, not a strength."

Benedict took a step closer, his voice low and urgent. "Just tell us where the women are."

"Your women will die regardless of the vote," Marthe revealed, flicking a menacing look at Benedict.

"No, they won't," Adrien said in an authoritative tone, "but you most assuredly will."

KATE COULD HEAR MUFFLED VOICES FLOATING AROUND HER, BUT she could not seem to understand the words. She attempted to open her eyes, but her eyelids were too heavy, the effort too great. A faint headache was forming, making it harder to think.

As she attempted to concentrate on the conversation going on around her, she heard an unfamiliar man's voice ask, "How much laudanum did you give her?"

"Less than half of what I normally dose," a gruff answer came in response. That voice seemed oddly familiar, but she could not place it.

She could feel someone tenderly caressing her hair and heard the unfamiliar voice say gently, "Kathryn, wake up."

*No, she would not be called Kathryn again.* "Kate," she rasped. "I go by Kate."

"Not anymore," the voice pressed. "You will go by Kathryn now."

Forcing her eyes open, she was met with the intense gaze of a handsome, older gentleman with short black hair greased to perfection and piercing blue eyes. As his face softened, a smile formed on his lips revealing charming dimples. "Good, you are awake," he said with a distinctive French accent.

"Where am I?" Kate asked as she tried to sit up.

The man's hands gently helped her until her back was leaning up against a wall. "Someplace safe."

Placing a hand to her head, she repeated her question. "But, where am I?"

"I told you she was an impertinent one," the familiar voice stated from behind the older man.

Kate's gaze drifted towards the voice, and she recognized an impeccably dressed Mr. Henley leaning against the opposite wall. *She was most definitely not safe.* She forced her eyes to look back at the older man. "Please release me and let me go home."

The man shook his head, oblivious to her disdain of Henley. "You are home."

Kate's eyes took in the small rectangular room with ripped

floral wallpaper along one wall. A boarded-up window allowed only minimal light into the room through small knotholes. The other walls revealed exposed rotting wood in sections where the plaster had fallen off, leaving clumps on the floor. Lifting her head, she could see the discoloration of the ceiling, primarily around the corners, and chunks of it had fallen onto the threadbare carpet.

At last, she focused on the other bed, observing Eliza breathing deeply, her hands bound with rope. When Kate saw her sister was alive, she let out a long sigh of relief.

Focusing back on the older man who was watching her carefully, she asked cautiously, "This is my new home?"

Letting his head drop back, the older man roared with laughter. "Heavens no, this is not your home. I'm afraid this is just a temporary stop before we take you back to France."

Confusion now clouded her features. She had no idea where she was, who this man was, or what Mr. Henley wanted with her. Why would she want to go to France? She knew no one there. "I'm afraid I do not understand."

Mr. Henley threw his hands up in the air in obvious frustration. His palms were bandaged with white cloth. "Phillipe, I told you she was addled."

Furrowing her brow, Kate shot back, "I am not addled, Mr. Henley."

Narrowing his eyes, Henley took a threatening step towards her but was stilled by the older gentleman's hand on his chest. "I will assume your rudeness is a lingering effect of laudanum, but next time I will not be as forgiving," the older man warned her as the warmness in his eyes dimmed.

Apparently, this man is not my ally either, she thought. She nodded her head in understanding, and the warmness in the older man's eyes returned. He carefully lowered himself onto the bed next to her. "What do you know about your father?"

"My father?" Kate repeated, growing more suspicious of the

man's motives. "My father, the Duke of Remington, will pay a ransom for his daughters' safe return if…"

Henley let out a bark of laughter. "She doesn't know. They never told her."

"Shut up, Edgar," Phillipe admonished, effectively silencing him before turning back to her. "The duke is not your father." He ran his hand gently over her cheek. "I am your father."

She stilled at the man's touch. "You, my father?"

Dropping his hand from her cheek, Phillipe's hands encompassed hers. "Your mother was the love of my life," he said, smiling fondly, "and I convinced her to take a chance on a penniless man from France. A few nights before her wedding to that English scoundrel, William, we eloped to Gretna Greens. We were married by a blacksmith, surrounded by witnesses, and had a marriage license to prove it. After we rented a room at the inn, we consummated the marriage, multiple times." He smirked with pride as he admitted that last part.

Suddenly, his face turned expressionless, but his eyes were filled with rage. "Diana's father, the Duke of Windcom, showed up and ripped her out of our warm bed. He demanded she put her clothes back on and forced her into an awaiting carriage. That arrogant duke came into my room and declared that our wedding was invalid," his voice hitched with emotion, "and ripped up the marriage license. After he stormed out of the room, his footmen beat me until I begged for death."

Phillipe lowered his head and a surge of compassion swelled in Kate's heart. "I am sorry for all that you had to endure," she softly acknowledged.

"I had hoped that we conceived a child that ill-fated day, but we were unsuccessful in that attempt," her supposed father continued, looking down at their encompassed hands. "As time went on, your mother's hatred toward William, now the Duke of Remington, grew, and we spent more time together. Eventually, I moved into the abbey for a few blissful years until your mother became pregnant with you."

Kate's eyes grew wide as she listened to this man's story. He was dressed as an English gentleman, but his mannerisms and speech marked him as French. Was he truly her father? None of this made any sense. "If you were my father, then why did you leave me to be raised by another?"

He gave her a tight smile. "I had no choice in the matter. The duke and your mother decided to raise his bastard alongside you, as twins."

Kate's mind whirled. So many things started to fall into place, but she needed to know more. "Why didn't Mother tell me?"

Phillipe placed his hand on her cheek. "To protect your future. You see, you were in a perfect position to spy for the French."

Careful not to show her distress, Kate wanted more clarification. "In what way?"

"After your by-blow sister was sent away, your mother and I arranged for Mrs. Evans to be your governess, to guard you in your youth," Phillipe informed her, puffing up with pride. "And when Michel was selected as the perfect candidate to impersonate Lord Camden, I knew you would be a suitable wife for him. Together, you and Michel should have been instrumental in toppling the English government from within, but he failed his country."

Tears welled in Kate's eyes at her father's admission, now knowing the part he played in her life. "You selected me to marry Michel?"

Oblivious to her pain, Phillipe smiled at her. "I did, and your mother confirmed it would be a good match. With you, the daughter of the Duke of Remington as his wife, no one would doubt the validity of Lord Camden. Besides, you two were good together," he asked, his eyes searching hers, "were you not?"

Tears streamed down her face. "He beat me, causing me to lose the babe I was carrying."

A calloused voice broke into their private conversation, reminding her that Henley was still in the room. "A husband has a right to discipline his wife," he stated flatly.

"Leave us, Edgar, now!" her father shouted without turning around.

As Edgar slammed the door shut to express his disapproval, large sections of plaster on the ceiling dropped to the floor, scattering even more white dust along the carpet.

"Michel should not have beat you to such a degree," Phillipe acknowledged, but his eyes reflected no sympathy. "However, in my experience, women need to be reminded of their place from time to time."

"Oh," was the only thing that Kate could think of saying.

Abruptly standing, her father held his hand out to her. With a wary glance, Kate placed her hand into his and allowed him to help her off the bed. He tucked her hand into the crook of his arm, and she felt the texture of his high-quality garment.

"I would like to show you around," he said, escorting her to the door.

Walking through the door, they entered a narrow, poorly lit hall with multiple doors on each side. Judging by their number and symmetry, she guessed they were in a dilapidated inn. The rickety walls were a testament to the years of neglect this inn must have endured.

Pointing at the doors, Phillipe continued his tour. "All these rooms contain wives, sisters, or loved ones of various lords. These women are being used for blackmail and will ensure we win the vote that will end the war with France."

Glancing at the passing doors, Kate asked in a hushed tone, "Will these women be returned to their families after the vote?"

He shook his head firmly. "No, they are mere casualties of

war." He patted her hand condescendingly. "Do not fret. They are just English."

"I am English," Kate reminded him, giving her father a side glance.

With a misguided twinkle in his eye, he smiled. "You are only half English; as far as I am concerned, you are French."

At the end of the hall, Kate could see a narrow staircase leading down to a large open room. As they approached the stairs, the boisterous noise from below sounded louder. Slowly, they descended the shaky steps, and the room grew silent.

Over a dozen tough-looking ruffians were staring at her, or more accurately, lewdly perusing her body. As her face scanned the crowd, more than one filthy man winked at her, while others made wildly inappropriate gestures.

Abruptly pulling her to a stop at the bottom of the stairs, Phillipe kept her tucked against him. "This is my daughter, Kathryn," he proclaimed, his voice echoing through the room. "Any unseemly behavior towards her will be dealt with swiftly and with no mercy."

Sitting in the middle of the room next to a large round table, was Mr. Henley. He glared at her, unleashed hatred radiating from his whole frame. What have I done to cause him to loathe me so much, she wondered.

A man sitting next to Henley nudged him and made no attempt to keep his voice low. "Your sister is a real looker."

Fearing she misunderstood, she kept her voice quiet as she asked her father, "Is Mr. Henley my brother?"

"Step-brother, actually…" her father confirmed, but his voice faded away in her mind.

A surge of overwhelming panic gripped her, making it difficult to calm her racing heart. As her vision started to blur, darkness seeped into her vision, and she found she had no desire to stop the inevitable. She welcomed the respite from her new prison.

# 23

YANKING OFF HIS OFFENDING CRAVAT, ADRIEN TOSSED IT ONTO the floor. Four days! It had been four days since Kate's abduction, and they were no closer to ascertaining her location than before. Reaching for the missive in his pocket, he reviewed the straight-forward words of Lord Beckett.

*STEARNS AND PETERS FOUND FLOATING IN RIVER THAMES. Henley's whereabouts unknown. Marthe refuses to cooperate. Hanging forthcoming. No leads on the location of abducted women.*

SLIDING THE NOTE BACK INTO HIS POCKET, ADRIEN FELT AN unfamiliar wave of frustration and hopelessness coursing through him. Even under the most extreme circumstances, he had always completed his mission. He was *Hawk*! Now, he was relegated to sitting behind his desk, reviewing documents that had been found at Henley's townhouse and encouraging pompous lords to vote against the bill to withdraw troops.

Lord Beckett continually denied his request to interrogate Marthe at Newgate, citing he was too close to the situation to act rationally. Apparently, the Crown employed agents whose sole task was to interrogate foreign spies in the most effective ways possible. Not only did they want Marthe to reveal the location of the women, but they wanted her to explain what they discovered on the list. Who were *G.M.* and *Rogue* and why was the date 6/15 important?

No! No more waiting! He refused to stand by any longer. He would go to Newgate and break Marthe. Grabbing the cravat off the floor, Adrien started for the door but was stopped when Benedict walked purposefully into his office.

Eyeing the cravat in his hand, Benedict arched an eyebrow. "Where are you going?"

"To Newgate."

"You will be going against Lord Beckett's direct orders," his friend reminded him.

"What in blazes do you expect me to do?" he exclaimed, as he began the arduous process of tying his cravat. "Kate and Eliza's lives are at risk, and I am tired of reviewing Henley's bloody financials."

With his cravat tied, albeit haphazardly, he began to brush by Benedict but stopped at his raised hand. "I was sure that Eliza would be back by now." He lowered his gaze, his eyes pools of deep sadness.

"I thought so, too," Adrien admitted, sadly.

His friend's eyes snapped back to his, determination blazing through them. "I am coming with you."

"And risk Lord Beckett's fury?"

Benedict responded with a low chuckle. "What can he do? Finally accept my resignation?"

"Do you think Larson will let us leave?"

"Larson is currently chasing down a lead on the south bank with a few other agents," Benedict revealed.

Exiting the room, they walked swiftly towards the main hall but stopped when a familiar, disgruntled voice shouted, "Camden!"

With an annoyed eye roll, he turned to face Benedict. "You sent for Jonathon?"

"Camden!" Jonathon's angry voice echoed throughout the entry hall. "Where the blazes are you?"

Placing a hand on Adrien's shoulder, Benedict just nodded. "I did. Both of his sisters have been abducted, remember?"

Sighing in frustration, Adrien turned just as Jonathon caught sight of them. "There you both are," he growled, as Adrien's poor, exasperated butler, Mr. Ward, followed close behind.

Jonathon started to open his mouth, but Mr. Ward interjected, "Lord Jonathon Beckett is here to see you, my lord." With that announcement, his butler turned on his heel and marched away. Adrien was positive he heard him muttering something under his breath about "uncouth lords".

"Jonathon, it is good to see you," Adrien lied as he took in Jonathon's disheveled appearance. His hair was wind-tossed, his white shirt and buckskin breeches were terribly wrinkled, and his face was still red from the crisp morning air. "Did you ride straight through?"

"I did," Jonathon stated with a disapproving curl of his lip. "Have you located my sisters?"

Adrien shifted his gaze and shook his head. "Not yet."

With fury in his eyes, Jonathon closed the distance between them. "Then why are you not out looking for them?"

Before he could respond, Benedict's voice of reason came from behind. "I suggest we have this conversation in private."

With a bob of his head, Adrien preceded them into his study on the main floor. As soon as the door was closed, Jonathon started pacing. It was not long till he stopped and glared irately at Adrien. "Can someone explain to me how Eliza and Kate were abducted right from under your noses?"

Adrien gave a quick sidelong glance at Benedict. It was only natural that Jonathon held them responsible for his sisters' abduction. He was as scared and frustrated as they were and needed someone to blame. As much as he wanted to dismiss Jonathon, he knew that they needed all the help they could get right now. So, he said the one thing he never thought he would say to Jonathon. "We need your help."

Those simple words seemed to calm Jonathon down to a rational level, because his next words were carefully phrased. "Just tell me what the blazes is going on."

Walking over to his drink tray, Adrien poured brandy into three snifters, handing one to Benedict and one to Jonathon. He lowered himself onto a wingback chair and took a sip of his drink. "We found the list in a locket around Kate's neck…" he began.

He laid out everything they had uncovered about the plot to remove troops and defund the war. When he finished, he reached into his pocket and pulled out Lord Beckett's missive. As he handed it to Jonathon, he concluded his explanation with, "That is the latest correspondence we've received from your uncle."

After reading the note, Jonathon lowered the paper and turned to look at Benedict. "What is your assignment in all of this?"

Benedict placed his snifter onto the table and frowned. "To ensure the bill does not pass by remaining in our seats in Parliament."

With a lift of his brow, Jonathon stared at them as if they each had sprouted an extra head. "And?"

Adrien tossed his drink down the back of his throat and slammed his snifter onto the nearby table. "And, nothing! We were relegated to desk duty."

"That is why I sent for you," Benedict spoke up. "I hoped that by the time you arrived we would either be celebrating your sisters' safe return, or we would be in desperate need of your services."

A wince creased Jonathon's brow as he listened to his friend, his eyes betraying his worry. "I was positive that Eliza would have escaped by now." No one wanted to voice the most obvious reason why Eliza might not have escaped, because they all were holding out hope she was still alive.

Benedict attempted a smile, but all he accomplished was the slightest of upturns at the corners of his mouth. "Did you bring your working clothes?"

"I did," Jonathon confirmed.

Adrien groaned in a deep voice. "There has to be another way."

Benedict shot him a look of understanding. "Agents have been scouring the city for days but have found no trace of the missing women. Jonathon has contacts in the rookery that could prove useful."

"Fine, but I refuse to ride in the carriage with you," Adrien stated. "You may use one of my other carriages."

Jonathon huffed, "I smell no worse than people who live in those areas. With those clothes, I can slip in and out, meet with my contacts at will, and avoid detection."

"Adrien and I will go to Newgate to interrogate Marthe, and you," Benedict said, pointing at Jonathon, "will meet with your informants. Someone must have seen something suspicious in the past few weeks."

Jonathon gave them a skeptical look. "If you ask me, I think going to see Marthe is a waste of time. If the agents at Newgate haven't gotten Marthe to break, you will have little chance of success by just talking to her."

"I have a plan," Adrien announced.

Benedict smirked. "A good one?"

"Let's hope so." Addressing Benedict, Adrien asked, "Does Eliza still have a drawing book and watercolors?"

"Yes, she does."

Jonathon snorted before a small grin flashed across his face. "Your plan revolves around ladies' watercolors?"

Adrien shrugged. "I have a hunch."

"Sounds good to me," Benedict agreed without a trace of reservation, arising from his seat. "Let's go."

As Adrien stood, he grimaced. "There is one more thing, Jonathon," he hesitated, reluctant to say his next words. "Kate's father is alive and is most likely behind the abduction."

Jonathon stared at him in disbelief before he roared, "Impossible! Phillipe is dead."

Running a hand through his hair, Adrien explained, "When I met with Henley, he confessed that Kate's father wanted her back, alive."

"For what purpose?" Jonathon asked, his eyes sparking with anger.

"My interrogation was hampered by Henley's thugs breaking down the door," Adrien said in irritation. "I know nothing else."

Closing his eyes, Jonathon put his hand to his face and pinched the bridge of his nose. "We should have told Kate the truth when we had the chance."

"What's done is done," Adrien quoted Shakespeare. "Kate will understand when you explain it to her later."

"I hope you are right," Jonathon said as he dropped his hand.

"I am." Not one to miss an opportunity to rile Jonathon, Adrien started walking towards the door as he revealed, "After all, your sister and I are engaged."

In true Jonathon fashion, he shouted, "Like bloody hell you are!"

AFTER OFFERING BRIBES TO OVER A DOZEN PRISON GUARDS, Adrien and Benedict were told how to locate Marthe's cell in the wing where the condemned were housed at Newgate. The thick walls in the passageway leading towards the cells allowed no natural light to enter. The only thing lighting their way was the small torch given to them by the guards.

Easily locating her dark, damp cell, Adrien stood outside of the rusted, deteriorating bars. He could barely see Marthe sitting on the cot, her shoulders slumped in defeat. A small, barred window cast a very dim sliver of light onto the floor.

He placed the torch into a wall sconce. "Marthe," Adrien called softly, just loud enough to get her attention.

With brown hair trailing down the sides of her face, Marthe did not move, preferring to stare at the filthy, straw-covered floor.

He directed his next question to Benedict. "Do you have enough light to create a proper sketch?"

"I have sketched in worse conditions," Benedict replied flamboyantly as he took the chalk and watercolors from his bag. "Besides, I have an excellent memory." He leaned up against the wall opposite the cell and pulled out a sketch pad.

Marthe's head tilted as she listened to their conversation, but she did not say anything. "I want it to be a perfect likeness of her," Adrien continued to explain.

"Why?" a raspy voice came from the cell. "Why are you drawing me?"

Turning his attention back to her, Adrien rested his hands between the cell bars. "As a precaution."

"For what?" The raspy voice became more strained, as though she hadn't used it lately.

"Agents have been scouring the city, but we have not located the missing women," Adrien explained. "In a few days, the vote will be over, and the women will be killed when they are no longer useful." Marthe's shadowed face revealed nothing as she shifted her body slightly towards him, so he continued, "If Kate…"

"Or Eliza," Benedict interjected.

"If Kate or Eliza are killed, then I will seek revenge," Adrien paused, waiting till she looked up at him, "on you."

Marthe's bruised face scrunched in confusion, causing her to hiss in pain. "I am to be hanged by the end of the week," she said, her voice regaining some strength.

Adrien nodded in response. "Your people have taken everything from me. French operatives killed my family, leaving them buried on the side of the road. Michel emptied the coffers of my estates, abused my serving women, and sullied my family's name."

Taking a moment to reign in his emotions, he swallowed slowly. "Now the French have taken the only thing I have left. If Kate is lost to me, then I have nothing to live for."

Marthe slowly rose, her body showing signs of abuse and torture. Hunching over, she crossed the distance in the tiny cell to stand near the bars. Purple discoloration marred her once beautiful face, and small, infected gashes trailed down both sides of her arms. "If it helps, Kate will not be killed," she revealed, resting against the damp wall.

"Is it because Kate's father has her?" Adrien inquired.

She shivered. "It is."

Shrugging out of his coat, he offered it to Marthe through the bars. She hesitated, then reached for it, and he found he was pleased to see her accept it. After she put it on, she crossed her arms in front of her as if attempting to conserve her new-found warmth.

"If Kate is lost to me then I am left with nothing," Adrien repeated, locking eyes with her. "And a spy with no reason to live is a dangerous force to be reckoned with."

"You are an English lord, for now," she added critically. "You have plenty to live for."

Leaning more on the bars, Adrien glanced over at Benedict who was adding color to his sketch. "With this sketch, I will go to Corsia, and I will track down every person; friend, family, or foe, that recognizes this likeness of you," he paused to emphasize his point, "and I will kill them."

Surprise flashed across Marthe's battered face. "I am not from Corsia," she denied weakly.

With a tsking noise, Adrien shook his head. "You have the same accent that Napoleon uses when he becomes angry." Turning his head to look at Benedict, he explained, "Napoleon was born in Corsia, but he perfected his Parisian and *langues d'oil* during his time in military school. However, whenever Napoleon uses his sharp tongue on his military advisors, his Corsian accent manifests itself."

Turning back to face Marthe, he lifted his brow to make his point. "It is a very distinct accent because it is a blend of Italian and French."

With her arms wrapped tightly around her, Marthe's eyes flashed in defiance. "Corsia is ruled by clans. You would never be able to infiltrate them without being killed first."

"You underestimate me," Adrien asserted, his voice taking on a hard edge. "For over seven years, I lived solely in France and completed various undercover assignments on French soil. Each mission required me to create a new identity, and I became a different person. For years, I sent sensitive French military documents back to England, right under Admiral Garnier's nose."

His eyes were drawn to the sides of Marthe's face and noticed portions of her ears had been sliced off. "Corsia would be a holiday compared to what I have had to endure."

"You would give up your life of leisure for unnecessary bloodshed?" Marthe asked, sounding skeptical.

"Yes!" Adrien shouted, his voice echoing off the thick walls. "If I have nothing to live for, I will have ample time to exact my revenge. I will take on a new persona, and I will bribe, plot, and kill anyone that crosses me until I find your loved ones." He watched the fear trickle through her eyes, knowing she was finally starting to believe his words. "I will kill every man, woman, and child who recognizes your likeness, and I will do it in your name. I will not rest till my revenge is complete."

"Please don't." Marthe's voice trembled. "They are innocent in all of this."

"So is Kate," he exclaimed, slamming his hand against the bars. Marthe jumped in surprise. "It is simple. Do you fear Henley or *Hawk* more?"

Marthe's eyes became filled with despair and grim acceptance. "Father has her," she said so softly that he almost didn't hear it.

Adrien opened his mouth but quickly closed it. Was that a slip of her tongue, or did she just make a mistake? "Father? Are you Kate's sister?"

Swiping a tear away, Marthe nodded. "Yes. Father has plotted his revenge for years. All he has ever cared about was getting Kate back to him, and making England pay for their sins," she stated bitterly.

"What has he plotted?" Adrien pressed.

"The day of reckoning."

"What is the day of reckoning?"

Marthe shook her head weakly. "I do not know. I was not privy to that information."

Adrien lifted his brow in disbelief. "You are lying to me."

"No, I was kept from the truth because I am a woman," she admonished with conviction. "My only role was to seduce Lord Lexington and position Edgar into the House of Commons. After Michel was killed, I was tasked with keeping my liaison with Lexington and making him turn."

"And did he turn?"

"No," she said. "He is loyal to England."

"You have ruined Lexington," Adrien informed her. "Did you care for him at all?"

She shrugged her shoulders. "He never beat me."

"I believe your standards are too low, Marthe," he responded. He was starting to get a sense of what this lady had endured.

Grabbing the bars near his hands, Marthe's defeated eyes peered up at him. "My own father and brother used my body to advance the agenda of France, and I was forced to go along with it." Closing her eyes, she added, "I am so tired. I just want this torment to be over."

Tilting his head, Adrien's instinct told him that she was not playing a role anymore. She was broken, defeated. "Tell me where Kate and the other women are," he urged.

"The Squeaky Wench," she confessed. "It is an inn Edgar bought with the money given to me by Lexington."

"Where is The Squeaky Wench?"

"It is on the south bank of the River Thames, accessible only by ferryman." Her hands dropped from the bars.

"Is your father's name Phillipe?"

"Yes, Phillipe Durant."

"P.D. was not on the list," Adrien said, anxious to learn the truth. "Where can I find *G.M.* or *Rogue*?"

Marthe tightened her lips into a thin white line as she brushed her hair off her face. "I do not know where *Rogue* is, but my father is using the assumed name Gasper Maminot."

"Why did Michel create the list and put it into the locket?" Adrien asked.

"Michel was responsible for receiving directives from *Rogue,* and then passing along the information to my father," she confessed. "When Michel died, the only way to prove to *Rogue* that Edgar was who he claimed to be was to produce the locket."

"Why is June 15th important?"

"June 15th is the day of reckoning," she revealed, as her bruised face became expressionless again. "I told you what you wanted to know. Do I have your word that you will not harm my loved ones?"

"Yes, you have my word," Adrien answered honestly.

Marthe's arms hugged her body dejectedly. "The word of a spy is typically worthless."

"We have finally come to a consensus," Adrien spoke with a half-hearted smile. "If I find that you lied to me, then…"

"I know," Marthe said with unshed tears in her eyes, "but I kept my end of the bargain."

As much as he wanted to turn around and run for the exit, Adrien felt pity for Marthe. He straightened and removed his hands from the bars. "If you make a full confession, Lord Beckett might be willing to spare your life."

"No," she protested, shaking her head. "I betrayed my father and brother, either way I am a dead woman." Her eyes closed, defeated, and her message was clear; she wanted to die.

Feeling a sudden surge of compassion towards the French spy, he gave her a polite bow. "Then this is goodbye."

When she attempted to remove his coat, Adrien put his hand up to stop her. "Keep it. You need it more than I do."

Relaxing her shoulders, a genuine smile touched her lips. "Thank you."

With an acknowledging nod and knowing there was nothing more to say, Adrien turned to walk down the dark and dreary passageway to exit this hell called Newgate.

After leaving the prison behind, Adrien turned to Benedict. "Can I see what you sketched?"

"I would be honored." Benedict smiled broadly as he opened the drawing pad. Flipping through the pages, Adrien saw it was filled with unrecognizable shapes and splotches of color, appearing to have no rhyme or reason.

"I am glad she did not call our bluff," Adrien huffed, clearly unimpressed with his friend's artistic skills.

"I agree," Benedict said as he placed the drawing pad and watercolors back into his bag.

Adrien mounted his horse and noticed that Benedict was watching him carefully. "Everything all right?"

Faint worry lines creased Benedict's forehead, and his voice was tight as he asked, "Would you really have slaughtered hundreds of people if Marthe didn't reveal Kate's location?"

He turned his head to avoid seeing the disappointment in his friend's eyes as he answered truthfully, "I wish I could tell you no."

After a few moments, Benedict mounted his horse and came alongside of him. "Then I hope for Marthe's sake that she did not lie to you, so you can avoid traveling all the way to Corsia," he stated with no censure in his voice. "After all, I look forward to having you as Jonathon's brother-in-law. It will make family dinners that much more exciting."

Relieved that Benedict hadn't pressed the issue, Adrien laughed and followed closely behind as they navigated the streets of London.

# 24

KATE TRIED TO OPEN HER EYES, BUT HER EYELIDS WERE HEAVY, as though they were weighted down. She blinked, finally managing to wrench them open. Her body ached in protest as she shifted her position on the straw pallet, instantly reminding her that she was not resting on her plush featherbed at home.

"Kate, wake up." Eliza's hushed but urgent tone came from across the room.

Turning her head towards the offending noise, Kate looked over at her sister. Slowly at first, the events of the past few days flooded her mind, and she shot into a sitting position. Her stomach churned at her impulsive move, and she longed to return to her dreamless rest.

"It is the effects of the laudanum," Eliza said. "Wait a moment, and the nausea will pass."

Nodding her understanding, Kate brought her knees up close to her chest and rested her chin on them. After taking a few deep breaths, the nausea eased, and she lifted her head to look at her sister. Eliza's hands were now tied to the metal frame behind her head, as she laid on a lumpy straw pallet, which looked just as uncomfortable as hers.

Frowning at her sister's awkward position, Kate inquired, "When were you tied to the bed frame?"

A quick, unrepentant smile formed on Eliza's lips. "After I tossed my dinner back in Henley's face."

"Why did you throw your dinner at him?" She was curious, because they were only given a weird-tasting cup of slop once a day. It wasn't much, but at least it provided some sustenance.

"I realized that the food is spiked with laudanum."

"Good enough for me," Kate replied, returning her sister's smile briefly. Then the reality of their situation came crashing down on her. "What are we going to do?"

Eliza shifted so she was tilted to her left side. "Would you be so kind as to retrieve my dagger?"

With her eyes flashing towards the door, Kate quickly crossed the room in a few strides, and sat down on her sister's bed. "What if someone comes in?"

"Our food is laced with laudanum, and I venture no one will come back till dinner time," Eliza rationalized. "I plan to escape before then."

Kate could not stop her eyebrow from lifting in amazement. "How do you propose to accomplish that?"

Her sister blew a stray piece of auburn hair out of her face before admitting, "I have no idea."

Reaching up Eliza's right thigh, she removed the jeweled dagger strapped there and started cutting the rope binding her sister's hands. Once the rope was worn, Eliza jerked her hands and broke from her restraints.

As Eliza started rubbing her reddened wrists, Kate took in her sister's haggard appearance, which was in stark contrast to the way she usually looked. Her auburn hair had fallen out of her chignon, and the dark circles under her eyes made her look exhausted.

Kate attempted to run her fingers through her own blonde hair, but she dropped her hands in defeat, feeling deflated by her failed efforts. It reminded her of their precarious situation. "I am sorry. This is all my fault," Kate stated.

"No, no, no..." Eliza repeated, sitting up on the bed. "This is not your fault."

Turning her attention towards the deteriorating wall, Kate's eyes welled with tears. "If I had not run away from your townhouse, then Roger would not be dead, and we would not be locked up in this forsaken inn." With tears running down her cheeks, she faced her sister. "I killed Roger."

Eliza pulled her into a tight embrace. "You did no such thing," her sister reassured her. "Henley killed Roger, not you."

"But it was my actions that led to his death, and our abduction." Kate stifled her sobs. "If I had just acted rationally, then we would not be in this mess."

"You must not blame yourself for Roger's death," Eliza said in a gentle, but firm voice. "You had no control of that situation. Now as for the abduction..." Her voice trailed off in amusement. "I have been in worse situations."

Leaning back from her sister's embrace, Kate was amazed at Eliza's reaction. "Have you?"

"Truthfully, this is my first abduction," Eliza revealed, smiling. "It is a new adventure for me. Lucky for us, Henley is not very clever."

"No, he is not." Kate's eyes lowered to the floor. "He is just evil."

"What is it?" Eliza asked. "Did Mr. Henley hurt you again?"

Hesitantly, she raised her eyes till she met her sister's concerned gaze. "Henley may be my brother," Kate informed her.

Eliza's eyes narrowed. "Can you repeat that?"

Wringing her hands tighter, Kate frowned. "Earlier, I woke up to a man hovering over me, and he claimed he was married to Mother, supposedly before she married father. He even claimed that we are not twins."

"What was this man's name?" Eliza asked, her voice calculating.

"Phillipe," Kate replied, confused by her sister's tone.

Eliza's eyes grew wide, and her face became unreadable. "Tell me everything," she insisted.

Tilting her head, Kate could not shake the feeling that Eliza did not seem as surprised as she should have been but recalled the conversation as best she could. When she was finished, Eliza jumped up from the bed and walked to the boarded-up window.

Pulling back the ripped section of the floral wallpaper around the window, Eliza attempted to pry off the boards, but after a few grunts, she stepped back, sighing. "It has been nailed shut, but I think I can pry out the rusted nails with my dagger." Reaching down to her undergarments, she ripped off a section and wrapped it around her right hand. "Can you keep watch?"

"Wait," Kate protested as Eliza reached for her dagger on the bed. "You don't have anything to say about the fact that a French man is claiming to be my father?"

In response, Eliza said the one thing that caught her completely by surprise. "Phillipe Durant was supposed to be dead."

The air stalled in Kate's lungs, and she lowered herself slowly onto the straw pallet. She had naively been holding out hope that Phillipe was mad, and there was no truth behind his words. "How long have you known?" she asked, when her voice was finally steady enough to emit sound.

Crouching down in front of her, Eliza's posture was strong and self-assured, but her eyes held a hint of uncertainty. "I have known for almost six weeks now, but we debated when we should tell you. We discovered the truth when we questioned Mother about Michel's involvement, and you were still at Beaumont Castle."

"We?" Her voice croaked. "Who else knows?"

"Jonathon, Uncle Charles, Benedict, Adrien, Mr. Larson, and Father," she listed.

Closing her eyes, Kate willed herself to disappear. Every good thing about her was a lie. She was the imposter. The duke was not her father, Eliza was not her twin sister, and she was the daughter of a French spy.

"Kate," Eliza ventured, her words cautious, "you must understand, this changes nothing."

"This changes everything," Kate stated, a little too vehemently.

"No, you will always be my sister." Eliza's eyes held compassion. "Father was adamant that you not be told the truth because he was worried you might question his love for you."

"Everything I have ever known has been a lie," Kate cried. "How can I even trust you?" As soon as the words were spoken, she wished she could take them back. Opening her mouth to apologize, Eliza put up a hand to stop her.

"I am truly sorry for hurting you, but when exactly would have been an appropriate time to inform you that you had a French father?" Eliza arched an eyebrow, challenging her to deny the truth. "You have had so much suffering these past few months that we wanted to spare you the pain of learning the truth about your father."

Crossing her arms over her chest, Kate was through being coddled by her loved ones. "I am tired of all the secrets in our family," she said, struggling to control her growing frustration. "I deserve a chance to know the truth, good or bad, about my own life."

Eliza conceded with a decisive head bob. "Fair enough. We will have a frank conversation when we get home, but I need you to trust me until then."

"I do trust you," Kate stated, feeling guilty. "That was unfair of me to say."

Eliza waved off her comment. "Considering the circumstances, I would have said the same thing." She came and sat next to her on the bed. "Tell me about Phillipe."

"Phillipe is a lot like Michel. He is charming and polished on the outside, but his eyes exude cruelty," Kate described, shuddering.

"I wonder why Diana was led to believe Phillipe was dead," Eliza questioned.

"Maybe she was misinformed?"

"No, Diana clearly believed Phillipe had died in war."

"Phillipe plans to take me back to France," Kate divulged, attempting to contain the gnawing fear that her father might succeed.

Eliza frowned hesitantly. "Do you want to go to France?"

With a huff, Kate pushed off the bed. "No, I do not want to go to France and live with Henley as my brother. How can you even ask that question?"

"Good," Eliza said, sounding relieved. "Then, we will need to escape before Henley, or anyone else, comes back into this room."

Trying not to be cynical, Kate asked, "And how do you propose we do that? Even if we can open that window and fit our bodies through, how do we survive jumping from a second story window?"

Turning her gaze towards the boarded window, Eliza started tapping her finger over her lips. "If I know our men, they are searching tirelessly for us. It is only a matter of time before they find us."

"I have no confidence that Adrien is looking for me," Kate expressed softly. "Why would he?"

Confusion lined her sister's features. "Why would you say such a thing?"

"The last time I saw Adrien, I said some cruel, hurtful things to him."

Eliza walked over to the boarded-up window. "Every couple fights," she responded flippantly over her shoulder.

Surprised by her casual remark, Kate gave her a look of disbelief. "I even had Roger escort him out of my room."

Turning back towards her, Eliza's eyes held a twinkle of humor. "Now that plan has merit. Whenever I get frustrated with Benedict, I should ask Mr. Larson to escort him out of my presence."

Kate threw her hands up in exasperation. "Do be serious, Eliza."

Focusing on the window, Eliza placed her dagger under a rusted nail and tried to remove it. "I am serious, Kate," she said, not sparing her a glance. "Adrien loves you, and he will come for you." After yanking out one nail from the board, Eliza glanced at her. "The question is, do you want him to?"

"I do," she answered wholeheartedly, "but he won't want me when he learns the truth about my father." She joined her sister at the boarded-up window and attempted to pry out a nail with her fingers. After a few unsuccessful minutes, she placed her sore fingers in her mouth.

Successfully removing another nail, Eliza began working on the next. "And what is that?"

"My father, Phillipe, helped orchestrate the plot to swap French spies for English lords," Kate shared, reaching down to rip a section of her undergarments as she saw Eliza do.

"And?" Eliza prompted, with a small grunt as she extracted another nail.

"Ultimately, my father was responsible for killing Adrien's family," Kate stated, laying it out plainly. "Besides, I'm half French and Adrien hates the French."

With an exaggerated eye roll, Eliza faced her sister. "And I could give you a hundred reasons why Adrien loves you. Sometimes, falling in love with someone doesn't make sense, but if you are lucky enough to find it," Eliza clutched her dagger tightly, "hold on to it and refuse to let go."

Before Kate could respond, the sound of heavy, booted footsteps walking down the hall reached their ears. For a terrifying moment, true fear resonated in her mind as she thought of the torture Eliza would endure if she was discovered without her restraints.

Henley or her father would have no qualms about trying to beat Eliza into submission, but her sister would never yield to them; she would die first. No, she needed to protect Eliza. It was her turn to save her sister.

Formulating an impulsive plan in her head, Kate turned towards Eliza. "I will distract whoever is coming, and you keep trying to take down that board."

Eliza shook her head firmly. "No, Kate, I won't let you do this."

Filled with determination, she straightened her shoulders and met Eliza's gaze with her own fervent expression. "You asked me to trust you, and I am now asking *you* to trust me. I am the only one that can leave this room by way of the hall. If you are discovered, then we are both dead." The thuds of the booted footsteps were coming closer, and she knew she had little time left. "Climb out the window and go get help."

Without giving Eliza time to object, she strode over to the door and turned the handle slowly. Just as she suspected, it was not locked. With a quick glance over her shoulder at her sister, she smiled and quickly slipped out the door.

Once the door was closed behind her, she came face to face with her brother, and judging by the scowl on his face, he was not pleased to see her.

Attempting to soften her brother's ire, Kate gave him a tentative smile. "Mr. Henley," she said as she pressed her back against the closed door to create a larger gap between them.

He stopped a few feet away, his dark eyes boring into hers. "You may as well call me Edgar, since we are family."

"I would like that very much," she lied through gritted teeth.

"Father sent me to escort you downstairs." His eyes appeared suspicious as he shifted his gaze towards the closed door. "I did not expect you to be awake."

Hearing the distrust oozing from her brother's voice, Kate was afraid he would try to open the door and check the room. If he did, then either Edgar would kill Eliza, or Eliza would kill him. Either way, it would be disastrous.

Kate needed to distract him, but how? She could play the role of a battered wife but being submissive right now would not serve her objective. Suddenly, the thought of Adrien offering her the dinner roll sprang to her mind, and she knew what she needed to do.

Tilting her chin in the air, she summoned all her aristocratic training, and returned Henley's hostile gaze. "In what way have I offended you, that you should loathe me so?" Her tone of superiority was a perfect likeness of her mother's.

Her directness must have surprised him, but it wore off in only a few moments. Taking a step closer to her, he seethed, "Your whole existence offends me."

Bristling at his insolent remark, Kate's gaze did not waver from his. "Would you care to expand on that?"

With a huff, he shifted his eyes over her shoulder. "I was first in my class in military school. I even served under the King of Naples, Joachim Murat, as he led the charge of the French army into Madrid." For the briefest of moments, his eyes softened, but then hardened again as he looked back at her. "But it was never good enough for my father."

"Any father would be proud of…"

"No!" he shouted. "I was never good enough because of *you*."

Stilling at his words, she hesitated. What could she say? Until recently, she didn't even know Edgar was her brother.

Henley continued, "Father always talked about you. He always wanted to share stories about his precious English daughter. Whenever a new letter came from the *duchess*," he spat it out, as if the word was bitter in his mouth, "Father would adjourn to his office for hours to feast upon her words." His next sentence was muffled under his breath. "He broke my mother's heart."

Feeling as though she should apologize, Kate ventured, "I am sorry. I did…" Henley's narrowed eyes shot her a warning, and she closed her mouth.

"My mother asked for her husband on her death bed, but my father was too busy plotting his revenge against your horrible, puny isle," he snarled.

"That is terrible," she admitted softly, knowing what it was like to want to be loved by your spouse, but falling short.

"You are not worthy of Father's love, yet he freely gives it to you." Edgar scoffed, "A titled, pompous English lady."

Used to being insulted by her late husband, Henley's cruel words were easy to ignore. "You cannot blame me for his cruel actions."

"I do blame you," he answered swiftly, "and your duchess mother."

"My mother is dead," Kate said, hoping the relief was not too evident in her voice.

"I am aware of your mother's sudden death," Edgar drawled. "Michel asked her to spy on the duke and pass along crucial information. Unfortunately, your mother was not up to the task and she was killed."

Kate looked perplexed as she asked, "Why did my mother believe your father was dead?"

"*Our* father did die on the battlefield," Henley informed her. "He assumed another identity when he arrived in England, severing all ties with past acquaintances and loved ones."

"Why did he not sever ties with you?"

"Napoleon felt I was well suited to play an English gentleman and assigned me to the mission," he admitted smugly. "If not for that, my father would have been lost to me, too."

Feeling a slight twinge of compassion for Edgar, she gave him a sad smile. "I am sorry for what you have gone through."

Kate was close enough to see Henley clench his jaw so tightly that a small muscle below his ear started pulsing. Apparently, her sympathy made him even more upset. "I don't need, or want your pity," he replied dryly. "You will soon learn your place, as did Marthe."

"Marthe?" she asked hesitantly. Were they speaking of the same Marthe? The one who seduced Adrien in Hyde Park?

With a set jaw, he revealed, "Marthe is my sister."

"Is she here?"

"No, but she will join us shortly."

Kate attempted to smile. "I look forward to meeting her."

"You English are all the same," he said in a repulsed tone. "You lie and cheat your way in the world. As soon as Napoleon conquers Britain, there will be a day of reckoning, and all your loved ones will be killed."

Tilting her head, she was beginning to understand what fed Henley's hatred of her. Not only was she the beloved lost daughter in his mind, but she was an English noble, albeit an imposter. As much as she wanted to argue with Edgar's misguided logic, she needed him to believe she was shifting her alliance towards her new family.

Taking a moment to pretend to smooth out her horribly wrinkled traveling dress, Kate kept her gaze lowered until she could control the turmoil growing inside of her. Pushing her anger deep down, she assumed the role she had used successfully in her dealings with her mother and later, Michel.

Lifting her gaze back to meet Edgar's, she gave him a hesitant smile. "I would like for us to start over and make amends."

"What makes you think I want to make amends with you?" he asked, arching a disbelieving eyebrow.

She did not dim her smile at his less than encouraging words. "We will soon travel back to France and be a family. It would be nice if we could live in harmony and set our differences aside."

Placing his blood-stained, bandaged palm on the wall behind her, Henley leaned in until she could feel his warm breath on her face. "We will never be a family," he growled with such ferocity that it caused her to jump in alarm. "Father will not let me kill you, but I look forward to making your life a living hell." His face was stone cold, and she suspected his heart was, as well. "There are many ways to torture someone without beating them," he said as his menacing eyes roamed her face, "and you will discover them all."

Daring herself not to whimper in fright, she held his gaze, praying fear was not evident in her expression.

Edgar pushed his hand off the wall and offered her his arm. "Shall we?" he demanded more than asked.

Placing her hand on Edgar's arm, she allowed him to escort her down to the lower hall. Her plan had worked, and she had succeeded in buying Eliza more time. Now she just had to stay alive until help arrived. If help arrived.

# 25

"THIS WAY, SIR," A DIRTY LITTLE STREET URCHIN SAID OVER HIS shoulder. His bare feet were covered in layers of filth as he ran up the side of a muddy road, skillfully skirting piles of horse dung.

Trailing close behind, Adrien and Benedict followed the boy, despite him running in and out of alleyways, jumping over broken fences, and now ducking between men and women as they trudged back to their homes for some well-deserved respite from the day's monotonous work. The sunken-in, pale faces barely acknowledged the little boy at their feet, but their eyes flashed with annoyance as the two men pushed their way through the crowd.

The sun had begun to set behind the blackened buildings, casting shadows across parts of the street. Fortunately, there was enough light to avoid stepping in the ditches, some of which housed foul-smelling liquid coated with slime.

The boy's steps slowed as he put his hand out to indicate they should stop. "It's that one, it is," he stated with pride, pointing at a darkened two-story brown building with boarded up windows.

A decomposing wood sign reading, The Squeaky Wench, leaned up against the side of the building.

With an inward groan, Adrien's eyes scanned the darkened building for any sign of occupancy but found none. "It looks abandoned," he mumbled to Benedict as anger constricted his chest. He was going to kill Marthe himself for betraying him.

The boy shook his head adamantly. "It's not. I told ye before, I saw myself men going in and out of there."

Reaching into his pocket, Benedict pulled out two shillings and placed them in the boy's outstretched hand. "You have done well, lad."

The boy's eyes lit up at the windfall he'd just received. "Thank you!" He clutched the money in his hand and disappeared into the shadows.

Their eyes strayed back to the building, noting the boarded-up windows that ensured no light escaped, thus making it appear abandoned.

"How do you propose we rescue our damsels in distress?" Adrien asked, tilting his head towards The Squeaky Wench.

Benedict's alert eyes perused the street. "I propose getting off the street in case anyone is watching for us."

As they passed by an alley, a hand reached out and grabbed Adrien's right forearm, yanking him into the dark narrow passage. Instinct kicked in, propelling him into action as he slammed his right elbow into the attacker's stomach, freeing his arm. His left hand reached for his pistol as he shoved his upper arm into the man's throat, throwing him against the wall.

As he cocked the pistol against his attacker's temple, he heard a familiar voice gasp, "Good gracious, Adrien. What in bloody hell is wrong with you?"

Taking a moment to truly look at his attacker, he finally recognized Jonathon's shadowed face. Lowering his pistol and arm, he stepped back. "Don't you know better than to sneak up on people?" he muttered under his breath as he tucked his pistol back into his trousers.

With a huff, Jonathon glanced over at Benedict. "How have you survived Adrien's company for so long?"

Benedict smiled, amused. "I find his presence mostly tolerable."

Adrien glanced at Benedict and saw Mr. Larson standing next to him. Two tall men were standing behind Mr. Larson, with pistols in their hands, continuously scanning the narrow alley.

"How did you locate this place?" Adrien asked, referring to The Squeaky Wench.

"We were searching the south side and were told about rich blokes going in and out of an abandoned inn," Mr. Larson explained, pointing to the two men behind him. "We came over to check it out and ran into Jonathon."

"I, on the other hand," Jonathon said, running a hand through his hair, "paid a small fortune to my informants so they'd give up this building." Dropping his hand, he continued, "Word on the street is there are dangerous men sequestered in The Squeaky Wench, and they will kill anyone who reveals their location."

"We have the element of surprise in our favor. We could storm through the main door," Adrien proposed.

With a shake of his head, Jonathon surmised, "That would not work. The main door is made of solid wood and is guarded. I witnessed a man knocking to gain entry, and some type of code word was exchanged."

"We took out two guards that were scouting the alleyway behind the inn before we ran into Jonathon," Mr. Larson explained. "The place is a fortified stronghold."

Before Adrien could suggest any other course of action, a woman's voice interrupted their conversation. "If you are finished with your woolgathering, I know how you can gain access."

All heads turned to see a disheveled Eliza standing near them with hands on her hips. Without saying a word, Benedict rushed past him and embraced his wife. Drawing back to stare at her face, a smile formed on his lips. "Wife, you are never to leave my side again."

Eliza's mouth opened to protest, but Benedict pressed his lips to hers, rendering her speechless. Adrien shifted his gaze towards the ground to provide them with privacy during their reunion. After a few moments, he started to get impatient and wanted to know where Kate was. Clearing his throat, he asked, "Is Kate with you?"

"No," Eliza replied sadly, shifting in Benedict's arms. "She helped me escape from my ropes, and we were trying to remove the boards from the window when Mr. Henley came to collect her."

Adrien balled his hands into tight fists. "Why would Henley need to collect Kate?"

"Let me start from the beginning," Eliza said with a tight smile. She began with how their food was laced with laudanum, rendering them unconscious for days. She revealed how Kate discovered her new family and ended with the conversation she had overheard between Henley and Kate in the hall.

Placing his hands over his face, Adrien was sickened with the knowledge that Henley was even near Kate again. How were they going to get to her? If they stormed the building, they would be killed, and Kate would be living in France with her newfound family, evidently a family of monsters.

"I know how we can rescue the other women imprisoned." Eliza's voice penetrated his thoughts.

Selfishly, he did not care one whit about rescuing the other women. He just wanted Kate! This is why agents sever ties with their loved ones, because they affect your rational thoughts, he reminded himself. As an agent, his main concern should be to bring in the French spies and save as many abducted women as possible. However, he only cared about saving Kate!

Dropping his hands, Adrien faced Eliza, indecisiveness playing on his face. Eliza slipped out of Benedict's arms to come closer to him. "Kate is clever and stronger than we give her credit for," she told him, her eyes flickering with emotion. "She sacrificed herself to ensure my freedom."

Choking back his emotions, Adrien attempted to speak, "I love…"

"You can tell Kate that when we rescue her," Eliza interrupted firmly. "Because we *will* save her."

"I agree with Eliza. We won't leave Kate behind," Benedict asserted, walking up and wrapping his arm around his wife's waist.

Jonathon scoffed. "We will save her, but she won't be marrying you," he said, pointing his finger at Adrien. "My sister will not be coerced into marriage."

Mr. Larson came up behind Jonathon and whispered something into his ear. Adrien watched as Jonathon's eyes grew wide, then bored into his. A weaker man might have cowered under Jonathon's angry gaze, but he was not weak.

"I have just been informed that you have been courting my sister, and that she agreed to your courtship… willingly," Jonathon stated, his voice laced with incredulous accusation. "Blazes, I have only been gone for six weeks."

"Jonathon, we do not have time for this," Eliza interjected, her tone reasonable. "I left the window open, and because of Kate's quick thinking, the door in the room was left unlocked. We can sneak back in and help the women escape the way I did."

Benedict placed his hands onto Eliza's shoulders, his eyes roaming her face. "Why don't you go back to the carriage and rest? We will take care of rescuing Kate and the other women."

"And let you have all the fun without me?" Eliza asked with an arched eyebrow.

Benedict leaned closer and lowered his voice. "You are with child now."

Eliza's face softened. "I understand your concern, but I am going with you to rescue Kate."

Frowning, Benedict said, "If that is the case, then I am not leaving your side."

Smiling lovingly at him, Eliza nodded her approval. "The women haven't had their dinner yet, so they might be awake enough to help with their escape. Just in case, we may need to carry them out, and I don't know how many women are being held." With her brow lifted, she asked Mr. Larson, "You in?"

"It sounds like a fun adventure," Mr. Larson replied, gifting Eliza with a rare smile. Reaching down, he picked up Eliza's longbow resting against the wall. "I anticipated you would need this when we finally tracked you down."

With a wide, bright smile, Eliza accepted the longbow and quiver filled with arrows from Larson before she threw her arms around her protector. "Thank you," she said softly.

"I do not want to be a nay-sayer, but how are we supposed to distract all those guards down in the main hall as we help the women escape?" Jonathon asked, his eyes calculating. "We need a diversion."

As Adrien watched England's top spies mulling over ideas for a diversion, he knew they needed one that would sidetrack French spies and a room full of killers. Suddenly, the perfect ruse came to his mind. "I have an idea." His voice did not waver, even though he knew he might very well be marching in to his own death.

SITTING QUIETLY IN THE CORNER OF THE MAIN HALL, KATE KEPT her hands in her lap as her eyes fanned the length of the rectangular-shaped room. Clusters of men sat around tables playing cards, seemingly oblivious to the disarray around them. Lighted sconces along the walls provided adequate lighting to show a mixture of dirty bowls and plates placed on empty chairs or on the floor, ensuring the large black rats that scurried about had enough to fill their bellies.

Shuddering at the sight of the four-legged creatures, Kate knew she needed to keep her wits about her and focus on trying to find a means of escape. She counted twelve men around the tables, and one lone man guarding the entry door. These men were a despicable lot. Their clothing was filthy and battered, their hair lice-ridden, and the smell permeating off their persons filled the room with a repugnant odor.

"Kathryn, you should eat," her father urged, suddenly appearing by her side. He placed a tin cup in front of her.

Glancing at the offered fare, Kate tried not to gag at the foul stench emanating from the thin, green fishy slop. "What is it?" she asked hesitantly.

"Soup," her father informed her, frowning. "It is sold near the docks."

Leaning back from the soup to avoid the offensive smell, she turned to her father. "What is in it?"

Picking up the tin cup, he brought it to his nose and inhaled. "My guess would be boiled fish guts, parsley root, and possibly watered-down ale," he listed, returning the cup to its original position.

"It tastes like mud," Henley confessed as he pulled up a seat across from her and sat down with a tin cup in his hand. "I would use some caution when eating the soup, because the fish aren't boned."

Even as her stomach rumbled in protest, she pushed the cup away from her. "Is there no other option?" she asked hopefully.

Looking sympathetic, her father shook his head. "I'm afraid not."

"What's the matter?" Her brother smirked, obviously amused at her discomfort. "You don't like fish?"

Placing his top hat on the table, her father pulled out a chair, turning it slightly so he could face her. He was handsomely dressed, looking out of place in a room full of ruffians. Noticing his lack of food, she asked, "Aren't you eating?"

Leaning back, he crossed his legs. "I do not eat that sludge."

"No, he eats at the palace." Edgar grimaced before taking a sip of the soup.

Attempting to keep the disbelief out of her voice, she questioned, "The palace?"

"It is true." Her father frowned, his eyes flickering to Edgar. "I am the head chef at the palace."

Kate had so many questions formulating in her mind, but she couldn't find the words to articulate any of them without sounding skeptical. Prinny had a reputation for being eccentric, but would his staff be foolish enough to hire a French chef while England was currently at war with their country? She wanted to ask questions, but in such a fashion that would hopefully demonstrate that her loyalties had shifted to her new French family.

Still desperately clinging to hope that Adrien would come for her, Kate wanted him to be proud of her. If she collected more details about the French's conspiracy, then maybe he would overlook her harsh treatment of him the last time they spoke.

Flattery flashed through her mind. Of course! Men always responded to flattery. At least, Michel did. Would her family be immune to her charms though? One way to find out, she thought, as she smiled at her father. "Pray tell, how did a French spy get hired at the palace? You must be so clever."

Her father puffed out his chest at her words, and she could see the pride in his eyes. "It was simple. Prinny had heard of Marie-Antoine Carême's culinary genius from other ambassadors, partly due to his *pièces montées*. He was so taken with them that he sent a missive to inquire if he would be willing to work at the palace."

Although she knew exactly what he was talking about, Kate looked puzzled. "What are *pee ess moan te*?" she asked, deliberately massacring the pronunciation.

Smiling at her indulgently, as if coddling an inquisitive child, he replied, "They are elaborate constructions made of food, used as centerpieces."

"Why would Prinny be taken with elaborate centerpieces?" Kate inquired, attempting to understand the logic behind the prince regent's request.

Uncrossing his legs and placing his forearm on the table, her father continued with his explanation. "His designs were no mere centerpiece. Not only did Chef Carême make these confections, which were sometimes several feet high, entirely out of food, but he modeled them on temples, pyramids, and ancient ruins."

After draining his soup, Edgar wiped his mouth, removing the green line above his lips. "Prinny did not realize that Chef Carême did freelance work for Parisian high society, including Napoleon. In fact, he did the cake and centerpieces at Napoleon's wedding."

Phillipe smiled smugly. "The missive was intercepted by Napoleon's forces, and we hatched a scheme to send Marie-Antoine Crème's sous-chef, Gasper Maminot, to work for Prinny. A forged letter by Chef Carême, sending his regrets but recommending his sous-chef wholeheartedly for the position, was sent off to your haughty prince regent."

Attempting to understand his role in the mission, she asked, "Do you work for Chef Maminot, then?"

"No. I am Gasper Maminot," her father revealed, flicking off some dirt from the table. "I assumed the identity of Gasper and retained the real sous-chef as my assistant, only his name is now Louis Martin."

"That's quite a feat! How did you manage it?" Kate inquired, acting impressed.

Edgar pushed back his chair on the wood floor, causing a loud screeching noise to echo in the room. "By threatening his family," he revealed nonchalantly, as if that was a normal thing to do.

With a tight smile, she declared, "Very clever of you."

Luckily, Phillipe did not notice her sarcasm, or chose to ignore it. "I thought so," he said with a humph. "It was never part of the original plan, though. For years, we scoured England's countryside, looking for the perfect reclusive lords that would not be missed. Once we located the lords, we had to find the perfect imposter, so they could assume their seats in Parliament. Thus, we were able to promote the French agenda."

"Is that how Michel was selected?" Kate was pressing for more information.

"Michel was a low-level military officer when we approached him with this role," her father explained. "The resemblance to the original Lord Camden was uncanny, and Michel was catapulted up the ranks." He frowned. "Unfortunately, the spy assigned to replace Lord Pembrooke was not as reliable and failed to assume his role. Sadly, the whole group of agents assigned to the undertaking went missing."

"If it was never part of the plan, why did you become Prinny's chef?" she asked innocently. "For what purpose?"

Clearing his throat with a low growl, Edgar announced, "That is enough questions."

Kate watched her father's eyes narrow as he turned to face his son. "Why is that? My daughter is entitled to know the truth about our family, since she will be helping to increase our legacy."

Rubbing his temples aggressively, her brother appeared vexed. "She is not family. She will never amount…"

With a gasp, Kate watched as her father flung himself around the table at a remarkable speed for his age, and threw Edgar against the wall, pressing his forearm against his chest. His voice was sinister, his expression full of menace. "She is my daughter and your sister. Everyone in this family has a role to play, and she will be an asset to us." He leaned in till he was nose-to-nose with his son. "Do I make myself clear?"

Kate's eyes roamed the room to see the mercenaries' reactions to this altercation, but their eyes appeared unconcerned by her father's show of force. She had no doubt that they would have jumped to attention if Edgar attacked her father. It was clear who the boss was.

Dropping his forearm from Edgar's chest, her father returned to his seat as if beating his son was a natural occurrence. Leaning back in his chair, he placed his right hand on the table and started drumming his fingers. "You asked me why I became Prinny's chef," he said with a brow lift. "It was a perfect opportunity to infiltrate the prince regent's household. Around the palace, I have created a peculiar persona that has allowed me to gain unparalleled access to His Highness. I have insisted on bringing him his breakfast, which is a French tradition. I placed small drops of laudanum into his food to cause drowsiness, giving me enough time to search his office without fear of discovery."

Kate furrowed her brow. "I thought the royal family employed food tasters to protect against food poisoning."

Leaning forward, her father reached for her hand in her lap. "My naive Kate. Everyone has a weakness. I simply exploited those. Some were threatened, others were eliminated, and the smart ones accepted bribes."

Without warning, a black, plump rat scurried over her ankle boots. She shrieked, causing the men in the room to roar with laughter. Attempting to regain her composure, she sat rigid in her chair and closed her eyes, praying this nightmare would be over soon.

After a few deep breaths, she opened her eyes to notice her father smiling at her. He seemed amused by her hysterical display. "Napoleon will be pleased with you. He has a fancy for beautiful blonde women, especially English noblewomen with delicate constitutions."

Fearing she misunderstood her father's intentions, she asked, "How exactly am I to entertain Napoleon?"

Placing his right elbow on the table, he looked pleased. "You are to seduce him and make him favor you. If you can accomplish that, then you could be one of his mistresses."

"You want me to bed Napoleon?" Her question held more astonishment than outrage.

Dropping his arm off the table, he smiled. "Think of the advantages of becoming Napoleon's mistress. You are an exquisite beauty, just like your mother, and you will charm our emperor. Besides, you are technically the daughter of a duke, a second cousin to the prince regent. You would be a sparkling jewel at his side."

Hiding the gnawing resentment that she felt for her father, knowing he wanted her to do something so despicable, was nearly impossible. However, she mustered up all her courage and plastered on a smile. "The role of a lifetime," she murmured, appeasing him.

But in her mind, she recoiled at her father's plans for her. She would never become Napoleon's mistress! How could a father encourage his daughter to seduce a man to gain leverage, or status? Suddenly, she felt sadness for Marthe, her sister. "Was Marthe's job to seduce someone?"

"It was," her father confirmed. "She successfully became Lord Lexington's mistress, and used her influence to get Edgar a seat in the House of Commons. Although, at first, she was uncertain about her role within the family, but we convinced her to change her mind."

"Marthe's misguided dream was to open a shop and sell fashionable gowns," Edgar interjected, scoffing. "She was stubborn, but we eventually beat her into submission."

Phillipe nodded his head in agreement. "It is the family business."

Kate brought her eyes up and searched her father's face for any sign of compassion, or love for Marthe, but his face was expressionless. He viewed Marthe only as an asset, and that is what he wanted her to be; merely a pawn in his game.

Sweeping her eyes over the room, Kate tried to appear interested in her next question. "When will we leave for France?"

Her father's face filled with pride. "Not until our French troops have seized London, and Napoleon rides triumphantly through the streets."

Kate swallowed her dread slowly. "When is that supposed to happen?"

"First, the day of reckoning will occur," Edgar said with a pointed look.

Tentatively, she pressed, "What is the day of reckoning?"

"On June 15th, Prinny is hosting a lavish affair of state, and only the crème of society will be there: King George, Prinny, dukes and lords," her father listed, looking entirely too pleased with himself.

With a cruel grin, Edgar informed her, "The Duke of Remington plans to be in attendance."

Phillipe nodded. "He will be, and I will be adding something special to my confection, which will eliminate everyone who partakes of my scrumptious dessert."

Trying to calm her beating heart, Kate inquired, "Won't you be arrested if everyone dies?"

"No, I will be long gone and Louis, my sous-chef, will take the fall while we go into hiding until the soldiers arrive from Scotland," her father shared, mirroring his son's sadistic smile.

She glanced at Edgar, who had his arms crossed over his chest as he continued to glare at her. "Scotland?"

"The English Channel is impenetrable," her father conceded, "so France is sending a frigate filled with our finest soldiers out into the Celtic sea and up the Irish coast, where it will land in Scotland in less than two weeks."

"But Scotland is nowhere near London," Kate contended, crinkling her nose.

Edgar stopped glaring to answer her question. "At twenty-five to thirty miles a day, the soldiers should arrive in London within a fortnight."

"Assuming the French soldiers meet no resistance along the way, how will they seize London without mass bloodshed?" Kate countered with pursed lips.

"With England in chaos over losing their precious king, the eccentric prince regent, and all their high-ranking members, it will be a perfect time to invade Britain. Seventeen-year-old Princess Charlotte will be thrust into the position of queen, one that she is not prepared for. Thus, she will be easily manipulated," her father bragged, rubbing his hands together in glee. "Furthermore, the British only retain a small army in London and will not be prepared for the onslaught of our highly-trained cavalry soldiers on their own soil."

Looking smug, Edgar added, "If the bill to end the war passes, the military will be in chaos as they attempt to withdraw their troops from Europe, guaranteeing their allies will be unable to stop Napoleon's forces."

"The day of reckoning is less than two weeks away," Kate softly said in disbelief. If her father succeeds, Napoleon will take over Europe, conquer Britain, and slaughter thousands in the process, ensuring his reign of wrath.

Listening to the chatter of the men in the room, she knew she was helpless to do anything. These men were being paid to commit treason, and they seemed at peace with it.

Unexpectedly, banging came from the entry door, and a loud, muffled voice exclaimed, "I am here to negotiate the terms for Lady Lansdowne's release."

# 26

IT WAS ADRIEN! KATE WOULD RECOGNIZE HIS SMOOTH, BARITONE voice anywhere. What was he doing here? Was Eliza able to escape and find help already? No, that was impossible. There had not been enough time for her to seek out other agents.

As questions continued to rise in her mind, Kate watched as the scraggily group of men pushed back their chairs and jumped up, anticipating a fight. Any signs of rowdiness had disappeared and been replaced with grim, stern faces as they turned to her father for direction.

Slowly rising from his seat, Phillipe buttoned the bottom two buttons of his tailcoat and straightened his cravat in a calm, orderly fashion. He removed an overcoat pistol from his pocket and placed it on the table. When he was ready, he nodded his approval for the guard to open the door.

Scanning the room, it appeared the only two men that had pistols were her father and Edgar. That made sense because pistols were expensive, and not everyone could afford such a luxury. A few of the ruffians had knives sticking out of their trousers, but most of the men appeared to enjoy settling their differences with fisticuffs.

As the guard opened the door, Adrien strode confidently into the room, wearing only a white shirt, tan trousers, and Hessian boots. He had no coat, cravat, or hat, which surprised her. A gentleman never went out in public dressed so informally, even if he was a spy. Between his wrinkled clothes, mussed-up hair, and the dark circles under his eyes, he appeared exhausted. Yet, to her, he never looked more handsome.

As Adrien's calculating gaze swept the room, their eyes momentarily met, and she was met with a cold, unrelenting stare before he continued his perusal of the hall. She understood his anger towards her, but she was not prepared for his disdain. Stifling a cry, her heart shattered, knowing that he was not pleased to see her. Was he truly only here to barter for Eliza and not her?

Luckily, no one heard her stifled cry, because Henley howled in rage, shot up from his seat, and charged Adrien, knocking his back against the wall. Yanking back his blood-soaked hand, he slammed his clenched fist into Adrien's face. Before he could deliver another blow, Adrien plowed his fist into Henley's stomach and finished by jabbing him under the chin. The amount of force behind the blow caused Henley's head to whip back, and he collapsed onto the floor, causing a pile of dirty dishes to scatter and roll around.

"Enough! Lord Camden is not here to engage in fisticuffs with you, Edgar, but to discuss Lady Lansdowne's release," her father shouted with thinly veiled contempt in his voice. He glared at his son, who was still on the floor nursing his tender jaw. Slowly turning his attention back towards Adrien, he asked, "How did you find this place?"

Adrien shrugged with one shoulder. "It was not that hard, in all honesty. Although, I do believe Napoleon is not paying you enough."

"And why would you think that?" Phillipe inquired curiously.

"Because this building is decrepit," Adrien declared, as he pointed at the ceiling. "I am surprised it has not already collapsed on you. What imbecile did you assign to find this place?"

Frowning, Edgar rose from the floor. "There is nothing wrong with this building. I picked this location because it is easy to defend."

"Ah," Adrien said, knowingly. "You're the imbecile. That makes sense."

"I am not an imbecile," Edgar growled as he pulled his pistol from his trousers and pointed it at Adrien's chest. "I have had enough from the likes of you."

"Edgar, lower your pistol, now." Her father's cold words spoke volumes. Everyone knew exactly how he felt about his son's behavior. "You are being rude to our guest."

Following Phillipe's order, Edgar lowered his pistol and brought his hand back up to his jaw. "He is not our guest," he grunted. "He works for the Crown."

Not speaking at first, Adrien lifted his brows at Edgar's words. "My role within the agency has nothing to do with why I am here," he stated, his tone imposing. "I am here to secure the safe release of Lady Lansdowne under the direction of the Duke of Remington."

Her father observed Adrien before he crossed his arms over his chest. "Just Lady Lansdowne?" Turning towards her, he asked, "Not Lady Camden, as well?"

Adrien shook his head. "We both know that Lady Camden is not the daughter of the Duke of Remington." With a quick press of his lips, he added, "In fact, the duke was pleased to learn that Lady Camden was with her real father, because he can now be done with the burden of financially supporting her."

That announcement stole Kate's breath, but she admonished herself to stay strong. Her father said that? True, the duke wasn't really her father, but those words cut her deeply. She loved him and thought he loved her in return. Willing herself not to cry, she kept a stony expression on her face, hoping she wouldn't give anything away. She refused to let Adrien see how much his comments hurt her.

Her father made a clicking noise with his mouth before he acknowledged Adrien's statement. "That does seem a little harsh from a man who raised my daughter for all those years."

"I am not here to discuss anyone's feelings on the matter," Adrien said coldly. "I am here to pay for the release of Lady Lansdowne before the Bow Street Runners break down that door and kill everyone in this room."

All the ruffians' eyes panicked as they simultaneously turned their heads to Phillipe for direction. He huffed in amusement. "And why should we believe you?"

Adrien's eyes widened and landed on Edgar. "You didn't tell him?"

"Tell him what?" Edgar asked in confusion.

With an amused half-smile on his face, Adrien turned his gaze back to her father. "Lady Lansdowne is not only the daughter of the Duke of Remington and the wife of the Marquess of Lansdowne, but she is pregnant with their first child, the Duke of Remington's first grandchild." He paused to let his words sink in. "Lord Lansdowne has hired every available Bow Street Runner to scour the streets of London, leaving no stone unturned."

Her father exploded with multiple expletives as he glared at his son. "You failed to mention that piece of information, Edgar," he drawled, his words dripping with scorn.

Edgar frowned deeply. "This is the first I have heard of this."

Adrien resumed his casual demeanor and leaned his shoulder against the wall. Even though he appeared relaxed, Kate had no doubt that his body was poised for an attack.

"I would like to buy Lady Lansdowne's release for £10,000, or £20,000 for the release of all the women that were abducted."

Her father walked closer to Kate and reached for her hand. “Is Lady Camden part of the deal?”

“No,” Adrien replied adamantly. “As far as the duke is concerned, she is back where she belongs.”

Edgar shot him a glare, full of hate and rage. “You are lying! Just a few days ago, you demanded her release, and now you stand here and claim you have no feelings for her. What game are you playing?”

Adrien glanced at Kate and offered a pitying smile. “No game. It is true that I offered to marry Lady Camden, but she jilted me. Lucky for me, there are plenty of women who want to warm my bed now that I am an earl.”

Kate could not control the whimper that slipped out as her hand covered her mouth, and she quickly ducked her head to hide her burning pink cheeks. His words were cruel, but she deserved them.

Phillipe studied Adrien before he reached down and slowly picked up his pistol. “Herein lies the problem with your plan to rescue the women before the Bow Street Runners come. If they charge the building, my men have strict orders to immediately kill the women.”

“If you accept the money, then no blood will be spilt today,” Adrien countered, eyeing the pistol in her father’s hand.

“But it will regardless,” Phillipe contended. “We cannot release these women until the bill to end the war has passed, but more importantly, you have seen my face.”

Adrien laughed. “I have seen many faces today. Why should I be killed for seeing yours?”

“Because my role is a secret, and I will not jeopardize this entire mission by letting you go free,” her father said, slowly raising his pistol.

“Even at the cost of your own daughter?” Adrien asked with a lifted eyebrow.

"As you can see for yourself, Kathryn is in no danger," Phillipe huffed, glancing over at her.

"I am not speaking of Kathryn," Adrien spat out. "I am speaking of Marthe."

The pistol stilled in her father's hand as his face paled. His voice was shaky. "You have my daughter."

"She is in Newgate awaiting hanging," Adrien informed him. "If you won't accept the money for Lady Lansdowne, at least accept a trade for your daughter's life."

Understanding dawned on Phillipe's face. "Marthe told you about this place."

"She did, amongst other things," Adrien confirmed.

In response, Phillipe shook his head. "No, she would not have betrayed me. She would have revealed nothing."

"Marthe informed me of your new name, Gasper," Adrien stated, his eyes scanning the room.

Her father's chest heaved with rage at Adrien's words. "My own daughter betrayed me!" he roared.

"I told you we should have killed her," Edgar growled.

"It matters not," her father said, frowning. "Marthe was expendable." He shifted his gaze towards her. "Kathryn and I will depart after I kill you, and Edgar can lead the charge against your Bow Street Runners."

With a flabbergasted expression, Adrien looked at Henley, standing only a few feet away. "You would leave your son to die while you live another day?" Then he turned to address the small group of ruffians. "And are all of you prepared to die for the French agenda?"

"Edgar knows his purpose. We are fighting for a cause dear to our hearts. As for these men, they understand their deaths will be for the greater good," Phillipe proclaimed prophetically, waving his pistol towards the men. "When Napoleon conquers England, he will be unstoppable, and no one will dare oppose his reign."

Adrien scoffed. "You are delusional, I see."

"And you, sir, will die today," her father declared, raising his pistol.

A flash of light caught her eye at the top of the stairs and Kate saw the tip of an arrow sticking out from behind the wall. It had to be Eliza! She must be waiting for a signal to intercede.

Biting her lower lip, Kate debated how she could save Adrien. If Eliza started releasing arrows from her longbow, her father would surely shoot Adrien before doing anything else. Suddenly, a thought sprang into her mind, but it would be very risky. It might even result in her death, but she had to try to save Adrien.

"Father," Kate interjected. As he tilted his head towards her, she walked to Phillipe's side and smiled at him. "I would like the privilege of shooting Lord Camden myself."

Lowering his pistol, her father gave her a puzzled look. "And why is that?"

"He confessed to me that he killed Michel aboard the *Brazen Hine*," she lied, finding it surprisingly easy to conjure up tears. "He killed my husband, then he tried to force me into marriage. If Edgar hadn't abducted me, thus saving me…" She let her voice trail off to emphasize her point.

"I understand," Phillipe replied, his eyes full of sympathy. "Michel was dear to me, too."

She willed herself not to shudder as he brought his hand up to cup her cheek. Kate placed her hand over his and said softly, "Thank you for understanding how much this means to me."

Her father pulled her closer and kissed her forehead. As he leaned back, he asked, his tone patronizing, "Do you even know how to shoot a pistol?"

"I do," Kate confirmed. She failed to mention that Adrien was the one who taught her in the first place.

"As you wish." Her father handed her the pistol and stepped back.

Testing the pistol's weight, it was similar in size to the one Adrien used to train her. Turning to face Adrien, she kept her face emotionless, fearing that she would give away her advantage.

"I am sorry it had to come to this, Lord Camden," she declared, raising the pistol till it was aimed at his chest.

Shock registered on Adrien's face as he straightened from the wall. "Don't do this, Kate."

"I'm afraid I have to." Kate tried to ignore the hateful glances being sent her way by Henley. "It is either me or you," she said, with a hitch in her voice, "and I choose you."

"Kate, wait…" Adrien's voice trailed off as he took a step forward but was stopped by Henley placing a hand on his shoulder.

"Just shoot the bastard," Henley barked.

"I intend to," Kate replied, meeting Adrien's pleading gaze. There were so many things she wanted to say to him, things he deserved to hear from her, but her fate would be sealed when she pulled this trigger. "I am sorry."

*I love you*, she mouthed to Adrien, before she slightly shifted the direction of the pistol and pulled the trigger.

# ❧ 27 ☙

BRACING TO BE SHOT, ADRIEN'S TEAR-FILLED EYES WATCHED HIS beloved Kate as she pulled the trigger. However, to his surprise, Henley collapsed next to him, and blood began saturating the wood floor.

"What have you done!" Phillipe growled as he knocked the smoking pistol from her hand. He grabbed both of her shoulders, forcing her to face him and shook her repeatedly. "What did you do?"

Kate tilted her head and locked eyes with Adrien, resigned to her fate. She had saved him, even though she knew her father might kill her for shooting Henley.

Preparing to intercede on Kate's behalf, Adrien took a step forward but was stopped by the group of dirty ruffians. They were eyeing him, but waiting anxiously for Kate's father to give a command. Even though these men would be left to die, their loyalties still resided with Phillipe.

A loud slap echoed through the hall before he saw Kate fall to the floor, her father towering over her. Turning his head to address the men, Phillipe pointed at Adrien and ordered, "Kill him first, then kill all the women upstairs."

The mob of men started bearing down on him, but the familiar whizz of arrows could be heard, followed by the sound of thuds as the men dropped. A tall, heavyset man came charging at him with his arm bent back, ready to swing. As the man brought his arm forward, Adrien caught his fist. Surprise registered on the thug's face. Twisting the fisted hand, he used his free hand to punch the thug in the stomach, knocking the breath out of him and folding him over. He kneed the man under his jaw, rendering him unconscious.

Over and over, he braced himself for an attack, using only his fists to fight these miscreants. The collection of men may have been thugs, but they were not skilled fighters. Henley probably picked them up near the docks or in pubs, because although they were large in stature, they were weak-minded, easily coerced by the enemy.

At some point, Jonathon and Larson joined him in the main hall, thrashing the men quite soundly.

A lanky man with brown pants, ripped at the ankles, slashed at him with a large, curved fishing knife. Jumping back from the assault, he reached for the knife in his boot. Before it was fully out of its sheath, the roar of a pistol resonated from the top of the stairs, and the lanky man dropped dead.

Adrien glanced up the stairs, and Benedict gave him a salute with two fingers before he ran down the stairs to join the fight. Within minutes, all the ruffians were either subdued or dead.

Panic filled Adrien's heart, as his eyes scanned the room for any sign of Kate. Where was she? "Kate!"

"Phillipe escaped out the main door during the chaos," Eliza revealed from the top of the stairs. "I tried to stop him, but he used Kate as a shield."

Turning his head towards the main door, he saw several arrows plunged into the wood near the door frame. It was obvious that Eliza had tried to intercede, but Phillipe had still escaped with Kate.

"Go," Benedict ordered, with a wave of his hand. "We will tie up these men and come after you."

Needing no further encouragement, Adrien ran out the main door into the dark, foggy street. Hastily, he located Phillipe's booted footprints deeply imprinted into the muddy road with smaller, smudged footprints next to his, as though the smaller person was being dragged. As he followed the footprints down the street, he was so distracted that he failed to notice a carriage barreling up behind him. The driver shouted out a warning, and Adrien jumped to the side, narrowly escaping being trampled to death.

Following the boot prints in the mud, he kept to the side of the uneven cobblestone street, until he saw Kate fighting against her father, attempting to free herself from his clutches. Yanking free of his hold, she ran further into the street, but Phillipe quickly caught and subdued her against him.

"Phillipe," Adrien bellowed as he ran closer to them. His voice echoed off the blackened buildings that lined both sides of the street.

Curious, dirty faces peered out their windows to watch the scene play out in front of them, allowing light to filter into the darkened street. He came to a stop a few yards away from Phillipe, the omnipresent fog swirling around them. "Release Kate or you will die here."

Keeping Kate firmly tucked up against him, he turned to face Adrien. "Go away, Lord Camden. This does not concern you."

"No?" Adrien mocked. "Your plan has unraveled. Henley is dead, Marthe will be hanged tomorrow, the women you abducted have been set free, and the bill to end the war will not pass. It is over."

Phillipe laughed loudly and sent him a spiteful, knowing look. "It doesn't matter. Your country is in chaos, led by a fool prince regent and no army to defend against an invasion. The bill was a means to an end."

"There you go again spouting nonsense." Adrien laughed as he reached down to pull out the spare pistol from his right boot. "You will have to expand on that when you are in Newgate. I will even arrange for you to share a cell with your daughter."

As he brought the pistol up to point at Phillipe, the coward placed Kate between him and the pistol, his arm slung around her throat. He smiled smugly. "You wouldn't shoot your former betrothed, would you?"

"No, I would not," Adrien confirmed with a shake of his head. "But look around you, there is nowhere to run."

"Napoleon will be victorious! England will fall!" Phillipe shouted, his eyes blazing with fury.

A mixture of boos and cheers came from inside the dirt-encased buildings as the people responded to Phillipe's words. Keeping his pistol aimed at Kate, he saw her looking back at him with trust in her eyes.

He kept his eyes trained on Phillipe, knowing desperate men would do anything in a final effort to stay alive. Hoping that Benedict and Jonathon were circling around to approach Phillipe from behind, he tried to stall.

"Why don't we take a walk down to Newgate and talk about Napoleon's plans?" Adrien said.

"I am no fool, Lord Camden," Phillipe replied, tightening his hold around Kate's neck.

Adrien let out a bark of laughter. "You are the definition of a fool. The question you should ask yourself is, am I going to die on this street or live another day?"

Phillipe huffed in contempt. "Oh, I am going to live another day, so I can have the chance to kill you." The sound of an approaching carriage came from behind him, and Phillipe's words were drowned out by the noise.

As the carriage drew closer, Adrien watched in horror as Phillipe threw his daughter into the path of the oncoming carriage, causing her to tumble to the ground. Dropping his pistol, he charged into the street and scooped her up, racing to beat the carriage. He almost reached the other side, but a horse clipped his leg, propelling him towards the buildings.

Turning to ensure Kate would not take the brunt of the fall, he twisted so his body hit the cobblestone street, and he felt Kate's weight bounce off his chest. Then, everything went black.

BOUNCING OFF ADRIEN'S WIDE CHEST, KATE SPRAWLED OUT along the narrow street, taking a long moment to get her bearings. As she lifted her head, she saw an unconscious Adrien lying a few feet from her, with a small pool of blood expanding beneath his head.

Gasping, she rushed to his side. She ripped a long strip from her petticoat and bandaged his wound. As she knelt next to him, she gently cradled his head and moved it up to her chest. She could not stop the tears flowing down her cheeks. A world without Adrien, her best friend, would be heartbreaking.

"Please don't leave me, Adrien," she pleaded softly. "I am so sorry for what I said to you. I was cruel, and I was scared to trust you with my heart." Removing one of her hands, she swiftly wiped the tears off her face.

A small group of people formed around her, mainly children with brown bare feet, and they were looking at her with sympathy in their eyes.

Ignoring all around her, she held Adrien tight in her arms. "I love you. Please don't die." She leaned down and placed a lingering kiss on the top of his head.

A deep clearing of someone's throat caught her attention. She looked up to see Benedict and Jonathon standing nearby.

Expecting to see compassion in their eyes, she was surprised by the amusement on their faces.

"Kate…" Benedict started as he wiped away a smile. "Adrien will no doubt make a full recovery."

Willing to believe his words, she asked with a tear-streaked face, "How can you be so sure? He has lost so much blood." Her eyes swept over the blood-stained cobblestone, and she noticed the blood had now seeped into the cracks.

Frowning, Jonathon stepped forward. "I hate to say it, but Benedict is right. Head wounds can cause a large amount of blood."

"Did either of you bring a carriage?" she asked, looking between them. "We need to get Adrien to a doctor as quickly as possible."

"Stop fussing, Kate," Jonathon ordered. "Adrien is just fine."

Feeling as if her entire world was falling apart, and no one seemed to care, her tears flowed freely again. "I can't lose him, Jonathon," she whimpered, utterly beside herself. "I made a mess of things, and I need to convince Adrien to forgive me. But for that to happen, he has to live."

Letting out a frustrated sigh, Jonathon kicked Adrien's boot. "Are you happy now? You made my sister cry."

"Why did you just kick Adrien?" Kate questioned, confused.

"Because Adrien has been awake since we got here," Benedict revealed, smiling. His expression sobered when her astonished gaze landed on him.

"Thank you for giving me away," Adrien said good-naturedly from his position. "I was enjoying being fussed over."

Bristling, she dropped her hands from Adrien's head. "That was a cruel joke, Lord Camden," Kate chastised, her words a mixture of relief and anger. "I thought you were dying."

As she started to rise, Adrien reached out and grabbed her hand, stopping her. Turning so he was looking up at her, he asked, "Did you mean what you just said?"

Pressing her lips together tightly, she tried to reign in her emotions. Now that she knew Adrien was awake, it was harder to confess her feelings. What was wrong with her? Lowering her eyes, she closed them, wishing she could conjure up strength. She could shoot Edgar, defy her true father, but she couldn't confess her undying devotion to a now-conscious Adrien.

Releasing her hand, he brought it up and cupped her cheek, the warmth of his hand causing her soul to rejoice. "Kate, did you mean what you just said?" His eyes implored hers to tell the truth. "I need to know."

Letting a lone tear fall from her eyes, she knew it was time to trust Adrien wholeheartedly. "Yes, I meant every word."

"Oh, Kate," he said tenderly, as his eyes shimmered with unshed tears. "I love you, too."

Staring deeply into Adrien's eyes, her whole body tingled with love for this man. How could she have ever questioned his loyalty, or his devotion to her?

"Kate," Eliza yelled as she broke through the crowd and dropped down next to her, throwing her arms around her. "I was so afraid I would have to go to France to rescue you."

Adrien took that as a sign to remove himself from the warmth of her arms, and she immediately longed to be near him again. Patting her sister's arm, she replied, "No need. Adrien rescued me after my father…" Kate's voice faded. With wide eyes, she looked up at the three agents. "Where is my father?"

All the men looked sheepish as Benedict confessed, "We lost him in the crowd. When Jonathon and I rounded the corner, we witnessed Phillipe toss you in front of the oncoming carriage, and we came to check on you two."

Mr. Larson walked over and extended his hand towards her. After he helped her stand, he said kindly, "I am relieved to see you well, Kate."

Smiling back at him, she replied, "Thank you."

Glancing at the growing crowd, Mr. Larson stated in a

hushed, but amused tone, "I suggest we stop making spectacles of ourselves, and adjourn to Eliza's townhouse."

Everyone murmured their agreement as Adrien offered his arm to her. Placing her hand into the crook of his arm, she yanked him tight against her side, causing him to momentarily lose his balance.

Recovering quickly, Adrien tenderly placed his other hand over hers. "Careful, my lady," he smirked, "if you continue in this scandalous behavior, I might assume you like me."

Feeling slightly giddy with relief, she laughed. "Well then, my lord," she playfully bantered back, "I guess I will have to do one thing shocking every day to prove to you how much I tolerate your presence."

"Only tolerate now?" Adrien asked, placing his hand over his heart, feigning disappointment. "You have wounded my pride, from which I may never recover."

"Good gracious." Jonathon's voice floated from behind them. "Please say that I was never this sappy around Hannah."

Everyone laughed, and Benedict slapped Jonathon on the shoulder. "You, my friend, were worse."

# ✠ 28 ✠

MUCH LATER, AND AFTER LONG, SOAKING BATHS, EVERYONE reconvened in the Lansdowne's drawing room. Eliza and Benedict sat on a settee, with Mr. Larson and Jonathon sitting on upholstered arm chairs. Kate sat next to Adrien on an opposite settee, his arm draped familiarly behind her.

Eliza and Kate took turns explaining what happened at The Squeaky Wench prior to Adrien's arrival and shared the specifics of their abduction. As they discussed the abduction, a moment of silence passed as they remembered their friend, Roger.

Adrien and Benedict shared details about locating the inn and how they obtained the information. Thankfully, Benedict did not address how Adrien threatened to annihilate an entire village to force Marthe to give up the location.

It turned out that Henley had abducted fifteen ladies and had been holding them captive, some for months. Mr. Larson shared the details about how the women were returned to their homes. All were safe, although most had lost some weight from their ordeal.

After everything was revealed, Adrien asked the group, "Where do you think the French will land in Scotland?"

"Based upon Kate's uncanny ability to interrogate a suspect," Jonathon said, smiling proudly at his sister, "Henley revealed that the soldiers' march would take fourteen days. It is safe to conclude that the ship will anchor relatively close to the border."

"That is still hundreds of miles along the Scottish coast that will need to be searched by agents," Benedict voiced, rubbing his hand over his chin. "That will take some time."

"And the Crown's resources are already stretched thin," Eliza pointed out.

"Uncle Charles will need to notify our army and send troops up to defend the Scottish border," Jonathon asserted. "We might not be able to stop the ship from anchoring offshore, but our army can stop the French from entering England."

"There is a possibility that our Royal Navy intercepted the French frigate and engaged them in open water," Adrien suggested. "Their soldiers could be at the bottom of the sea right now."

Benedict nodded his head in agreement. "There is that chance, but we will still need to inform our lord high admiral, the Duke of Clarence, in case the French frigate slipped past the British blockade of the channel."

"I dare say that Prince Frederick, our dear commander-in-chief of the forces, will not be pleased to hear a French landing might be imminent," Mr. Larson spoke up, "but at least we are better prepared after learning of Napoleon's planned invasion in 1805."

"I remember that," Jonathon piped in. "In addition to the Army of Reserve and the militia, Britain was relying on the patriotism of the people to volunteer in guerrilla-type warfare against the French troops."

Eliza smiled. "Luckily, Napoleon's plans never came to fruition, and he abandoned them at the last minute."

"Our troops are stretched thin, fighting with our allies in Europe, as well as the skirmish in the colonies, but Britain is not defenseless," Adrien confirmed. "Now that Phillipe has fled, the threat of poisoning our monarchy is over, and I have no doubt that the bill to defund the war will be voted down. There is a possibility the French will reject the misguided notion of landing in Scotland since Phillipe has lost the advantage."

Before anyone else spoke, deep muffled shouting could be heard in the main hall. "Kate! Eliza!" Within moments, the tall, and unequivocally dominating Duke of Remington stormed into the room. His new wife, Anne, who was a perfect likeness to her daughter, Eliza, followed closely behind. Everyone rose to greet their family.

As the duke's eyes landed on Eliza, he rushed over and hugged her, as the duchess embraced Kate. "I am so relieved you are all right," she murmured close to Kate's ear.

Leaning back, Kate gave her step-mother a genuine smile. "Thank you."

The duchess patted her cheek affectionately and then turned to embrace Eliza. As the duke turned his attention towards Kate, she curtsied and stated respectfully, "Your grace."

Everyone stopped and turned to stare at Kate, astonishment on their features. "Kate?" Eliza said, hesitantly. "What is wrong?"

Taking a shaky breath, Kate smiled politely at the duke. "I recently learned the truth of my parentage, and I know I have been quite a burden to you. Thank you for taking me in all those years ago, and raising me as your own daughter, even though you never wanted me." Shifting her gaze from the duke's face, she added genuinely, "I was blessed to have you as a father, even if it was for only a short time."

"Kate…" The duke's voice trailed off, and he looked completely baffled. "Why… I am at a loss for words." He put his hand out to touch her arm, but then thought better of it and lowered his hand. "You have never been a burden to me. Why would you believe that to be the case?"

Turning her head slightly, Kate's eyes met Adrien's. Realization dawned on him, and he realized he was to blame for this confusion.

"Kate, I need to explain something," Adrien confessed, noticing that the duke's eyebrows rose at his use of her given name. "What I said at the inn," he winced, "your father, the duke, never said those things. I was trying to distract Phillipe and Henley while Eliza and the other agents rescued the abducted women."

A frown tugged at Kate's lips as she kept her gaze steady on him. "Everything you said at the inn was a lie?" she asked in a hushed voice.

He nodded. "Everything."

A mask of indecision hung over her facial features as she processed what he was telling her. Keeping her voice low, she stated, "Even so, it was the truth. I must face the facts that my father is a French spy."

"What did you say to my daughter that would cause her to think this way?" the duke addressed him, a hint of threat in his tone.

Knowing that his ploy at the inn had hurt Kate, he had to set the record straight. Ignoring the duke's direct question, he placed his hand on Kate's forearm, turning her to face him. "I wish I could have spared you the pain of being abducted, or the deceitful words I used to divert Phillipe's attention towards me. My heart is breaking knowing that I caused you such pain. However, nothing I said in that room was how I felt, or a representation of what the duke felt." His eyes pleaded for her to understand his dilemma. "Sometimes, spies must come up with a plan on the spot, and our only focus is to stay alive."

After Kate gave him a nod to acknowledge his words, he shifted to face the Duke of Remington again. "My ploy involved Phillipe thinking you felt Kate was a burden and was pleased that she was back with her real father. Furthermore, I implied you never cared for her, as a tactic to trick Phillipe into loosening his tongue."

"And did it work?" the duke asked, his jaw clenched.

"Like a charm," he admitted, giving Kate an apologetic smile. "Furthermore, the only reason I am standing here is because Kate's quick thinking saved me from being shot."

"Pity," the duke replied, his eyes stormy. "I feel as if I have every reason to shoot you."

"Father…"

Putting his hand up to stop Kate from speaking, his eyes softened, reflecting a deep love for his daughter. "After you were born, I refused to see you until the day I brought Eliza over to be placed in your mother's care. The nursemaid brought you into the room and asked if I wanted to hold my daughter," he revealed, his voice hitching. "I wanted to ignore your existence, but the moment you were placed in my arms…" A tear slipped down his cheek. "You were mine."

He stepped closer, and gently placed his hands on her shoulders. "I don't know what was said at that inn, but you will always be my daughter. The very notion of you being a burden is offensive to me and has no grain of truth to it."

Kate offered him a sad smile. "But my father is French…"

"No. Forget that imposter. I am your father," the duke declared. "When I held you in my arms, and saw blonde tufts of hair sticking up, and your lovely blue eyes, you stole a piece of my heart."

Without saying a word, Kate threw her arms around her father's waist, embracing him firmly. After a moment, she straightened and stepped out of his arms, but not before Adrien saw her purse her lips. He was starting to read her expressions, and he could tell she was worried about something.

"My fa…" Kate stopped, and corrected herself, "Phillipe might seek revenge on me for killing Edgar, and I don't want to place you or Anne in danger."

The duke's eyes shifted and narrowed, obviously displeased. "I may not have been able to protect you earlier, but I will ensure you are protected from now on. You will not need to fear for your safety. I will hire a militia to keep my family safe."

With a shake of her head, Kate insisted, "I will not be kept locked away as a prisoner again."

"You won't be a prisoner," her father assured her. "I will hire guards to keep you safe."

"Like Roger?" she contended softly. "Because of me, Roger is dead. I won't ask anyone to risk their life to guard me again."

"We will keep you safe," Eliza stated as Benedict, Jonathon and Mr. Larson bobbed their heads in agreement.

"I know, but…" Her voice faded as she looked longingly at Adrien. "I was hoping for a different sort of arrangement."

"Were you?" he replied slowly, not entirely sure how to proceed. Did this mean she would still welcome his courtship? He was hoping that is what she meant.

"Yes," Kate said, her voice steady. "I am hoping your offer of marriage still stands."

Eagerly, he reached for her hand, tenderly intertwining their fingers. "It still stands. Are you sure you want to marry me? Even though I am a spy?" His eyes searched hers for any sign of hesitation.

Tilting her head coyly, Kate's eyes roamed his face. "I married a French spy first, but I think I would very much prefer to be married to an English spy this time."

Ignoring the duke's gasp, Adrien laughed. "It will be a very different experience, my dear."

"I should hope so," she jested cheekily.

Restraining himself, Adrien felt it wouldn't be prudent to pull Kate into his arms and kiss her in front of her father, the Duke of Remington, one of the most powerful men in England. Instead, he turned to address the duke. "Could I have a moment of your time, your grace? I have a question I would like to ask you."

"You don't have to marry him, Kate," Jonathon pointed out, walking closer to his sister. "If you want to remarry, I could introduce you to a plethora of eligible bachelors that will vie for your attention."

Squeezing his fingers, Kate smiled at her brother. "I know, but I love Adrien. I choose him, not because I long to get married, but because I never want to leave his side again."

With a grin, Jonathon dipped his head in acknowledgement. "Hannah will be pleased to have Adrien in the family."

The duke cleared his throat loudly. "Lord Camden, you come with me," he demanded, pointing at him. "We have a lot to discuss before I even think of consenting to this marriage."

As the duke began to turn, knowing Adrien would follow his order, Kate's firm voice stopped them in their tracks. "Father, I wish to marry Adrien." Her father opened his mouth to speak, but she put her hand up to stop him, causing his eyes to widen. "I truly hope to have your consent, but regardless, if Adrien will have me, I will marry him with or without it."

Adrien was surprised to see the duke's face softening as he listened to his daughter. When she was finished, his eyes filled with pride. "Well said, Kate," the duke stated, his voice reflecting the joy displayed in his eyes. "I always knew you had an incredible amount of inner strength, but seeing you stand there, defending your position, I now know that you are strong, inside and out." His eyes filled with moisture, but he blinked away the tears. "You are finally becoming the woman you were meant to be."

Giving Adrien a pointed look, the duke turned and started walking out of the room, intent on finishing his conversation in private.

"Your grace," Mr. Larson spoke up, stopping him in his tracks. "You should ask Lord Camden about the door."

With a questioning look, the duke asked, "What door?"

"The door that Adrien created between our townhouses," Benedict answered smiling, fully enjoying himself. "The burden of exiting his main door, walking a few yards, and knocking on my door, was too arduous while he was courting Kate."

"Your grace, the door was intended…"

"Lord Camden, spare me your pathetic excuses," the duke growled before he exited the room.

Risking a glance at Kate, Adrien could see her hiding a smile behind her hand. "Are you truly enjoying this?" he muttered under his breath.

Wiping the smile away, she looked at him, her eyes still filled with merriment. "Of course not, my lord."

"Traitor," he said good-naturedly as he went to face her father.

KATE SAT IN ADRIEN'S LIBRARY, ENJOYING THE SOUND OF A slow-burning fire crackling in the fireplace while a book sat in her lap, unopened. She should be in her room sleeping, but she did not want to adjourn to her bedchamber until she had spoken to Adrien. Her father and Adrien had been meeting in Benedict's study for over an hour, and her nerves were wreaking havoc on her ability to sleep.

She groaned inwardly at her bold speech about marrying Adrien earlier, causing her stomach to churn with anxiety. Kate had wanted to prove to him, and herself, that she could stand up for what she wanted, but Adrien hadn't said he wanted to marry her. What if Adrien didn't really want to marry her, and now only obligation bound him?

For the first time in over a week, her hand rose to finger the locket around her neck but stilled when she remembered she had long since given it to Adrien. Instead, she smoothed out her white lace overlay dress, touching the delicate flowers sewn into the neckline. Maybe she should order tea to calm her stomach? As she placed the book on a small round table, she rose when she saw Adrien leaning against the door frame.

Part of his face was shadowed, but there was no mistaking the way he watched her. His eyes were filled with a mixture of emotions that she could not identify. Pushing off the door frame, Adrien walked further into the room and stopped a few feet away.

Suddenly feeling very shy, she dipped her head and fingered the book on the table, attempting to distract herself from Adrien's intense gaze. What could she say to someone she had pushed away, only to discover later that she could not live without?

Lifting her chin, Kate gave him a tentative smile as she began wringing her hands together. Attempting to formulate the right words, she whispered, "Adrien." However, that was all that she could manage.

His face broke out into a wide smile. "Would you like me to go first?" he asked, his eyes twinkling in amusement.

Not trusting her words, she bobbed her head.

"I spoke to your father, and he has agreed to our union," Adrien said. Then his smile dimmed. "However, he has a few conditions."

"Oh?" Kate murmured as her heart constricted at his lack of excitement.

Taking a step forward, Adrien rubbed the back of his neck with his hand. "Your father requested that you are to determine where we reside when we are not in London for the season, and that you are to have a well-stocked library at all of our residences. Furthermore, he insisted, demanded really, that you will be reintroduced to society when you are ready."

"Is that all?"

"No, that is not all. He wants grandchildren," Adrien smirked, "loads of grandchildren."

Ducking her head as a deep blush came over her cheeks, she tried to distract herself from the thoughts of the marital bed with Adrien.

"But first, I have a question," Adrien said, luring her out of her thoughts.

Expecting to be teased, she was surprised to see any trace of humor was stripped from his expression. "And that is?" she asked, her mind reeling with the possibilities of what Adrien might say.

Taking another step forward, he stood within arm's distance, but he did not reach out to touch her. "I want to know if you truly mean to marry me, a fool that pushed you away in the first place by my irrefutable horrible actions, all while hiding behind the mask of a spy."

She matched his step forward with one of her own. "I admit I was devastated watching you and Marthe in Hyde Park, but honestly, I would have found another reason to push you away. I wasn't ready to give you my full heart. I was only prepared to give you pieces of my shattered heart."

"Your heart is not shattered," Adrien replied gently. "Misused, yes, but not shattered."

Feeling bold, she reached out to take his hand and was pleased to feel his hand engulfing hers. "While I was in captivity, my only thoughts were hoping I could apologize to you for my cruel words, and tell you how much you mean to me," she admitted, her eyes focusing on their entwined hands.

Tilting her head back, she gazed deep into his eyes as she continued, "I am sorry for what I said to you. My words were biting and cold..."

"And accurate." Adrien finished her words for her.

"No, it was unfair for me to accuse you of such depravity." She attempted to reassure him.

Adrien's eyes flickered over her shoulder before they again rested on her. This time his eyes held vulnerability. "I have lived a long time as a spy, and I have done some horrible acts in defense of the Crown; things that could never be forgiven. For so long, I have lived behind a mask, afraid that the person I had become was not worthy of happiness, or love."

His voice became hoarse as he stated, "It is easier to put on an air of joviality than it is to accept that I am not worthy of polite company."

"What mask are you wearing now?"

A look of surprise flashed in his eyes. "That is the ironic part, I've never had to wear a mask when I was around you. From the moment I met you, I never had to pretend I was something that I was not. You accepted me for who I was."

With an optimistic feeling, she pressed, "Will you tell me more about your life as a spy?"

"I have told you some," Adrien confirmed, his eyebrows pulled together. "Although, most of the stories are not meant for the drawing room."

"Good, you can tell me in our bedchamber," she joked.

He chuckled. "Life with you will never be dull."

Knowing her heart was filled with an all-encompassing love for this man, she smiled up at Adrien. "I love you enough to take you as you are, your perfections and imperfections, your strengths and weaknesses, and I am finally ready."

"Ready for what?" Adrien asked, keeping his gaze on her.

"I am ready to love a spy, with my whole heart," Kate responded. She smiled nervously. "If you will still have me."

"If I will still have you?" he repeated back in astonishment. Taking his free hand, he reached for her other hand and brought it up to his lips for a kiss. "From the moment I laid my eyes on the mysterious Kate at Beaumont Castle, you have entranced me with your beauty, charm, and compassion for others. Even as you were fighting your own demons, you helped me overcome mine."

Slowly, Adrien sank to one knee, keeping his gaze firmly on her. "I love you, Kate." His fingers grazed over her knuckles as he spoke. "Originally, my plan was to be your friend and reintroduce you into society, but my plans went awry as I spent more time with you. I have found a new purpose in my life; to love you with such an intensity that you could never question my undying devotion to you."

With happiness bubbling up inside of her, Kate wanted to throw her arms around Adrien and shout for joy, but one thing was still missing. Arching an eyebrow, she quirked one corner of her mouth up into a tiny smile. "Was there a question in there?"

A boyish grin lit Adrien's face. "Will you marry me?"

"Yes," she exclaimed, "Yes, yes, yes…"

Jumping up, Adrien pulled her into his arms before he leaned back and brought his hand up to cradle the back of her neck. Her lips parted, and her breath quickened with the anticipation of his kiss as he lowered his head towards her.

As their lips met, Kate's heart began to mend itself, knowing that Adrien would safeguard it always. Tenderly, he deepened the kiss, his lips marking her as his own, and allowing the heartache from her past to be swept away.

Never again would she be forced to be someone she wasn't, and she would be free to express herself without fear or punishment. More importantly, she wouldn't have to walk her journey alone anymore. She had her best friend to walk beside her.

Overcome with love for Adrien, her hands slid up his chest, and her arms wrapped around his neck, pulling him closer. Chuckling against her lips, he kissed her with equal enthusiasm, and their passion threatened to consume them both.

Loud clearing of throats echoed in the small library as Adrien rested his forehead on hers, his deep breathing matching hers. "I was only given ten minutes," he apologized.

"Foolishly, you spent nine of those minutes talking," Benedict commented good-naturedly from outside the door.

With one final kiss on the lips, Adrien stepped back but stayed close. Turning, he addressed Benedict, Jonathon, and Eliza at the door. "A lot needed to be said first," he admitted, "and Kate has finally agreed to marry me."

Rushing into the room, Eliza embraced her warmly before whispering, "I was shamelessly eavesdropping, and I am so happy for you."

Mr. Larson walked in, handed a key to Benedict, and announced, "It is done."

With a disbelieving huff, Adrien stated, "You didn't?"

Wagging his eyebrows at Adrien in an exaggerated fashion, Benedict smirked. "Of course, I did."

"What did he do?" Kate curiously asked Eliza.

Eliza smiled. "Benedict had Mr. Larson put a lock on the door between our townhouses."

"I suggested removing the door entirely, but Benedict would rather leave it up, so you and Eliza can visit each other freely," Jonathon revealed, as he came over to embrace her.

"The door will only need to be locked until the wedding takes place," Benedict said, as he shook Adrien's hand and gave Kate a hug.

"We could post the banns tomorrow, which gives us three weeks to plan your wedding," Eliza informed her. "We need to plan an engagement ball, a luncheon after the ceremony, and we need to buy you a whole new bridal trousseau."

An image of her previous engagement ball came to her mind as she danced awkwardly in Michel's arms. She shook her head. "I do not want an engagement ball, and I do not want to wait three weeks for the banns to be posted."

Turning to address Adrien, she nervously bit her lower lip,

before asking, "Would you mind obtaining a special license? I would prefer to be married the day after tomorrow."

All the men in the room burst out laughing, and Kate did not understand why. She looked at Eliza, her eyes holding questions.

Eliza appeared amused at her confusion. "No man wants to endure an engagement ball and a long engagement unless his fiancée desires it."

Kate frowned apologetically to Adrien. "I know it will cause a scandal to marry so quickly after the death of my husband, and society may give me the direct cut, but…"

He placed his finger against her lips, stilling her words. "No one will ever mistreat you again, I vow it."

Bringing her hand up, Kate lowered his finger. "I do not care how the ton treats me, but I worry your reputation will suffer from being married to me."

"The only reputation I care to have is that of a loving husband and father." Adrien flashed her a mischievous grin. "Do not fret. All will be well, you shall see."

Kate gave him a grateful smile before she turned to Eliza. "It appears we have two days to plan a wedding."

# 29

SLAMMING DOWN HIS QUILL PEN, ADRIEN JUMPED UP FROM HIS desk chair and put on his black superfine coat with tails.

As he started buttoning it, his butler, Mr. Ward, walked into his office, leaving the door open. "My lord, the carriage is ready to take you to St. George's."

"Excellent!" Adrien exclaimed as he came around the desk, trying to avoid rubbing his hands together in anticipation. He had not seen Kate for two days, not since he proposed to her in his library, and he was more than anxious to see his bride.

Mr. Ward held up a small box. "Your gift for Lady Camden has just been delivered from the jeweler."

"Thank you, Ward," he said, placing the golden box into his coat's front pocket. He had spent hours debating on the perfect wedding gift for Kate, and he had finally decided on two gifts. Both were meaningful and wildly expensive.

"What did you buy for Kate?" Benedict inquired, striding into the room with his wife on his arm.

"I hope it is thoughtful," Eliza commented.

As Jonathon walked through the door, he added, "I highly

doubt you could beat my wedding gift to Hannah. I bought her a horse farm."

"If you must know, I bought her two gifts, but this one just arrived," Adrien announced, removing the box from his pocket. He opened it up to reveal a heart shaped gold locket with a large diamond in the center. "I noticed that Kate still reaches for the locket around her neck, and I thought I would replace it with one from me."

"That is a splendid gift for Kate. She will be most pleased," Eliza gushed, before glancing over at her husband. "For our wedding, Benedict gave me a lovely diamond necklace."

"Lovely?" Benedict huffed teasingly. "That diamond necklace is a family heirloom and cost more than Beaumont Castle."

Eliza fingered the diamond necklace around her neck. "Exquisite then?"

Tilting his head, Benedict pretended to mull over her correction. "I will allow that, only because you are looking especially beautiful today, and are carrying my babe."

Smiling coyly, Eliza patted his arm. "Thank you, husband." Turning to face Adrien, her playful expression was gone. "I received a letter from Lady Rachel today."

"And I received a letter from Luke," Jonathon added.

Not understanding what this had to do with his wedding, he put his hands out to herd them out the door. "Well, that is great news, but we have a wedding that we must attend."

Ignoring his efforts, Jonathon walked over to his drink cart and poured three snifters of brandy. "I told you that he would not make the connection," he stated, offering one of the glasses to Benedict.

"Be nice to Adrien. Men in love tend to not think clearly," Eliza defended him.

Jonathon handed him a glass, then clinked their glasses together. "True, at least I was spared that malarkey."

Still confused, Adrien nevertheless took the opportunity to

rile Jonathon. "At least Kate knew I was proposing to her." He was referencing Jonathon's failed attempt at his first marriage proposal to Hannah.

"Touché," Jonathon replied, before taking a sip of his drink.

Pulling out a few sheets of paper, Eliza lowered herself onto a wingback chair, then took a moment to smooth out her elegant, slate gown with a wide, square neckline. "Lady Rachel is Lord Exeter's daughter…"

"And you ordered her to visit her family in Scotland," Adrien said, finishing her sentence. "Can this wait till after the wedding?"

"I'm afraid it can't," Benedict answered, standing next to Eliza. "We will be departing immediately after the luncheon. In fact, our trunks are already strapped onto the coach."

Taking a sip of his drink, Adrien unbuttoned the bottom button of his jacket and sat down across from Eliza and Benedict. "Start from the beginning."

"Lady Rachel wrote a letter, informing me that she is becoming quite fond of Lord Downshire's lead horse trainer, John," Eliza shared, with an amused smile on her face.

Adrien turned his baffled gaze towards Benedict. "And that is important why?"

Chuckling, Jonathon spoke up, "My brother, Luke Arthur *John* Beckett, or Lord Downshire, does not employ a lead horse trainer at his stud farm, since he prefers to train the horses personally. And, he also spoke of a growing attachment towards a *Miss* Rachel."

Chugging back his drink, Adrien slammed it on the table next to him. "If you will excuse me, I have more important matters to deal with than the particulars of Lady Rachel's love life."

"Wait, that is not the important part," Benedict claimed, indicating he should remain seated.

"No?" Adrien asked. "Will someone just tell me what needs to be said and be done with it?"

Eliza's eyes twinkled with excitement. "It turns out that Lady Rachel's uncle's estate borders my brother's horse stud farm near a small village called Rockcliffe in Scotland, and both letters contained details about witnessing small dinghies carrying French soldiers."

"Why did they send letters to both of you?" Adrien asked curiously.

"Lady Rachel knows that I am *Shadow*, but Luke does not, and she was seeking out my help," Eliza explained.

Leaning against the wall, Jonathon acknowledged, "And Luke knows of my association with the Crown. He reached out to me, urging me to investigate the matter."

"What does Lord Beckett have to say about all this?" Adrien questioned, squashing the growing desire to travel to Scotland with them. As much as he wanted to beat the French, he would rather spend his time getting acquainted with his wife. A smile touched his lips as he thought of Kate and how much he wanted to marry her.

"Adrien," Benedict shouted, followed by snapping of his fingers. "I told you we lost him."

Clearing his head, Adrien focused back on the conversation. "I apologize, my mind started to wander," he admitted, much to the amusement of his friends.

"As I was saying," Eliza continued, with an arched eyebrow, "my uncle asked us to go to Scotland and employ countermeasures, while the army is rerouted to the England-Scotland border."

"All right," Adrien said, with a bob of his head. "What do *you* intend to do about it?"

Smirking, Jonathon still leaned against the wall, his ankles now crossed in a casual pose. "I never thought I would live to see the day *Hawk* would back down from a fight."

"Love can change a man," Adrien announced with a silly grin on his face. "And for the first time, I like the changes I see inside of me."

Arising quickly, Eliza reached for Benedict's arm. "We will have plenty of time to discuss our plans in our carriage ride to Scotland, but I would hate to experience Kate's wrath if we make her groom late for the ceremony."

"ALMOST DONE, LADY CAMDEN," ELIZA'S LADY'S MAID, Martha, said as she finished weaving pearls throughout her hair. Stepping back to review her work, she clapped her hands in glee. "Done, and you look beautiful."

Staring at the large mirror, Kate turned her head, side to side, to look at her elaborately coiffed hair, causing the curls framing the side of her face to swish back and forth. "I love it," she declared, as she stood up and walked over to Eliza.

"And now for the dress," her sister stated, helping her into a beautiful, silver, high-waisted gown with crushed red rubies sewn into the bodice. Small, ornate buttons ran down the back, and a silk train, embroidered with flowers, fanned along the floor behind her.

Stepping back to look in the mirror, the magnificence of the dress took her breath away. "It is exquisite," she breathed. "What happened to the gown Madame Lancaster altered yesterday for my wedding?"

"I have a confession," Eliza admitted as she joined her at the mirror. "I commissioned this wedding gown from Madame Lancaster after we visited her weeks ago. I had a feeling that you would be marrying Adrien."

"Truly?" Kate asked.

Her sister smiled brightly. "Even though you fought it, I could see the way you looked at Adrien. I hope it is the way I look at Benedict."

A loud knock reverberated around the wood-paneled room. Martha slowly opened the solid paneled door, before dropping into a curtsy. The Duke of Remington, dressed in a black coat with tails, a starched, white waistcoat with a stiff collar, and a white cravat, walked into the small room.

"You both look beautiful," he acknowledged as he walked over to Kate, taking her hands into his own. "And you look breathtaking."

"Thank you, father." Kate smiled, as tears sprang to her eyes.

Pulling out a handkerchief, he handed it to her. "I hope these are happy tears, because if they aren't, then you know you don't have to marry…"

"These are most definitely happy tears," she rushed to reassure him. "How could they not be? I am marrying the man I love, and my father will walk me down the aisle."

Her father's eyes filled with moisture, but he blinked them away. "I have a surprise for you," he announced, walking over to the door and revealing the prince regent.

Dressed in his superfine clothes, Prinny's brown hair was brushed forward, and his long-chiseled nose highlighted his high cheekbones and bright green eyes.

Dropping into a low curtsy, Kate waited for the prince to approach her. "Lady Camden," he said kindly. "I have been told that I owe you my life, my family's lives, and my court's lives by sparing us the unfortunate experience of being poisoned by dessert."

As she rose, she returned his smile. "I did not do it alone, your highness."

"I have been made aware of your help," Prinny remarked, his

amused gaze transferring to Eliza. "It would appear *Shadow* has come out of retirement, yet again."

"It would appear so, your highness." Eliza nodded as the corners of her lips upturned slightly, and a twinkle shone in her eyes.

Turning his attention back to Kate, Prinny declared, "I know you did not ask it of me, but I approve of your match to Lord Camden, and I will make it known amongst the ton. Furthermore, if you would permit me, I would be honored to walk you down the aisle."

Recognizing she might bring shame on her family by her next words, she swallowed her trepidation. "With all due respect, your highness, I was hoping my father would walk me down the aisle, since he was unable to attend my previous wedding."

Instead of seeing censure in the prince regent's eyes, she saw his expression soften. "I understand. I hope my Charlotte will feel the same way when she is to be married." Shifting his gaze to the duke, he gave him a tight smile, as if attempting to reign in his emotions. "You should be proud of your daughters. They both are exceptional women, in their own right."

Her father's eyes shone with tenderness as he dipped his head in acknowledgement. "I have always been proud of them, but now so much more."

Reaching for Kate's gloved hand, Prinny brought it to his lips. "May you have a lifetime of happiness, Lady Camden. If you are ever in need, I am your humble servant." While Prinny gently lowered her hand, he added in a hushed voice, "You have endured much these past few years, but the future is yours. Take hold of it with joy."

"Thank you, your…"

"Please, call me Prinny," he said, cutting her off. "After all, I gave permission to your sister years ago to call me that."

"Thank you, Prinny," Kate replied. "And I thank you for coming to my simple wedding."

"Simple?" Prinny asked in surprise. "My dear, there is nothing simple about your wedding. All of the pews are filled, and there is a line of people outside hoping to get a glimpse of you."

"How is that possible? We didn't send out invitations, and Adrien just obtained the special license two days ago," Kate said, turning her gaze to Eliza. "How did people find out?"

The duke wiped a smile off his face, before answering, "Lord Camden has been very busy these past two days. He visited every lord that had their loved one abducted by Phillipe and explained how your quick action saved the lives of all the women."

Prinny chuckled. "From what I heard, Lord Camden told all the lords that you single-handedly took out fifteen armed mercenaries and foiled a plot by the French government."

"Then Adrien personally invited all of them to attend the wedding. He wanted the church to be filled to the rafters with your admirers, and to ensure you will always be welcomed amongst the ton," Eliza shared with a knowing smile.

"He did that all for me?" Kate asked, in awe at this sweet gesture.

Eliza nodded. "And everyone is invited to the luncheon."

"Oh no," Kate replied, her hand flying to cover her mouth. "We didn't plan for that many people to attend the luncheon."

"Do not fret. Anne took care of all the arrangements and even moved the luncheon to our townhouse," her father informed her. "She also ordered all the flowers for the church."

"Flowers?" Kate repeated, bewildered.

Prinny chuckled again. "If you will excuse me, I believe it is time I take my seat, and for Lady Camden to witness the grandeur of St. George's."

After Prinny excused himself, her father smiled down upon her. "Are you ready to marry Lord Camden?"

"I am," she stated enthusiastically.

With her arm in the crook of her father's arm, they entered the chapel and Kate's feet faltered at the sight she beheld. The beautiful chapel overflowed with men and women, dressed in their finery, all greeting her with cheery smiles. However, the enormous collection of white flowers, lining the pews and hanging down from the rafters, caused her to gasp in awe.

A bright red carpet lined the center of the chapel and led to the elevated, black-and-white checkered platform where the priest was standing, cloaked in his ceremonial robes. The decorative stained-glass turned the sun's rays into multi-colored splashes of light that shone throughout the room, rendering the ornate gold chandeliers unnecessary.

With her father's slight tug at her arm, Kate began walking towards the front where she saw Adrien standing tall with his hands at his sides. Knowing she would not remember what he wore this day, or what vows they shared, she would always remember the love radiating from his eyes.

Seeing his love reminded her that no matter what she'd had to endure in her past, it was worth the cost to be standing here, right now, allowing her to marry the man that she had always dreamed of, but didn't think existed.

As Adrien extended his hand towards her, Kate willingly placed her hands in his, eagerly anticipating their future together.

# EPILOGUE

SIX WEEKS LATER, ADRIEN SAT BACK IN THE CARRIAGE AS HE listened to his beautiful wife recount every detail about the ball, held in their honor, at Lord Wessex's estate. Her eyes twinkled with merriment as she described the women she was introduced to and the dresses they wore.

Kate had become lively and charismatic with everyone she met, and the burdens of her past seemed to have faded away. For the first month of their marriage, they spent their time tucked away at Pratt Hall, but were coaxed to London by the elite of the ton, who wanted to celebrate their nuptials.

Eventually, they would have traveled back to London anyway, because Kate's gift was ready for unveiling. He had to call in every favor he was owed, and then some, to obtain this present for his wife.

"Why are we traveling to our country home?" Kate inquired, glancing out the window. "I thought we were going back to Pratt Hall."

Adrien smiled. "We are, but first, I needed to show you something."

Lifting an eyebrow, Kate asked, "What?"

Leaning in, he kissed her squarely on the mouth. "You will see, my impatient wife."

The carriage lurched to a stop, and Adrien jumped out excitedly, not waiting for the footman to open the door. Turning back, he offered his hand to Kate and waited till she was on solid ground before he tucked her hand into his arm.

They walked towards the main door, and he stopped. Turning to face Kate, he gazed into her eyes. "I remembered when you told me that this home was your refuge, your safe haven from the world."

Kate smiled tenderly up at him, and he continued, "I also remembered when you saw that girl at Timpleton Square, and I knew your heart swelled with compassion for her." He placed a hand on her cheek. "I know you wanted to act and help her, but you were constrained at the time."

"I do remember that girl. She reminded me of myself," Kate admitted. "I wanted to help her, but I had nothing to offer."

Adrien looked at her incredulously. "Nothing to offer? You are the most kind-hearted person I know."

"I fear you are a little biased, my love," Kate said, smiling. "But, if I remember correctly, you helped her by giving her some coins."

He shook his head. "You are wrong. I would have walked right by the girl, without a second thought, if you hadn't stopped. You are the reason I helped her. You made me see her."

He took a step back and pointed at a plaque next to the main door. "I present to you, *Lady Camden's Home - A Refuge for Women.*"

Kate started to open her mouth, obviously wanting to ask questions, but he reached for her hand. "Come, I will show you."

He opened the door and the entry hall was lined with women of all ages, some dressed as servants, and others dressed in simple frocks.

Mr. Oakes stepped forward with a knowing smile on his face.

"Welcome home, Lady Camden. I hope you are pleased with the changes Lord Camden implemented."

Kate's gaze was on the line of women, but she turned to acknowledge her butler. "I am still trying to sort out all of the changes."

Adrien placed his hand on her back as he addressed the women. "This home is a refuge for women that have been mistreated by a family member or spouse; a place to encourage them to learn skills that will help them find reliable employment," he paused, as his eyes sought out Kate, "or they may stay here, tucked away from the world."

Kate's eyes filled with tears as she looked away from him to survey the women. Her eyes stopped, and widened, when she saw the girl from Timpleton Square.

Stepping away from him, Kate moved to stand in front of the girl. "It is you." Her eyes roamed the girl's face and dark-brown hair. "What is your name?"

Keeping her eyes trained low, she curtsied. "Josette, my lady."

"You are French?"

She shook her head. "No, my mother was."

"How old are you, Josette?"

"Sixteen."

"Did your father pass away, too?"

A mask settled over the girl's features as she replied in a surprisingly firm tone, "To me, my father is gone."

Kate's eyes shone with compassion, and she reached out to embrace Josette. The girl stiffened, but within moments her hands circled around Kate.

Leaning back, Kate said, "You are most welcome here, and I cannot wait to hear your story of survival."

Josette huffed, unconvinced. "My story isn't worth sharing."

Adrien watched as his wife stepped back with a determined tilt of her chin. "I will be the judge of that," she said.

He walked closer to her and whispered, "I have one more surprise for you in the drawing room."

As he led her towards the drawing room, he suddenly was anxious. He hoped he had made the right decision. As he opened the door, he stepped aside, and Kate walked into the room. He saw her steps falter.

Marthe was standing next to the window, her hair pulled back into a low bun, which hid her deformed ears, and her gaze was firmly lowered towards the Persian carpet. She was dressed in a modest beige gown, with a high neckline and long sleeves that were embroidered with small flowers.

Kate glanced over her shoulder at him, as he walked into the room and closed the door. This conversation would be best in private. Walking up, he placed his hand on the small of Kate's back and said, "I would like to introduce you to Cosette."

"Cosette?" Kate frowned forming a small pucker between her brows.

In a weak voice, she revealed, "Cosette is my given name. Father demanded I change my name to Marthe when we arrived in England."

Kate hesitantly walked closer to her, stopping a few feet away. "How is this possible?" she asked, keeping her eyes on her sister. "I thought you were to be…" Her voice trailed off.

Cosette's eyes flickered up for a moment, but then she lowered her gaze again without saying a word.

Adrien stepped closer to Kate. "When I first approached Lord Beckett about releasing Marthe to me, he thought I was mad. It took a lot of convincing, but your uncle agreed, contingent on a few things."

"Which were?" Kate asked.

"I had to get Prinny's consent, which cost us a small fortune," Adrien admitted. "Furthermore, Cosette is my responsibility and…"

Cosette's voice was resigned as she spoke over him, "I am not allowed to leave this country home without permission."

Kate nodded her understanding slowly. "I can't believe you are here."

With a downtrodden expression, Cosette's eyes flickered to her. "Lord Camden has been gracious enough to allow me to recover here from the injuries I sustained at Newgate, but I plan to return to France soon. I beg your patience for just a little while longer."

"Do you wish to return to France?" Kate inquired.

She shook her head. "No, but I have nowhere else to go."

"I would love for you to stay here."

Cosette's eyes widened in disbelief. "Why would you want me here after everything I've done?" she asked, her eyes flickering towards Adrien.

Kate took a step closer. "You are my sister."

"It is better for me to leave," Cosette stated sadly.

Adrien interjected, "Cosette has been kind enough to teach the women how to embroider."

"You have?" Kate asked.

Cosette nodded regretfully. "My dream was to open a dress shop one day, but that dream is dead." Her voice grew soft as she lifted her hands to reveal crooked fingers. "A side effect of being a condemned spy."

"Our father wanted me to become Napoleon's mistress," Kate revealed, "but that was before he tossed me into the path of an oncoming carriage."

"Don't feel badly. Father only cared about me when I was useful to him in some way, too," Cosette expressed softly. "I was forced to play the role of Marthe because my own father threatened to kill me if I refused."

Kate stepped forward until she was in front of her sister. "Please stay here and recover. I would like to get to know you."

"But I have done some horrible things…"

"It is in the past, Cosette," Kate said, cutting her off. Turning her head, she tenderly looked Adrien in the eye. "And I find I want to live in the present."

He smiled at his wife, knowing that no truer words had ever been spoken. His place of refuge, and future, was in the arms of his beautiful new wife.

## COMING SOON

A Tangled
Ruse

"He was determined to remain a recluse, but she had other plans."

by

Laura Beers

# ABOUT THE AUTHOR

Laura Beers spent most of her childhood with a nose stuck in a book, dreaming of becoming an author. She attended Brigham Young University, eventually earning a Bachelor of Science degree in Construction Management.

Many years later, and with loving encouragement from her family, Laura decided to start writing again. Besides being a full-time homemaker to her three kids, she loves waterskiing, hiking, and drinking Dr. Pepper. Currently, Laura Beers resides in South Carolina.

Printed in Great Britain
by Amazon